365
DAYS

DISCARD

365
DAYS

A NOVEL

Blanka Lipińska

Translated by Filip Sporczyk

EMILY BESTLER BOOKS
—
ATRIA
New York • London • Toronto • Sydney • New Delhi

EMILY
BESTLER
BOOKS

ATRIA

An Imprint of Simon & Schuster, Inc.
1230 Avenue of the Americas
New York, NY 10020

First Emily Bestler Books/Atria Paperback edition May 2021

EMILY BESTLER BOOKS / ATRIA PAPERBACK
and colophon are trademarks of Simon & Schuster, Inc.

For information about special discounts for bulk purchases,
please contact Simon & Schuster Special Sales
at 1-866-506-1949 or business@simonandschuster.com

The Simon & Schuster Speakers Bureau can bring authors to your live event.
For more information or to book an event, contact the Simon & Schuster Speakers
Bureau at 1-866-248-3049 or visit our website at www.simonspeakers.com.

Interior design by Dana Sloan

Manufactured in the United States of America

3   5   7   9   10   8   6   4

Library of Congress Cataloging-in-Publication Data is available.

ISBN 978-1-9821-7430-9
ISBN 978-1-9821-7431-6 (ebook)

365

DAYS

CHAPTER 1

"Do you know what this means, Massimo?"

I turned my head toward the window, looking at the cloudless sky, and then fixed the man with a stare.

"I'll take over that company whether the Manentes like it or not."

I stood up, and Mario and Domenico slowly followed suit, assuming their places behind me. The meeting had been pleasant enough, but it was getting decidedly too long. I shook hands with the men gathered in the room and headed to the door.

"It will be better for everyone this way." I lifted my hand, index finger outstretched. "You'll thank me for it later."

I took my jacket off and undid another button of my black shirt. I was sitting in the back seat of the car, savoring the silence and the coolness of the conditioned air.

"Home," I growled at the driver, scrolling through the messages on my mobile.

Most were business related, but one was from Anna. It read, I'm wet, I need to be punished. My penis stirred in my pants. I sighed, grabbing it through the fabric and squeezing hard. Oh yes, my girl always knew my moods.

She knew the meeting wouldn't be enjoyable, and that it would only make me weary. She also knew how I liked to unwind. **Be ready at eight**, I replied, and sat back comfortably, observing the world outside the window as it whizzed by. I closed my eyes.

There she was again. My cock instantly grew hard as steel. *God, I'll go crazy if I don't find her.* It had been five years since the accident. Five long years since the—how did the doctor put it?—the miracle of death and resurrection. Five years of dreaming about a woman I had never seen in real life. I had met her in my comatose visions. I could almost smell her hair, feel the smoothness of her skin—I could almost feel it. Each time I made love to Anna or any other woman, I made love to her. I named her my Mistress. She was my curse, my obsession, and apparently—my salvation.

The car stopped. I grabbed my jacket and stepped out. Domenico, Mario, and the other guys I'd taken with me were already waiting on the tarmac. Maybe I'd overdone it, but sometimes you just need a show of force to catch your enemy off guard.

I greeted the pilot as I entered the plane and sat down in the soft seat. A flight attendant passed me a glass of whisky with a single ice cube. I glanced at her. She knew my tastes. I sent her a blank look, while she blushed and smiled flirtatiously. *Why not?* I thought, and pushed myself up in a fluid motion.

I seized the surprised woman by the hand and pulled her with me toward the private part of the jet.

"Take off!" I called to the pilot, and closed the door, locking the girl and myself in.

I shot out an arm, clasping my hand over her neck and pushing her against the wall. I fixed her with a gaze. She was terrified. I closed the distance between us, allowed our mouths to touch, and bit her lower lip. She moaned. Her arms hung limply along her body and she stared straight into my eyes. I seized her by the hair and pulled, tilting her head back. Her eyes closed and she moaned again. Such a beauty, so girlish. I required all my employees to be aesthetically pleasing. I liked my things pretty.

"Kneel," I growled, pushing her down. She did as she was ordered without hesitation. I purred, praising her submissiveness, and trailed a thumb along her lips. They parted obediently.

I had never even talked to this girl before, but she immediately knew what she was supposed to do. I gently pushed her head against the wall and unzipped my pants. The flight attendant swallowed loudly, her enormous eyes still fastened on mine.

"Keep your eyes closed," I said gently, my thumb moving across her eyelids. "You'll only open them when I tell you."

My cock sprang from my pants, rock-hard, almost painfully stiff. It rested on the girl's lips, and she obediently opened her mouth. Wide.

You don't have any idea what's coming, darling, I thought, and pushed my prick all the way in, holding her head so she couldn't move. I felt her choking, and thrust even deeper. Oh yes, I loved it when their eyes snapped wide open in terror, as if they really thought they'd suffocate. I withdrew. Slowly. Then I stroked her cheek in a tender, delicate gesture. I observed her calming down, licking her lips clean of the thick spittle that came deep from her throat.

"I'll fuck your mouth," I said. She was trembling. "May I?"

My face expressed nothing—no smile, no emotion. For a moment, the girl stared at me with those huge eyes, finally nodding her consent.

"Thank you," I breathed, caressing her cheeks with both hands. I leaned her head further back against the wall and slid myself along her tongue all the way to her throat. She clasped her lips around my cock. *Oh yes!* My hips began to thrust, hard. I could feel her fighting for breath, so I gripped her harder. *That's it!* Her nails bit painfully into my thighs. At first she tried to push me away, then to simply hurt me, scratching my skin. I liked it. I liked it when they fought when they were helpless against my strength. I closed my eyes and saw my Mistress kneeling in front of me, her jet-black eyes piercing me like daggers.

She loved it when I took her like that. I clenched my hands on her hair even harder, seeing the lust in her stare. I couldn't last any longer. Two more hard strokes and I froze, while my jizz spurted out from my shaft, filling the girl's throat, choking her. I opened my eyes and looked at her smeared makeup. I withdrew a fraction, making some space.

"Swallow," I growled, pulling her hair once more.

Tears rolled down her cheeks, but she complied. I pulled my cock out of her mouth and she collapsed back on her heels, sliding down the wall.

"Now lick it." The girl froze. "Lick it clean."

I propped my arms against the wall in front of me and glared at her menacingly. She hoisted herself up again and grabbed my manhood in one slender hand, starting to lick off the remains of my seed. I smiled faintly, watching as she did her best. When I decided it was enough, I pulled away and zipped my pants.

"Thank you." I offered her a steadying hand as she pushed herself up, stood next to me on slightly shaky legs. "The bathroom is there," I said, pointing her in the right direction, despite the fact that she must have known the plane intimately. She nodded and headed toward the door.

I returned to my companions and sat, taking a sip of the exquisite liquor, though its temperature had ceased to be perfect sometime before. Mario put down his newspaper and sent me a look.

"Back in your father's day, they'd shoot us all dead."

I sighed, rolling my eyes, and clinked the glass against the tabletop with irritation.

"Back in my father's day we used to bootleg booze and drugs instead of running the biggest companies in Europe." I leaned back in the chair, pinning my consigliere with an angry stare. "I am the head of the Torricelli family and I got where I am by no quirk of fate. It was my father's decision. I have been brought up prepared to lead the family and bring it into a new era." I sighed again, relaxing a little when the flight attendant flitted silently to the front of the plane. "Mario," I said. "I know you used to like shooting." The older man, my adviser, allowed himself a slight smile.

"We'll have an opportunity for that soon enough." I sent him a grave look. "Domenico." I turned to my brother, who was stealing glances at me the whole time. "Tell your men to start looking for that whoreson Alfredo." My eyes traced back to Mario. "You want a shootout? You'll get one."

I took another sip of the whisky.

The sun over Sicily was setting when we landed in Catania. I put my jacket on and we exited the plane, then headed out toward the terminal entrance. I pulled out my sunglasses, feeling a blast of the scorching-hot air on my skin. Mount Etna loomed over the horizon—perfectly visible today.

The tourists should be happy, I thought, entering the air-conditioned building.

"The guys from Aruba want to meet with you over that issue we talked about earlier," Domenico said, walking by my side. "We have to take care of the Palermo clubs, too."

I listened to him intently, silently making a list of things that still needed tending to. Suddenly, it was like everything became dark, even though my eyes were wide open. I saw *her*. I blinked frantically. I'd only ever seen my Mistress when I wanted to. My eyes widened, but she was already gone. Was my condition deteriorating? Were the hallucinations growing stronger? I needed to go back to that idiot doctor to get examined. Later. For now, I had to get things done. Like find the cocaine dealer who had mysteriously disappeared. Well, not "disappeared" per se, but the term was the closest one that fit the situation. We were approaching the car when I saw her again. *Fucking hell, but that's impossible!* I stepped into the parked car and nearly pulled Domenico inside when he opened the other door.

"It's her," I whispered, my throat constricting. I pointed at a girl marching down a walkway, away from us. "It's the girl."

My head was spinning. I couldn't believe my eyes. Or maybe I was just seeing things. Losing my mind. The car started.

"Slow down," my younger brother said as we were closing in on the girl. "Holy shit," he breathed as we caught up with her.

My heart skipped a beat. Her head turned; she was looking straight at me, not seeing me through the reflective window. Her eyes, nose, her lips . . . It was her—just like I'd dreamed. I reached for the handle, but Domenico stopped me.

A muscular bald man was calling over to my Mistress, and she turned and started walking his way.

"Not now, Massimo."

I sat there, paralyzed. She was right *there*! She was real! I could have her, touch her. Take her with me and spend the rest of my life with her.

"What the fuck are you doing?" I shouted.

"She's with others. We don't know who they are."

The car accelerated and I could do nothing but stare at the fading silhouette of my Mistress.

"I'm sending people after her right now. You'll know who she is before we reach home. Massimo!" Domenico was saying, raising his voice. I didn't react. "You've waited so long—you can wait a couple hours more."

I pinned him with a gaze so furious and hateful he shrunk away. I could have killed him right there. The quickly diminishing rational part of my brain knew he was right, but the rest—the prevalent part—didn't want to listen to a word he said.

"You have one hour," I growled, staring dumbly at the seat in front of me. "You have sixty fucking minutes to tell me who she is."

We parked at the driveway and stepped out. Domenico's men immediately walked over, handing him an envelope. He passed it to me, and I headed toward the library without another word. I needed to be alone so I could wrap my head around all this.

I sat behind my desk and tore off the upper side of the envelope, my hands suddenly shaky. I spilled its contents to the desktop.

"Motherfucker!" I clutched my head in disbelief as the photos— no more paintings ordered from various artists—finally revealed the face of my Mistress. She had a name, a past. And a future she had no idea about. I heard someone knocking on the door. "Not now!" I yelled, not removing my eyes from the photos and notes. "Laura Biel," I whispered, touching her face on the glossy paper.

After about thirty minutes of analyzing all the new information, I got up from my desk and sat down in an armchair and froze, staring at the wall.

"Can I?" Domenico asked, peeking through a crack in the door. I didn't react, so he entered and sat in the other chair.

"What now?"

"We'll bring her here," I said numbly, not looking at him. He stayed locked in place, nodding his head slowly.

"But . . . how are you going to do that?" He sent me a disbelieving look, as if I were an idiot. Irritating little prick.

"You'll go to her hotel and tell her you used to have these visions back when you nearly died and that's where you saw her . . ." Domenico trailed off, looking at the note lying on the table in front of me.

Yes, I added in my head. *Laura Biel, you are mine now.*

"I'll kidnap her," I said. There was no hesitation in my voice. "Send people to the apartment of that—" I broke off, searching for the name of the bald guy in my notes. "Martin. They are to find out who he is."

"Maybe I should ask Carlo? He's right there," Domenico said.

"Good. Tell his men to get everything on the man. I need to find a way to bring her here as soon as possible."

"You don't have to look far, you know." I shot a glance at the door, from behind which a woman's voice had sounded. Domenico looked, too.

"I'm right here." Anna, all smiles, was walking my way in sky-high heels.

Fuck, I swore silently. I had completely forgotten about her.

"Well . . . I'll leave you two." Domenico grinned stupidly, pushed himself up, and headed to the door. "I'll take care of that thing, and we'll finish our business tomorrow," he said.

The blonde approached me. With one of her long, slender legs, she delicately spread my own. Her scent was intoxicating, as always. A mix of sex and power. She drew up her revealing black silk cocktail dress and sat astride me, pushing her tongue into my mouth.

"Hit me," she pleaded, biting my lip, rubbing her clit on the zipper of my pants. "Hard!"

She licked and bit my ear, and all I could do was stare at the photos scattered on the table. I pulled off my tie, which I had loosened earlier, and got up, pushing Anna down to the floor. I turned her around and blindfolded her with the tie. She smiled, her tongue tracing a line over her lower lip. She found the table with an outstretched arm, stood up, legs spread wide, and bent over the oak slab. She was wearing nothing under that dress. I walked over to her and smacked her on the ass. Hard. She yelped, head turning to the side, opening her mouth wide. The sight of the photos spread over the table and the thought that my Mistress was so close immediately made my dick hard as steel.

"Oh yes," I purred, gently rubbing her wet snatch, keeping my eyes on the pictures of Laura. I grabbed her by the neck, lifting her for an instant and removing all the papers she had lain over. I let her lie over the desktop again, lifting her arms above her head. Then I arranged the photos so they all faced me. To possess the woman from those pictures . . . There was nothing I wanted more.

I was ready to come at once. I pulled my pants down quickly and slid two fingers into Anna. She moaned, squirming under my touch. Her pussy was wet and hot and so tight. My fingers started to circle her clit and she grabbed the edge of the table harder.

My left hand shot out to grab her by the neck, and my right smacked her on the ass cheek. I felt an inexplicable relief. I shot another glance at one of the photos and slapped her again, even harder. She screamed, but I hit her again and again, as if it could really change her into Laura. Her ass was purpling. I bent over and licked it. It was hot and pulsating. I spread her ass cheeks and began trailing my tongue around her sweet hole, visualizing my Mistress all the time.

"Yes," she moaned softly.

I need to have her. Laura. I need her to be mine, I thought, straightening and impaling Anna with my throbbing cock. She bent her back into an arch and then lowered herself to the wooden table, now wet with sweat. I fucked her hard, keeping my gaze fixed on Laura. *It won't be long now. Soon, those black eyes will look at me as she kneels before me.*

"You bitch!" I clenched my teeth, feeling Anna's body go rigid.

I pushed myself inside her hard and aggressive, heedless of the orgasmic waves rippling all over her body. I didn't care. Laura's eyes made me want more, but at the same time I couldn't last any longer. I needed to feel more. Experience everything fully. I slid my cock out of her pussy and slammed it into her tight ass. I heard her scream wildly in pain and ecstasy and felt her tighten around me. My prick exploded with cum, but the only thing I could see was my Mistress.

Eight Hours Earlier

The sound of the alarm clock pierced my brain.

"Get up, honey. It's nine already. We have to be at the airport in an hour. Our Sicilian vacation awaits. Wakey, wakey!" Martin stood at the bedroom door, sporting a wide grin.

I opened my eyes slowly, reluctantly. It's the middle of the night for me, for God's sake. *What a barbaric idea to fly at this time*, I thought. Since I'd left work a few weeks ago, time of day stopped making any sense. I would go to sleep too late, wake up too late, and the worst of it was that I didn't have to do anything. I could do what I wanted. I'd spent too much time in the quagmire of the hotel business, and when I had finally gotten my dream position as a sales manager, I quit. I just lost the passion for my work. I never thought that at the age of twenty-nine I'd feel burned-out, but those were the facts.

Working at the hotel had been satisfying and fulfilling, and it was good for my ego. Every time I negotiated a big contract, I felt the thrill of excitement, and when those negotiations involved competing with more experienced people—adept at the art of manipulation—I was exhilarated. Especially when I won. Each little victory in my financial battles had given me the feeling of superiority.

It satisfied the vainer side of my character. It might sound stu-

pid, but as a girl from a small Polish town who hadn't even gradu-
ated university, proving my value to everyone around was a priority.

"Laura! You want cocoa or tea with milk?"

"Martin, please! It's the middle of the night!" I rolled over on the
bed and covered my head with a pillow.

Bright August light illuminated the bedroom. Martin never
liked darkness, so even our bedroom windows lacked any kind of
blinds. He used to say that darkness caused depression. Well, for
him to fall into depression was easier than getting a coffee at Star-
bucks. The windows were all on the eastern wall, so each morning
the sun made it pretty much impossible for me to sleep late.

"I made both cocoa and tea." With a smug expression, Martin
remained standing in the doorway, holding a cup in each hand.
"It's scorching hot outside. I bet you want the cold one," he said,
and passed me the cocoa. Then he began pulling the sheets from
the bed.

By that time I was getting pissed at him, but I crawled out of
my cave. I knew he wouldn't relent. Martin flashed his teeth in a
wide grin. That was so much like him—every morning he had too
much energy. He was a heavily built, bull-like man with a bald head
perched on top of a wide neck. People called him a muscle head.
Aside from the purely physical aspect, he had nothing in common
with that kind of man. He was the best human being I'd ever met.
He had his own company, and each time he scored a big hit, he'd
transfer a large sum to a children's hospice. He liked to say: "I need
to share God's blessing with others."

Martin had blue eyes. They were gentle and full of kindness. His
nose was large and crooked—it had been broken in the past. Nobody's
perfect, and Martin hadn't always been this wise and well mannered.
What I loved about him the most were his full lips and his spectacular
smile that always disarmed me each time I was mad at him.

His enormous arms were covered with tattoos. His entire body was, in fact, aside from his legs. He was a strong man, weighing a good deal more than two hundred pounds. I always felt safe with him, though I have to admit that at five feet five and 110 pounds, I might have looked a bit mismatched with him. My mom had always told me that sports are good, so I trained in whatever took my fancy at any given time, from Nordic walking to karate. I never stuck to any discipline for long, though. What it ultimately boiled down to was that my body was extremely fit, my tummy was hard as rock and perfectly flat, my legs were slim and muscled, and my buttocks toned and curvy. I must have done more than a million squats to achieve that effect.

"All right, I'm getting up," I mumbled, then drank the delicious now-cold cocoa in one great gulp.

I put the cup down and went into the bathroom. As I stopped by the mirror I realized just how much I needed this vacation. My dark eyes were sad and resigned, and the lack of anything to do had made me apathetic. My chestnut hair flowed around my lean face and fell to my shoulders. That it reached this length was a success— usually I wore my hair a lot shorter. In normal circumstances, I would have thought myself pretty hot, but I didn't right then. I was overwhelmed with the burden of my own failings and my aversion to work. I had no idea what to do with myself. My professional life had always determined my self-esteem. Without a calling card and a work phone in my purse, I didn't feel too confident.

I brushed my teeth, put some pins in my hair, applied some mascara, and . . . that was about it. I didn't have it in me to do much else. Besides, it would be enough. A while ago I had splurged on permanent brow, eye, and lip makeup out of sheer laziness. It allowed me to have more sleep and limit the morning bathroom routine to the bare minimum.

I went to the closet to get the clothes I had prepared for today. One thing always remained the same for me, irrespective of my moods and all the things I had no power to change—I had to be dressed as perfectly as possible. Wearing the right clothing made me feel better. Obviously, it made me *look* better, too.

My mother always said that a woman should always be beautiful even if she is hurting. And if my face couldn't be as attractive as it was on a good day, I had to take everyone's attention off it. So for the trip I selected light denim shorts, a loose white shirt, and despite the scorching heat outside, a light, gray mélange cotton cardigan. Planes were too cold for me, and even if it meant I'd boil outside first, at least I'd feel comfortable on board. Well, as far as I could, anyway—I was terrified of flying. I slipped my feet into my Isabel Marant wedge-heel gray-white sneakers and I was ready.

I went to the living room, which was connected to the kitchen annex. The apartment had modern decor—cold and minimalist. The walls were covered with black glass, the bar was illuminated with LEDs, and instead of a table like you'd have in a normal home there was a small counter with two leather-covered stools. An enormous gray corner sofa sitting in the middle of the room was a testament to its owner's size. The bedroom was divided from the living room by a great aquarium. It was clear that a woman hadn't designed this apartment. It was the perfect fit for a committed single, which the lord and commander of this particular apartment had been until recently.

Martin was sitting with his nose in his laptop as usual. It didn't matter what he was doing at any given time—working, on a call, or watching a movie—he always kept his laptop close by. It was his best friend and an integral part of who the man was. I hated it with a passion, but it had always been like that, so I really had no right to change it. Even though I had appeared in his life more than a year ago owing to that little device, it would be hypocrisy if I suddenly wanted it out of his life.

I remember it had been February, and I hadn't been in a relationship with anyone for more than six months. I was growing bored, or maybe lonely, so I decided to set up a profile on a dating site. It turned out to be fun, not to mention that it ended up boosting my already high self-esteem. During one of those sleepless nights, browsing through hundreds of men, I finally stumbled on Martin. He was looking for a loyal woman to fill his world all at once. Anyway, we clicked and thus a petite girl tamed the tattooed monster. Our relationship wasn't your run-of-the-mill affair. We were both the strong, dominant types and were prone to explosive outbursts. We were also both intelligent and had significant knowledge of our respective professions. It pulled us both to each other, intriguing and impressing us. The only thing our relationship was lacking was the animal magnetism, the unbridled attraction and passion that had simply never been there. As Martin had once said, he'd already had his share of fucking. I, on the other hand, was a volcano of sexual energy threatening to explode at any time. I had to search for release by masturbating on a daily basis. But still, I felt good at Martin's side. Safe and calm. It was more important than sex. Or at least that's what I thought.

"I'm ready, honey. I just have to zip up my travel bag, which is not going to be easy, and we can go."

With a laugh, Martin pushed himself up, stuffed the laptop into its bag, and headed toward my luggage.

"I think I'll manage, baby doll," he said, squeezing my gigantic suitcase. "It's the same thing all over again, eh? Excess baggage, thirty pairs of shoes and half the closet flying with us while you're not going to wear more than, like, ten percent of all that."

I frowned and crossed my arms.

"At least I'll have choices!" I retorted, putting on my sunglasses.

I always felt apprehensive and anxious in airports, afraid even. I had claustrophobia and hated flying. Besides, I had inherited my mother's pessimism. It was always doom and gloom for me, so I tended to overthink things that at least theoretically might end up in some kind of trauma. So a flying can with a pair of engines strapped to the sides wasn't something I'd likely trust without a shadow of a doubt.

We were traveling with Martin's friends, who were already waiting for us in the brightly lit departures hall. Karolina and Michał had been together for years and had chosen our destination. They were thinking of getting married, but at least for now, thinking about it was enough. He was your typical womanizer. With short blond hair, a deep tan, and blue eyes he was also pretty good-looking. All he was ever interested in was boobs, though. He didn't even try denying that. She, on the other hand, was a tall, long-legged blonde with a delicate, girlish face. Nothing special at first glance, but when you came to know her, she became remarkably interesting. Karolina all but ignored Michał's bothersome inclinations. I wasn't sure how she managed it. With my possessiveness, I wouldn't be able to stay with a man whose head turned every time he glimpsed another woman. I swallowed two antianxiety pills to be sure I wouldn't have a full-blown panic attack on the plane.

We were supposed to have a stopover in Rome. An hour's break and then another hour flying straight to Sicily. Last time I had been to Italy I was sixteen, and since then I didn't have a high opinion of Italians. They were noisy, intrusive, and didn't know a word of English. And English was like a native tongue to me. After all those years spent in various hotels, there were times I even thought in English.

When we finally landed in Catania, the sun was already setting. The guy at the car rental office took his bloody time handling customers. We got stuck in the queue for an hour. Martin was hungry and edgy, and his foul mood was rubbing off on me, so I decided to take a look around the place. There wasn't much to see, truth be told. I exited the air-conditioned building and felt the overwhelming heat. In the distance, I saw the smoking summit of Mount Etna. It was a bit disturbing, really, though I had known the volcano was still active. Walking with my head in the clouds, I didn't notice the end of the pavement, and before I gathered my wits, an enormous Italian popped out of nowhere and I nearly walked into him. I stopped, dumbfounded, a couple of inches from the man's back, but he didn't even flinch, failing to notice I nearly slammed into him. A group of men wearing dark suits were walking out of the airport terminal. The man in front of me looked like he was escorting them. I didn't wait for them to pass, instead turning on my heel and walking back to the car rental office, praying for the car finally to be ready. When I was close, three black SUVs drove by. The middle one seemed to slow down a bit for an instant, but I couldn't see anything inside through the darkened windows.

"Laura!" I heard Martin call out, the keys to our car clasped in his hand. "Where the hell are you going? We're off!"

———

Hilton Giardini Naxos welcomed us with an enormous vase in the shape of a head, holding a bundle of tall white and pink lilies. The scent of the flowers filled the impressive entrance hall decorated with golden motifs.

"Real ritzy, darling," I said, turning to Martin with a smile. "A bit Louis XVI. I wonder if there's a bathtub with lion paws upstairs."

Everyone burst out laughing. We all had all been thinking the same thing, it seemed. The hotel wasn't as luxurious as a Hilton should have been. There were a lot of shortcomings I could discern with my professional eye.

"The only things that matter are a good bed, a freezer filled with vodka, and some sunny weather," Michał said. "I don't care about anything else."

"Right, well, I forgot this is going to be just another trip of binge drinking. Now I feel bad for not being an alcoholic like the rest of you," I replied with a grimace of mock irritation. "I'm hungry. I had my last meal back in Warsaw. Can we get a move on and eat out today? I can already taste that pizza and wine . . ."

"Spoken like the absolutely-not-alcoholic afficionado of large quantities of wine and champagne," Martin said with a smirk, wrapping his great arm around my shoulders.

All similarly hungry, we unpacked our things quickly, and after fifteen minutes met in the corridor between our rooms.

With what little time I had, unfortunately I didn't have the opportunity to adequately prepare myself for going out, but on my way to the room earlier I'd been mentally combing through the contents of my baggage. I wanted something that would end up the least crumpled after the long trip. Finally, I'd picked a long black dress with a metal cross on the back, a pair of black flip-flops, a black leather fringe bag, a gold watch, and large round earrings. I'd hastily applied some eyeliner and mascara, touching up my earlier work, which was already fading after the flight, and then powdered my face lightly. I'd grabbed a tube of golden-speckled lip gloss and drew a line along my lips without looking in the mirror.

Karolina and Michał shot me surprised glances as I left the room. They were still in the same clothes they had had on during the flight.

"How did you manage to change clothes already? You look like you had hours to prepare!" Karolina muttered as we were walking to the elevator.

"Well . . ." I shrugged. "You've got your talent for excessive drinking, but I have a trick or two up my sleeve, too. I prepare in my head, so then I can ready myself in a couple minutes."

"All right, quit it with the chitchat. Let's go have a drink!" Martin boomed.

All four of us crossed the hotel lobby to the exit.

Giardini Naxos at night was a beautiful, picturesque place. The narrow, winding streets pulsated with life and music. There were all kinds of people everywhere, from young partygoers to mothers with children. Sicily only woke up after sundown, it seemed. The scorching heat of the day was too much for everyone to go out earlier. We reached the densely populated port district. There were dozens of restaurants, bars, and cafés along the seafront.

"I'm about to die of hunger here," Karolina said.

"And my blood alcohol content is definitely too low," added Michał. "Look at this place. It'll be perfect."

He pointed to a restaurant by the beach called Tortuga. It was a classy place with glass tables, white chairs and sofas, and candles everywhere. Overhead, enormous sheets of white sailcloth waved and rippled in the wind, making it seem like it was floating. The restaurant was divided into cozy nooks enclosed by heavy wooden beams supporting the cloth roofing. The effect was magical—bright and breezy and simply perfect. The prices were a bit steep, but it was filled with people. Martin waved at a waiter, and with a quick incentive of a few euros, we were sitting comfortably and reading the menu in no time. My dress did nothing to make me blend in with my surroundings. I felt everyone's eyes on me. With all that white, my black outfit made me stand out like a black beacon.

"I'm feeling watched, but who could have known we'd end up

in a big milk jug," I whispered to Martin with a stupid, apologetic smile.

He took a quizzical look around, leaned in to my ear, and whispered, "You're paranoid, babe. Besides, you look astonishing. Let them look."

I scanned the place again. At first glance, nobody was looking my way, but I had this strange feeling of being watched nonetheless. I pushed away the nagging thought of having inherited some kind of mental disease from my mother and focused on the menu. I quickly found my favorite, grilled octopus, and chose a rose Prosecco. The waiter, despite being a Sicilian, was also an Italian, which meant we couldn't expect anything done fast. We'd have to wait a good long while before he came back to take our order.

"I have to go to the restroom," I said, my eyes darting around.

There was a small door by the beautiful wooden bar in the corner of the restaurant. I headed that way. I passed through, but it was just the dishwashing room. I turned back, only to hit the stone-hard chest of a tall man. Frowning and rubbing my forehead, I raised my eyes. The man in front of me was handsome. An Italian. *Haven't I seen him somewhere before?* His icy stare transfixed me. I couldn't move as he gazed at me with his black eyes. There was something in him that terrified me. I froze.

"You seem to be lost," he said in perfect, fluid English with an immaculate British accent. "I can help you if you tell me what you're looking for."

He smiled, presenting a set of perfectly straight, white teeth, and placed a hand on my back, between my shoulder blades, touching naked skin. He pushed me gently in the right direction and led me to the door. Feeling his touch made shivers run down my spine. It made walking no easier. I was light-headed, bewildered. I couldn't speak. The only thing I could do was smile, or rather grimace. I headed back to Martin. With all these emotions running through me, I completely forgot why I had left our table in the first place. As I returned, my friends were already having their drinks—they had managed to down one round already and were just ordering another. I collapsed on the sofa, grabbed my glass of Prosecco, and finished it in one gulp. At the same time, the glass still at my lips, I gestured to the waiter that I needed another one.

Martin shot me an amused glance.

"You boozer!" He laughed. "And you tell me I have a problem with alcohol."

"I just needed a drink," I replied, a bit dizzy with the wine I had drunk too quickly.

"That restroom has to be a magical place if that's the way it worked on you." Hearing that, I glanced around nervously in search of the tall Italian who had made my legs shake like they had on the day I had first ridden a motorbike after getting my driver's license.

And he'd be pretty easy to spot in the white interior—just like me, he wore black. Loose black linen trousers, a black shirt with a wooden rosary sticking out from underneath the collar, and black loafers. I might have only glimpsed the man, but I remembered him well.

"Laura!" Michał's voice pulled me out of my reverie. "Stop staring at people and have a drink!"

I didn't even notice the second glass of Prosecco arriving at our table. I decided to take my time with it, though I felt the urge to pour it all into my mouth just like the first one. My legs were still shaky. Dinner was served and we devoured it. The octopus was perfect—accompanied only by small, sweet tomatoes. Martin got a gigantic squid, cut into pieces and scattered over his plate with garlic and coriander.

"Holy shit!" Martin exclaimed suddenly, jumping to his feet. "Do you know what time it is? It's past midnight, so, Laura . . .

'Happy birthday to you, happy birthday to you . . .'" he sang. Michał and Karolina stood, too, and joined in the merry, loud, and raucous rendition of the birthday song. The other guests were looking at us, intrigued, and then joined as well, singing in Italian. The restaurant reverberated with loud applause, and all I wanted to do was vanish. I hated that stupid tune. I don't think anybody really likes it. Nobody really knows how to behave as everyone is singing it—sing along, clap their hands, smile like an idiot? All options seemed bad, and you are just left the center of attention, looking out of place. With a fake smile plastered to my face, I rose and waved at everyone, bowing and thanking them for their wishes.

"You just had to do this to me, didn't you?" I growled at Martin, the smile still stretching my lips. "Reminding me of my age isn't too polite. Besides, did you have to involve everyone?"

"Well, babe, it seems the truth is a hard pill to swallow. But, by way of apology, I've ordered your favorite drink."

The waiter appeared with four tall glasses and a bottle of Moët & Chandon Rosé in a bucket filled with ice.

"Oh, I love it!" I squealed, jumping up and down and clapping my hands like a little girl.

My glee wasn't unnoticed by the waiter, who opened the bottle and filled our glasses. He then smiled at me widely and put the cooler and the nearly empty bottle on the table as he left.

"*Na zdrovye!*" called Karolina in Polish, raising her glass. "May you find what you're looking for, always have what you want, and fulfill all your dreams. Cheers!" We clinked glasses and drank the champagne.

After midnight, the restaurant turned into a club. The colorful lighting drastically changed the atmosphere of the place. The elegant, classy white and sterile interior suddenly exploded with all kinds of gaudy colors. The white was all the more understandable now. With a bit of lighting, you easily could change the character of the room.

I really had to go to the restroom now. This time, however, I decided to find it with some help. The waiter pointed me in the right direction. I elbowed my way through the crowd toward the ladies' room, when I had that strange feeling of being watched again. I stopped and took a careful look around. On a pedestal, leaning over one of the wooden beams, stood the black-clothed man, pinning me with his icy stare again. He measured me with his eyes, his face showing no emotion. He looked like your typical Italian, though he might have been the least typical man I'd ever seen. His black hair cascaded down his forehead. His jaw was covered with a meticulously trimmed dark stubble. His lips were full and well defined. *Perfectly suited to pleasure a woman*, I thought. His stare was cold and piercing. It was the stare of a wild animal just waiting to pounce. Seeing him from that distance, I realized just how tall he was. He loomed over the women standing nearby. He must have been at least six three. I don't know how much time passed with us just staring into each other's eyes. It might have stopped for all I cared. My bewildered stupor was broken by a man who walked into me on his way somewhere. With all that staring I had grown rigid and numb at the same time, so I just wheeled around on one foot and toppled to the ground.

"You okay?" the Man in Black asked, appearing suddenly at my side. "If not for the fact that I saw it wasn't you who walked into him this time, I would have thought bumping into people was your way of picking up guys."

He grabbed me by the elbow and lifted me up effortlessly. He was so strong it seemed like I didn't weigh a pound. This time I gathered my wits, and the alcohol made me braver.

"I would have thought the problem is that you're always in my way, pretending to be a wall or a crane," I retorted, shooting him the coldest stare I could muster.

He withdrew, but kept his eyes focused on me, looking me up and down, as if he couldn't believe I was real.

"You've been watching me the whole evening, haven't you?" I asked fiercely. I might be paranoid sometimes, but when I have a hunch, it's rarely wrong.

The man smirked.

"I watch the club," he replied. "I supervise the staff, check on the guests, and look for women in need of a wall or a crane."

I found his response amusing and discomfiting in equal parts.

"In that case, thank you for being my crane. Have a good night." I sent him a provocative gaze and headed toward the restroom. When he stayed behind, I sighed with relief. At least this time I didn't look like a complete idiot and had been able to speak like a normal person.

"See you around, Laura," I heard him say.

I spun on my heel, but the Man in Black was nowhere to be seen anymore.

How did he know my name? Had be been eavesdropping on us? No, he couldn't have. I would have noticed him. Karolina grabbed me by the hand all of a sudden.

"Come on, or you'll never reach that ladies' room and we'll be stuck here forever."

When we finally returned to our table, there was another bottle of Moët waiting for us.

"Well, well. I see we're not skimping on the drinks today, darling," I said with a laugh.

"I thought you ordered it," Martin replied, visibly surprised. "I already paid, and we wanted to leave."

I took a look around the club. I knew it wasn't a mistake. The bottle arrived at that moment on purpose. *He* was still watching me.

"It's probably on the house. After your 'Happy Birthday,' they couldn't leave us with nothing," Karolina said. "But, since it's already here, drink up!"

I fidgeted on the sofa until the bottle was finished, wondering about who that man dressed in black had been. Why had he looked at me like that? How did he know my name?

We spent the rest of the evening wandering around clubs, only returning to the hotel when the sun was rising.

I woke with a terrible headache. Oh, right . . . Moët. I adore champagne, but the hangovers it causes are the worst. What normal person binges on champagne? With the last of the strength I could muster, I crawled out of bed and reached the bathroom. I rummaged through my toiletry bag and found my painkillers, taking three and returning straight to bed. When I came to a few hours later, Martin was gone, and I could hear the sounds of people lounging in and around the pool. I needed to get up and catch some sun. It was my vacation, after all. Energized with that thought, I took a quick shower, jumped into a bikini, and thirty minutes later was ready for sunbathing.

Michał and Karolina were sprawled on chaise longues by the pool, sipping on ice-cold wine.

"Here. It's medicine," Michał said, passing me a plastic cup. "I'm afraid plastic is all they've got. Regulations."

The wine was delicious. Cold and . . . wet. I downed the glass in one go.

"Have you seen Martin? He wasn't there when I woke up."

"He's working in the lobby. The Internet was too bad in the room," Karolina explained.

Right—man's best friend, the laptop. And work was Martin's favorite lover. I lay down on the chaise and spent the rest of the day alone, with only the constantly smooching couple next to me. Once in a while, Michał would push away from Karolina and exclaim, "Look at those tits!" at passing women.

"Want to grab some lunch?" he asked at one point. "I'll go fetch Martin. That man can't enjoy a proper vacation with that laptop of his."

He got up, put on a T-shirt, and headed to the lobby.

"Sometimes I can't stand him." I turned to Karolina and she stared at me, eyes wide. "I'll never be number one with him. You know, more important than work, friends, or hobbies. Sometimes I think he's with me just because he's got nothing better to do. It's a bit like having a dog—you pet it when you want, play around a little bit, but when you're bored you just shoo it away. It's there for you, not the other way around, right? Martin spends more time chatting with his friends on Facebook than with me at home. Not to mention in bed."

Karolina rolled to the side and propped up on an elbow.

"You know, Laura, relationships are like that sometimes. Passion just vanishes at some point."

"But after a year and a half? Not even that! Am I that ugly? Is something wrong with me? Is it wrong that I just want to have a good fuck once in a while?"

Karolina jumped to her feet with a laugh and gestured to me to get up.

"You need a drink. Overthinking it won't change a thing. Just look around! It's perfect and you're beautiful and so thin! If not Martin, you'll find someone else! Come on!"

I threw on a light floral tunic, wrapped my beach scarf into a turban, put on my Ralph Lauren sunglasses, and followed Karolina to the bar in the lobby. My companion went to her room for a while to leave her bag and ask Michał about those lunch plans.

Our men weren't downstairs. I went to the bar and waved at the bartender, asking for two glasses of cold Prosecco. That was just what I needed.

"That's it?" I heard a man's voice behind me. "I thought your heart belongs to Moët?"

I turned around and froze. There he was, standing right in front of me. Only he wasn't the Man in Black anymore. He wore off-white linen pants and a bright shirt. It was the perfect counterpoint to his sun-kissed skin. He pulled his sunglasses lower down his nose and fixed me with that cold stare of his again. He called out to the bartender in Italian. As soon as the mysterious man arrived, the man behind the counter had pointedly ignored everyone else, standing at attention and waiting for my stalker's order. Hidden behind my sunglasses, I felt especially courageous and gutsy today—furious and hungover.

"Why do I get the feeling you're following me?" I asked, crossing my arms. He raised his right hand and slowly took my glasses off to see my eyes. It felt like he was taking away my shield. Suddenly I was out in the open.

"It's not a feeling," he said, looking me straight in the eyes. "It's not coincidence, either. Happy twenty-ninth birthday, Laura. May the coming year be the best in your life," he whispered, and placed a delicate kiss on my cheek.

I was so shocked that I just stood there, dumbfounded and mute. How did he know my age? And how the hell did he find me on the other end of town? The bartender's voice shook me out of that train of thought. I turned his way. He was just setting a bottle of rose Moët and a small colorful cupcake with a single candle on the counter.

"Goddamn it!" I spun to face the Man in Black, who had vanished in the meantime. Again.

"Well, well," Karolina said with a smile, approaching the bar. "We were supposed to have a glass of Prosecco and suddenly I find another bottle of champagne waiting for me."

I shrugged and scanned my surroundings nervously in search of the mysterious man, but he wasn't there. I pulled out a credit card and offered it to the bartender. In mangled English he refused the payment, assuring me that the tab had already been paid. Karolina graced him with a charming smile, grabbed the cooler with the bottle and cups, and went straight back to the pool. I blew out the candle on the cupcake and followed her.

I was pissed off, to say the least. But also disoriented and intrigued. There were dozens of different scenarios playing out in my head, suggesting different personalities for the mysterious man. The first thing that came to my mind was that he was some kind of pervert. But it didn't entirely agree with the image of the breathtakingly handsome Italian—he was probably spending more time trying to avoid admirers than actively seeking them out. Judging by his shoes and expensive clothes, he was far from broke. And he had mentioned something about checking up on guests in that club. So my next theory was that he was the manager there. But that wouldn't explain what he was doing at the hotel. I shook my head, trying to get rid of the nagging thoughts, and reached for a cup. *What do I care?* I thought, sipping the champagne. It must have been a coincidence after all.

When we finished the bottle, our men arrived, looking happy.

"So how about that lunch?" Martin asked with a satisfied grin.

The champagne I had drunk, today and last evening, made me combative. I was furious about his carefree attitude.

"What the fuck, Martin?" I snapped. "It's my birthday and you vanish for hours and don't even care what I'm doing or how I'm feeling and now you just show up and simply ask about lunch? Enough of this! It's always about you. I always do what you want, and you always tell me what to do. I'm never the most important thing in your life. And lunchtime was hours ago!"

I wrapped my tunic more tightly around me, grabbed my bag, and stormed off to the lobby. I crossed the hall and found myself on the street. My eyes were watering. I put my glasses on and started walking.

The streets of Giardini were lovely. There were trees speckled with flowers growing all along the pavement. The buildings were well cared for and beautiful. Sadly, my state of mind didn't allow me to really take in the charm of the place. I felt so alone. I realized I was crying. Tears flowing freely down my cheeks, racked with sobs, I nearly ran. Was I running away from something?

The sun was slowly setting, but still I walked. When the first wave of anger abated, I became aware of just how much my feet hurt. My wedge-heeled flip-flops, despite being a work of art, were no shoes for long walks. I noticed a small café in one of the nooks and crannies of the town. It was the perfect place to catch my breath, and I found out one of the items on the menu was sparkling wine. I sat down outside, watching the serene surface of the sea. An old woman brought me a glass of wine and said something in Italian, gently stroking my hand. Jesus, I didn't even have to understand the words to know what she was talking about—that all men were bastards unworthy of our tears. I sat at the table and stared out at the sea until it grew dark. I wouldn't have been able to get up after how much I had to drink, but meanwhile I had ordered a *quattro formaggi* pizza that had turned out to be a better salve for my sadness than the wine. Then I had tiramisu and it was one of the best I had in my entire life. Better than the best champagne.

I felt ready to return and face what I had left by running away. Calmly and slowly, I headed back to the hotel. The winding streets were nearly deserted—they were too far from the main boulevard running along the coast. Two black SUVs passed me by. I had seen cars like those before, back at the airport.

The night was hot, I was drunk, my birthday was ending, and everything felt wrong. I turned when the walkway ended and realized I had no idea where I was. *Shit. Me and my sense of direction.* I looked around, but the only thing I could see were the lights of approaching cars.

CHAPTER 2

When I opened my eyes, it was night. I looked around and realized I still had no idea where I was. I was lying in an enormous bed in a room faintly lit only by the streetlamps outside. My head hurt and I needed to puke. What the hell happened? Where was I? I tried getting up but didn't have the strength. I felt like I weighed a ton. Even my head was too heavy to lift from the pillow. I closed my eyes and fell back into unconsciousness.

When I came to again, it was still dark. How long had I been asleep? Maybe it was the next night? There was no clock anywhere, and I didn't have my bag or my phone with me. This time I managed to push myself up and sit on the edge of the bed. For a while, I waited for my head to stop spinning. There was a night lamp by the bed. When its light filled the room, I saw it was part of an old house. I didn't know this place.

The window frames were gigantic and richly carved. Opposite the great wooden bed there was an enormous stone fireplace, the kind I'd only ever seen in movies. There were old wooden beams running across the ceiling. They matched the color of the window frames. The room was comfortable, classy, and very Italian. I walked toward the window and went out to the balcony overlooking a garden. The view was breathtaking.

"So good to see you awake."

I froze, hearing the words. My heart must have skipped a beat. I turned around and saw a young Italian. I knew he was a local by the accent with which he had spoken to me in English. His appearance only reinforced my assumption. He wasn't tall, just like 70 percent of Italians I had seen. He had long, dark hair that flowed freely over his shoulders, delicate facial features, and very large lips. A beautiful boy, you might say. He wore an immaculate elegant suit, but it did nothing to make him look any more adult. He evidently worked out. His shoulders were wide.

"Where am I? Why am I here?" I barked, stomping toward the man.

"Why don't you go and refresh yourself? I'll be back for you and you'll learn everything," he said, and walked out, shutting the door behind him. He had left me, while it was me who was scared witless by this whole situation.

I tried prying the door open, but it was no use. The man must have used a key to lock me in. I swore under my breath. I was completely helpless.

There was another door by the fireplace. I opened it and turned the light on, revealing a spectacular bathroom. There was a gigantic bathtub in the middle, a dressing table in the corner, right next to a sink with a tall mirror. In the opposite corner there was a shower that could probably fit an entire football team. It had no shower caddy or walls—only a large glass panel and a floor made out of minuscule mosaic tiles. The bathroom was probably as large as Martin's entire apartment. *Martin . . . he must be worried sick. Or maybe not? Maybe he's happy he got me out of his hair.* I felt another pang of anger, this time laced with fear caused by the situation I had gotten myself into.

I walked up to the mirror and gazed at myself. I looked good, incredibly good in fact. My skin was tanned brown and I appeared well rested. The bags I had under my eyes lately had vanished. I was still dressed in the black tunic and the bikini I had been wearing on my birthday, when I had run from the hotel. How was I supposed to *refresh myself* without my stuff? I dropped my clothes and took a shower, grabbing a fluffy white bathrobe from the hanger. Here you go—refreshed!

As I walked around the room where I had woken up, looking for any clues as to my whereabouts, the door opened. The young Italian was there again. With a wide gesture, he showed me out. We walked down a long corridor decorated with flowerpots. The house was engulfed in darkness, illuminated only by the streetlamps outside, shining through the numerous windows. We weaved our way through a labyrinth of corridors until the man stopped by a door and opened it. He shut it behind me, staying outside. This room must have been a library—the walls were lined with bookshelves and paintings in heavy, dark frames. There was another beautiful stone fireplace in the middle, with a fire burning brightly within. Around it stood soft dark-green sofas stacked with dozens of pillows in various shades of gold. There was a small table next to one of them, with a champagne cooler perched on top. I shuddered. Alcohol was the last thing I needed right now.

"Please, have a seat. You didn't react well to the sleeping pills. I had no idea you had a heart condition," I heard a man say, and noticed a silhouette standing on the balcony, facing away from me.

I didn't even flinch.

"Have a seat, Laura. I will have to use force if you don't comply. I will not ask again."

Blood was pounding in my head. I could hear the thumping of my own heart. I was about to faint and could see dark spots floating in front of my eyes.

"Why aren't you listening to me, goddamn it?"

The silhouette leaped from the balcony into the room and caught me before I could collapse to the floor.

I blinked, trying to clear my sight, and felt the man sitting me down in an armchair and putting an ice cube into my mouth.

"Suck it. You've been asleep for nearly two days. The doctor gave you an IV so you didn't dehydrate, but you may feel thirsty and dizzy." I knew that voice and that characteristic accent.

I opened my eyes only to meet that ice-cold, animal stare. It was the same man I had met at the hotel, in the restaurant, and . . . oh my God—at the airport! He was dressed the same way he had been when we had landed on Sicily and when I had walked into his burly bodyguard. He was wearing a black suit with a black shirt with the top button undone. Very elegant and very imperious. I spat the ice cube into his face.

"Why am I here? Who are you and how dare you keep me here?"

He swept away the water spattered over his face, picked the cold translucent cube from the rug, and flung it into the fireplace.

"Answer me, you motherfucker!" I screamed, momentarily forgetting my dizziness. I tried to jump to my feet, but he put his hands over my shoulders and pushed me back into the armchair.

"I told you to sit down. I will not tolerate any insubordination," he growled, leaning over me with his hands propped on the armrests.

Furious, I raised my hand and slapped his face. His eyes blazed with wild fury, and I shrank back in terror. The man rose, very slowly, straightened out, and inhaled loudly through his nose. I was so afraid of what I had done I stayed down, frozen, unable and un-willing to test his limits. He headed toward the fireplace, stopped with his back to me, and put his hands on the wall over the mantel, leaning on it heavily. Time was passing, and he stood there, utterly quiet. If not for the fact that he was keeping me there against my will, I would probably have felt pricks of conscience by now and would have started apologizing profusely, but in my circumstances, I couldn't help feeling only anger.

"You're so disobedient, Laura, I have difficulty believing you're not Italian."

He turned back and looked at me. His eyes were still blazing. I decided to keep quiet, hoping to learn what I was doing here and how much longer this whole business would take.

The door opened and the same young man who had brought me here entered.

"Don Massimo . . ." he stammered.

The Man in Black shot him a warning glance, making his subordinate freeze. Then he walked over to the younger man and stopped only a few inches short of touching him. He needed to bend down, being a lot taller than the second man—at least a few inches.

Their conversation was in Italian—the youngster spoke, and my captor stood perfectly still and listened. He replied with a single utterance and the other man disappeared, closing the door behind him. The Man in Black paced the room for a while, then left for the balcony. He leaned over the railing and started to repeat some phrase in a soft whisper.

Don . . . I recalled people referring this way to Marlon Brando in *The Godfather*. But he was the head of a Mafia family. Suddenly it all came together: the bodyguards, the cars with black windows, that enormous house, and the terrifying imperiousness. I had thought the Cosa Nostra a figment of Francis Ford Coppola's imagination, but here I was, in the middle of the real thing.

"Massimo?" I asked quietly. "Is that what I am supposed to call you? Or Don?"

The man turned around and walked back to me with a confident stride. The whir of thoughts in my head made me gasp for air. The fear was paralyzing.

"So, you think you understand now?" he asked, reclining on the sofa.

"I think now I know what your name is."

He smiled slightly, growing a bit more relaxed. "I imagine you'd like some kind of explanation. Nevertheless, I don't know how you'll react to what I am going to say. Better have a drink first."

He stood up and poured us two glasses of champagne. He took one and passed it to me, and then sipped from the other one before taking his seat on the sofa again.

"A few years ago, I had a . . . let's call it an accident. I was shot. It's part of the risk you need to accept when you're part of my family. As I lay dying, I saw . . . ." He trailed off and got up. After walking to the fireplace, he placed the glass down on top of the stone mantel and sighed heavily. "What I'm about to tell you will be hard to believe. Before I saw you at the airport, I never hoped to meet you in person. Please, look up at the painting over the fireplace."

My eyes trailed upward, to the place he had pointed to. I stiffened. It was a portrait of a woman. With my face. I grabbed my glass and downed it. The alcoholic bite made me wince, but it had the calming effect I had expected. I reached out for the bottle to pour myself another glass. Meanwhile, Massimo continued.

"When my heart stopped, I saw . . . you. After weeks in a coma, I regained consciousness, and my fitness came back sometime later.

As soon as I was able to communicate the image I had before my eyes the whole time, I called an artist to paint the woman I saw in my dreams. He painted you."

That couldn't be disputed. It was me in the painting. But . . . how was that possible?

"I looked for you everywhere. Well, that might be a bit of an overstatement. Deep down, I knew someday you'd show up. And here you are. I saw you at the airport, leaving the terminal. At first I wanted to grab you then and there and never let you go again, but that was just too much of a risk. But since then, my people have been keeping an eye on you. Tortuga, the restaurant you ended up in, is my property. But it wasn't my doing that you went there. It was fate. When you were inside, I just couldn't resist. I had to talk to you. And then fate intervened again, and you went through that door you shouldn't have. Providence seems to favor me. The hotel you stayed in is also mine . . . In part."

That's when I realized where the champagne on our table had come from, and why I had felt watched. I wanted to interrupt the man and shower him with a million questions, but I decided to wait.

"You must be mine, too, Laura."

That was it. I snapped. "I'm not anyone's property! I'm not a thing to own! And you can't just *have* me. Kidnap me and count on me just accepting that," I hissed.

"I know. That's why I'll give you a chance to fall in love with me and stay with me out of your own volition, rather than any compulsion I might impose."

I snorted with hysterical laughter, and then slowly and calmly rose from the armchair. Massimo didn't object to that. I walked over to the fireplace, turning my champagne glass in my fingers. I finished the rest and then turned to my captor.

"You're kidding, right?" I narrowed my eyes, pinning the man with a hateful glare.

"I have a boyfriend who will look for me. I have a family. Friends. I have a *life*. And I don't need your goddamn chance at love!" I nearly shouted that out. "So you'll let me go right now and allow me to return to my world."

Massimo walked over to the opposite side of the room. He opened a cabinet and took out two envelopes before returning and stopping right next to me. He was close enough for me to smell his scent—an overpowering mix of power, money, and warm, spiced perfume. It made me feel dizzy all over again.

He passed me the first envelope, saying, "Before you open it, I'll explain what is inside . . ." I didn't wait, instead spinning on my heel away from him and ripping the envelope open.

Photos spilled to the floor.

"Oh my God . . ." I breathed. Then a great sob wracked my body and I collapsed to my knees, hiding my face in my hands.

My heart cramped and my eyes teared up. The photos showed Martin fucking another woman. They had been snapped secretly, but there was no doubt they showed my boyfriend.

"Laura . . ." Massimo knelt beside me. "I will explain what you're seeing now, so listen, please. When I tell you to do something, and you decide to do the opposite, it will always . . . *always* end up badly for you. Please understand that and stop fighting me. You've already lost that battle."

I raised my teary eyes and looked at him with such uncontrollable hate that he withdrew a bit. I was furious, desperate, ripped to shreds with grief. I didn't care anymore.

"You know what? Fuck off and die!" I threw the envelope at him and leaped for the door.

Still on his knees, Massimo shot out a hand and grabbed my

ankle, pulling me toward him. I toppled to the floor again, slamming into it with my back. He didn't mind, instead pulling me across the rug until I found myself directly beneath him. Lightning fast, he released my ankle and clasped his hands around my wrists. I thrashed wildly, trying to break free.

"Let me go, you fucker!" I roared, struggling.

He shook me, trying to make me stop fighting, and a gun slipped from beneath his belt, tumbling to the floor. I froze, but Massimo didn't seem to care at all, instead keeping his eyes focused solely on me. His hands clamped around my wrists harder, like vises. I stopped struggling, growing limp. I was helpless. I cried. His cold eyes pierced me with their icy stare. His eyes trailed down my body, half-naked now. The bathrobe I had on had rolled upward, revealing a lot. Massimo inhaled through his teeth, biting his lower lip. He moved his mouth near mine. I stopped breathing. He was taking in my scent and getting ready to taste me now. His lips touched my cheek and trailed a line across it. He whispered, "I will not do anything without your consent and willingness. Even if I think I already have it, I'll wait for you to want me, to need me, and to come to me out of your own will. Which doesn't mean that I don't want to enter you, deep, and stifle your screams with my tongue."

Those words, spoken so softly and silently, caused a wave of heat to ripple through my entire body.

"Now stop squirming and listen. I have a hard night ahead of me. The previous ones haven't been a walk in the park either, and you're not making it any easier for me. I'm not used to having to tolerate insubordination. I don't know how to be delicate, but I don't want to hurt you. So either I strap you to a chair and gag you, or I let you go and you start doing what I say."

His body was stuck to mine. I could feel each of his perfectly toned muscles working beneath his skin.

He slid his left knee, which had been locked between my legs, higher when I didn't react to his words. I moaned softly, stifling a scream when he pushed his knee between my thighs and it rubbed against my sensitive skin. My back arched unwillingly as I turned my head away from him. My body only reacted this way when I was aroused. Despite Massimo's aggression, that was exactly how I felt.

"Don't provoke me, Laura," he hissed.

"All right. I'll be good. Just get off me."

Gracefully, Massimo stood up and put his gun on the table before taking me by the hands and leading me back to the armchair.

"This way it'll be a lot easier for the both of us, believe me. So, back to those photos . . ." he said.

"On your birthday, I witnessed a quarrel between you and your man at the pool. When you left, I knew it was the day I'd bring you into my life. After your man didn't even move a muscle to stop you when you ran away, I knew he wasn't worthy of you. I knew he wouldn't grieve for you too long. When you disappeared, your friends went to lunch as if nothing happened. That's when my people took your things from your room and left a letter in which you wrote to Martin that you're leaving him and returning to Poland, moving out of his apartment and disappearing from his life. There's no possibility that he didn't read it when he went to his room after lunch. In the evening, when they walked by the reception dressed fashionably and in a great mood, your friends were approached by a staff member who recommended a club to them. It's called Toro and it's also my property. This way I could control the situation. When you look through those photos, you'll see the whole story play out just the way I told you. What happened at the club . . . well, they drank, had fun, and Martin took an interest in one of the dancers. You saw the rest. The pictures speak for themselves."

I sat still, looking at him in disbelief. My whole life had been turned upside down in a matter of hours.

"I want to go back to Poland. Please, let me go home."

Massimo got up from the sofa again and walked over to the fireplace. The dying fire bathed the room in a warm half-light. He propped one hand on the wall and said something in Italian. With a deep sigh, he turned to me again and replied, "Unfortunately, that won't be possible during the next three hundred and sixty-five days. I want you to sacrifice a year for me. I will do everything in my power to make you fall in love with me. If I fail by your next birthday, I will set you free. Don't get me wrong, this is not a proposal. I'm telling you what is going to happen. I will not touch you or do anything you won't want. I will not make you do anything against your will. I will not rape you, if that's what you're afraid of. Because you're my angel. I want to show you all the respect in the world. Your value to me is as high as my own life's. Everything in my residence will be at your disposal. You will get your own bodyguards, but not because I want to control you. It's only for your own safety. You will pick the men yourself. You will be able to access all my property. I will not keep you locked up. If it is your wish to leave the house and go to a club or wherever else, I have nothing against it—"

I interrupted him.

"You're not being serious, are you? You think I'll just sit here like nothing ever happened? What will my parents think? You don't know my mother. She'll cry her eyes out when she learns I've been abducted. She'll spend the rest of her life looking for me. Do you know what this will do to her? I'd rather you shot me right here and now than make me blame myself for my mother's pain. If you let me out of this room, I'll run away, and you'll never see me again. I will *not* be anyone's property. Not yours, not anyone else's."

Massimo closed the distance between us, as if he knew something unpleasant was going to happen again. He reached out, passing me the other envelope.

Holding it in my hands, I wondered if I should rip it open like I had done the first one. I studied Massimo's face closely. He was watching the fire, waiting for my reaction to what was inside the envelope.

I ripped it open and pulled out another set of photos, my hands shaking. *What the fuck?* Those were photos of my family: Mom, Dad, and my brother. In normal, everyday situations. Taken near our house, or at lunch with friends, through the bedroom window as they slept.

"What is this supposed to mean?" I asked, disoriented and pissed to the brink of completely losing it.

"This is my insurance policy. You will not risk the life and safety of your family, will you? I know where they live, what they do, where they work, when they go to sleep and what they eat for breakfast. I will not keep an eye on you the entire time. I know I won't be able to keep you in place when I'm out. I won't keep you under lock and key, either. The only thing I can do is to give you an ultimatum: you give me a year and your family will be safe and sound."

I sat rooted to the spot and wondered if I could kill him. There was a gun lying on the table between us and I was ready to do what it took to protect my family. I sprang up and snatched the firearm, aiming it at the man. He remained in place, calm and impassive, but his eyes were ablaze with anger.

"You're driving me crazy, Laura. Crazy and mad. Please, put the gun down or the situation might get out of control and I may be forced to hurt you."

As soon as he was finished, I closed my eyes and pulled the trigger. Nothing happened. Massimo pounced on me, wrested the gun from my hand, and jerked me off the armchair, flinging me to the sofa he had jumped off of a second ago. He rolled me to my stomach and bound my hands with a decorative rope attached to one of the pillows. Then he sat me up, or rather threw me against the soft seat.

"You have to flick off the safety first! You want to talk that way? You comfortable? Want to kill me? Think it's so easy? As if nobody tried before you . . ."

He trailed off, brushed his hair with a hand, sighed, and threw me a cold and furious glare.

"Domenico!" he called out.

The young Italian immediately appeared at the door. He must have been waiting on the other side, ready to enter at any time.

"Take Laura to her room but keep the door unlocked," he said in English with that British accent of his. He wanted me to understand. Having done that, he turned to me and said, "I will not keep you here against your will, but will you risk escaping?"

He lifted me by the rope and passed it to Domenico, who accepted the thing with utter impassivity. Massimo tucked his gun behind his belt and left the room, shooting me a last warning glance as he did so.

The young Italian gestured to the door and led me by the "leash" Massimo had bound me with. After walking the same labyrinth of corridors, we reached the room where I had woken up a few hours ago. Domenico untied my hands, nodded, and closed the door as he left. I waited a couple of minutes and grabbed the handle. The door wasn't locked. I wasn't sure if I wanted to cross the threshold. I sat down on the bed, thoughts spinning in my head. *Was he telling the truth? Was he being serious? The entire year without my friends? Without my family? Without Warsaw?* I broke out crying. Would he be able to do something that cruel to my family? I wasn't sure, but I didn't want to test him. A wave of tears flooded from my eyes. I don't know how long I spent crying, but finally, exhausted, I fell asleep.

I woke up curled into a ball, still wearing the fluffy white bathrobe. It was dark outside. I wasn't sure if it was the same horrible night, or maybe the next one.

I heard hushed male voices from the garden, so I went to the balcony. I couldn't see anyone. The sounds were too quiet for the men to be anywhere close by. *Something must be happening on the other side of the property*, I thought. Reluctantly, I grabbed the door handle to check if I was free to go. The door was open, and I crossed the threshold, only to spend a long while thinking whether to continue or retreat back into the room. My curiosity won that struggle and I headed down a long hallway, in the direction of the voices. It was a hot and breezy August night. The drapes in the windows fluttered in the breeze that smelled of the sea. The house was dark and calm. I wondered how it looked by day. Without Domenico, I couldn't find my way through the tangled corridors. In just a short while, I was hopelessly lost. The only thing I navigated by were the voices. They were growing louder with each step I took. Passing through a half-open door, I found myself in an enormous hall with gigantic windows overlooking the driveway. I approached the pane of glass and leaned against the thick, tall frame, trying to hide behind it.

In the dark, I could see Massimo and several other people. There was a man kneeling before them shouting something in Italian. His expression suggested terror and panic as he stared wide-eyed at the Man in Black. Massimo was standing at ease, his hands in the pockets of his casual pants. He was fixing the pleading man with an icy stare, waiting for him to finish. As soon as he did, Massimo impassively uttered a short sentence or two, took out his gun, and shot the man in the head. The victim's body flopped to the stone driveway.

I yelped and put my hands to my mouth to stop myself from screaming. It was no use. Massimo heard me, turned away from the body, and looked straight at me. His stare was cold and emotionless, as if killing a man was nothing to him. He grabbed the silencer of his gun and passed the weapon to one of the men standing next to him. I slumped to the floor.

I couldn't breathe. I gasped for air. My heart was thumping, but its rhythm was quickly slowing and so was the pumping of blood in my head. I saw darkness and my stomach cramped, signaling the inevitable release of the champagne I had drunk earlier. With trembling hands, I tried untying the belt of the bathrobe that seemed to constrict me so tightly I could barely breathe. I had witnessed the death of a human being. In my head, I could see the scene of the execution replaying over and over again. The image made me choke, my lungs completely void of air. I let it go, succumbed to the feeling, stopped fighting. During the last moments of consciousness, I felt the belt of the bathrobe loosening and someone's fingers touching my neck, searching for a pulse. One hand slid under my back and went up, passing my neck and holding my head. Another supported my legs. I felt movement. I wanted to open my eyes but couldn't lift my eyelids.

There were sounds around me, but only one clear enough to hear, "Breathe, Laura."

That accent. I knew it was Massimo with his arms around me. The arms of a man who had killed just a moment before. He took me to my room, kicking the door open. I felt him laying me down on the bed. I was still struggling to breathe. My heaving breath was getting less chaotic and panicked, but I still couldn't inhale deeply. There was still too little oxygen.

Massimo opened my mouth with one hand and slid a pill under my tongue.

"Don't be afraid, darling girl. It's heart medicine. The doctor left it in case of just such a situation."

A while later my breathing went back to normal. Oxygen finally got into my lungs and my heart steadied its rhythm. I sank into the sheets and fell into a deep sleep.

CHAPTER 3

When I opened my eyes, it was day. I was lying in white sheets, wearing a T-shirt and briefs. I seemed to recall falling asleep with the bathrobe on . . . Had the Man in Black changed my clothes? In order to do that, he'd have to first remove the bathrobe. And that meant he had seen me naked. That thought wasn't exactly pleasant, even though it had to be said that Massimo was as handsome as they got.

The events of last night flitted before my eyes. I gasped in fear and pulled the duvet over my head. All this information—the 365 days he was giving me, my family, Martin's betrayal, and the death of that man—was too much for one night.

"It wasn't me who changed your clothes," I heard a muffled voice saying through the duvet.

I slowly pulled it off and looked at the Man in Black. He was sitting in a grand armchair by the bed. This time, he was wearing a more casual outfit—gray joggers and a white tank top, accentuating the muscles of his wide shoulders and perfectly chiseled arms. He was barefoot, and his hair was in disarray.

If not for the fact that he was looking so fresh and tempting, I'd have thought he had just woken up.

"Maria, my cousin, did it," he was saying. "I wasn't even there. I promised you I won't do anything without your consent, though I won't pretend I wasn't tempted to watch. Especially because you were unconscious, so defenseless. And I was sure you wouldn't slap me in the face this time," he said, raising his brows in amusement. I saw him smile for the first time. He looked carefree and happy. For him, the dramatic events of last night were already forgotten.

I sat up and rested my head against the wooden headboard. Massimo, his roguish smile not disappearing, reclined in the armchair, crossed his legs, and waited for me to speak.

"You killed a man," I breathed, my eyes tearing up. "You shot him just like that. Without emotion, as if it was just another thing."

His eyes immediately lost their playfulness, and the smile vanished from his face, replaced with an unflinching mask of severity that I already knew.

"He betrayed the family. I am its head, so he betrayed me." Massimo leaned closer. "I told you, but apparently you thought I was joking. I do not tolerate defiance and insubordination, Laura. There is nothing as important as loyalty. You are not yet ready for all this, and you can't ever be ready for what you saw yesterday."

He trailed off and stood up, walking over to the bed and sitting on its edge. He combed through my hair with a hand, as if checking if I was real. At some point, he slid his hand under my head and grabbed me by the hair, hard. He swung his leg over me and sat astride me, pinning me down. His breathing quickened, and his eyes flared with passion and animalistic ferocity. I went rigid with terror, and it must have shown on my face. Massimo saw it and he liked it.

After the events of last night, I knew this man was no joke. If I wanted my family to be safe, I needed to accept his terms.

Massimo clamped his hand even harder on the back of my head, trailing his nose across my face. He inhaled deeply, taking in the scent of my skin. I wanted to close my eyes to show him the depth of my contempt, to overcome my own fear, but I was hypnotized by the savagery of his gaze and couldn't take my eyes off him. He was a beautiful man. Exactly my type. Black eyes, dark hair, large and full lips, a light stubble on his face, now delicately tickling my cheeks. And that body! Long, lean legs around my hips, strong and muscular arms, and a wide chest that I could see through the tight tank top.

"I said I won't do anything without your consent, but I don't know if I'll be able to stop myself after all," he whispered, looking me in the eyes.

He grabbed my hair and jerked my head back, pushing it into the pillow. I moaned softly. Massimo sucked in a gust of air, and then slowly and delicately inserted his right leg between my thighs. He rubbed against me with his manhood. I could feel it on my hip. He wanted me so bad. I, on the other hand, could only feel fear.

"I want to have you, Laura. I need to have you whole . . ." He was trailing his nose along my face. "When you're so fragile and helpless . . . I want you even more. I want to fuck you like nobody ever did before. I want you to feel pain and rapture. I want to be your last lover . . ."

He was saying all this while his hips were rhythmically rubbing against me. I understood that the game I was going to be a part of had just begun. I had nothing to lose. My options were to either spend the next 365 days fighting this man, which could only end in defeat, or learn the rules of the game and play it. Slowly, I lifted my hands above my head, resting them on the pillow, showing submission and defenselessness. Seeing that, the Man in Black let my hair go and intertwined his fingers with mine, pinning my hands to the bed.

"That's better," he breathed.

"I'm glad you understand me."

Massimo's impressive cock was rubbing against my hip faster and harder. I could feel it slide over my tummy.

"Do you want me?" I asked, lifting my head slightly, tracing my lower lip across his chin.

He moaned, and before I could react, his tongue was already in my mouth, pushing itself in frantically, deep, in a desperate search for my own. His grip on my hands slackened and I could free my right arm. Engrossed by the kiss, he didn't notice. I raised my right knee and pushed him away, simultaneously slapping him in the face with my free hand.

"Is this the respect you said you'd show me?" I screamed. "I remember you saying something about waiting for my express consent instead of misinterpreting any perceived signs!"

Massimo froze, and when he turned his head back to me, his eyes were calm and expressionless.

"If you hit me one more time—"

"What are you going to do? Kill me?" I barked before he could finish.

He withdrew, sitting on the edge of the bed. For a while he just stared at me, and then suddenly he burst out in loud, clear, and completely sincere laughter. In that moment, he looked like a young boy. For all I knew he might have been one—I had no idea as to his real age, but in that instant, he looked younger than me.

"How are you not Italian?" he asked. "This doesn't feel like Slavic temperament."

"How many Slavic girls do you know?"

"Oh, one is enough," he replied, still mirthful, and jumped off the bed. He turned to me, smiling, and said, "This is going to be a great year, but I do have to learn to dodge faster. You caught me off guard this time, sweetheart."

He headed to the door, but before crossing the threshold, he stopped and shot me another glance.

"Your things are here. Domenico arranged them in the closets. Not too many of them, but still, for someone who was supposed to be here only five days, you have a surprising amount of clothes. Not to mention shoes. We need to do something with your outfits, though. I'll be back in the afternoon, and we'll go buy you something new. Underwear and whatever else you'd like. This room is yours, unless you find another one you like more. The servants know who you are. Call Domenico if you need anything. The cars and drivers are at your disposal, though I'd prefer it if you didn't travel alone. You will get a security detail. They will do their best not to look too conspicuous. I will give you your telephone and computer in the evening, but we'll have to discuss some terms before I do that."

I stared at him, eyes wide, wondering what I was actually feeling. My thoughts were racing, and I couldn't focus with the taste of Massimo's mouth still on my lips. His penis was still erect, throbbing, and I couldn't take my eyes off it. I think I had a crush on my captor . . . There was no way to know if it was my subconscious reaction to Martin's betrayal, a need to take some kind of revenge, or else the desire to show Massimo just how tough I could be.

Meanwhile, Massimo continued. "The residence has a private beach, Jet Skis, and motorboats, but you aren't allowed to use them just yet. There is a pool in the garden. Domenico will show you around. He will be your personal assistant and translator if it comes to that. Some people don't know English around here. I chose him for his great love of fashion. Besides, he's about your age."

"How old are you?" I interrupted him. He let go of the door

handle and leaned against the doorframe. "Shouldn't godfathers be old guys?"

Massimo narrowed his eyes and replied, keeping his stare fixed on me, "I am not *capo di tutti capi*. They are older, you're right. I am a *capofamiglia*, or a don. But that is a long story. If you're interested, I'll tell you later."

He turned around and walked down the hallway until he vanished through one of the dozens of doors. I stayed still for a while longer, analyzing my predicament. Thinking about it felt exhausting, so I decided to keep myself busy. I had my first real chance to see the mansion in daylight. My room must have been at least 860 square feet and it had everything I could want. A great walk-in closet straight out of *Sex and the City*, for instance. Only nearly empty. The things I had taken with me to Sicily filled only about a hundredth of the gigantic room. The shoe shelves were empty, too. Most drawers only contained satin lining and nothing else. The place needed some filling.

Aside from the walk-in closet, I also got an enormous bathroom—the one I had used during the night. I had been too shocked and dazed then to really take in the impressive room. The huge open shower had a steam sauna function and was lined with massage jets that looked like towel hangers. Inside the dressing table with the mirror, I was delighted to find cosmetics of all my favorite brands: Dior, YSL, Guerlain, Chanel, and lots of others. Bottles of perfume crowded the counter next to the sink and one of them was my beloved Lancôme Midnight Rose. At first I wondered how he knew, but he knew everything about me, so such mundane little details like my favorite perfume, which he must have found in my baggage, shouldn't have been a mystery to him. I took a long, hot shower, washed my hair (it needed it desperately by that time), and went to the closet to choose something comfy to wear.

It was at least eighty-six degrees Fahrenheit outside, so I selected a long, flowy, raspberry-colored bare-back dress and wedge-heeled sandals. I wanted to dry my hair, but before I finished dressing, it was already dry. I bound it into a casual bun and headed out to the hallway.

The house looked a bit like the mansion from *Dynasty*, only more Italian flavored. It was gigantic and very impressive. Passing through dozens of rooms, I found more portraits of the woman from Massimo's visions. They were beautiful, presenting *me* in various poses. I still couldn't understand how he was able to depict me so closely without having seen me before.

I went down to the garden, meeting no one on my way. I wondered where the servants were as I strolled the paths lined with meticulously pruned greenery. Finally, I stumbled on the entrance to the beach. There was a little dock there, with a beautiful white motorboat and several Jet Skis floating at the quay. I took my shoes off and stepped onto the boat. The keys to the ignition were right there, lying unguarded next to the steering wheel. For a moment I entertained the thought of breaking Massimo's laws. As soon as I touched the key ring, I heard a voice from behind me.

"I would prefer if you didn't do that today."

I spun around, startled, and saw the young Italian.

"Domenico! I just wanted to know if they fit . . ." I stammered with an idiotic grin on my face.

"I can assure you they do. If you would like a little trip on the boat, we can arrange it after breakfast."

Food! Oh my God, when had I last eaten? I wasn't sure how much time I had spent asleep. In fact, I didn't have an inkling as to what day or hour it was. The thought of eating made my stomach rumble loudly. I was starving, but with all those conflicting emotions I had simply forgotten about it.

With an expansive gesture, Domenico directed me to get off the boat, offered me a hand, and led me up the quay.

"I allowed myself to prepare you breakfast in the garden. It's not that hot today and I thought you'd enjoy it," he said.

Yeah, right, I thought. But eighty-six degrees wasn't *that* hot around here, I realized. Why not eat outside after all?

Domenico led me through the garden to a great terrace on the other side of the mansion. The view seemed familiar. My room had to be somewhere on this side of the house. There was a makeshift gazebo on the stone floor, closely resembling the enclosures at the restaurant where we had eaten the first night. It had thick wooden supports that served as anchors for great sheets of sailcloth stretched overhead as protection from the sun. Beneath the gently waving roof, there was a long table made of the same wood as the supports, and a set of comfortable-looking chairs with white pillows.

The breakfast was worthy of a queen, and my hunger had only intensified. There were platters of cheeses, olives, aromatic cold cuts, pancakes, fruit, eggs—everything I loved. I sat at the table and Domenico vanished. I was used to eating alone, but dealing with the heaps of delicious food would be all the more pleasant with someone to accompany me. A while later, the young man returned, carrying a bundle of newspapers.

"I thought you might want to read today's papers, ma'am."

Having said that, he turned away and walked into the villa.

I glanced at the papers and realized they were all Polish—*Rzeczpospolita*, *Wyborcza*, a Polish issue of *Vogue*, and some British tabloids. I felt better immediately. I could at least read about the goings-on in my home country. Helping myself to all the delicacies and leafing through the papers, I wondered if for the next year this would be the only way I would read the news from Poland.

Sometime later, I finished my breakfast. I had no strength to do anything taxing—I was too stuffed. Apparently, eating so much after several days of fasting was not the brightest idea. In the distance, in a remote corner of the garden, I noticed a large beach sofa in the shade of a canopy. It would be the perfect place to wait through the stomachache. I headed that way, taking the rest of the papers with me.

I took my shoes off and crawled onto the soft couch, tossing the magazines next to me and making myself comfortable. The view from the sofa was amazing—small boats floated lazily on the sea, a motorboat was towing a parachute with two people enjoying the ride, and the azure water looked so inviting with the monumental rock formations jutting from the waves offering the promise of equally beautiful views below the surface. A cool breeze was blowing from the sea and all the sugar in my blood was making me drowsy. I allowed myself to recline deeper into the soft pillows.

"Are you going to sleep through another day?" A quiet whisper with a British accent woke me up.

I opened my eyes only to see Massimo sitting next to me, observing me.

"I missed you," he said, lifting my hand in his and placing a kiss on the back of my palm. "I've never said that to anybody. I never felt this way. I've been thinking about you the whole day. That you're finally here."

Still a bit dazed after the nap, I stretched out lazily, arching my body. The thin dress must have exposed my curves. Massimo shot up and took a step back. His eyes were full of that animal lust again.

"Can you stop that?" he asked, shooting me a warning glare. "If you keep being so provocative, you may regret it."

Seeing his stare, I jumped to my feet and stopped right in front of him. Without my high heels, I didn't even reach his chin.

"I was stretching. It's a natural thing you do after waking up, isn't it? But since you're so touchy, I won't do it again with you around," I said, pouting.

"I think you know perfectly well what you did there," Massimo retorted, lifting my chin with his fingers.

"But since you're up, we can go now. You'll need a few more things bought before we leave."

"Leave? Am I leaving all of a sudden?" I asked, crossing my arms.

"You are, with me. I have a couple of things to do back on the mainland, and you'll accompany me. After all, I only have three hundred and fifty-nine days left."

Massimo was clearly amused, and his carefree attitude quickly rubbed off on me. For a while, we stood face-to-face, like a couple of flirting teenagers. I could feel the tension between us, the fear and the lust. I thought we were both feeling the same thing—only the cause of our fear was different.

Massimo kept his hands in the pockets of his loose dark pants. His shirt of the same color, with the top button undone, showed a glimpse of the short hairs on his chest. He looked so sensual and seductive when the wind ruffled his combed hair. I shook my head again, getting rid of the unwanted thoughts.

"I would like to talk," I stammered.

"I know. Not now. There will be a time for that during dinner. You'll have to be patient. Come with me."

He took me by the hand, picked up my shoes from the ground, and led me to the villa. We passed a long hallway and found ourselves on the driveway. I stopped on the stone surface, rooted to the spot. The horror of last night returned. It was *the place*. Massimo felt my hand growing limp. He took me in his arms and carried me to the black SUV parked a few feet away. I blinked nervously, trying to clear my sight. I wanted to pinch myself to wake up from the nightmare that kept repeating itself over and over again in my head.

"If you're going to black out each time you leave the house, I'll have my people replace the whole driveway," Massimo said matter-of-factly, keeping his fingers on my wrist and looking at his watch. "Your heart is going to burst if it continues like that. Try to calm down. Otherwise I will be forced to give you your medication, and that would only make you go to sleep again."

He grabbed me and sat me on his knees, bringing my head against his chest, stroking my hair, and swaying softly.

"My mother did this to calm me when I was little," he said. "In most cases it worked wonders." His voice was gentle, and his hand didn't stop its rhythmic movement.

This man was so full of contradictions. A tender barbarian. The perfect way to describe him. Dangerous, imperious, intolerant of any defiance, but at the same time so caring and delicate. The mixture of all those things was terrifying, but also fascinating and intriguing.

Massimo said something to the driver in Italian and pushed a button on a panel, which caused a darkened window to rise between us and the man. The car accelerated and the Man in Black did not stop stroking my head. A few moments later I was calm again, and my heartbeat returned to its normal rhythm.

"Thank you," I breathed, slipping from his knees and sitting down next to him.

He studied me intently, making sure I was okay.

In order to avoid his piercing eyes, I looked out the window, only to realize we were going uphill. I raised my eyes and gasped at the beautiful vista stretching before us. A city built on a rocky slope.

"Where are we?" I asked.

"My villa stands on the slopes of Taormina, and we're going to town. I think you'll like it," he said, looking out his own window.

CHAPTER 4

Giardini Naxos, where I had stayed with Martin, was located a few miles away from Taormina. The town on the rock was visible from practically everywhere in Giardini. We were supposed to go sightseeing there. What if Martin, Michał, and Karolina went along with the plan? What if we met them? I fidgeted restlessly in my seat and the Man in Black noticed. As if reading my mind, he said, "They left the island yesterday."

How could he know what I was thinking? I sent him an inquiring look, but he didn't so much as look my way.

When we reached our destination, the sun was already setting, and thousands of tourists and locals were swarming the streets of Taormina. The town was brimming with life, and the narrow, picturesque streets were lined with hundreds of small cafés and restaurants. Signboards of expensive boutiques beckoned to me. Exclusive brands? In the middle of nowhere? There were no stores like that in the center of Warsaw. The car stopped, and the driver stepped out, opening the door for us. The Man in Black offered his hand and helped me out of the large SUV.

After a while, I realized there was another car with us, just behind ours. Two tall men dressed in black emerged from it. Massimo grabbed my hand and led me to one of the main streets. His people followed us at a distance that was supposed to be inconspicuous. It all looked kind of grotesque—if they really wanted to remain unseen, they should be wearing shorts and flip-flops, not undertaker suits. It would be pretty difficult to hide those guns in tourist outfits though.

The first shop we visited was a Roberto Cavalli boutique. As soon as we stepped over the threshold, we were greeted by a shop assistant, who sprinted from behind her desk, eager to please. A well-dressed older man appeared from the back room. He kissed Massimo on both cheeks, saying something in Italian, before turning his attention to me.

"*Bella*," he said, reaching for my hands.

It was one of the few words in Italian I did understand. I smiled at the man, thanking him for the compliment.

"My name is Antonio. I shall help you choose some more . . . appropriate attire," he said in fluent English. "Size thirty-six, I presume?" He sent me a probing stare.

"Sometimes thirty-four. Depending on the bra size. As you can see, Mother Nature hasn't been too generous to me," I said, pointing to my breasts with a wide grin.

"Darling!" Antonio exclaimed. "Roberto Cavalli adores such shapes! Come! Let don Massimo stay here and wait for the show."

The Man in Black began to sit down on a silvery satin couch. Before he even touched the soft pillows, he was offered a bottle of ice-cold Dom Pérignon, and one of the shop assistants filled his glass. Massimo shot me a lustful glance before hiding behind a newspaper. Antonio was hauling dozens of dresses to the changing room, helping me into them, all the time clicking his tongue with appreciation. I stared wide-eyed at the price tags of the outfits.

That little heap of dresses Antonio prepared for me would probably buy you an apartment in Warsaw. Nearly an hour later, I finished picking clothes, and my choices were packed neatly into beautiful decorative boxes.

The story repeated in other boutiques: an enthusiastic welcome followed by an unending shopping spree . . . Prada, Louis Vuitton, Chanel, Louboutin, and Victoria's Secret to top it all off.

Each time Massimo would sit down and patiently wait for me, reading his newspaper, talking on the phone, or scrolling on his iPad. He seemed completely disinterested in what I was doing. On the one hand, I was happy, but on the other—it was getting on my nerves. What was wrong with him? Earlier, in the morning, he couldn't take his eyes off me, and now—when he had the opportunity to admire me in all these beautiful outfits—he wasn't paying attention.

This definitely didn't go hand in hand with my concept of shopping straight out of *Pretty Woman*—me, showing off in new hot and sexy outfits and him playing the role of my horny fan.

Victoria's Secret greeted us with pink. It was everywhere: on the walls, the couches, the shop assistants, even—I felt like I'd been thrown into a cotton candy machine. I was about to puke with all that sweetness. The Man in Black glanced at me, taking his eyes off his mobile for a moment.

"This is the last one. We've got no more time. Please take that into account when choosing your outfits here," he said nonchalantly, turned his back on me, sat down on one of the couches, and got back to his phone.

I grimaced, glaring at him with disapproval. It wasn't about the fact that we were nearing the end of our shopping trip—I had enough by that time—but rather the way he had addressed me.

"Signora," the shop assistant called out, inviting me to the changing room with a gesture.

As I entered the cubicle, my eyes were drawn to a neat heap of swimsuits and underwear waiting for me.

"You don't have to try on everything. Just one will be enough. I'll make sure the size I've chosen for you is appropriate," the woman said, and disappeared, drawing the heavy pink curtain behind her.

Why would I want so many pairs of underwear? I haven't had this many throughout my entire life. I stood there, gaping at the tower of colorful fabric—mainly lace. I peeked outside and asked, "Who picked all these?"

Noticing me, the shop assistant jumped to her feet and came over immediately.

"Don Massimo asked me to prepare those specific styles."

"I understand," I replied, retreating into the changing room.

Scouring through the heap, I noticed something: all this stuff was made of lace—thin lace, thick lace, regular lace . . . maybe a couple of cotton briefs thrown in, just in case. *Great. Very comfy*, I thought ironically. I picked a red lace and silk set and started to pull off my dress to get this over with. The fine bra closely fit my small breasts. Even though it wasn't a push-up, they looked really sexy in the new lingerie. I bent over and pulled up the lace. As I stood back up and looked in the mirror, I realized Massimo was standing behind me. He was leaning against the changing room wall with his hands in his pockets and observing me, taking in the view. I spun around, glaring at him.

"What are you—" I managed before he shot out his arm, grabbing me by the throat and slamming me into the mirror.

He stepped closer, his body pressed against mine as he delicately trailed his thumb along my lips. I froze, paralyzed. His taut, muscled body made it impossible for me to move anyway. He took his thumb away and lowered it to my neck. His grip wasn't too tight. It didn't have to be. It was a message—he was in charge here.

"Don't move," he purred, pinning me with his wild, icy stare. He dropped his eyes and moaned softly. "You look pretty. But you can't wear these. Not yet."

The words "you can't" sounded like an encouragement to me. Like a provocation. I felt like doing the exact opposite of what he was saying. I pushed myself away from the mirror and took a step forward. Massimo didn't resist. He pulled away, matching my movements, keeping me at an arm's length, his hand never leaving my neck. When I was sure we were sufficiently far from the mirror, and that he could see me entirely, I lifted my eyes and looked into his. As I suspected, his stare was fixed on my reflection. He was appraising his trophy, and I could see his pants becoming too tight for him. He was breathing loudly, and his torso was heaving faster and faster.

"Massimo," I whispered.

He tore his eyes from my ass and looked me in the eyes.

"Leave or I guarantee this will be the last time you see me like this," I growled, trying to make a threatening expression.

He smirked, accepting the challenge. His hand tightened on my neck. His eyes flared with fury and lust as he took a step forward, and then another one. I felt the mirror on my back again. That's when he let go of me and said, "I picked everything for you. I will decide when I want you to wear this." He turned away and left without another word.

I stood there for a while longer, boiling with fury, but somehow satisfied at the same time. I was beginning to learn the rules of our little game. I was getting to know his weak spots.

As I put on my dress, I could still feel the anger inside. I snatched the heap of lingerie from the drawer and stormed out of the changing room. The shop assistant sprang to her feet, but I walked straight past her. Massimo was back on the couch. I marched across the room with all the underwear in my arms.

"You picked that? Then here you go! It's all yours!" I screamed, flinging the lingerie at him before running out of the boutique.

The security detail waiting outside didn't move a muscle as I passed them. They sent Massimo wary looks but kept to their posts. I ran along crowded streets, thinking about what I'd done and what I was about to do. What my behavior could bring about. I glimpsed a flight of stairs between two buildings, took a turn, and ran straight up, taking another turn and disappearing into the first narrow street I saw. It ended in another flight of stairs. I climbed higher and higher until I found myself two blocks away from the place I had escaped from. Then I leaned against the wall, panting. My shoes might have been works of art, but they definitely hadn't been made for running. I stared into the sky and the grand castle looming over Taormina. *Fuck this*, I thought. *I can't go on like this.*

"It used to be a fortress," I heard someone say. "You want to run all the way up there or will you spare my boys the exertion? They're not as fit as I am." I turned my head. It was Massimo. Standing at the top of the stairs. It was clear he had followed me in a run—his hair was disheveled. He hadn't even broken a sweat. Unlike me. The Man in Black leaned nonchalantly against the wall, sliding his hands into his pockets.

"We need to go back now. If you'd like a workout, there's a gym and a pool back home. Or, if you're more of a staircase marathon kind of girl, there's a lot of those back at the villa, too."

I knew I had no choice. I had to go back with him, but at least for a moment I had felt my fate was in my own hands. Massimo extended a hand, which I ignored, heading back down the stairs where the two suited bodyguards were already waiting. I passed them both with a disapproving frown and walked over to the SUV parked a couple of feet away. I got in, slamming the door behind me.

A while later, Massimo joined me. He took the seat next to me and put his phone to his ear, talking all the way, until we reached the driveway. I had no idea what he was saying—I could still understand very little Italian. Massimo's voice was calm, though, and down-to-earth. He listened more than he spoke, and I couldn't read his body language.

We stopped at the mansion. I grabbed the handle, but the door was locked. The Man in Black finished his call, tucked the mobile into his breast pocket, and fixed me with a stare.

"Dinner will be served in an hour. Domenico will come for you."

The car door opened, and I saw the young Italian, his hand outstretched to help me out. I let him do so, sending him a wide, ostentatious smile. Then I ran to the building, looking straight ahead, not wanting to catch even a glimpse of the spot where the nightmare of last night had taken place. Domenico followed me.

"Turn right," he said quietly as I was starting to lose my way in the labyrinth of corridors.

I turned back, thanking him for the assistance, and a while later I was back in my room.

The young Italian stopped in the doorway, as if waiting for me to allow him in.

"They'll bring you all the things you've bought in a minute. Do you need anything else?" he asked.

"Yes. I could use a drink before dinner. Unless I'm not allowed, of course."

Domenico smiled and nodded understandingly, disappearing in the darkness.

I went to the bathroom, took off my dress, and locked the door behind me, stepping into the shower and turning on the cold water. It was freezing—I could barely breathe, but after a while I got used to it. I needed to cool off. When the chilling stream calmed me down, I turned up the temperature. I washed my hair, massaged in some conditioner, and sat down with my back against the wall. The water was pleasantly warm. It cascaded down the glass shower wall, relaxing me. I had a moment to think about what had happened in the morning, and then in the afternoon, back in the shop. I was confused. Massimo was a complicated man—totally unpredictable. Slowly, it was dawning on me that if I wouldn't accept my newfound circumstances and start living normally, I'd simply die of exhaustion.

That's when it struck me—there was nothing to fight, nothing to run away from. There was nothing for me back in Warsaw. I wasn't losing anything, because everything I had was now gone. The only thing I could do was let this adventure unfold. *It's time to accept your situation, Laura*, I thought, standing up.

I rinsed my hair and wrapped it in a towel, put on a bathrobe, and left the bathroom.

My bedroom was filled with dozens of boxes. I couldn't help feeling elated at the sight. In the past, I would have given everything to be able to go on a shopping spree like that. Nothing was going to stop me enjoying this now. I had a plan.

I rummaged through everything, finally finding the Victoria's Secret bags and digging through the dozens of lingerie sets until I found the red lace one. Then I picked a black see-through dress and a matching pair of Louboutin high heels. Massimo would have a heart attack! I headed toward the dressing table, snatching the bottle of champagne from the table on my way. I poured myself a glass and downed it in one gulp—I could use some liquid courage. Pouring another glass, I sat down by the mirror and took out the makeup set.

When I was finished, my eyes were heavily accented, my skin perfectly coated with foundation, and my lips shone with Chanel nude lip gloss. I dried my hair, curling it slightly for a wavy effect, and tied it in a high chignon.

I heard Domenico calling from outside.

"Dinner's served, miss."

Putting on the underwear, I called back through the door, "Give me two more minutes."

I pulled on the dress, stepped into the impossibly high heels, and sprinkled myself with a generous dose of my favorite perfume, stopping in front of the mirror for a second to nod with approval. I looked gorgeous. The dress fit perfectly and the red lace visible beneath it matched the red soles of the stilettos. It was provocative, but also elegant. I downed another glass of champagne, feeling ready to face the world and a little tipsy.

As I left the bathroom and presented myself to Domenico, his eyes widened.

"You look—" He broke off, looking for the right word.

"Yes, I know. Thank you," I replied, smiling coquettishly.

"Those high heels are incredible," he added in a whisper, and offered me his arm.

I took it and let him lead me down the corridor.

We went to the terrace I had had breakfast on earlier. The canvas-roofed gazebo was illuminated by hundreds of candles, and Massimo was standing beside it, his back turned to the building, staring into the distance. I let go of Domenico's arm.

"I'll manage on my own, thank you."

The man retreated into the darkness while I headed toward the Man in Black with a steady gait.

Hearing the *click click* of the heels on the stone floor, Massimo turned around. He was wearing gray linen pants and a light gray sweater with its sleeves rolled up. He walked over to the table and put down the glass he had been holding. His eyes trailed my every step as I closed the distance between us. When I stopped just a step away, he leaned back against the table, widening his stance. I took another step, halting between his legs, keeping my eyes on him. He was burning with passion. Even if I'd been blind, I would have felt his desire through my very skin.

"Will you pour me a glass?" I asked quietly, biting my lower lip.

Massimo straightened up, showing me that even in my heels I was still a lot shorter than him.

"Are you aware," he said in a whisper, "that if you keep provoking me, I might not be able to control myself?"

I placed a hand on his stone-hard torso and delicately pushed him away, suggesting he should take a seat. He didn't resist and did what I asked. Instead, he watched me with curiosity, still flushed, devouring me with his eyes—my face, dress, shoes, and especially the red lace dominating my outfit.

I stood close to him so he could enjoy the scent of my perfume. My right hand went to his nape, and my fingers combed through his hair, pulling down his head. He didn't resist, but his eyes never left me. I neared my lips to his and asked once more, "Will you pour me a glass, or should I help myself?"

A moment later, I let go of his hair and went over to the cooler, filling my glass. Massimo was still sitting propped against the table, watching me closely. His lips spread into something approaching a smile. I sat down, playing with the foot of the wineglass.

"Dinnertime?" I asked, sending him a bored look.

He got up, drew near me, and placed his hands on my shoulders, leaning over and whispering into my ear, "You look gorgeous." His tongue delicately skimmed over my ear. "I can't remember any woman having such an effect on me." His teeth trailed along the skin on my neck.

I felt shivers going up my spine, all the way from between my legs.

"I want to lay you on your belly right on the table, pull up that short dress of yours, and fuck you hard without taking that thong off."

I gasped, aroused. He went on. "Your smell . . . I felt it as soon as you stopped in the doorway. I'd like to lick it off you." Saying that, he started to tighten his grip on my shoulders rhythmically. "There is one spot on your body that scent is absent, I'd wager. And it's the same place I'd like to explore the most."

He broke off and started to kiss and gently bite my neck again. I didn't resist, instead turning my head, giving him more space. His hands slowly slid down my cleavage and closed on my breasts. Hard. I moaned.

"You see, Laura. You do desire me." I felt his hands and lips retreating.

"Remember. It's my game. I make up the rules." He kissed me on the cheek and sat down on the chair next to me.

He was triumphant. We both knew that. It didn't change the fact that I could clearly see the bulge in his pants.

I pretended not to care, but it only made him laugh. He sat back, playing with his champagne glass, with an impish smile on his face.

Domenico arrived at the door, only to disappear an instant later. Two young men showed up in his place, serving us appetizers: octopus carpaccio. It was delicious and delicate, and the dishes that kept arriving were even better. We ate in silence, shooting each other glances from time to time. After dessert, I pulled back from the table, took a glass of rosé wine, and said, my voice unwavering, "The Cosa Nostra."

Massimo shot me a warning stare.

"As far as I know, it doesn't exist. Is that true?"

He laughed mockingly and asked in a low voice, "What else do you know, baby girl?"

Disoriented, I started turning the glass in my fingers. "Well, I've seen *The Godfather*, but who hasn't? I'm wondering how much truth there is to it."

"About us?" he asked. "There's nothing there about me. As for the rest, I don't know."

He was making fun of me. I knew it.

"What do you do?" I asked.

"Business."

"Massimo." I refused to back down. "I'm asking for real. You want a year of my life and my unswerving obedience. Don't you think I should know what I'm getting into?"

His face became serious and he caught me in his gaze.

"You are entitled to some kind of explanation. You're right. I will tell you as much as you need to know." He took a sip of his wine. "After my parents died, I was chosen as the next head of the family. That's why people call me don. I own several companies, clubs, restaurants, and hotels—we're just like a regular corporation. I'm the head. But all that is just a part of a bigger picture. If you need a list, you'll get it, though I believe that the less you know, the better." He kept his eyes trained on me, looking deathly serious.

"What do you want to know specifically? You want me to tell you if I have a consigliere? Yes, I do. You'll meet him soon enough. You already found out if I have a gun and if I am dangerous. Whether I tackle my own problems head-on. What else? Ask away."

There were a million thoughts whirling around my head, but I didn't really *need* to know anything else. Most of what was happening was already clear. To be honest, since last night, I knew everything I wanted to know.

"When will you give me my phone and laptop?"

The Man in Black calmly turned in his chair and crossed his legs. "Whenever you want. We only have to agree on what you're about to say to the people you'd like to contact."

I took a breath, preparing to say something, but he lifted his hand before I could start.

"Before you interrupt me, I'll tell you where we stand. You can call your parents, and if you think it necessary, I'll let you return to Poland."

My eyes grew brighter and my face bloomed in happiness.

"You'll tell them you've received a very lucrative work proposition in one of the hotels on Sicily and that you're going to take it up. There will be a one-year probation period. You won't have to lie to your relatives when you feel like calling them. We've taken your things from Martin's apartment before he returned to Warsaw. They should be here by tomorrow. I consider the entire subject of that man closed. Permanently. I don't want you to see him anymore."

I stared at him questioningly.

"Am I making myself clear? No? Let me elaborate on that, then. I forbid you to contact that man," Massimo said icily. "Anything else?"

I remained silent for a while. He had thought this thing out pretty solidly. It was all planned and logical.

"Right. What if I need to visit my family?" I asked. "What then?"

Massimo frowned.

"Well . . . in that case I will be happy to see your beautiful country with you."

I laughed, sipping my wine. I was picturing him, the head of the Sicilian mob, strolling around Warsaw.

"Can I disagree with you?" I ask.

"That was not a proposition. I was just describing things as they are and will be." He leaned toward me. "Laura, you're smart. Haven't you realized that I *always* get what I want?"

I grimaced, recalling last night's events.

"As far as I know, don Massimo, not always." I dropped my eyes to my lace underwear, still perfectly visible beneath my dress, and bit my lower lip.

Then I slowly pushed myself up. The Man in Black carefully

watched my every movement. I kicked off those gorgeous red-soled high heels and headed toward the garden. The grass was wet, and the air tasted of salt. I knew he wouldn't be able to resist. That he'd come right after me. That is just what happened. I walked through the darkness, the only thing I could see being the faraway lights of boats afloat on the sea. Having reached the beach sofa under the rectangular canopy I had taken a nap in earlier, I stopped.

"You feel right at home here, don't you?" asked Massimo, stopping beside me.

He was right. I didn't feel like an outsider here. I felt like I've been living here all my life. Besides, show me a girl who wouldn't want to live in a beautiful mansion, surrounded by servants and all kinds of luxuries.

"I'm slowly starting to accept my situation. I'm getting used to all this. I know I have no other choice," I replied, taking another sip from my glass.

Massimo grabbed it out of my hand and threw it to the grass. He took me in his arms and delicately lay me down on the white pillows. My breath quickened. I knew anything could happen. He flung one leg over me and here we were again, lying just like in the morning.

The difference was that earlier I had been afraid, and the only things I felt now were curiosity and arousal. Maybe it was all the alcohol I had had, but maybe I had simply accepted my fate, making everything easier.

Propping his hands on both sides of my head, Massimo leaned over me.

"I would like to . . ." he whispered, gently nudging my lips with the tip of his nose. "I'd like you to teach me how to be gentle with you."

I froze. Such a dangerous man, a powerful man, was asking me for my consent, tenderness, and love.

My hands wandered up, stopping on his cheeks. For a while I held his face, staring into his calm black eyes. With a gentle motion, I pulled him closer. As our lips met, Massimo rushed in with all his strength, opening my mouth wider. Our tongues danced to the same rhythm. His body lay on mine, and his arms surrounded me. It was clear that we wanted each other. Our tongues and lips fucked, hard and full of passion, our sexual temperaments matching.

A moment later, when the adrenaline rush subsided and I composed myself a bit, I realized what I was doing.

"Wait! Stop," I breathed, pushing him away.

The Man in Black did no such thing. He grabbed me by the wrists, despite my protestations, and pinned them to the sofa. Then he lifted me, tightly clamping his hand around both my wrists. His other hand trailed along my thigh, climbing, until it felt the lace thong. He grabbed it, pulling his lips away from mine. The pale light of streetlamps in the distance faintly illuminated my terrified face. I didn't fight him. I stood no chance. I lay motionlessly and tears streaked down my cheeks. Seeing that, he released me, pushed himself up, and sat on the edge of the couch, resting his feet on the wet grass.

"Baby girl . . ." he breathed heavily. "When you've been using nothing but violence for your whole life and you've had to fight tooth and nail for everything you have . . . it's difficult to react in any other way when someone takes away what you desire."

He got up and ran a hand through his hair, while I stayed down, frozen. I was livid, but at the same time, I felt bad for Massimo. I had thought he wasn't one of those men who take their women by force, but this behavior must have been normal for him. Such roughness came as naturally to him as shaking someone's hand. He had probably also never really cared for anyone—never having to struggle for anyone's feelings or to nurture them. Now he was trying to make me reciprocate his feelings, and the only way he knew how to do it was by force.

The terrifying silence was finally broken by Massimo's mobile vibrating in his pocket. He took it out, glanced at the screen, and accepted the call. While he talked, I wiped away my tears and got to my feet. With calm, leisurely steps, I went back to the villa. I was tired, a bit drunk, and utterly disoriented. It took me a while, but finally I reached my room and collapsed on the bed, exhausted. I immediately fell asleep.

CHAPTER 5

When I woke up, it was already bright outside. I felt some-one's hand lying heavy on my waist. Massimo was sleeping next to me, curled into a ball, his arm around me.

His hair fell over his face and his mouth was half-open. He was breathing deeply and steadily, and his tanned body—dressed the same as last morning—looked very pleasing surrounded by white sheets. *God, he's so hot*, I thought, licking my lips and inhaling the scent of his skin.

That's all well and good, but what is he even doing here? I was afraid to move, to wake him, and I had to go to the bathroom. I started to slip from under his arm, lifting it delicately. Massimo took a deep breath and turned over on his back. He was still asleep. I got up and headed to the bathroom. Stopping in front of the mirror, I grimaced. Yesterday's makeup was smudged all over my face, resembling Zorro's mask now. The thin black dress I had on was crumpled and creased, and the intricate bun I had tied on my head last evening now looked like a bird's nest.

Just great, I thought, wiping the black smudges around my eyes with a cotton pad. Done with that, I took my clothes off and went to the enormous shower. I turned the water on and poured some bath gel over my palm. The door slammed open suddenly. It was the Man in Black. He was ogling me, not even trying to act cool.

"Good morning, baby girl. May I join you?" he asked, rubbing the sleep off his eyes and smiling happily. At first all I wanted was to rush at him, pummel him with my fists for what would have been the thousandth time, and throw him out. But my experience of the last couple of days told me that it would come down to nothing and only elicit an abrupt, violent, and unpleasant reaction. Instead, I replied, spreading the soap over my body, "Sure. Be my guest."

Massimo stopped rubbing his eyes, frowned, and froze, dumbfounded. He must have thought he had misheard me. I had thrown him off balance.

I couldn't change the fact that he had just gone in behind me and seen me naked, but at least I could take the chance to see him without his clothes, too.

Slowly, Massimo approached the expansive shower, grabbed the shirt from the back of his neck and tore it off with one fluid motion. I stood leaning against the wall, taking my time spreading the soap over my skin. All the time, my eyes didn't leave the Man in Black, and he in turn kept watching me. I realized I was staring and that my hands had been caressing my breasts longer than necessary.

"Before I take my pants off, I have to warn you. I'm a man, it is morning, and you're naked, so . . ." He trailed off, shrugging nonchalantly and spreading his lips in a roguish smile.

My heart skipped a beat. I thanked God I was under the shower. His words made me wet instantly. *When had I last had sex?* I asked myself. Martin had always treated it as a sporadic and unpleasant duty. I hadn't been pleasured by anyone except myself for what felt like weeks. And I had just menstruated, so the hormones did their part in skyrocketing my libido. "This is torture," I muttered under my breath, and turned toward the shower head, turning the water temperature down until it became ice-cold.

I was so aroused at the thought of seeing Massimo naked I drew up my toes on instinct, and all my muscles started flexing. For my own good and safety, I closed my eyes and entered the freezing stream, pretending to wash the soap off. Unfortunately, the temperature of the water did nothing to cool down my titillation.

Massimo entered the enormous cubicle and turned on the second shower head. There were four of those in total, not counting the gigantic water jet panel that looked like a bathroom radiator, only riddled with little holes.

"We're leaving today," the Man in Black said impassively. "We're going to be away for a couple of days. Maybe weeks. I don't know yet. We'll drop by some galas and parties, so take this into account while packing your things. Domenico will take care of everything. You just tell him what you need."

I heard him but didn't really listen. I was still trying my best to keep my eyes closed. In the end, my curiosity won. I turned his way and saw Massimo standing with his arms propped on the wall, letting the water flow freely down his naked body. The view was overwhelming—his toned legs, beautiful, shapely buttocks, and his muscled belly were all testament to the enormous work he had to do to keep his body in such perfect shape. Then my eyes stopped wandering and stopped on one particular point. I saw what I had been fearing the most. His beautiful, straight, and thick prick stood erect like the candle stuck in the birthday cake I had had back at the hotel. It was perfect—not too long, but as thick as my wrist. Flawless. I stood still in the cold stream, swallowing loudly. Massimo's eyes remained closed, his face upturned. He was turning his head this way and that, allowing the water to rinse his hair.

Then he bent his arms and leaned against the wall with his elbows so his head left the stream of water.

"You want something, or are you just watching?" Massimo asked, his eyes still shut.

My heart was pounding like crazy. I couldn't take my eyes off of him. In my thoughts, I was cursing the moment I had allowed him to join me in that fucking shower, though truth be told, my protestations would have probably amounted to nothing. My body was rebelling against me, every cell in it yearning to touch him. I licked my lips, wondering how it would feel to have him in my mouth.

I imagined myself standing behind him, water dripping from my body, and grabbing his manhood with my hand. Tightening my fingers around it. And him, moaning in ecstasy, aroused by my touch. I turn him around and push him against the wall. Then I take a step closer, my hand never leaving his rock-hard cock. Slowly I lick his nipples and trace my fingers up his dick, to the very tip, and then back to its base. I feel him getting even harder, and his hips starting to rock gently to the rhythm of my strokes.

"Your expression, Laura, tells me you're not thinking about the things you're going to pack for our trip."

I shook my head as if I'd just woken up and was trying to drive off a lingering dream. Massimo was standing in the same position with his elbows against the wall. The only difference was that now he was watching me, clearly enjoying himself. I panicked and couldn't think of anything to say. The only thing I could think of was sucking his dick. My panic lured him, like a wounded animal attracts a predator.

Massimo started heading toward me, and I was doing everything I could to keep my eyes trained on his. He closed the distance between us in three steps. That was good. The object of my obsession vanished from my field of view. Unfortunately, the feeling of relief didn't last. As he stopped right in front of me, his erect phallus delicately touched my belly. I withdrew, but he followed me. Each two steps I took, he only had to take one to get close again. Despite the shower being so big, I knew there wasn't much space left behind me. When I reached the wall, the Man in Black pressed against me.

"What did you think about, looking at it?" he asked, leaning over me. "You want to touch it? For now, it is touching you . . ."

I wasn't able to reply. I opened my mouth, but no words came out. I stood there, defenseless, dizzy and drunk with lust, and he rubbed against me, pressing harder against my belly. The steady pressure grew rhythmic, pulsating. Massimo moaned and leaned his forehead on the wall behind me.

"I'll do it with your help or without it," he breathed.

I couldn't resist anymore. I clutched at his buttocks. As I sunk my nails into his skin, he growled with delight. With a firm motion, I turned around and pushed him against the wall. His hands fell loosely along his body, and his eyes were alight with desire. I knew that I had to stop right now. If I didn't, I wouldn't be able to control myself, and I'd do something I'd regret later.

I spun around and rushed out. I grabbed a bathrobe on my way and threw it over myself, running through the door. I kept running down the corridor, even though I couldn't hear his steps behind me, only stopping when I passed the garden and the stairs leading to the little marina. Gasping for air, I jumped onto the motorboat and collapsed on one of the couches.

Trying to catch my breath, I analyzed what happened. The images in my head weren't going to allow me to think clearly. The only thing I could see was Massimo's gorgeous, erect cock. I could almost taste it in my mouth, feel the touch of its delicate skin in my hand.

I don't have the slightest idea how long I stayed in that boat, staring out into the sea, but at some point, I gathered my wits and returned to the residence.

Carefully opening the door to my bedroom, I saw Domenico, arranging gigantic Louis Vuitton travel bags.

"Where is Massimo?" I asked in a whisper, sticking my head into the room.

The young Italian raised his eyes and smiled.

"The library, I'd wager. Would you like me to take you to him? He's currently talking to his consigliere, but I was instructed to take you to him whenever you'd like."

I entered the room and closed the door behind me.

"Oh, believe me, I *don't* want that," I replied, waving my hands at him. "Did he tell you to pack my things?"

Domenico didn't interrupt his work.

"You are leaving in an hour, so I thought you could use some help, miss. Unless you don't want me to . . ."

"Stop calling me miss. I can't stand it. Besides, we're probably the same age, so let's skip the formalities."

Domenico smiled and nodded, signaling his consent.

"Can you tell me where we're going?" I asked.

"To Napoli, Rome, and Venice," he replied. "And then the Côte d'Azur."

I opened my eyes wider, surprised. I had never been to all those places. I hadn't seen so many places in my whole life!

"Do you know what we're to do in each of those places?" I asked. "I'd like to know what to take with me."

Domenico stopped what he was doing and walked over to the closet.

"I do, in fact, but I was told not to spoil it for you. Don Massimo will make everything clear in time. I'll help you pick the right outfits, don't worry." He winked at me. "Fashion is something of a hobby to me."

"I'll trust you fully if that's the case. If we only have an hour to prepare, let's get to it, shall we?"

Domenico nodded and disappeared in the cavernous closet.

I went into the bathroom, which was still filled with the scent of lust. My stomach cramped. *I can't do it*, I thought. I went back to the bedroom, crossed the room, and went into the closet, calling out to Domenico, "Have my things from Warsaw arrived yet?"

The man opened one of the large armoires and pointed his hand at a heap of boxes.

"Yes, but don Massimo asked me to tell you not to wear those."

Great, I thought.

"Can you leave me for a second?"

Before I managed to turn around, I was alone.

I threw myself at the boxes, searching for the only thing I really needed right now—my pink, three-pronged best friend.

After some fifteen minutes of frantic searching through dozens of boxes, I finally had it. I breathed with relief, hiding my trophy in a pocket of the bathrobe. I hurried back to the bathroom.

All the while, Domenico stayed on the balcony, awaiting my signal. Crossing the room, I nodded to him and he returned to the closet.

I took out the pink toy and washed it thoroughly. It really was my best friend at the moment. I let out a soft moan in anticipation. Taking a look around the bathroom, I searched for the perfect place. I liked to masturbate lying down. I could never do it in a rush or when I felt uncomfortable. The bedroom would be best, but my assistant's presence would only distract me. There was a modern white chaise longue in the corner of the bathroom, though. It wouldn't be the most comfortable spot, but it'd have to do. I was desperate enough to lie on the floor anyway.

The chaise was surprisingly soft and perfectly suited my body. I untied the bathrobe, letting it slip to the sides of my body, and reclined, naked and yearning for orgasm. I licked two fingers and slid them inside me to reduce the friction. Amazingly, I was still so wet it proved completely unnecessary. I switched the vibrator on and slipped its middle prong into my pulsating snatch. As the thickest part slid deeper into me, a second protrusion—shaped like a bunny—entered my back door. My body spasmed. I shivered, knowing it wouldn't take me long at all to slake my desire. The third part of my rubber companion vibrated the hardest, caressing my puffed-up clitoris. I closed my eyes. There was only one image in my head, and I wouldn't want it any other way. It was Massimo, in the shower, holding his beautiful cock in his hands.

The first orgasm came after only a couple of seconds. The next waves came in increments of half a minute at most. After a short while, I was so exhausted I had difficulty pulling the pink vibrator out. I brought my legs together.

Thirty minutes later, I was standing in front of the mirror, packing my cosmetics into one of the leather bags. I glanced at my reflection. I looked nothing like the woman I had been just a week ago. My skin was tanned, healthy, and fresh. I'd tied my hair into a neat bun, lined my eyes delicately, and applied some dark lip gloss. Domenico picked a white Chanel outfit for our trip. Long, wide, off-white pants made of paper-thin silk blended in with a delicate flowy shirt with wide shoulder straps, giving the impression of being a single, unbroken overall. The peep-toe Prada stilettos complemented the outfit perfectly.

"Your things are packed," Domenico said, passing me my bag.

"I'd like to see Massimo now."

"He hasn't finished his meeting yet, but—"

"Then he will," I snapped disdainfully, leaving the room.

The library was one of those rooms whose location I had committed to memory. I headed down the corridor, and the patter of my stilettos reverberated from the stone floor. As I reached the right door, I took a deep breath and pulled on the handle. I went inside and felt a shiver running down my spine. I hadn't been here since my first conversation with the Man in Black, only a while after waking up from my deep sleep.

Massimo was sitting on the couch. He wore a light linen suit and an unbuttoned shirt. Next to him sat a man with graying hair—very handsome and a lot older than Massimo. *A typical Italian*, I thought. Longish hair combed back and a well-groomed goatee. Seeing me, both of them jumped to their feet. The first look I got from the Man in Black was ice-cold. As if he wanted to scold me for interrupting his meeting. But as soon as his eyes swept my entire silhouette, his stare seemed to grow less severe. He said something to the other man, keeping his eyes on me, and started walking my way. He approached me and leaned over, kissing me on the cheek.

"A pity. I had to cope without you," he whispered, planting the kiss.

"I've done the same," I replied in a whisper as his mouth retreated.

The words made him freeze for an instant. His stare was full of passion and anger. He took my hand in his and led me to his friend.

"Laura, meet Mario—my right hand." I walked over to the man to offer him a hand, but he swooped in, grabbed me by the shoulders, and kissed me on both cheeks. I still hadn't grown used to that. Where I come from, you only kiss your closest friends and relatives.

"Consigliere," I said with a smile.

"Just Mario is all right." The older man returned my smile. "It is good to finally see you in the flesh. Alive."

Those words rooted me to the spot. What did he mean, "alive"? Had he assumed I wouldn't live to see him? My face must have shown some of my emotions, as Mario quickly explained, "There are paintings of you all over the mansion. They've been there for years now, but nobody ever believed you were real. You must be as astounded as we are."

I could only shrug.

"I won't lie: this whole situation is a bit surreal and daunting. But we all know I have no power over don Massimo, so I humbly accept each and every one of the three hundred and sixty-five days he has given me."

Massimo burst out laughing.

"Humbly . . ." he repeated, turning to his companion, who immediately joined in the merriment.

"I'm happy I could improve your mood. Now, I'll wait in the car so you can enjoy my absence," I hissed, sending them both an ironic smirk. As I turned my back on them and headed to the door, I heard Mario say, trying to hold back the laughter, "Indeed, Massimo, it's just as if she was Italian."

I ignored that and shut the door behind me.

I stopped before I exited the house and went out to the driveway. The image of the dead man lying on the paving stones flashed before my eyes. I swallowed, took a furtive look around, and headed in the direction of the SUV parked outside. The driver opened the door for me and gave me a hand as I stepped inside.

My iPhone was lying on the back seat, right next to my laptop. I squealed with glee, seeing both devices. I quickly pressed the button that closed the darkened window between the driver and the back seat. I turned the phone on and quickly my joy evaporated—there were dozens of missed calls from my mom, but not even one from Martin. It was weird and sad to discover that the man I had been with for more than a year cared so little about me.

I dialed Mom. Her terrified voice greeted me immediately.

"Oh, darling, I've been crying my eyes out. Dying of fear for you, goddamn it!" my mother exclaimed, on the verge of bursting into tears.

"Mom, you only called me yesterday. Everything's fine."

It seemed her motherly intuition told her otherwise. She didn't back down.

"Are you sure? Is everything okay, Laura? Are you back from Sicily? How was your trip?"

I took a deep breath. It wouldn't be that easy to fool her. Was everything okay? Well . . . I glanced down at myself, then around me.

"It is more than okay, Mom. I'm back, yes, but I need to tell you something." I squeezed my eyes shut, praying that she took the bait.

"I was offered a great job in one of the best hotels on the island." I tried sounding super excited. "They're giving me a one-year contract and I've decided to accept. I'm just getting ready to go back to Sicily." I waited for some kind of reaction. There was only silence.

"You can't speak a word of Italian," Mom said.

"Oh, please, what does it matter? Everyone here speaks English."

The situation was getting out of hand. If we kept speaking, she'd see through my deception. Wanting to avoid that, I continued.

"I'll come and visit in a few days and I'll tell you everything. For now, I have a lot of stuff to take care of."

"Okay. What about Martin?" she asked cautiously. "I know he won't leave his company. He's too much of a workaholic."

I sighed.

"He cheated on me during our trip. I left him. I know now that this is a great opportunity for me," I said in the calmest and most dispassionate voice I could muster.

"I told you! He wasn't the guy for you, child."

Yeah, right. You should be happy you don't know the new one.

"Okay, I have to go now, Mommy. I'm entering the town hall now. Call me and remember that I love you."

"I love you, too. Be careful out there, darling."

I sighed with relief as I pressed the red button. It worked, hopefully. Now I only had to tell the Man in Black about my visit to Poland. It was inevitable now. In that moment, the car door opened, and Massimo deftly slipped inside.

He took a look at my hand. The iPhone was still in it.

"Have you talked to your mother?" he asked with something approaching concern as the car began moving.

"Yes, but it didn't change the fact that she's still worried," I replied, keeping my eyes on the window. "Unfortunately, speaking to her on the phone did next to nothing, and I'll have to go to Poland within the next couple of days. Especially since she thinks I'm already there." I turned my head to the Man in Black, wanting to gauge his reaction. He was watching me.

"I expected as much. That's why I've already planned for it. The last stop of our trip will be Warsaw. It won't be as soon as you'd like, but calling your mother more often from now on should assuage her concerns and give us more time."

That was good news.

"Thank you. I really appreciate this."

Massimo kept his eyes on me for a moment longer. Then he lay his head on the headrest and sighed.

"I'm not so bad. I don't want to keep you here against your will. I don't want to threaten you. But, tell me: would you stay of your own will?" He fixed me with a searching stare.

I turned away. Would I stay? Of course not.

The Man in Black was still waiting for a reply, but didn't get one, so he turned to his iPhone, scrolling and reading something on the Internet.

The silence was unbearable. I needed someone to talk to. Maybe it was because of my longing for home, or maybe it was the morning shower. Still looking through the window, I asked, "Where are we going now?"

"The airport in Catania. If the traffic is light, we should be there in less than an hour." Hearing the word "airport," I shivered. My back stiffened and my breathing quickened. There weren't a lot of things I hated as much as flying.

I fidgeted restlessly in my seat, and the pleasant chill of the air-conditioning suddenly seemed like arctic winter. Nervously, I rubbed my arms, trying in vain to warm myself. The goose bumps didn't vanish. Massimo glanced at me with his cold eyes, but the ice suddenly turned into fire.

"Why aren't you wearing a fucking bra?" he snapped.

I frowned and sent him a questioning look.

"I can see your nipples."

I glanced down and realized he was right. They were visible through the delicate fabric. I dropped one of the straps of my shirt, revealing my shoulder. The tanned skin was covered by the lace strap of a beige bra.

"Not my fault that all the underwear I own now is made of lace," I said, impassive. "I don't have a single padded bra, so excuse me, but I'll just have to keep drawing everyone's attention. I didn't pick any of those things." I looked Massimo in the eyes, waiting for a response.

He watched the thin lace strap for a moment before reaching out with a hand and pulling my shirt even lower. The light fabric flowed gently down my arm, revealing my breasts. Massimo sat rooted to the spot, taking in the view. I did nothing to hide. After my morning meeting with my pink friend I was feeling sated and in control of my own head, even if it was only an illusion. The Man in Black drew his leg up the seat and sat on his side. Slowly, he pushed his thumb between the lace shoulder strap and my skin. His touch made me shiver again, but this time it had nothing to do with the fear of flying.

"Are you cold?" he asked, trailing his thumb lower and sliding his whole hand under my bra strap.

"I hate flying," I said, trying to mask my arousal. "If God wanted us to fly, he would have given us wings," I said, lowering my voice to a whisper and half closing my eyes. Fortunately, I had my sunglasses on, so he couldn't see that.

Massimo's hand was still moving toward my breast, his fingers lazily fiddling with the lace fabric, sliding ever downward. When his hand finally reached its destination, his face took on an expression of desire, and his eyes flared. I had seen that stare before. Each time, I had run. I had nowhere to run now.

Massimo was tightening his grip on my breast and edging closer to me. My hips started to move of their own accord, and my head leaned back as he played with my nipple, holding it between two fingers. With his free hand, he snatched me by the neck, as if knowing how long it had taken me to tie my hair, and how much I'd hated him doing that. He dropped his head and gently bit on my nipple through the fabric of the bra.

"This," he said, lifting his head for an instant, "is mine."

Hearing his rugged voice and those words, I let out a quiet moan.

Massimo pulled the shirt from both my shoulders, letting it fall to my waist. He pulled away the bra and reached for my nipple with his lips. Everything inside me was pulsating, throbbing. My morning masturbation had been for nothing, it seemed. I was still horny. I imagined him ripping my pants off and fucking me from behind without taking them all the way down, rubbing against the lace of my panties. My fire kindled by my own thoughts, I slid a hand into his hair and pulled him closer.

"Harder!" I whispered, taking off my glasses with my free hand. "Bite me harder."

That was like pushing that big red button inside his head. He nearly ripped the bra off of me, hungrily biting into my breasts, sucking and licking. I felt a wave of lust overcoming me. I wouldn't be able to resist much longer. I lifted his head by the hair and allowed his lips to find mine. Very delicately, I pushed him away so I could look him in the eyes. He was burning up, his pupils dilated, and his eyes completely black. He panted, breathing into my mouth, trying to catch my lip between his teeth.

"Don . . . don't start something you can't finish," I said, licking him gently. "I'll be so wet in a moment I'll need a new outfit."

The Man in Black dug his fingernails into the side of the seat hard, making the leather creak under the pressure. He drilled holes in me with his wild gaze, and I knew he was fighting an internal battle.

"The second part of your statement was entirely unnecessary," he said finally, leaning back in his seat. "The thought of what's between your legs now is driving me crazy."

I shot a glance at his pants, swallowing loudly. That beautiful erection wasn't just an image in my mind anymore. I knew what his thick cock looked like, standing at attention under his clothes. With clear relish, Massimo watched my reaction. I shook my head to clear my mind and started to put my shirt back on.

He kept his eyes on me as I brushed down the crumpled fabric. I combed through my hair with a hand and put on my sunglasses. When I was finished, Massimo reached into the glove compartment and took out a black paper bag.

"I have something for you," he said, handing me the package.

The elegant gold lettering on its front formed the words "Patek Philippe." I knew that name. There could only be one thing inside. I also knew how expensive those watches were.

"Massimo . . . I . . ." My eyes wandered back to him. "I can't accept that."

He laughed out loud, sliding on his aviators.

"Baby girl, this is one of the cheaper gifts I'm going to give you. Besides, don't forget you don't get to decide for another few hundred days. Open it."

I knew this was going nowhere—arguing with him never did. It could only lead to misery for me, especially since there was nowhere to run now. I pulled a black box from the bag and opened it. The watch was marvelous—pink gold encrusted with little diamonds. Simply perfect.

"You have been pretty isolated for the last few days. I know I've taken much from you, but you'll start getting it all back now," Massimo said, fastening the watch on my wrist.

CHAPTER 6

We reached the airport without any problems. The driver opened the door for Massimo while I was stuffing my things into my bag—they must have spilled out to the seat during our drive. Massimo rounded the car and opened the door on my side, offering me a hand. He was being very gallant, and in that linen suit of his he looked simply overpowering.

As both my feet touched the ground, he discreetly grabbed my ass, pushing me gently toward the entrance. I sent him a shocked glance—that was behavior worthy of an adolescent boy. But he only smirked, sliding his hand up to my back and leading me to the terminal.

I'd never had all the check-in formalities done so fast. All we had to do was pass through the building. When we emerged on the other side, another car picked us up and drove us to a small plane. I got nauseous as soon as I saw it. It looked too small—like a tube with some wings attached. I hated flying charter planes, and those looked like Goliath to this David.

"Go up the stairs," I heard from behind me.

"I can't do it, Massimo! I can't!" I pleaded. "You didn't tell me we were going to fly a toy plane. I'm not going inside." I panted, panicked, trying to back away from the aircraft.

"Please, don't make a scene, Laura. I'll have to carry you in by force," he hissed, but I simply couldn't take another step.

Without another word, Massimo took me in his arms, and not reacting to my panicked screams and flailing arms, he carried me up the stairs and squeezed through the small entrance. He greeted the pilot and the hatch closed with a hiss.

I was terrified. My heart was pounding. I couldn't hear my own thoughts. In the end, my desperate flailing got me what I wanted, and Massimo put me down.

As soon as my feet touched the floor, and he took a step back, I slapped his face.

"What the fuck were you thinking? Let me out! I want out!" I was yelling, still frightened to death, before throwing myself at the door.

He grabbed me by the shoulders and flung me back to a leather couch that filled nearly the entire side of the plane. Then he pinned me down with his body. I couldn't move.

"Goddamn it, Massimo!" I kept wailing and swearing.

Intending to gag me, he pressed his lips to mine and pushed his tongue into my mouth. I was in no mood for play, though, and as soon as he did it, I bit. Hard. The Man in Black leaped back, raising his arm, as if he were going to hit me. I squeezed my eyes shut and waited for the inevitable. The strike did not come. When I opened my eyes again, he was undoing his belt. *Oh my God, what's he going to do?* I thought. I started to crawl back along the couch, kicking with my feet to give me purchase on the floor. He continued, pulling the leather belt out of the loops in his pants with one fluid motion. Then, he took off his jacket, hanging it on the backrest of one of the seats next to him. He was furious. His eyes flared with anger and his jaw was working rhythmically.

"Massimo, please, don't . . ." I stammered.

"Get up," he ordered coolly. When I didn't react, he burst out, "Get your ass up!"

Terrified, I jumped to my feet.

He stepped toward me, pinched my chin between his fingers, and lifted it so I had to look him in the eyes.

"You'll choose your punishment now, Laura. I warned you not to resist. Now give me your hands." Still staring into his eyes, I did as he asked. He grabbed both my wrists and deftly tied them with the leather belt. Then he sat me down and fastened our safety belts. A while later, I realized the plane was already taxiing.

Massimo sat opposite and glared at me, still boiling with fury.

"So you don't have to think too hard, I'll tell you what your choices are," he said slowly, keeping his voice cold. "Each time you hit me in the face, you show a lack of respect. It is insulting, Laura. Therefore, I'll make you feel what I feel. You might not like it, but your punishment is going to be corporeal. You can choose now: either you suck me off or let me pleasure you with my tongue."

The plane took off and shot upward, and I fainted.

When I came to, I was lying on the couch, but my hands were still tied. The Man in Black was sitting in his seat, his legs crossed, his eyes trained on me, playing with a glass of champagne.

"So?" he asked impassively. "What'll it be?"

I opened my eyes wide and sat up, staring at him all the time.

"You're joking, right?" I asked, swallowing nervously.

"Do I look like I'm joking? Do you think hitting me in the face is a joke?" He leaned closer. "We've got an hour in this plane ahead of us, Laura, and you *will* have your punishment before we land. I'm nothing if not fair. At least I let you choose." He squinted at me, licking his lips. "But my patience will run out. Soon. And then I'll do the same thing you did, which is whatever I want."

"I'll suck you off," I said numbly. "Will you untie me, or do you simply want to fuck me in the mouth?" I asked, my voice growing hoarse.

I could not show him that I was afraid. I knew it would only spur him on. He was like a predator on the prowl—when he smelled blood, he pounced.

"I thought as much," he said, getting up and unzipping his pants. "I will not untie you. You'd probably do something stupid then, and I'd have to come up with another punishment."

As he approached me, I closed my eyes. Let it happen. I wanted it to be over. Instead of his prick on my face, I felt him lifting me. I opened my eyes. The corridor was getting narrower in this part of the plane. Massimo had to turn sideways to squeeze us through. We entered a dark room with a bed in the middle.

The Man in Black slowly lowered me to the soft sheets. He left me there and disappeared in the small adjoining room. When he returned, he had a black bathrobe belt in his hand. I watched his movements. Despite my fear, I realized that what I was about to do wouldn't exactly be unpleasant. It might not be a punishment, after all.

Massimo untied the belt wrapped around my wrists. Then, he rolled me over and tied the soft bathrobe belt in its place. When he was finished, he rolled me to my back again. I couldn't move my hands an inch.

He reached to the nightstand and picked up a sleeping mask. I had been using one just like it back in Warsaw to sleep through the mornings.

He leaned over and put it over my eyes. The only thing I could see now was the silky fabric.

"You don't have any idea how many things I'd like to do to you now, baby girl," he whispered.

I kept still, disoriented. I didn't know where exactly he was or what he was doing. I licked my lips nervously, getting ready for his manhood.

Suddenly, I felt him unzipping my pants.

"What are you doing?" I asked, trying to squirm out of the mask. "Don't you just need my mouth for what you're about to do?"

Massimo laughed wryly but didn't stop undressing me.

"Pleasuring me wouldn't be any kind of punishment for you," he whispered. "I know you've been wanting to do it since morning. But if I do it to you, without your control, we'll be square." He tore my pants off abruptly.

I lay still, squeezing my legs together as hard as I could. I knew I wouldn't be able to resist him if he really wanted to go on with his plan.

"Please, Massimo, don't do it."

"I asked you, too, not to hit me . . ." He trailed off, and I felt the mattress sagging under his weight.

I had no idea what was happening. I could only listen. I felt his breath on my cheek, and then he gently bit my earlobe.

"Don't be afraid, baby girl," he said, pushing his hand between my legs. "I'll be gentle, I promise."

I squeezed my legs together even harder, whining softly with fear.

"Shush," he whispered. "I will part your legs now and start with just one finger. Relax."

I knew he'd do as he was saying whether I wanted it or not. So I relaxed.

"Good. And now spread those legs wide for me."

I did as I was told.

"You'll be a good girl and do what I say now. I don't want to hurt you."

Delicately, he started to kiss me on the lips while his hand slid down. With his other hand, he held my head, deepening the kiss. I yielded, and an instant later, our tongues were dancing, quicker and quicker. I wanted him. My lips were growing greedier.

"Calm down, baby. Not so fast. Remember—this is supposed to be punishment," he breathed into my ear as his hand reached the lace fabric of my panties. "I love how your skin feels in that lace. Now, be still and don't move."

Massimo's fingers slipped into the most intimate spot of my body. Slowly, with his lips right next to my ear, he explored the inside of my thighs, gently stroking them with two fingers, teasing me. He rubbed my lips down there and finally slid inside. I felt his touch, so wonderful, and my back arched. I moaned in ecstasy.

"Don't move and be silent. Don't make a sound. Do you understand?"

I nodded quickly. His finger sank deeper, until it was all the way in. I clenched my teeth, trying to remain silent, while he started to move, subtly and sensually, inside me. His middle finger slid in and out, while his thumb softly fondled my clit. I felt his weight subsiding and then shifting downward. I stopped breathing. His fingers didn't stop.

He reached his destination. Suddenly, he slipped his fingers out, making me wince. But then I felt his breath through the lace of my panties.

"I've dreamed about it since I first saw you. I want you to talk to me when I start. Tell me if I'm doing it good. Direct me. I want to give you ecstasy," he breathed, pulling my thong down my legs.

On instinct, I brought my legs together, embarrassed.

"Spread them wide for me! I want to see it."

That's when I realized why he had given me the mask—he wanted me to feel more comfortable during our first intercourse. It made me feel like he was seeing less than he actually was. It's a bit like with children who close their eyes when they're afraid, thinking that if they can't see, they can't be seen, either.

I slowly did as he told me and heard him inhaling deeply. He spread my legs wider, piercing me with his gaze, sinking deeper into my most intimate, secretive places.

"Lick me," I moaned, unable to keep quiet anymore. "Please, don Massimo!"

Hearing that, he started steadily rubbing my clit with his thumb.

"You're patient. You like to be punished."

He leaned down and sank his tongue in my snatch, his movements dynamic. I wanted to grab him by the hair, but my hands were tied behind my back. With the fingers of one hand he spread the lips of my pussy, wanting to reach that most sensitive spot.

"I want you to come, and I want to torture you with more orgasms until you beg me to stop. But I won't stop. I need to punish you, Laura."

He ripped the sleeping mask off my face.

"I want you to look at me. I want to see your face as you come, again and again."

He pushed himself up and slipped a pillow beneath my head.

"You need to see everything clearly," he said.

Between my legs, Massimo was at the same time sexy and terrifying. I've never liked it when a man looked at me when I was orgasming. Somehow it felt too intimate. This time, I had no choice. He swooped in again, his lips caressing my clit, and two of his fingers impaled me. I closed my eyes, feeling myself on the very brink of rapture.

"Harder," I whispered.

His fingers kept stroking expertly, while his tongue never stopped.

"*Kurwa mać!*" I shouted in my native tongue as I came for the first time. The orgasm was long and strong, overwhelming. My body was taut like a string, trapped by what Massimo was doing. When I felt the orgasm subside, he rushed at my exhausted, tender, and sensitive clit again, almost painfully. I clenched my teeth until they grated, squirming—impaled by his two fingers.

"I'm sorry!" I cried after the next wave of painful bliss overcame me.

The Man in Black slowly relented, let my body cool down, softly kissed and stroked all the places that were hurting now. My hips collapsed to the mattress when he was finished. As I lay still, he slipped his hand beneath me and loosened the strap around my wrists so I could slide my hands free. I opened my eyes and looked at him. Slowly he pushed himself up, reached for the nightstand, and fished out a box of wet wipes. Gently he wiped the spots he had been attacking with such brutality just a moment ago.

"Apology accepted," he said, and disappeared back into the main compartment.

I kept still for a moment longer, analyzing everything, but I couldn't believe what had just happened. I only knew one thing: I was so calm now, and so sore, as if I had been fucking him for hours.

When I returned, Massimo was sitting in his seat, biting his upper lip. He turned his head, sending me a look.

"My lips smell of your pussy now. Suddenly I'm not so sure if you were the one punished."

I sat down opposite him, seemingly unmoved by what he said.

"So, what are our plans for today?" I asked coolly, snatching the champagne glass from his hand.

"You're getting adorably insolent." He smiled and poured himself another glass. "I can see the size of the plane stopped bothering you."

I swallowed a sip of champagne with difficulty. I *did* forget about my fear.

"Getting to know its interior changed my perspective. So what's the plan?"

"You'll learn in time. I'll do some business and you'll get to play the mobster's girl," he said, boyish amusement illuminating his face.

When we landed, a pair of black SUVs and a whole security team was already waiting for us. One of the men opened the door for me, then shut it as I made myself comfortable in my seat. Each time I saw those cars, I thought it was a little bit magic—the way they moved all that stuff from place to place. How did those guys and those cars manage to keep pace with Massimo? What broke my chaotic reverie, probably fueled by all those orgasms, were the words of my oppressor, uttered into my ear.

"I'd like to be inside you," he whispered, and his hot breath paradoxically chilled me to the bone. "Deep and brutal. I'd like to feel your wet snatch close around my cock."

The words I heard woke each and every ounce of my rich imagination. I could feel what he was saying almost physically. I closed my eyes and tried to calm down the frantic beat of my heart. It grew a bit steadier. Suddenly, Massimo's warm breath vanished, and I heard him saying something to the driver. The words were unintelligible, but after a few seconds, the car veered off the road and stopped. The man stepped out, leaving us completely alone.

"Sit in the passenger seat in the front," Massimo said, pinning me with his cold, black stare. He didn't look like he was about to move himself, which seemed a bit strange.

"Why?" I asked, disoriented.

Massimo's face took on an expression of annoyance, and his jaw clenched.

"I'll repeat it one last time: move or I'll move you myself."

Again, I couldn't help it—his tone made my hackles rise. I wanted to resist, if only to see where it took us. I also knew he was pretty good at punishing me and making me do things, but was that something I was entirely against?

"You order me around like a dog. I am no dog."

I inhaled, intending to berate him for treating me like that, but I didn't manage to say another word. Massimo pulled me out of the car by force and then threw me into the front seat. He pulled my hands back, behind the backrest.

"Not a dog. A bitch," he hissed, tying my hands with some kind of strap.

Before I realized what was happening, I was sitting tied to the passenger seat, and the Man in Black sat behind the steering wheel. I started to wriggle my fingers, trying to feel my way around, and discovered that I was tied with the same bathrobe belt as back in the plane.

"You like to tie women up?" I asked as he was fiddling with some settings on the dashboard.

"It's not a question of preference in your case."

He pressed the ignition button and a woman's voice from the GPS directed him as he started to drive.

"My back hurts. And my arms," I said after a couple of minutes.

"Well, I'm hurt, too, but for an entirely different reason. Want to compare?"

I knew he was angry or frustrated. I couldn't differentiate between those two feelings in him, but I had no idea what I had done to cause this. And even if it wasn't my fault, he was taking it all out on me.

"*Ty cholerny, uparty egoisto,*" I whispered in Polish. You damned, stubborn egomaniac. "As soon as you untie me, I'll smack you so hard you'll have to look for your teeth on the ground," I ranted, still in Polish.

Massimo slowed down and stopped at a traffic light, turning to me and fixing me with a furious glare. "Now repeat that in English," he growled.

I smiled disdainfully and spewed a whole litany of profanities in Polish—all directed at him. He didn't move, but his glare was growing more furious by the second. As soon as the light turned green, he stepped on the accelerator.

"I'll get rid of your pain. Or at least take your mind off it," he said, and started unbuttoning my pants with his right hand. His left hand was still on the steering wheel, but the right one slipped under my panties. I squirmed and jerked in my seat, cursing him and begging him not to do it, but it was too late.

"Massimo, I'm sorry!" I cried, trying to get out of his reach. "I'm not in pain anymore! And what I said in Polish—"

"Not interested in that anymore," he said. "But if you don't pipe down, I'll have to gag you. I'd like to hear the GPS if you don't mind, so shut up."

His hand slid deeper into my underwear, and I felt a wave of panic flooding me. At the same time, I grew completely docile and stopped resisting.

"You promised you wouldn't do anything against my wishes," I whispered, leaning back.

Massimo's fingers irritated my clitoris, smearing it with wetness that appeared as soon as he touched me.

"I'm not doing anything against your wishes. I'm just making sure your hands aren't in pain anymore."

His touch was growing harder, and the circular motions were sending me down the abyss of his absolute power over me. I squeezed my eyes shut and reveled in the feeling he was giving me. I knew he was acting on instinct—he had to divide his attention between two things: driving and punishing me.

I squirmed in my seat, rhythmically rubbing my hips against

the leather, when the car suddenly stopped. I felt his hand leaving, though he really should have kept working on it for a couple of minutes more. Then my ties loosened.

"We're here," Massimo announced, killing the engine.

I stared at him from half-closed eyelids. A voice in my head was screaming, raging and cursing him. How could he leave a woman on the cusp of ecstasy and despair like that? I didn't have to say it aloud. I knew well enough what his motivation had been. He wanted me to beg him. He wanted to show me how much I desired him, despite rebelling against anything and everything he said and did.

"That's great," I replied, rubbing at my wrists. They hurt so much I nearly went mad. "I hope whatever was hurting you has stopped," I called provocatively, shrugging at the same time.

Here it was—that big red button in his head again. The Man in Black shot out with an arm, pulling me over himself, so I sat astride him with my back to the steering wheel. He grabbed me by the back of my neck and pressed my snatch against his hard cock. I moaned, feeling him rubbing against my sensitive clit.

"What hurts me," he hissed, his fury threatening to boil over, "is that I haven't come in your mouth yet."

His hips were undulating lazily. That movement and the pressure of his penis made me breathless.

"And you won't for a long, long time yet," I whispered, my mouth close to his. I licked his lower lip then. "I'm beginning to enjoy the game you make me play," I added cheerfully.

He froze, watching me closely, looking for answers to questions yet unasked. I don't know how long we spent there, looking at each other, but our silent battle was interrupted by knocking on the window. Massimo lowered the glass, revealing the not-too-surprised face of Domenico. *That guy certainly looks like he's seen everything,* I thought.

He said a couple of sentences in Italian, ignoring our position, and Massimo shook his head quickly. I had no idea what they were talking about, but it was clear the Man in Black wanted to have nothing to do with what Domenico was suggesting. When they were finished, Massimo opened the door and stepped out, keeping his hold on me. We headed toward the hotel he had parked the car next to. I was still clutching him, my legs around his hips. I could feel the surprised stares of the other guests as we passed them without a word, Massimo keeping a poker face.

"I'm not paralyzed or anything," I said, raising my eyebrows and shaking my head slightly.

"I hope not, but there are a few reasons why I won't let you go. At least two I can think of off the bat."

We passed the reception desk and entered the elevator, where Massimo propped me against the wall. Our lips touched.

"The first one is that my erect cock is about to rip through my pants, and the second that yours have a wet stain on them and the only things that could cover it were my hands and your hips."

I bit my lip, hearing this. He was making sense.

The bell in the elevator signaled that we reached our floor. Having taken a few steps outside, Massimo used the card he had gotten from Domenico to open the door to our monumental apartment. He put me down.

"I'd like to take a shower now," I said, looking around for my bags.

"Everything you need is in the bathroom. I need to go out and deal with a few things," he said, putting his cell phone to his ear and vanishing into the cavernous living room.

I took a shower and applied a hefty dose of vanilla lotion, which I found in the bathroom cabinet. I left the bathroom and walked through the apartment, finally finding what I was looking for—a bottle of my favorite bubbly beverage. I helped myself to a glass, then another, and another. I watched TV, drank champagne, and wondered where my oppressor had gone. Sometime later, out of boredom, I started to explore the apartment. It took up most of the hotel floor. When I reached the last door, I opened it and went in. Suddenly I found myself in pitch darkness. My eyes had to adjust for a while.

"Sit," I heard the voice I had grown to recognize by now.

I did as I was told. Resistance would be pointless. A while later, I saw Massimo in the gloom. He was drying his hair with a towel. I swallowed loudly, amazed by the view and animated with the alcohol I had had. Massimo was standing by a giant bed supported by four monolithic beams. The mattress was strewn with dozens of purple, gold, and black pillows. The room was dark, classily furnished, and very luxurious. I grabbed the armrests of the armchair I was sitting in as he started to walk my way. I could not take my eyes off the penis now dangling in front of my face. I was staring, my mouth agape. He only stopped when his legs touched my knees. Massimo threw the white towel over his shoulders, grabbing its ends. When his predatory stare met my eyes, I began to pray silently. I was begging God for the strength to resist what I was seeing. What I was *feeling*.

Massimo was perfectly aware of his effect on me. I wasn't too hard to read then, not to mention that I was sucking on my lower lip without realizing it. It wasn't exactly helping to mask my feelings.

Slowly he reached for his prick with his right hand and started stroking it, from the base to the very tip. I prayed harder. His body was flexing. The steely hard muscles of his stomach grew taut, and the penis I was doing everything in my power not to look at was growing, swelling.

"Will you help me?" Massimo asked without taking his eyes off me. Without stopping to play with himself. "I won't do anything without your consent. Remember that."

Oh, God, he didn't even have to do anything. He didn't have to physically touch me to ignite my passion and focus my entire being on him, that magnificent cock, and the thought of sucking it. The last clear-thinking vestiges of my psyche were screaming at me now—if he got what he wanted, the game would stop holding his interest. And I wouldn't feel pleased with myself for succumbing to him this fast. At this point I was sure he would have me, sooner or later. The only question was when. My reptilian brain reminded me that the man masturbating before me was the same man who wanted to kill my family. In an instant, my arousal evaporated, replaced with anger and hate.

"You've got to be joking," I scoffed. "I'm not going to help you with anything. Besides, you've got people for everything. Why don't you ask them?" I raised my eyes. "Can I go now?"

I tried getting up from the armchair, but Massimo grabbed me by the neck and pinned me to the backrest. He leaned over and smirked.

"Are you sure that's what you want, Laura?"

"Let me go, for fuck's sake," I hissed.

He did just that and walked away toward the bed. I got up and grabbed the door handle, wanting to leave this room right then before my thoughts started to focus on things I didn't want to think about. The door was closed. The Man in Black picked up his phone from the nightstand, dialed a number, and said something before hanging up.

"Come here," he ordered.

"Let me out! I want to leave!" I was pulling at the handle, screaming.

Massimo swung the towel to the bed and was standing with his arms hanging loose now, fixing me with his icy gaze.

"Come over here, Laura. I won't repeat myself."

I leaned against the door, intending to follow none of his orders. Massimo let out a deep roar and charged at me. I squeezed my eyes shut, fearing what was going to happen. Then I felt my body being lifted and hitting the bed an instant later. The Man in Black muttered something in Italian under his breath. When I felt myself sink between the pillows, I opened my eyes only to see Massimo looming over me again. He grabbed my right hand and handcuffed it to one of the four pillars of the bed. Then he went for the left one, but I managed to squirm free and hit him first. He clenched his teeth before letting out a furious bellow. I knew I crossed a line there. He clutched my wrist again, painfully hard, and pulled my arm toward the handcuff affixed to the other pillar, all the while pinning my body to the mattress.

"I'll do what I want with you," he growled, sneering.

I kicked out, thrashing on the bed, until he sat astride my legs, his back turned to me, and drew out a short tube. I had no idea what that was. I only wanted him to finally get off me. But then he fastened two soft collars sticking from both ends of the tube around my ankles, reaching to the third pillar. From behind it, he pulled out a chain, fixing it to the collar wrapped around my right ankle. He repeated the operation with my left ankle. Finally, Massimo stood up, admiring his work. He had a satisfied smirk on his face and was clearly aroused by the whole situation. I, on the other hand, was disoriented and dazed. I jerked with my legs, but the tube to which they were cuffed only elongated in response, locking them stiffly in place. Massimo bit his lower lip.

"I was hoping you would do that. This is a telescopic bar. It can elongate but will not shorten unless you know where to push."

I started panicking. I was immobilized with my legs spread wide—an invitation for my tormentor. Suddenly, someone knocked on the door. I stiffened.

The Man in Black moved closer, pulled the sheets from under me, and covered me with them.

"Don't be afraid," he said with that same smirk on his face as he walked to the door.

He opened it and led a young woman inside. I couldn't see her clearly, but she had long, dark hair and wore impossibly high-heeled stilettos accentuating the shape of her toned legs. Massimo told her something and the girl froze. That's when I realized he was still naked. The woman didn't seem to care.

Then he covered the distance between us and leaned over me, lifting my head and putting a pillow beneath it so I could see the whole room without having to exert any muscles.

"I'd like to show you something. Something that you're going to miss out on," he whispered, biting my earlobe gently.

He returned to the other side of the room and sat back in the sofa chair opposite the bed I was strapped to. Keeping his eyes on me, he called out to the woman in Italian. Hearing it, she burst into motion, stepping out of her dress and standing before Massimo in her underwear. My heart started pounding as she dropped to her knees and promptly started to suck my oppressor's cock. His hands landed on her head, his fingers entwining her hair. I couldn't believe it. His black eyes were fixing me with a steady gaze. He was breathing heavily, greedily gulping air. The girl knew what she was doing. She was a pro. Once in a while Massimo would say something in Italian, as if instructing her. In response, she moaned lusciously. I watched them, trying to come to grips with what I was feeling. His piercing gaze made my body burn with desire. I couldn't take my eyes off of him—his ecstasy.

The fact that it wasn't me between his legs chafed at me. Was I jealous? Did I envy this woman? Over that bossy prick? I pushed that thought away. I wouldn't want what she was having. But I couldn't stop staring all the same. At one moment, Massimo tightened his grip on the girl's head and brutally pushed his cock into her throat, making her choke. She wasn't sucking him off anymore—he was fucking her mouth. He went in deep and fast. I squirmed on the bed, making the chains holding me in place rattle against the wooden posts. I was breathing heavily now, my chest heaving too fast for my liking. The show Massimo was starring in was exciting me, stoking the flames of my passion, but at the same making me angry. I understood the words he had said to me before the girl approached him. Yeah, I was jealous. It required a conscious effort, but I managed to close my eyes and turn my head to the side.

"Open your eyes and look at me right now," Massimo hissed.

"I will not. You can't make me," I replied with a croaky voice, barely audible.

"If you won't look at me right now, I'll lie next to you and she'll finish the job rubbing against you. Your choice, Laura."

The threat was enough to make me open my eyes again.

When my stare met his, I could see the satisfaction in his eyes. His parted lips spread into a faint smile. The Man in Black rose from his seat and moved closer to me so the girl kneeling before him was now sitting with her back to the bed, some five feet from me. My hips were moving of their own accord, brushing against the satin sheets. My tongue trailed along my parched lips. I wanted him. If not for the fact that I was tied down, I would probably have thrown that woman out and finished what she had started. And Massimo knew that. After a while, his eyes grew darker and emptier, and beads of sweat formed on his chest. I knew he was going to come. The movements of the girl kneeling in front of him grew faster.

"Yes, Laura, yes!" Massimo moaned, as all the muscles in his body tensed. He came, flooding the girl's throat with sperm.

I was ecstatic, burning up with desire. I felt like I was orgasming with him. A wave of heat crossed my body. Massimo's eyes didn't waver even for a second—he was looking straight at me.

I breathed out slowly, relieved that the show had come to an end. The Man in Black barked something in Italian and the woman pulled away, got up, picked up her dress, and quickly left the room. Massimo left, too, disappearing into the bathroom. I heard the sound of the shower. A few minutes later, he emerged and walked over to me again, rubbing his head with a towel.

"I can put you at ease, baby girl. I'll lick you slow, make you come. I'll make it last. Unless you prefer to feel me inside you."

I opened my eyes wide. My heart was thundering fast and hard, like applause after a Beyoncé concert. I wanted to defy him, but I couldn't speak. Not even a word came out of my mouth.

With a quick snap, Massimo tore the sheets from over me and untied the bathrobe I was wrapped in.

"I like this hotel for two reasons," he said, taking a seat on the bed. "First, it's mine, and second, it has this apartment. I've been looking for the perfect furniture for it for a long time." His voice was calm, sexy. "You see, Laura, you're immobilized now so efficiently that you have no chance of escaping or offering any resistance." He licked the inside of my thigh. "At the same time, I can enjoy each and every part of your gorgeous body."

He grabbed my ankles, spreading my legs wider. The telescopic rod snapped a couple of times and locked in place, holding my legs in the shape of a very wide V.

"Please," I whispered. It was the only thing that came to my mind.

"Are you asking me to begin already? Or stop?"

This was a simple question, but the answer to it wasn't coming. I only let out a soft yelp of resignation. The Man in Black crawled toward me and hovered over my face, pinning me with his eyes. His lower lip brushed against my nose, lips, cheeks.

"I'll fuck you so hard, all of Sicily will hear you scream."

"Please, no," I croaked with the last of my strength, and squeezed my eyes shut. They were watering. Complete silence fell then. I was too afraid to open my eyes—terrified of what I'd see. I heard a click and felt my right hand falling to the mattress, free. Then more clicks. After a while I was completely free.

"Put some clothes on. We need to be in one of my clubs in an hour," Massimo said, leaving the bedroom, still naked.

I stayed on the bed for a moment longer, analyzing what had happened. Suddenly, a tsunami of fury rolled over me. I jumped to my feet and rushed out, chasing him. He was already standing in his suit pants and sipping on champagne.

"Would you care to explain this to me?" I shrieked as he slowly turned, hearing me stomping out of the adjoining room.

"What is there to explain?" he asked, nonchalantly leaning against the table.

"That girl took your interest? She's nothing but a whore. I own a few brothels and you didn't want to help me blow off some steam. The bed and the toys on it didn't seem to be to your liking. That doesn't require any further comment, does it? Just like Veronica and what she did. Judging by your reaction, at least." He lifted his brows. "What more is there to say?" Massimo crossed his arms. "I won't force myself on you. Not before you give me your consent. I promised. It's hard for me to control myself fully, but I won't rape you." He turned away and headed toward the door. "Despite that we both know perfectly well that it would be the best sex of our lives. And that you would beg for more when it ended."

I stood rooted to the spot, not able to deny what he was saying. He was right—there was no point fighting the obvious. Back in the bedroom, he had been just a couple of minutes from finally making me cave in. What Massimo wanted, though, was for me to give myself over out of love, instead of animalistic desire. He wanted to possess me whole. Sticking his cock inside me wasn't enough. God, he was devious and manipulative. After what he had said as he was leaving, I wanted him even more. Now it was I who needed to keep it together, just to stop myself from throwing myself on him on one of those gigantic sofas. I screamed, helpless, balling my fists. Then I went to take a cold shower. It was what I needed. When I left the bathroom, I met Domenico in the living room. He was leaving another bottle of champagne on the table.

"I'm surprised you aren't sick of him yet," he said, pouring me a glass.

"Who said I'm not? And you never ask me what I'd like, instead making me drink all those fizzy carbs all the time," I said with a laugh, sipping the beverage. "What is this place we're about to go to?"

"It's called Nostro. Massimo's favorite club. He keeps an eye on all the comings and goings personally. It's a pretty classy spot. Only politicians, businessmen, and . . ." He trailed off, making me all the more curious.

"And who? Their whores? Like Veronica?" I spun on my heel, facing him.

Domenico sent me a probing look, as if checking my bluff. I didn't allow my face to show any emotion, instead focusing on rummaging through my clothes, pretending to look for something appropriate for the evening. Once in a while I pressed the champagne glass to my lips, sipping.

"Maybe not exactly like Veronica, but yes. It is a place for people who cannot act as freely anywhere else."

"After she sucked Massimo off in front of me, I had the impression she knew him well. They probably spent some quality time together in that club of his, eh?"

I said it. I had meant to think it only, but it came out aloud.

Now I didn't know what to do. I shrugged and went to the bathroom, silently scolding myself. I didn't close the door and, after a while, as I was doing my makeup, Domenico appeared at the door and leaned against the wall. He couldn't hide his amusement at my sincerity.

"You know, it's not really my business who blows whom. Or employs, for that matter."

"So, you're telling me you're not even interested in how you get your recruitment done?"

Domenico raised his brows and burst out laughing.

"Forgive me, Laura, but . . . are you jealous?"

I felt a shiver running down my spine. Was I that bad at pretending not to care? "I'm just losing my patience. I want this year to end and I want to go home. Now. What should I wear today?" I asked, changing the subject and turning away from the mirror.

Domenico smiled charmingly and turned to head back to the living room. "You can't be jealous about a whore, you know. She's only doing her job. And I've already prepared a dress for you."

As he left, I collapsed, hiding my head in my hands, bent over the sink. If it was so clear that I couldn't keep my wits about me, it would only become worse with time. *Focus!* I said to myself, slapping myself in the face.

"If this is your way of disciplining yourself, I can gladly hit you harder."

I raised my eyes and saw Massimo sitting in an armchair behind me.

"You'd like to slap me in the face?" I asked, grabbing my eyeliner.

"If that's your thing . . ."

I tried to focus on doing my makeup, but those piercing eyes of his were making everything harder. Even the easiest things, it seemed.

"You want something? If not, leave me."

"Veronica is a prostitute. She comes over, sucks my dick, and sometimes I fuck her if I'm in the mood. She likes the violence and the money. And she works with the most discerning clients—myself included. All the girls working for me—"

"Do I have to listen to this?" I spun around and crossed my arms. "Would you like me to tell you how Martin used to fuck me? Or maybe you'd like to watch?"

His eyes darkened and his sly smirk vanished, leaving a face that could have been made of stone. Massimo got up and walked over to me, grabbing me by the shoulders, lifting me, and perching me on the counter next to the sink.

"Everything you see here is mine."

He seized me by the head and turned my face to the mirror. "Everything. You. See," he hissed furiously. "And I'll kill anyone who takes what's mine." He turned his back on me and left without another word.

Everything was his. The hotel, the whores, and the game. All of a sudden, I had a plan. I would punish Massimo's hypocrisy. I went to the bedroom and glanced at the dress splayed on the bed—it was golden, bare backed, covered with sequins. A beauty. Regretfully, it wouldn't do for my plan. I went to the closet and looked at all my dresses.

"You like whores? I'll show you a whore . . ." I murmured in Polish.

I picked a dress and a pair of shoes, and then went back to the bathroom to redo my makeup. Thirty minutes later, as Domenico knocked on my door, I was fastening my boots.

"Fuck me," Domenico breathed, nervously closing the door behind him. "He'll kill you. And then he'll kill me. You can't go out like that."

I laughed mockingly and went to the mirror. The flesh-colored dress with thin shoulder straps looked more like a slip than a full outfit. It revealed the entire back and the sides of my breasts. It didn't really cover much at all, but that was the whole plan. As the dress had a high neckline, I hung the necklace—a large cross studded with black crystals—on my back, so nobody could miss my nakedness. I also picked thigh-high boots—they served to emphasize the fact that the dress barely covered my ass. It was hot outside, but fortunately Emilio Pucci, the designer of this particular pair, had foreseen everything. Women who loved high boots wanted to wear them all year round, so he had designed them to be airy, with laces going all the way up, and toeless. They were obscene. And obscenely expensive. I tied my hair into a very tight ponytail on the top of my head. The sexy, simple, and lifting hairdo perfectly complemented the smoky eyes and bright, glossy lips.

"Who bought me all those things, Domenico? If he paid for them, he had to realize I'd wear them," I said, adding, "You look pretty nice yourself. Are you coming with us?"

The Italian stood immobile, with his hands clutching at his head. His chest was heaving.

"I'm going with you because Massimo has some other business to attend to first. Do you realize I'll be in big trouble if he sees you like that?"

"So you'll tell him you tried to stop me but I overpowered you. Come on!"

I grabbed a black clutch bag and a tiny white fox bolero, passed Domenico with a happy smile, and left the apartment. He muttered something, which I didn't catch, but followed.

As we left the elevator and crossed the hall, the staff all froze. Domenico nodded at them, and I just kept walking with a big grin on my face. We stepped into a limo parked by the entrance and drove to the party.

"This is the day I die," Domenico said finally, pouring himself a glass of amber liquid. "Why are you doing this to me?" He drank it all in one gulp.

"Oh, Domenico, don't be such a crybaby. I'm not doing this to you. I'm doing this to *him*. Besides, I think I look very stylish and sexy."

The young Italian helped himself to another drink and poured the third. He looked especially dapper that evening in light-gray pants, similarly colored shoes, and a white shirt with the sleeves rolled up. There was a beautiful golden Rolex shining from his wrist, paired with a set of bracelets—some wooden, some gold, and the other made of platinum.

"Sexy, that's for sure, but stylish? I sincerely doubt that Massimo will appreciate this particular brand of elegance."

CHAPTER 7

Nostro reflected Massimo's personality perfectly. Two tall bouncers stood guard at the red-carpeted entrance. A flight of stairs led down, straight to the elegant, dark interior. Tables were nestled in alcoves divided with dark, heavy drapes. Walls of ebony and the dim light of candles gave the impression of sensuality, eroticism, and luscious appeal. There were two platforms, where scantily dressed women in masks writhed to the rhythm of Massive Attack.

The bartenders standing behind a long black bar covered in quilted leather were women. They were all dressed in tight-fitting bodysuits and wore high heels. Their wrists were adorned with leather straps imitating manacles. Yes, everything was unmistakably Massimo's idea.

We passed the bar and the crowd of bodies lazily moving to the rhythm of the music. A massive bouncer who was making way for us drew another drape open, revealing another room—a cavernous hall. Massive dark wood sculptures shaped in the form of conjoined bodies dominated the space. I was awed by their sheer size rather than by what they depicted.

In the corner, on a pedestal, obscured by semitransparent curtains, was an alcove where we were led. It was decidedly larger than the other ones. I could only speculate as to what normally happened here—there was a dancing pole in the middle.

Domenico sat down, and before he touched the satin lining of the sofa, alcohol, appetizers and a tray covered with a silver dome were brought into the alcove. On instinct, I reached out for the tray, but Domenico caught my hand before it touched the metal surface, shaking his head. He passed me a glass of champagne.

"We won't be alone today," he said cautiously, as if afraid of what he had to say. "We'll be joined by several people with whom we have to tend to some business."

I nodded and repeated after him, "Some people, some business. Right. You boys will play gangsters." I poured the content of the glass down my throat and stuck my hand out so Domenico could refill it.

"We'll be doing business. Best get used to it." Suddenly, his eyes bulged.

He was staring into the distance, at something behind me.

"Shit is going to hit the fan now," he breathed, running his hand through his hair.

I turned around and noticed several men entering our alcove. Massimo was among them. Seeing me, he stopped and froze in perfect stillness. He stared at me coldly.

I swallowed hard, and suddenly my plan to dress like a hooker didn't seem like such a good idea. Massimo's companions passed me on their way to greet Domenico, while the head of the family kept his distance. His fury was clear and apparent.

"What the fuck are you wearing?" he growled, grabbing me by the elbow.

"Only what you picked for me," I replied, freeing my arm.

My retort wasn't to his liking. I could see the red-hot rage boiling over in him, wondering why he hadn't started spewing steam from his ears yet. That's when one of the men shouted something to Massimo, who replied, keeping his eyes aimed at me.

I sat at the table and reached for yet another glass of champagne. If I was to play a piece of decor, I might as well be a very drunk piece of decor.

It was a good day to drink. Bored witless, I observed the room, listening in on the conversation. When Massimo spoke Italian, he was really sexy. Suddenly, Domenico broke my reverie by lifting the dome from the silver platter. I shot a glance at what was on it and nearly choked—it was cocaine. The drug, divided into several dozen neat little lines, covered the entire platter. Where I come from plates like that are what you serve roast turkey on. I exhaled slowly and left the alcove, but I didn't even manage to turn my head to take a look around, as the gigantic bouncer materialized in front of me. I shot Massimo a look. The man was keeping his eyes trained on me, standing right behind me. I bent over, pretending to scratch my leg, but really to show him how short my dress was before I left. I straightened up and met his predatory glare.

"Don't provoke me, girl," Massimo said.

"Why? Are you afraid I'm doing it well?" I asked, trailing my tongue along my lower lip. Alcohol always has that effect on me—I feel bolder—but with Massimo, when I got drunk it seemed to always bring out the demon in me.

"Alberto will keep you company."

"You're changing the subject," I purred, clutching the lapels of his suit and inhaling the scent of his cologne. "My dress is so short you could enter me without even taking it off." I grabbed his hand and led it down my waist and then under the fabric of the dress. "White lace, just the way you like it," I breathed. "Alberto!" I called out suddenly, and headed toward the dance floor.

I took a look back, shooting a glance at Massimo, who was standing propped against one of the pillars with his hands in his pockets and a wide smile on his face. He was into that stuff.

I crossed the hall and found a place where the rumbling music was the loudest. People were dancing, drinking, and fucking in the private alcoves. I paid them no mind. I needed to switch off. I nodded at the bartender, and before I could count to three there was a glass of rosé champagne in front of me. I needed another drink, so I downed it and grabbed another glass, which magically appeared on the counter. That's how I spent another hour, or maybe more. As soon as I decided it was enough and I was suitably drunk, I headed back to those junkies in the alcove, surprised to see that the gentlemen were not alone anymore. There were women all around them, purring and brushing against their legs, arms, and crotches like horny cats. They were all beautiful and all hookers. Massimo was sitting in the middle, but alone. Was that coincidence or something he had planned? I didn't care. I was happy with what I saw, because otherwise I might have reacted violently. And I wouldn't even hold that against myself. Before I could continue this train of thought, my eyes focused on the dancing pole. It was free.

When I had moved to Warsaw, I started taking pole dancing lessons. At first I thought it was all about sexy squirming, but my instructor quickly taught me better. Pole dancing was the perfect way to keep your body in shape. It was a bit like gymnastics, only on a pole. So, without thinking, I went to the table, aimed my eyes at Massimo, and slowly took off the cross hanging from my back. I kissed it and placed it gently on the table in front of the Man in Black. "Running Up That Hill" by Placebo was blasting from the speakers. It felt like an invitation. I knew I couldn't do everything I had in mind. My dress was too short and there were all those guests around. One thing I knew was that the moment I touched that pole, Massimo would blow a gasket anyway. When I grabbed the metal pillar and turned in a fluid pirouette, trying to gauge his reaction, he kept still. All the men suddenly lost interest in the women around them and instead looked at me. *I got you now!* I thought, and started the show. A few seconds later I already knew that the few years I hadn't practiced had done nothing to blunt my talent. I remembered all the motions and could do it without breaking a sweat. Dancing came naturally to me; I had danced since I could remember. Whether it was pole dancing, ballroom dancing, or Latino, it always soothed me.

I allowed myself to sink into it: the alcohol, the music, the atmosphere of the place—all that had changed me. After a longer while I shot a glance at the place where Massimo had been standing a while ago. The space was empty now, but all eyes were on me, including Domenico's. The young Italian was sitting wide legged on the couch. I pirouetted once more and froze. That wild, icy stare was drilling holes in me. Massimo was standing right next to me. I wrapped one leg around him and ran my fingers through his hair, leaning him back against the pole.

"A very interesting choice of music for a nightclub," I said.

"As you've noticed this is a club, not a disco."

I turned around and pressed my buttocks against his crotch, gently swaying. Massimo grabbed me by the throat and pushed my head into his shoulder.

"You'll be mine. I promise you that. And then I'll take you when and where I want."

I laughed flirtatiously and slipped down the pedestal, heading toward the table. One of the men pushed himself to his feet and grabbed me by the wrist, pulling me to himself. I lost my balance and fell face-first into the sofa. The man pulled up my dress and clasped his hand on my buttock, slapping it and shouting something in Italian.

I wanted to get up, hit him on the head with a bottle, but I couldn't move. As some point, I felt someone dragging me by the arms along the soft fabric of the sofa. I raised my eyes and saw it was Domenico. I turned my head, noticing Massimo, who was holding the man who had been groping me just a moment ago by the throat. He held a gun in his other hand, pointing it at my unfortunate admirer.

I wrestled out of Domenico's grip and rushed toward the Man in Black.

"He didn't know who I am!" I said quickly, stroking Massimo's hair placatingly.

He roared something in response, and Domenico jumped toward us, grabbing me again, but this time tightening his grip so I couldn't escape. Don Massimo turned his head to a man standing next to the sofa, and a moment later all the women were gone. As we were left alone, he pushed the man he had been holding by the throat down to his knees, aiming the gun at his head. The sight made my heart start thumping wildly. I could see the scene that had taken place on the driveway. It was still too nightmarish for me. I faced Domenico, huddling my face against his shoulder.

"He can't kill him," I yelped, certain that a man couldn't be murdered in cold blood in a public place like this.

"Oh yes, he can," the young Italian replied very calmly, holding me tight. "And he will."

I felt all blood drain from my face when I heard the horrific sound of a gunshot. My legs buckled and I started to slide down Domenico's chest. He held me tighter and called something out. I felt myself being lifted and carried somewhere. The music died, and my body hit soft pillows.

"You like to leave with a bang, don't you?" I heard Domenico saying and pushing a pill under my tongue. "Now, now, Laura, calm down."

My heart was pounding like crazy, but soon it started slowing down. Then the door to the room swung open and Massimo barged in, with the gun stuck behind his belt.

He kneeled by my side and stared at me, his face a mask of fear.

"Did you kill him?" I asked in a whisper, praying that he didn't.

"No."

I breathed out and turned onto my back.

"I only shot off his hands. He won't be touching you again," he replied, getting up and passing the gun to his assistant.

"I want to go back to the hotel. Can I?" I asked, trying to stand up. The mix of the pill with the alcohol made the whole room whirl. I swayed and fell back to the pillows.

The Man in Black held me in his arms and hugged me. Domenico opened the door, through which we went to the back office, then to the kitchen, and finally to the back exit. There was a limo waiting there for us. Massimo stepped in, still holding me in his arms. He placed me in a seat and covered me with his jacket. I fell asleep huddling against him.

I regained consciousness back at the hotel, hearing Massimo fighting with the laces of my boots, swearing like a sailor.

"There's a zipper on the back," I whispered, my eyes half closed. "You didn't actually think anyone would be able to tie those shoelaces each time . . ."

Massimo raised his eyes and sent me an angry look, pulling the boots from my feet.

"What did you think, coming dressed like a . . ." He trailed off.

"Finish the sentence," I growled, irritated, instantly awake. "Like a whore, you mean. Isn't that what you were going to say?"

The Man in Black balled his fists. His teeth were clenched, and the muscles of his jaw worked.

"You like whores, don't you? Isn't Veronica proof of that?"

His eyes grew empty—devoid of emotion. I stopped talking, pursing my lips and waiting for a reply. Massimo didn't speak, but I could see his knuckles whitening, his fists squeezing tightly. Finally, he shot up and sat astride me, his legs around my hips. He grasped my wrists and lifted my arms above my head, pinning them to the mattress. My chest started heaving frantically as he brought his face close to mine, then thrust his tongue inside my mouth. I moaned, writhing beneath him, but I was not going to fight him this time. I didn't want to. His tongue pushed inside me, deeper and deeper and harder.

"When I saw you dance . . ." he whispered, pulling away from me. "Fuck!" He dropped his head, hiding his face in the crook of my neck. "Why do you do this, Laura? Are you trying to prove something to me? Checking my limits? I decide what they are. Not you. Or maybe you want me to take what I desire? If that is so, I'll do it."

"I was having a good time. Wasn't I supposed to have a good time?" I asked. "Now get off me, I need a drink," I added.

He raised his head, sending me a surprised look.

"You need what?"

"A drink," I repeated, crawling from under him as he loosened his grip and fell to his side over the mattress. "You're getting on my nerves, Massimo," I muttered, and walked over to the table, pouring myself a glass of amber liquid from a carafe.

"Laura, you do not drink spirits. And after taking your medication and all the champagne you've had at the club, this is not a good idea."

"I don't drink spirits?" I asked, raising the glass. "Watch me, then."

I tilted the glass and downed it in one gulp. *God, it tastes bad*, I thought, wincing. My dislike of spirits didn't stop me from pouring myself another glass. Plodding to the terrace, I turned my head and sent the Man in Black a look. He was watching my little show with his head propped on his arm.

"You'll regret this, girl!" he called out when I left through the door leading outside.

The evening was wonderful—the heat had dissipated, and the air seemed fresh, even though we were in downtown Rome. I sat on a long sofa and gulped down another sip of my drink. Sometime later, as I finished it, I felt drowsy and sleepy. My head swam. I usually didn't drink spirits, just like Massimo said. Now I knew why. The spinning in my head made walking difficult—not to mention finding my way through the door. I squeezed one eye shut, focusing hard to appear in control of my body, intending to go back to bed. As gracefully as I was able, I stood up and grabbed the doorframe. Massimo could be watching. An instant later I realized I was right—he was lying in bed with a laptop on his legs. He was naked, not counting the tight-fitting CK boxers. *God almighty, he's too beautiful*, I thought as he raised his eyes and looked at me. My drunken brain was suggesting that I slowly drop my clothes and leave him to himself. I took a step forward, fiddling with the shoulder strap of my dress, letting it slip off. The dress slid down my body and landed on the floor. I wanted to smoothly raise my knee and disappear into the bathroom, but at this point my legs had another idea. My right ankle got tangled in the dress, while my left foot stepped on the fabric. I fell to the carpet with a yelp and burst out in nervous laughter.

Massimo materialized above me, like that first night when I had bumped into him at the club. This time, he didn't lift me by the elbows, instead taking me tenderly in his arms and laying me on the bed, checking if I had hurt myself in the fall. When my hysterical giggling finally died down, he sent me a worried look.

"Are you all right?"

"Take me," I whispered, pulling off the last elements of my attire. As the white lace thong slid down to my ankles, I lifted a leg and snatched the piece of underwear between two fingers. "Take me now, Massimo!" I crossed my arms behind my head and spread my legs wide.

The Man in Black sat still, staring at me in his intense way, and a slight smile illuminated his face. He bent over me and kissed me lightly on the lips, covering me with the duvet.

"I told you it was a bad idea for you to drink more. Good night."

His reaction flustered me. I attacked, lifting an arm to slap him again, but either I was too slow or he was too fast—he caught my wrist and tied it to the pillar of the bed just like he had before, when Veronica had been doing her show. Then he jumped on the bed, and before I knew it, I was strapped to the bed, thrashing wildly.

"Let me go!" I yelled.

"Good night," Massimo repeated, leaving the room and turning off the light.

I was woken by the summer sun shining through the window. My head was heavy and throbbing with pain, but it wasn't my biggest problem—I couldn't feel my hands. *What the hell is happening?* I thought, my eyes shooting sideways, taking in the straps tying me down. I jerked my hands, but the sound of metal scraping against wood nearly made my brain burst. I wailed silently and took a look around. There was nobody there. I tried remembering what had happened last night, but the only thing I could recall was my pole dance. I groaned, thinking about all the things that must have happened when we got back—Massimo must have gotten what he wanted. How else would I have ended up like this? Now the only thing I could do was die of shame and hangover. A few more minutes of self-pity, and I started to think more logically. I fiddled with the locks with the tips of my fingers, but whoever had designed my trap had made sure that freeing myself on my own was practically impossible.

"Fuck, shit, fuck!" I swore helplessly. That's when I heard a quiet knock on the door.

"Come in," I said haltingly, fearing who I would see at the door.

It was Domenico. I can't remember being this happy in my life. The young man froze and watched me for a while, clearly amused. I dropped my eyes to see if my breasts were visible, but I had been covered with the sheets very meticulously.

"Don't just stand there! Help me out!" I growled, irritated.

The young Italian walked over and freed my hands.

"The evening was a success, I gather?" he said, lifting his eyebrows.

"Give me a break." I covered my head with the duvet. I wanted to die.

When I took a peek under the sheets, I realized I was naked.

"Oh no," I yelped.

"Massimo left. He has a lot of work, so you'll have to bear with me. I'll be waiting in the living room with breakfast."

After thirty minutes, a shower, and a bunch of Tylenol, I sat at the table, sipping tea with milk.

"Have fun yesterday?" Domenico asked, putting his newspaper down.

"As far as I know, not really. But judging by the state you found me in, I did have some fun after we returned. Thank God I don't remember any of it."

Domenico burst out in booming laughter, nearly choking on his croissant. "How much do you remember?"

"My pole dance. Nothing more."

He nodded understandingly. "I have to say, that dance of yours is hard to forget. You're very flexible." He grinned.

"Ugh . . . kill me," I groaned, my head hitting the table with an audible thump. "But first tell me what happened next."

Domenico raised his eyebrows and took a sip of espresso. "Don Massimo took you to your room and—"

"Fucked me."

"I doubt that, though I wasn't there. I met him a minute after we returned and then saw him leaving the room and going to sleep in the second bedroom. You know, we're family, me and Massimo, and he didn't look"—Domenico searched for the right word—"satisfied. And after a night spent with you, I believe that is how he would have looked."

"Oh my God, Domenico! Why do you torment me so? You know what happened. You can just tell me."

"I can, but it won't be as fun." The expression on my face must have told him I was in no mood for jokes right now. "All right. You got drunk and got naughty, so he tied you to the bed and went to sleep."

I sighed with relief. I couldn't stop thinking about what had really happened, though.

"Oh stop it, you. Eat something. We have a lot to do today."

We only spent three days in Rome, but I didn't see Massimo even once the whole time. After our night at the club, he had disappeared without a trace, and Domenico wouldn't talk about it.

So we spent the whole time together, with Domenico showing me the Eternal City. We ate together, shopped together, and went to the spa together. Was this how all our trips would be?

When on the second day we were having lunch in a breathtaking restaurant with a view of the Spanish Steps, I asked him, "Will he let me work at all? I can't just sit around, waiting for him all the time."

Domenico kept quiet for a long while, before replying. "I can't speak for Massimo. I don't know what's in his head. So please,

Laura, don't ask me about these things. You have to remember who he is. The less questions, the better."

"Goddamn it, I have a right to know what he's doing! Why he isn't calling and if he's even alive," I growled, dropping my fork with a loud clink.

"He's alive," Domenico retorted gruffly, avoiding my eyes.

I grimaced and returned to my meal. On the one hand, this life was as comfortable as it got, but on the other, I wasn't the kind of person who just wanted to sit around doing nothing. I wasn't a trophy wife. Especially since Massimo wasn't even my man.

On the morning of the third day, Domenico and I had breakfast as normal. His cell phone rang, and the man excused himself and left the table. He talked for a couple minutes before returning to me.

"You will leave Rome today, Laura."

I sent him a surprised look. "We've only just arrived."

The young Italian smiled at me apologetically and headed toward my closet. I downed my tea and followed him.

A few minutes later, I tied my hair in a high ponytail and put some mascara on—I was getting more tanned by the day, which meant I needed less makeup. Each day, the temperature outside reached eighty-five degrees. Without knowing where we were going, I put on dark blue denim shorts and a scanty white top that barely covered my small breasts. Today's outfit was a bit of a declaration— I refused to be elegant. Besides, I dropped the underwear. As for shoes, I picked my beloved Isabel Marant wedge sneakers. I put on sunglasses and grabbed a bag when Domenico walked into the room. He stopped, rooted to the spot, and gazed at me for a while.

"Are you sure you want to go out like this?" he asked awkwardly. "Don Massimo won't be happy."

I spun on my heel nonchalantly, slid my glasses halfway down my nose, and shot him a disdainful look.

"What makes you think I care? After he left me for three days?" I turned my back on him and went to the elevator.

My absurdly expensive watch told me it was 11 a.m. when Domenico showed me the car I would be driven in.

"Aren't you going with me?" I asked, pouting like a little girl.

"I can't, but Claudio will tend to you during your trip." He shut the door and the car drove off. I felt alone and sad all of a sudden. Was it possible I was missing Massimo?

My driver, Claudio, who doubled as my bodyguard, was not too talkative.

I grabbed my phone and dialed Mom. She seemed calmer now but wasn't too happy when I told her I wouldn't be joining them this week.

When we finished talking, the car took a turn off the highway, and a few minutes later entered a town called Fiumicino. Claudio drove steadily, expertly navigating the narrow, picturesque streets in the enormous SUV. At one point, he hit the brakes, and I saw we were in a large port filled to the brim with luxury yachts.

An elderly man dressed all in white opened the door for me. I sent the driver a questioning look, and in response, he nodded to me, allowing me to step out.

"Welcome to Porto di Fiumicino, Laura. I am Fabio and I will take you to your boat. Follow me." The man gestured at me.

When, after a short while, we stopped to board the yacht, I raised my head and gaped. Before me was the *Titan*.

Most boats in the port were white, but this one was a cold steel gray, with tinted windows.

"The yacht is nearly three hundred feet long. It has twelve guest cabins, a Jacuzzi, a cinema, spa, gym, as well as a large pool and a helicopter pad."

"Not too shabby," I mumbled, picking my jaw up from the floor.

When I entered the first of six decks, I found myself in a grand living room, only partially roofed. It was elegant, but very minimalistic. Most of the furniture was white with steel-gray details. The floor was made of glass. Then there was the dining room and the stairs to the bow and the Jacuzzi. Most tables were laden with vases filled with white roses. I focused on the one without any flowers. Instead, there was a gigantic ice bucket filled with bottles of Moët Rosé.

Before I finished the tour of the deck, Fabio showed up next to me with a glass filled with the champagne. Did they all think I was some kind of alcoholic, my only way of dealing with free time being binging on champagne?

"What would you like to do before we set sail? A tour of the rest of the yacht? Some sunbathing? Or maybe you'd like lunch?"

"I'd like to be left alone, if that's not a problem." I put my handbag down and headed toward the bow.

Fabio nodded and left me. I stayed on the deck, observing the sea, slowly downing my glass. Then I had another one, and one more, and so on until the bottle was empty. The hangover I was still suffering from started dissipating, but only because I was drunk again.

The *Titan* left port. As the land disappeared over the horizon, I could only think about how I regretted ever visiting Sicily. I dreamed of not meeting Massimo and not becoming his savior. I could have lived my normal life in my normal world instead of sitting here, caged like a bird.

"What the hell are you wearing this time?" I heard the familiar voice behind me. "You look like—"

I spun and nearly bumped into Massimo, who was standing right behind me, just like when we had first met. I was pretty tipsy already, and I stumbled, falling to the sofa.

"I look how I want and it's none of your business," I muttered. "You've left me without a word and you're treating me like some doll you play with whenever you feel like it. But today that doll wants to be left alone." I got up from the sofa clumsily, grabbed another bottle of champagne, and staggered toward the stern. The shoes I had on didn't make walking any easier, and I realized how pathetic I must have looked. I kicked them off angrily.

The Man in Black followed me, calling out, but his voice failed to penetrate the buzz in my head from the alcohol. I didn't know the ship, but I needed to escape him. I ran down the steps and . . . that was the last thing I remember.

CHAPTER 8

"Breathe," I heard someone saying, as if through a wall. "Breathe, Laura. Can you hear me?" The voice was growing clearer by the moment.

I felt my stomach cramping and I threw up, coughing and spitting out something salty.

"Thank God! Can you hear me, baby girl?" Massimo asked, stroking my hair.

I managed to open my eyes and saw the Man in Black, hovering above me, soaking wet. He had his clothes on but had lost the shoes. I watched him, unable to say anything. There was a roar in my head and the sun was blinding me. Fabio passed us a towel and Massimo wrapped me in it and took me in his arms. He carried me across the yacht, through all the decks, until we reached a bedroom, where he put me down. I was still in shock, utterly clueless about what had happened. Massimo was drying my hair, looking at me with eyes filled with worry and anger in equal measure.

"What happened?" I croaked.

"You fell from the deck. Thank God we weren't going faster and that you fell to the side of the boat. Still, you nearly drowned."

Massimo knelt by the bed. "Goddamn it, Laura, I feel like killing you myself now. At the same time, I'm so happy you're alive."

I touched his cheek.

"You saved me?"

"You were lucky I was close. I don't even want to think what would have happened otherwise. Why are you being so stubborn? Why don't you listen to me?" He sighed.

The alcohol was still buzzing in my head, and I could taste the salt water in my mouth.

"I'd like to take a shower now," I muttered, and tried to push myself up.

The Man in Black didn't let me. He grabbed me by the shoulder delicately.

"I can't allow you to do it by yourself. Just five minutes ago you weren't even breathing. If you need it so badly, I'll wash you."

I shot him a glance, exhausted, unable to refuse. Besides, he had already seen me naked. Not only seen, but also touched, so there wasn't any part of my body that would still be unknown to him. I nodded slightly. For a moment, Massimo left, but when he reappeared, I could hear water running in the bathroom.

He took off his wet shirt, pants, and boxers. In normal circumstances that view would have worked me up, but not this time. Massimo took the towel I was rolled up in and gently took my top off, seemingly untouched by what he was seeing. He unbuttoned my shorts, discovering that I wasn't wearing any underwear.

"You don't have your panties on?"

"How astute of you." I smiled. "I didn't think we'd see each other."

"How does that help?" His stare grew ice-cold. I decided to leave it at that.

He took me in his arms and carried me to the bathroom, just

a couple of feet from the bed. A huge bathtub stood by the wall, partially filled with water now. Massimo stepped in, sat down, and leaned back, turning me around and setting me down between his legs with my head resting on his chest. First, he washed my body, not skipping a spot, and then went on to my hair. I was surprised at how delicate he could be. In the end, he took me out of the tub, covered me with a towel, and carried me back to the bed. With a button on a remote control, he made the shutters roll down the windows, shading the room. I immediately fell asleep.

I woke up terrified, gasping for air, panicking. Where was I? It took me a while to recall the events of the previous day. I got out of bed and turned the light on, revealing the impressive cabin. White, rounded sofas in the living room perfectly complemented the black floor. The interior was minimalistic and very masculine. Even the flowers in their vases perched on top of bright columns seemed somehow masculine.

Where was Massimo? Had he left me again? I put on a bathrobe over naked skin and went to the door. The corridors were wide and well lit. I had no idea where I was going. That's what you get when you choose champagne over a tour of the yacht. The thought of alcohol made me wince. Finally, taking the steps up, I reached the deck I remembered. Despite only learning about what happened from Massimo's story, I felt afraid. The deck was empty and dark—the glass floor was only illuminated by faint beams of light coming from the sparsely positioned floor lamps. I headed toward the semiroofed lounge, crossed it, and reached the bow.

"Sleep well?" I heard a voice from the darkness. I scanned my surroundings and there he was, the Man in Black, sitting in the Jacuzzi with both hands resting on the edge of the tub.

"I can see you're feeling better. Care to join me?"

He tilted his head from side to side, as if trying to relax his neck muscles. Keeping his eyes on me, he took a sip of the amber liquor from his glass.

The *Titan* was anchored, and I could see the lights of land in the distance. The calm waves were gently sloshing against the side of the yacht.

"Where is everybody?" I asked.

"Where they are supposed to be, which is somewhere else," Massimo said, and put the glass down. "Are you waiting for another invitation, Laura?"

His voice was serious, and his eyes reflected the light of the lamps illuminating the deck. Looking at him, I realized I had been missing him for the past few days.

I reached for the belt of the bathrobe, pulled at it, and allowed the robe to fall to the floor. Massimo watched in rapt attention, his jaw working rhythmically. Slowly I walked toward him and slid into the water, taking a place opposite him.

I looked at him as he took another sip. He was so lovely when he was trying to hold himself back.

I moved closer and sat on his knees, pressing myself against him. Without asking for consent, I ran my hand through his hair. He moaned softly and leaned his head back, closing his eyes. I stared at him for an instant before leaning closer and biting his lip gently. He grew harder beneath me. I swayed my hips delicately, sucking on his lips, trailing my teeth along them, until I slid my tongue into his mouth. He dropped his hands, grabbing my ass, pulling me closer.

"I've missed you," I whispered, pulling away for a moment.

He pushed me back and shot me a wide-eyed stare.

"Is that how you display your longing? Because if this is your way of saying thank you for saving your life, baby girl, I can't accept it. I won't do it with you until you're absolutely sure you want it."

That hurt me. I pushed even farther away and jumped out of the Jacuzzi, then grabbed my bathrobe and threw it over my shoulders, suddenly ashamed. I wanted to cry. I needed to be as far away from him as I could.

I ran back down the stairs and immediately got lost in the labyrinth of passageways. All doors looked the same. Thinking I found the right one, I grabbed the handle and entered a berth. Trailing my hand along the wall, I looked for the light switch, finally realizing this was not the place I had been looking for. The door behind me closed and I heard the click of the lock. The lights grew dimmer and I froze, afraid to turn around, though I knew he wouldn't hurt me.

"I love it when you touch my hair," Massimo said, stopping behind me. He snatched the sash of my bathrobe and tore my only cover away.

As I pressed myself against him, I felt he was naked, wet, and hot. He turned me around and his lips clasped around mine. He kissed me hungrily. His hands moved around my body, stopping on my ass. He lifted me up, kissing me all the while, and carried me to the bed, laying me on the mattress. For a while, he stood there, looking at me. I met his stare and lifted my arms above my head, spreading them to my sides, showing him my helplessness, but also my trust.

"If we do it now, I won't be able to stop. You know that, right?" he asked in a serious voice. "If we cross this line, I'll fuck you whether you like it or not."

The way he said it sounded like a promise. It only ignited my passion.

"So fuck me," I said, sitting in front of him on the edge of the bed.

He muttered something through his teeth in Italian and took a step closer, stopping a few inches away. With the faint light still on in the room, I could see his throbbing erection. I put my hands on his buttocks and pulled him closer, grabbing his manhood. It was amazing—thick and hard. I trailed my fingers down its length, licking my lips.

"Put your hands on my head," I said, looking him in the eyes. "And punish me."

Massimo exhaled loudly and grabbed my hair hard.

"Are you asking me to treat you like a whore? Is this what you want?"

I leaned my head back obediently and opened my mouth wide.

"Yes, don Massimo," I breathed.

His grip on my hair tightened. He moved closer, and with a fluid, decisive motion, shoved his swollen cock into my mouth. I moaned, feeling it reach as far as my throat. His hips started pumping forward and back. I couldn't breathe.

"If at any point you stop enjoying it, tell me. Just make sure I know you're not teasing me," he said, keeping his movements steady.

I withdrew a bit and took him out of my mouth, continuing to stroke his cock with my hand.

"Same goes for you," I replied, meaning it, before continuing to suck him.

The Man in Black laughed, but as soon as I picked up the tempo, he gasped. I blew him harder and faster than his hands on my head were suggesting. He was panting, his hands balling into fists in my hair. I felt him growing even larger in my mouth. I took it as an invitation to show him who was in control now. He was sweet, his skin so smooth, and his body exuded the scent of sex. I delighted in him, wanting to sate myself with what I had yearned for from the beginning. Another part of me wanted to prove something to him—to show Massimo that holding him in my mouth, I held him in my power. I picked up the pace. He wouldn't last long. I knew it, and he did, too. He tried slowing me down, but I didn't let him.

"Not so fast," he hissed, but I ignored him.

A moment later, when I didn't slow down even for an instant, he pulled out, pushing me away. I licked my lips lasciviously as he stood and stared at me, breathing heavily. He pushed me over on the bed and turned me onto my belly, clinging to me with his whole body.

"Are you trying to prove something to me?" he asked, licking two fingers. "Relax, baby girl," he purred, sliding them both inside me. I let out a loud moan. Two fingers were all it took to fill me.

"I think you're ready." Those words made a shiver run down my spine. The anticipation, the uncertainty, the fear, and the desire all whirled inside my head.

Massimo slowly entered me, and I could feel each and every inch of his thick phallus.

His arms wrapped themselves around me, almost painfully. As he slid inside me fully, he froze, only to pull out and rush in, harder. I moaned as my arousal and pleasure mixed with pain. His hips hastened, and his breath with them. The wonderful friction I felt was rippling in waves across my entire body. Suddenly, he slowed down, and I exhaled with relief.

Massimo's hand slid underneath me, raising my hips, and his knee spread my legs wider.

"Show me that beautiful ass of yours," he breathed into my ear, caressing my asshole.

I startled. Was he going to try something I wasn't ready for?

"Don . . ." I whispered fearfully, looking back at him.

He grabbed my hair and pushed my head into the pillow.

"Don't worry, baby girl," he breathed, leaning over me. "We're going to get there, but not tonight."

Slowly and rhythmically he pushed himself against me, bending my spine so that my butt thrust upward.

"Oh yes," he panted with excitement, holding my hips tighter.

I loved being fucked from behind, and the control he exerted over my body in this position made me equally afraid and aroused. He bent down a bit, sliding one hand over my clit. I spread my legs even wider so he could play with me.

"Open your mouth," he ordered, pushing his fingers between my lips.

When they were wet enough, he moved the hand back down to rub my pussy. He was an expert and knew perfectly well where to aim his hand to take me to the brink of ecstasy. I grabbed the pillow harder, unable to bear the frantic pace of his hips. I moaned and writhed beneath him, calling out in Polish.

"Not yet, Laura," he said, and turned me over. "I want to see you orgasm."

Massimo slid both hands under me and hugged me tightly as his penis slid inside and out, harder and faster, until I felt myself contracting inside. I swung my head back and allowed the orgasm to take me over.

"Harder," I moaned.

He pushed at me twice as hard. I could feel him close on my heels, but I couldn't stop the rapture anymore. I screamed, my body tightening as I came, and Massimo's hips didn't stop stroking, impaling me. Another stroke, and another. I heard ringing in my ears. It was too much. With a wild howl I came for the second time and my sweaty body collapsed to the mattress.

The Man in Black slowed down, becoming almost lazy in his movements. He clutched my wrists and lifted my arms, towering over me on his knees and observing my breasts—satisfied and triumphant.

"Come on my belly. I want to see it," I breathed, exhausted.

Massimo smiled and tightened his grip on my wrists.

"No," he replied, and picked up the pace, pushing wildly again.

A while later, I felt him spilling inside me with a warm wave. I froze. He knew I wasn't using birth control. He didn't stop coming for a long time, fighting me as I thrashed wildly to escape his sweet seed. When he was finished, he collapsed onto me, sweaty and burning.

I frantically tried to gather my thoughts. I wanted to wrest myself from under him, but his weight didn't let me move.

"Massimo, what the hell are you doing?" I asked, furious. "You know I don't use pills!"

He laughed and propped his head on his hands, staring at me as I jerked and fought.

"You're right—you can't trust those pills. But you have a contraceptive implant. See?"

Saying that, he touched the inside of my left bicep. There was a short tube barely visible under my skin. He let me go, and I realized he wasn't joking.

"When you were asleep that first night, I ordered it implanted. I didn't want to risk anything. It'll work for three years, but you can remove it after the first," he explained with a smile.

That was the first time I saw him smile like that. It didn't change the fact that I was livid. Satisfied but livid, nonetheless.

"Will you get off me?" I asked, looking at him dispassionately.

"Unfortunately, I won't be able to do it for a while yet. It would be hard to fuck you from a distance," Massimo retorted, biting my lip. "When I saw your face for the first time, I didn't desire you. I was terrified by that vision. But with time, when your portraits were all around my house, I began to notice the details of your soul. You and I are so alike, Laura," he said, kissing me softly.

I kept still, looking into his eyes and feeling the anger leave me. I adored it when he was open with me—it didn't come easy to him, and I appreciated the effort.

His hips started to gently move, and I felt him getting harder inside me again. He kept kissing my face and talking.

"That first night, I watched you until the sun came up. I could feel your scent, the heat of your body. You were alive. Real. And you were right there, next to me. I couldn't believe it. I had this irrational fear that I when I came back, you wouldn't be there anymore."

His voice grew sad and apologetic, as if he wanted me to know that keeping me here against my will didn't bring him any joy. But the truth was that if not for the fear, I would have slipped away at the first opportunity. His hips picked up their pace, and his arms wound around me, tightening, and I could feel his skin burning up, beading with sweat.

I didn't want to listen anymore—it made me remember that all of what was happening was not what I had wanted. I couldn't help but think just how cruel, brutal, and ruthless the Man in Black could be. Not that he had ever been like that to me, but I had seen what he was capable of.

Those thoughts made my head flood with anger again. His moving body was getting on my nerves, causing the fury in me to rise.

Massimo pulled back for a second and looked me in the eyes. What he saw made him freeze.

"What's happening, Laura?" he asked, his eyes searching for an answer in mine.

"You don't want to know. Now get off me already!" I jerked, trying to escape his clutch, but he didn't budge. His eyes were cold again—the don had returned—and fighting him made no sense at all.

"I want to be on top," I said through clenched teeth, grabbing his buttocks.

The Man in Black watched my face for a while longer, finally wrapping his arm around my waist and turning us over, never slipping out of me. He reclined, lifting his arms, just like I had a while ago.

"I'm all yours," he whispered, closing his eyes. "I don't know what made you so angry, but if you need some control over me to calm down, here you go," he added, opening one eye. "The gun is in the drawer on the left. The safety's off."

Slowly I rose above him, falling back down onto his hard cock. What he had said amused me, but at the same time I grew disoriented. I was still angry, too. I clamped my right hand over his cheeks like a vise and squeezed hard. His eyes stayed closed, but he started to clench and unclench his jaw. Steadily, I lifted myself and slid right back down, letting him slide deeper inside. I wanted him to know what I felt. I needed to punish him for everything. Hurt him. And I only knew one way to do that.

I pushed myself up, and when he felt what I was doing, he opened his eyes. I shot him a warning glare and went to find the bathrobe by the door. His seed was dripping down my legs. I dragged my finger through it, gathering some of the sticky cum, and licked it off my finger, keeping my eyes trained on the Man in Black. His prick started to throb.

"You're sweet," I said, licking my lips. "Want to try?"

"I'm not a fan of my own taste, so I'm going to have to pass," he replied, disgusted.

"Sit up," I ordered, sitting astride him.

Calmly, Massimo did as he was told, crossing his arms behind his back, as if knowing what I was about to do.

"Are you sure about this?" he asked me in a tone more serious than normal.

I chose to ignore his question and tied his hands so hard he hissed with pain.

Then I pushed him to the bed and reached out to the drawer on the left, pulling out the gun. The Man in Black didn't even flinch. He pinned me with a stare that said: *I know you wouldn't dare.* He was right, of course. I wasn't brave enough to do it, but I also didn't want it. I rummaged through the drawer again but didn't find what I was looking for. I reached for another one and . . . bingo! I pulled out a sleeping mask.

"Now we're going to have some fun, don Massimo," I purred, putting the mask over his eyes. "Before I begin, remember—if you don't like something, you have to tell me. Do it so that I believe you. Though I don't think I'll listen anyway."

He knew I was mocking him, and it elicited a smile on his face. He reclined his head on the pillow, making himself comfortable.

"You've kidnapped me, kept me against my will, and threatened my family," I said, clamping my hand on his cheeks again. "You've taken from me everything I had. And even though I find you irresistible, I still hate you, Massimo. I want you to know how it feels to be made to do things you don't want to do."

I pulled my hand away, but only to strike him with an open palm. His head jerked to the side, and I heard him swallowing loudly.

"Again," he hissed through clenched teeth.

What I did and the reaction I got were working me up. I grabbed his chin.

"I decide when I do that," I replied. Then I slid up, my wet clit hovering above his head. "Suck it," I said, brushing it against his lips.

I knew he wouldn't be happy about having to taste himself, but that was the only reason I decided to do this in the first place. When he didn't react, I lowered my moist pussy to his mouth, making him feel the taste that so disgusted him. He had no choice. A couple of seconds passed, and I felt his tongue caressing me inside. He lifted his chin and moved toward my clit. I moaned and propped my forehead against the wall behind the bed. He was too good at this. It only took him a while to take me to the brink of orgasm. I lifted myself on my knees and glanced down—he was licking me off his lips, purring quietly. That part of the punishment was clearly to his liking. I slid down over his torso and abdomen, finally feeling him entering my snatch, dripping with his saliva. His cock was hard, thick, and fit my pussy perfectly. I moaned, wrapped my arms around his back, and sat him up. I could feel him helping me, knowing that I wouldn't be able to pull him toward me on my own. Grabbing the headboard, I pulled us closer to the padding on the wall and leaned his back over it. I loved this position—it gave me absolute control over my partner, at the same time allowing for very deep penetration. I grabbed Massimo by the hair and slowly started to rub my clit against his belly. His penis gently rose inside me, and I pushed against it faster and harder. I fucked him, holding him by the hair with one hand and by the throat with the other. Massimo was breathing heavily. I could feel him edging closer to the end. I slapped him once more.

"Come!" I said, and hit him again.

It turned me on so much I felt myself starting to climax. But I didn't want that yet. When a second later the Man in Black filled me to the brim, letting out a mighty roar, and I felt his arms wrapping themselves around me, pressing me against him, he tore off the sleeping mask and kissed me greedily. He moved his hands over my ass and rocked my hips gently.

"I don't want to come yet," I whispered, trying to catch my breath.

"I know," he replied, moving my hips faster. "Hit me!" he hissed. With the mask off, when he could see me clearly, I was suddenly afraid to do it.

"Fucking hit me!" he roared, and I slapped him again.

As my hand connected with his face, I felt a tsunami wave of orgasm rolling over me. I wasn't able to move anymore—my whole body was spasming, with every muscle taut and hard as steel. Massimo was impaling me on himself hard and fast until I grew limp and collapsed into his arms in a heap. As we sat in silence, he stroked my back very gently.

"When did you free your hands?" I asked, my face resting on his shoulder.

"As soon as you were done with the tying," he replied, laughing. "You're not particularly good at this, Laura. I, on the other hand, am something of an expert on tying and untying."

"So why didn't you use your hands earlier?"

"I knew something I did or said angered you. I decided to allow you to blow off some steam. I was certain you wouldn't do me any harm. You missed me, remember?" he said, pushing himself to his feet with me still wrapped around him. Kissing me on the lips, cheeks, and hair, he carried me to the bathroom. He put me down in the shower and turned the water on. "We should go lie down," he said, spreading soap over my skin. "We have a long day ahead of us tomorrow. I can't deny I'd rather keep fucking you until morning, but evidently you haven't used that sweet pussy for some time, and I think it's had enough for now," he said, delicately washing me, trailing his hand between my legs. "You're very aggressive. It turns you on, baby girl, doesn't it?" His hands stopped, and his eyes pierced me.

"I just like rough sex," I replied, grabbing him by the testicles.

"What you do in bed is a kind of game—you can be whoever you want and do whatever you want. Within reason, of course,"

I continued fondling his balls. "It's only a bit of fun, not a matter of life and death."

"We'll be happy together, Laura. You'll see," he said, kissing me on the forehead.

CHAPTER 9

When I opened my eyes, soft light fell into the room through the closed blinds. I was alone in the immense bed, which still smelled of sex. Thinking of last night made me sweat. I didn't know if that had been a good decision—if I should have done it—but it had happened, and mulling it over wouldn't change anything.

The fact was that I really had been missing Massimo, and what he had done by saving my life showed me just how important I was to him. At long last someone was treating me like I wanted. Like a princess—someone valuable and important. I stayed in bed for a while, trying to figure out why I'd lost it yesterday, and I realized that the only thing that really ticked me off in this situation was that Massimo had threatened my family. I tried explaining his behavior with the fact that I would have escaped him if he hadn't made that threat, which would make it impossible for him to get to know me better. This was confusing. I shook my head, chasing away all thoughts too gloomy for this time of day.

The door swung open and Massimo greeted me with a smile. He was wearing white knee-length shorts and a white tank top. His feet were bare and his hair wet. I purred softly, seeing him, and stretched out, kicking the sheets off with my feet. He walked over to the bed, sweeping me with his gaze.

"Sleeping seems to be your favorite thing, eh?" he said, kissing me on the forehead.

I put my arms up and stretched out some more, ostentatiously flexing my body.

"I *love* to sleep," I replied, smiling.

The Man in Black rolled me over, his hand on my hip, and smacked me on the ass. Holding me with one hand by the back of my neck, pushing my face into the pillow, he leaned over and whispered to my ear, "You're provoking me again, baby girl." Well, he wasn't wrong there.

The hand resting on my buttock slid down, spreading my thighs. His long, slender fingers slid inside me.

"What have you been thinking just now? You're wet," he said.

I pushed my butt upward, and his fingers started to move inside me. He stood, keeping his eyes on me, looking at his hand working in me.

"Oh, just that if not for that implant of yours I would be ovulating now and would have been wet all day long," I said with a smile, rocking my hips.

Massimo's expression changed—he was clearly pleased.

"I'd like to take my pants off and fuck you from behind, leaning you against that window," he said, pulling his fingers out. Then he pressed a button on a panel adjoining the bed, and the room was flooded with light.

"So you could enjoy the view. But you're too swollen down there after our night. Besides, the guy that's supposed to teach us scuba diving is already here, so we don't have as much time as I would have wanted." He licked his fingers. "Fabio brought him in too early. Come on."

Massimo snatched me from the bed and threw me over his shoulder. Crossing the room, he grabbed the bathrobe and covered me with it. He headed down the passageway and I wiggled in his grip, unable to stop laughing. We passed a series of identical doors and some surprised staff members. I don't know what Massimo's expression must have been as I dangled from his back, but I suspect it was as serious as it got. After a while, we reached my berth. Massimo put me down and tossed the bathrobe onto the bed.

"I think I'll give the staff a day off, just so you can go around naked," he said, slapping my butt.

There was a tray laden with food on the table, and next to it jugs of tea, cocoa, and milk and a bottle of Moët Rosé.

"Interesting choice for a breakfast," I said, pouring myself some cocoa. "I think champagne should become a staple of my everyday menu."

"I already know you like champagne. And I suspect you'll like some of the other things here."

I sent him a questioning look, and Massimo leaned against the window and grimaced.

"When my people were packing your things back in Warsaw, there were two cups in the sink—one had some cocoa in it, and the second was filled with tea, with milk. Somehow I don't think your ex liked either of those beverages. But who knows?" He shrugged. "What's important is that you like at least one of them. Besides, you drank them in Rome, too. So it wasn't that hard to guess," he added, walking over to the cooler with the champagne.

"You'll start boozing right now, I presume?" I asked, sipping from my mug.

Massimo took the ice-filled bucket and put it down to the floor.

"No, I'm only making some space for myself," he replied, sliding the tea and milk jugs away.

"I thought I'd be able to control myself, but since you're still stark naked, I find it rather hard to focus. So I'm going to lay you on the table and take you. Delicately, yet resolutely."

I stood rooted to the spot, watching him sliding everything to the side of the table. I must have made an extremely weird face, as Massimo couldn't hide his amusement as he was laying me on the tabletop. He spread my legs, kneeled between them, and snuck his tongue inside me. It lasted for only an instant and was evidently not something that was supposed to pleasure me—only reduce friction. Then he did what he had said he would—delicately, yet resolutely.

———

I went outside to the deck with only my sunglasses and a wonderful white Victoria's Secret bikini on. There was scuba diving equipment on the stern. The young man preparing it didn't look like an Italian. He had bright golden hair and facial features that made me think he came from somewhere in the East. His eyes were large and blue, and his smile was infectious. Massimo was standing on the other side of the yacht, talking to Fabio and gesticulating wildly. I decided not to approach them. Instead I walked over to the diver. Descending the stairs, I stumbled and nearly fell into the water again.

"Jesus Christ, I'm going to kill myself one of these days," I muttered in Polish.

The young man's face brightened. He extended a hand and greeted me in perfect Polish. "Hi, I'm Marek, but everyone here calls me Marco. You have no idea how great it is to hear Polish again, ma'am."

I stopped, paralyzed, grinning at the man for a while. Then I burst out laughing.

"Trust me, I do! Thinking in English makes my brain hurt. I'm Laura, and please call me by my name."

"So how do you like your Italian vacation?" he asked, turning back to his equipment.

I took a moment to think about the answer.

"Well, it's not really a vacation," I stammered, looking overboard. "I've a one-year-contract on Sicily and had to settle here for a while," I added, taking the rest of the steps down. "Is your presence here a coincidence, or have they brought you here for me on purpose?"

"It's a coincidence, though a pretty happy one, won't you say? Paolo was supposed to dive with you today, but he broke his leg yesterday and I had to step in for him." Suddenly Marek straightened and his smile vanished.

I turned around and saw Massimo, slowly walking down the steps. The two men greeted each other and talked in Italian for a while. Then Massimo turned to me.

"I'm sorry, but I have an urgent meeting, so I can't go with you two," he said, clenching his jaw with anger.

"A meeting?" I took a look around. "We're in the middle of the sea!"

"A helicopter is coming for me. I'll see you in a while."

I spun to Marek and said in Polish, "So, we're all alone. I don't know whether to laugh or cry."

Massimo kept still, but his eyes flared with fury.

"Marco is Polish! Isn't this great? This is going to be an awesome day," I said, and kissed Massimo on the cheek.

As I stepped back, he shot out an arm and grabbed me by the wrist, whispering so only I could hear, "I don't want you to speak Polish when I'm around. I can't understand anything." His hand clamped painfully around my arm.

I jerked away and hissed angrily, "Well, I'd like you to stop speaking Italian. Can you do that?"

I shot him an admonishing glare and headed in the direction of the motorboat, where Marek was packing the diving equipment. I closed the distance between us, patted him on the back, and asked him in Polish if he needed any help and if we had everything we needed. Then I waved happily at Massimo and turned to go to the boat.

Honestly, I don't know if Massimo could teleport or something like that, but I hadn't managed even one step when he had me in his arms again, kissing me. He leaned over me slightly and lifted me from the ground, his arms crossed over my butt. His lips greedily latched on to mine, as if we were never to see each other again. The sound of the approaching helicopter broke our frantic kiss.

Massimo held my face in his hands, smiling widely, and winked at me, saying, "If he touches you, I'll kill him."

He planted a kiss on my forehead and left, taking the stairs up.

I stood and watched him go, feeling a wave of nausea at what I had just heard. He would do it. I knew that. I had no intention of taking responsibility for someone else's life.

"He must love you very much," said Marek, reaching out with a hand.

"More like control me all the time," I retorted, getting onto the motorboat.

We headed out. I turned my head back and saw Massimo, waiting for the helicopter, his hair blowing in the downdraft. He looked seriously annoyed. I didn't have to see his face to know that. All I needed was the position of his body—his toned legs planted wide and arms crossed on his muscular chest were never a good sign.

"Do you teach diving for a living?" I asked.

Marek laughed and slowed the boat so we didn't have to shout over the wind.

"Not anymore. I had a lot of luck and found a niche in the market. I'm the owner of an underwater empire now," he chuckled.

"Can you imagine? A Pole in Italy owning the biggest diving equipment company, handling all the stuff all by himself."

"So . . . what are you doing here with me, then?" I asked with a laugh.

"I told you! Destiny and a broken leg. This is how it was supposed to be." He raised his voice as the motorboat was accelerating again, rushing through the waves with the engines roaring.

When Marco was packing up our equipment after the diving session, the sun was deep orange in color.

"It was amazing," I said, chewing on a mouthful of watermelon.

"It's good you've dived before. Didn't have to waste any more time than necessary for the teaching part."

"Where are we, exactly?"

"Off the coast of Croatia." Marek pointed to the land on the horizon. "It's getting late, and I have to be in Venice today."

When we got back, it was already getting dark. I noticed Fabio on the deck of the *Titan*. The older man helped me out of the motorboat. I said my goodbyes and headed toward the stairs.

"The hairdresser and the makeup artist are waiting in the lounge by the Jacuzzi. Would you like me to serve dinner?" I heard Fabio saying.

"A hairdresser? Why?" I asked, surprised.

"You're going to a banquet. There's an international film festival in Venice, and don Massimo is the majority shareholder of one of the film companies. Unfortunately, you only have an hour and a half to prepare, what with you being so late."

Great, I thought. I've been sloshing around in salt water the whole day to dazzle everyone at the party with the dryness of my skin. I shook my head, wondering if the day when I'd know the plans in advance would ever come. Not to mention making those plans on my own. I headed upstairs.

Poli and Luigi were a pair of stereotypical gays. Wonderful, fantastic guys—a woman's true friends. And more feminine than most ladies . . . In an hour they managed to get the bird's nest that my hair had become and the flaking-dry skin on my face in order. When they were finished, I went to my room to pick some clothes for the evening. I entered the bedroom only to notice a Roberto Cavalli evening dress, which I had bought back in Taormina, hanging on the bathroom door. It had a small card attached saying Wear This One. Well, at least I knew the answer to the question of my evening outfit. The dress was amazing, but also very revealing. It was made of black, see-through material—a bit like mesh—with inserts that looked like zippers or lacing. Its long sleeves made my arms look thinner, but the pièce de résistance was the back—or rather lack of it. The dress had only a thin strap at the shoulder blades, then a long, wide cutout all the way to the derriere.

I can't wear underwear with this, I thought, grimacing, looking at myself in the mirror.

Roberto Cavalli had foreseen this, though, and in strategic places, the dress lost its translucence. It didn't change the fact that I simply would have felt better with at least a G-string on.

I grabbed my bag, sprayed on some perfume, slid my feet into a pair of elegant sandals, and went to the door. I stopped by the mirror for one last time. I looked mind-blowing. The incredible, smoky, black-and-gold makeup complemented the tan of my skin perfectly, and the chignon on the top of my head made me look slimmer and classier. *The heap of faux hair was worth it*, I thought, running my hand along the intricate structure on my head.

I went out and took a look around. There was a bottle of champagne and a glass—already filled—on the table. I was getting used to that. So the Man in Black must be somewhere close. I walked over to the table and poured another glass. For a while I wandered around the boat, peeking into darker spots, but didn't find anyone. At some point I noticed that the *Titan* had reached land. There was a magnificent vista of lights flickering in the distance for me to enjoy.

"This is Lido, which they call the beach of Venice," I heard the familiar voice say.

I turned my head toward the speaker. It was Domenico, sipping on his champagne.

"I knew that dress would be perfect. You look absolutely stunning, Laura." He stepped closer to me and planted a kiss on both my cheeks.

"I missed you, Domenico," I replied, hugging him.

"Now, now, dear, or else Poli and his girlfriend, Luigi, will have to start all over," he said with a laugh, and led me to a pair of leather armchairs, offering me a seat.

"Where is don Massimo?" I asked, taking a sip. Domenico sent me an apologetic look. I hadn't noticed before that he was wearing a tuxedo. That could only mean one thing—the Man in Black bailed on me again.

"He had to—"

I raised a hand, silencing Domenico. "Let's just have some fun tonight," I said, tilting my glass and downing it in one gulp.

The motorboat that we took was slowly angling toward one of the canals of Venice, while I allowed myself to fall deep into thought. Did I want this year to last, all of a sudden? Or maybe even more? Or was that too much? Maybe if Massimo got what he wanted, he'd let me go now . . . But did I want to go back to my old life? Why did I keep yearning for him so? Domenico woke me up from this reverie.

"We're nearly there. Are you ready?" he asked, offering me a hand.

I stood up, but the sight of all those people, lights, the pomp and splendor suddenly terrified me.

"No, I'm not. I'll never be. I don't want to be ready. Why are we doing this, Domenico?" I asked, eyes wide with fear when the boat drew up to the shore.

"For me, of course." I head the familiar accent and felt a warm wave flood over me. "Sorry for the confusion. I didn't think I'd get here on time, but we arrived at an agreement fairly quickly, so here I am."

I raised my eyes, seeing my resplendent captor waiting on the quay. He was wearing a double-breasted black tuxedo and looked straight out of a fairy tale. I was overawed. His white shirt brought out the color of his skin and the elegant bow tie was so classy. He looked so dignified.

"Come." Massimo offered me a hand, and a moment later I was standing next to him on solid ground.

I smoothed down my dress and lifted my eyes, meeting his gaze. He held me tightly by the hand, looking as dazed as I was.

"Laura . . ." he said, then trailed off, frowning. "You look so ravishing tonight, I don't know if I want anyone else but me to see you like this."

I smiled at those words in mock modesty.

"Don Massimo!" It was Domenico. "We have to go. They've seen us already. Please, your masks."

Who saw us? Why did we have to go all of a sudden? I took the beautiful lace mask offered to me.

Massimo turned to me, tied it over my face, and purred, brushing his nose against its rim. "What is it about you and lace . . . I love it," he whispered, planting a gentle kiss on my lips.

Before he managed to pull away, the flashing lights of the paparazzi illuminated the night. I started to panic. Massimo slowly took a step back and turned toward the photographers with his arm around my waist. He did not smile, instead just waiting until they were done. The crowd of paparazzi reverberated with calls in Italian, while I just tried to look as dignified as I could, though my legs were shaking.

The Man in Black waved a hand as if signaling that this was enough, and we headed toward the entrance along the red carpet. Having crossed the hall, we reached the ballroom lined with monumental pillars. There were candles and white flowers on round tables. Most guests wore masks, which suited me—my own mask gave me the illusion of anonymity.

We sat down at one of the tables. We were the last people to join that particular table. Waiters arrived a moment later, serving appetizers followed by other dishes.

CHAPTER 10

The banquet was as boring as they got: I'd organized hundreds of similar affairs, so my only diversion was to silently point out all the errors the staff was making. Massimo was conversing with the men sitting at our table, discreetly stroking my thigh once in a while.

"I need to go to the other room," he said. "Unfortunately, you may not participate in that conversation. I'll leave you under Domenico's care." He kissed me on the forehead and left for the door, trailed by the other men.

My assistant materialized immediately, taking Massimo's chair.

"That woman in the red dress looks like a giant furball," he said, and we both erupted in laughter, watching an elderly lady in a dress reminiscent of a Christmas tree decoration. "If not for those fashion curios, I'd be dying of boredom," he added.

I knew how he felt, and I was so glad he joined me. For nearly another hour, we talked and drank champagne. When we were suitably tipsy, we decided to take a shot at dancing.

The dance floor was crowded, but this was a formal party. *Can't go too crazy here*, I thought, glancing at the string quartet. After a couple of ballroom dances I had enough. As opposed to Domenico, I was an exquisite dancer—my dearest mother had always made me go to dance lessons until I finished high school.

As we were moving toward our table again, I head someone speaking in Polish.

"Laura? Guess we were meant to spend that night together after all, eh?"

I turned around and saw Marek, dressed up elaborately, wearing a glossy gray suit.

"What are you doing here?" I asked, surprised.

"My company works for most hotels around here. Besides, it's a charity ball and I'm one of the sponsors," he said with a shrug.

Domenico cleared his throat loudly.

"Oh, right," I said, switching to English. "This is Domenico—my assistant and friend."

The men greeted each other in Italian, and we were about to walk off when the string quartet was joined by other musicians and the entire room was filled with the sounds of Argentinean tango. I squealed with glee. Both men sent me puzzled looks.

"I *love* tango," I said, sending Domenico a meaningful look.

"For the last fifteen minutes I've been stepping on your toes and you're telling me you haven't had enough yet?"

I grimaced. He was right.

"I've been taking ballroom dancing classes for eight years, so . . . if you're not afraid, I'd be honored," Marek cut in, offering me a hand.

"Just one song," I said to Domenico, and we went to the dance floor.

Marek took me in his arms and a moment later the other dancers made space for us to show off our skills. He led expertly, with confident motions, a feeling of the music and perfect knowledge of all the steps. Everyone must have thought we had been dancing partners for years. A couple of minutes into the song, the dance floor emptied, and we whirled together, putting all our training to good use. When the music stopped, the entire room burst into applause. We bowed to the audience and turned in the direction where we had left Domenico. Instead of my young assistant, we saw Massimo standing in his place, surrounded by several men. As we approached him, they nodded with appreciation—all but Massimo. His face contorted in an ugly grimace of rage, and his eyes flared with fire. If looks could kill, I would have turned into a heap of ash. Not to mention my companion.

I stepped close to him and kissed him on the cheek. Marek took my hand off his shoulder, passing me over to the Man in Black.

"Don Massimo . . ." he said, bobbing his head.

They froze, looking each other in the eyes, and the air between them suddenly grew so cold it was hard to breathe. Not releasing my hand, Massimo turned to his companions and said something in Italian, causing general laughter.

"You know who he is?" I asked Marek in Polish, certain that Massimo wouldn't understand a word.

"Sure. I've been living in Italy for a dozen years now." The Pole winked at me.

"And you danced with me despite that?"

"What's he going to do? Kill me? I don't think so. Not here, anyway." He chuckled. "Besides, he can't really do that for a whole lot of reasons. So, I hope this wasn't our last dance."

He kissed my hand and disappeared among the tables. Massimo followed him with his eyes before turning back to me.

"You're a great dancer. That explains the range of movement of those hips in . . . different situations."

"I was bored, and Domenico isn't much of a dancer," I said,

shrugging by way of apology. A rhythmic paso doble reverberated through the hall.

"I'll show you how to dance," Massimo said, throwing off his tux jacket and passing it to Domenico.

He grabbed me by the hand and led me back to the dance floor. The remaining couples hadn't had time to crowd the floor yet, and seeing me appear with another partner, they left us some space. Massimo nodded at the orchestra to start over.

I was so tipsy and sure of my own abilities that I took a step back, lifting the hem of my dress, revealing my leg. God, what had I been thinking to go out without any underwear? The musicians played the first few chords. The position adopted by Massimo told me it wasn't his first time with this dance. Our dance was wild and full of passion—perfectly reflecting Massimo's authoritative character. This time it wasn't just a dance, though. It was my punishment and my reward—the portent of what was to happen when we left the banquet and the promise of a surprise waiting for me later. I was spellbound. I wanted the music never to stop, and our dance to last forever.

The finale had to be spectacular and extraordinary, of course. I prayed that he didn't lift my leg too high, thus revealing what I wanted hidden. The music stopped, and I stayed in Massimo's arms, breathing heavily. After a long while the whole crowd roared with applause. Massimo gracefully lifted me from the back bend and allowed me to pivot a couple of times before we bowed. In a calm and assured gait, holding me by the hand, he led me off the dance floor and put on the jacket that Domenico passed him.

We took a French leave then, nearly running out. Massimo dragged me along hotel corridors without a word, his fingers clamped around my wrist like a vise.

"Marvelous show," I heard someone say. A woman. Massimo stopped, as if rooted to the spot.

Slowly he turned around, keeping me at his side.

In the center of the hall there was a beautiful woman with blond hair, wearing a short golden dress. Her long legs ended around the level of my first rib. She had gorgeous fake breasts and an angelic face. She approached us, kissing the Man in Black.

"So, you found her," she said, her eyes trained on me.

Her accent told me she was British, and her looks suggested she had just left the catwalk at a Victoria's Secret show.

"Laura," I introduced myself, offering her a hand.

She shook it with an ironic smile, staying silent for a while.

"I'm Anna, Massimo's first and true love," she replied finally, not releasing my hand.

Massimo's hand, still clamped around my wrist, grew sweaty.

"We're in a hurry. Forgive us," he hissed through clenched teeth, pulling me with him down the corridor.

Taking a look back, I saw the blonde still standing in her place, spewing words in Italian. Massimo gritted his teeth. He released my hand and stomped back in her direction. Keeping his face carefully impassive, he replied something in Italian—a couple of sentences, maybe—and returned to me. He grabbed my hand again and we walked away, getting into an elevator and ascending to the top floor. Quickly, Massimo pulled out his key card, opened the door, and slammed it shut behind us. Without switching the lights on, he threw himself at me. His kisses were quick and hungry as his tongue slid into my mouth. After what happened downstairs, I was in no mood for that. I didn't react. After a while, Massimo realized something was wrong. He stopped, controlling himself, and flicked the lights on.

I straightened up, crossing my arms. Massimo sighed and ran a hand through his hair.

"Jesus Christ, Laura," he said, collapsing to a great armchair behind him. "She's . . . the past."

I kept silent for a moment, and he observed my reaction closely.

"I'm aware you had women before me. That's perfectly all right," I began, my voice calm. "I'm also not going to ask you about your past or judge you. But I am interested in what she said that made you decide to go back. And also: why was she so angry?"

The Man in Black didn't respond, instead glaring at me.

"It's all very new to Anna," he said finally.

"How new?" I refused to back down.

"I left her the day you landed on Sicily."

Well, that would explain a lot, I thought.

"I never lied to her. Paintings of you hung in the house for years, and nobody but me had ever believed that I'd find you. Her least of all. But the day I saw you, I told her to leave." He watched me, awaiting a reaction. "Is there anything else you'd like to know?"

I said nothing, staring at him and thinking about my feelings. Jealousy is weakness, and throughout the years I had learned to eliminate weaknesses of character. Besides, I didn't feel threatened, because I didn't care about Massimo. Or, at least, that's what I was telling myself.

"Say something, Laura," he hissed.

"I'm tired," I replied, sitting in the other armchair. "Besides, it's none of my business. I'm here because I have to be, and each day brings me closer to my birthday and my freedom."

I knew that what I said wasn't the whole truth, but I was in no mood to talk about it. The Man in Black kept his eyes on me for a long while, his jaw working rhythmically. I knew that my words had hurt and angered him. I just didn't care.

He got up and headed to the door, grabbing the handle. He turned his head, sent me a cold look, and said impassively, "She told me she'll kill you, to take away the thing that I cherish the most. Just as I have taken it away from her."

"Excuse me!?" I called out, shocked. "And you're just going to leave after telling me that?" I stormed in his direction. "You damned egomaniac . . ." I trailed off when I saw he was actually hanging the Do Not Disturb sign on the door. I stopped, my hands hanging limply at my sides, staring at him.

"That dance today," he said, approaching, "was the most electrifying foreplay I have ever experienced. That does not change the fact that I really wanted to kill that annoying little Polack when I saw him touching you. He knows who I am."

"I heard you can't actually kill him," I said, raising an eyebrow.

"Unfortunately, you're right. A pity," he replied, taking the last step toward me.

He wrapped his muscular arms around me and hugged me. He had never done that before. Dumbfounded, I didn't know what to do with my hands. I put my face on his chest, feeling the thumping of his heart. He sighed, sliding down to his knees.

In that position, with his forehead nestled between my breasts, he grew immobile. I ran a hand through his hair, stroking his head. He was defenseless, exhausted, and totally reliant on me.

"I love you," he breathed. "I can't fight it. I've loved you long before you showed up here. I've dreamed about you. I knew what kind of person you were. I felt it. And it all turned out to be true," he said, his hands wrapped around my hips.

Alcohol buzzed in my head, where fear was warring with a strange calmness.

I took Massimo's head in my hands and lifted his chin to look him in the eyes. He raised them, sending me a look completely filled with love, trust, and humbleness.

"Massimo, honey," I whispered, caressing his cheek. "Why did you have to fuck it all up so badly?"

I sighed and collapsed to the rug next to him, feeling my eyes watering. I thought about how wonderful it would be to meet him in different circumstances, where I wouldn't be his prisoner, where all those threats and blackmail wouldn't have happened, and—most important—where he wouldn't be who he was.

"Make love to me," he said gently, laying me down on the soft carpet.

My heart skipped a beat. I didn't expect this and froze, watching him through half-closed eyelids.

"This might be a problem," I said, making myself comfortable in his arms.

He hung above me, propped on his elbows, with his body pressing against mine, covering it all, and his eyes searching for answers in mine.

"You see," I continued, ashamed. "I've never made love to anyone. I only fucked. And I liked it. No man has ever taught me how to make love. So . . . there you are. You might be disappointed," I finished and turned my head away, embarrassed.

"Hey, baby girl," he said gently, turning my face back toward himself. "You're so vulnerable. I haven't seen you like this before. Don't be afraid. This will be your first time, but it will be a first one for me too. Don't go. I'm being serious."

"Ask me. Say please," I suggested, turning onto my belly. "You only need to ask. You don't have to command."

Massimo hesitated for a moment, watching me. His stare wasn't cold this time. It gave way to desire and passion.

"Please, stay with me," he burst out, and laughed.

"Not a problem," I replied, rolling over on the carpet.

Curious, I watched, waiting for his next move. He took off his jacket and hung it over the backrest of the armchair, unclasped his cuff links, and rolled up his sleeves. He was getting ready for something big. I giggled quietly. When Massimo disappeared behind the door, the only thing left for me was to scan my surroundings. The thick bright rug on which I was lying neatly harmonized with the rest of the huge room. The only other furniture were the two soft armchairs and a small black coffee table. The door led to other rooms—probably the living room first—but down on the floor I could only see the tall windows obscured with heavy drapes, and a wide terrace behind them, followed by the sea in the distance.

Waiting expectantly for my lover, I was suddenly struck by a worrying thought.

I had a couple of pounds of fake hair on my head! I started to pluck out the hundreds of pins holding my hair in position. For a long while I kept tugging at the elaborate chignon, praying that Massimo didn't catch me like that. When I was finally free, my eyes started darting around, looking for a place to stow the bundle of hair. The rug! I sat up and stuffed it all under the heavy thing, and brushed my fingers through my hair, letting the wavy strands fall over my face. I pushed myself up, looking in the mirror, which took up most of the wall behind the armchairs. Surprised, but also quite satisfied, I realized I still looked attractive. I let myself drop back to the rug.

"Close your eyes," I heard from the next room. "Please."

I rolled over to my back and did as I was asked. With no idea what position to take, I felt Massimo standing above me.

"You look like a body in a coffin that way, Laura," he said, laughing.

Right, those hands lying on my chest with fingers knitted might have looked a bit like that.

"I'm not here to talk about death," I retorted, opening one eye and smirking.

The Man in Black bent over and took me in his arms. As always, he did it so easily it seemed that I weighed next to nothing. Massimo carried me down a short corridor and soon I felt a blow of warm air carrying the smell of the sea.

He put me down and gently took my face in his hands, kissing me softly.

I reached out with my arms to touch him. He didn't resist. I started unbuttoning his shirt while his lips wandered up and down my neck.

"I love the smell of you," he whispered, pinching my chin between his teeth.

"Can I open my eyes now?" I asked. "I want to see you."

"Yes, you can," he replied, and his hand hovered toward the zipper holding my dress in place.

I raised my eyelids, revealing a stunning vista. We were on the terrace of the top floor of the hotel and could see most of the island of Lido. Flickering lights illuminated the night, shining over the waves breaking on the beach. The terrace was enormous—it had a private bar, a Jacuzzi, a few chaise longues, and a canopied gazebo with a bed inside, which made me think of the one in Massimo's garden. The difference was that the interior of this one was completely covered by canvas walls, and the mattress itself had a full set of sheets and a couple of pillows on it. I was pretty sure we'd be spending the night right here.

My dress slipped off and slid silently to the floor. Massimo's hands slowly traced a path along my naked skin, and his tongue lazily slid between my lips.

"You're not wearing underwear again, Laura," he breathed, his lips still close to mine. "And you haven't done that for me this time, either. You couldn't know I'd be here."

There was no anger in his voice now. Only surprise and amusement.

"When I put the dress on, I thought you had picked it for me. I had no idea I would be going with Domenico," I replied, pulling off his shirt and falling to my knees.

Steadily, I unbuckled his belt, glancing upward, looking for a re-action from that magnificent man. His hands were hanging limply beside his body. He didn't resemble the man who had so terrified me just a few weeks ago. With a quick, confident motion, I pulled his pants down, revealing an impressive erection.

"I can see you've been in a hurry, too. Or the meeting you've gone to wasn't of the kind I imagined," I said, looking at Massimo with a question in my eyes. "Where are your boxers?"

With a growing smile, Massimo shrugged and ran his fingers through my hair.

Slowly, I reached around his hips, placing my hand on his buttock and pulling him toward me. I was only inches away from his penis now. I gently grabbed the base and kissed the tip. Massimo moaned, the fingers in my hair drawing circles. I caressed him softly with my tongue and my lips until he grew steel-hard and swollen. I opened my mouth and slid it slowly into my mouth—all of it—wanting to feel every inch. I pulled away and pushed back at him, played with it, kissed it, and bit it until I felt the sticky fluid seeping down my throat. Massimo watched me the whole time, panting heavily.

He bent down, slid his arms under my shoulders, and lifted me. He kissed me on the lips, stepping toward the steaming Jacuzzi built into the terrace. Stepping inside, he sat me down astride himself. With his eyes looking deep into mine, me brushed his lips against the skin of my face and neck, until he reached my breasts. He softly sucked and bit my nipple, while his hands tightened on my but-tocks. Suddenly his finger slid to a place that I hadn't really felt ap-propriate if we were to make love. I stiffened.

"Don't be afraid, baby girl. Do you trust me?" he asked, letting go of my erect nipple.

I nodded, and his finger started to gently rub the spot between my buttocks. Massimo lifted me and steadily but carefully impaled me on his phallus. I moaned, throwing my head back. The hot water intensified my every sensation. Massimo's movements were steady and delicate at the same time. He was passionate, greedy, but also tender.

"Don't be afraid of me," he said, sliding the tip of his finger into my anus.

I let out a loud moan of delight, which he immediately stifled with his tongue. He was impaling me harder and harder. The water sloshed against the walls of the Jacuzzi to the rhythm of his stroking hips, and a different wave—a wave of ecstasy like I hadn't known before—rose inside me. Everything around me grew as if damped and subdued. I focused entirely on Massimo. With his free hand, he reached under the water and gently rubbed my clitoris. It was like pushing a red button deep inside me. The finger exploring my anus slid deeper and sped up its motion.

"One more," I whispered, keeping the orgasm at bay with difficulty. "Slide another finger into me."

That nearly caused the Man in Black to lose control. He pushed deeper inside my mouth with his tongue, and his teeth bit on my lip harder, causing a pang of beautiful pain.

"Laura," he breathed, obeying. "You're so tight."

Without thinking if I should, if I was allowed, I simply came as he said that. With a gasp and then a cry I reached the climax of pleasure. My entire body flushed and cooled down in a few seconds.

Massimo waited until I was calm again and carried me to the bed. I was only semiconscious when he pressed his body to mine and entered me again. He snuggled his face in my hair, and his hips rushed at me, hard. I could feel he was about to come, too. I writhed and moaned, my nails biting into the skin of his back. My kisses on his neck were greedy, and I bit his shoulders, listening to his breathing—growing faster and faster, heralding an explosion.

He pushed both hands beneath my back and hugged me so tightly I could barely breathe. His hand clutched at the back of my neck, and he looked me in the eyes.

"I love you, Laura," Massimo said, and I felt a wave of hot seed spilling inside me. His bliss was intense and lasted for a long while. His eyes never wavered from my face the entire time. It was so sensual and sexy that I felt my own muscles tightening with his, and I joined him. Finally, Massimo collapsed on me, his body taking away my breath.

"You're heavy," I said, trying to slide from beneath him. "And your cock is perfection."

Massimo burst out laughing and rolled over, freeing me.

"I'll take it as a compliment, baby girl."

"I need to wash myself," I said, trying to get up.

The Man in Black pulled me toward himself.

"I can't agree to that." He reached out with a hand and took a box of tissues from the night table.

Just as in the airplane, when he had first tasted my pussy, he gently wiped me clean before covering me with the duvet.

We lay in bed, talking, until the sun came up. He told me how it felt growing up in a Mafia family, and about his uncles. About the beauty of an exploding Etna and about his favorite dishes. We ordered breakfast and watched as a new day began, never leaving bed.

"Which one is it today?" he asked, sitting up.

I frowned, looking at him without understanding. "What are you asking?" I wrapped myself in the duvet. "The day? It's Wednesday."

"Which *day*?" he asked again, and it dawned on me what his question really meant.

I tried counting in my head, but the events of last night made it seem like something so irrelevant.

"I don't know. I stopped counting," I said, sipping my tea.

The Man in Black got up and went to the terrace railing, propping his hands on it. I rolled to the side and observed him. His buttocks were beautifully toned, small and shapely. His lean legs made his back and shoulders look even wider than they really were.

"Would you like me to set you free?" he asked, his eyes locking on me. I could see the tension in his face. "I'm taking a great risk now, but I just can't really enjoy your presence when I know I'm making you unhappy. So if you'd like to leave, you can return to Warsaw. I can get you there today."

I looked at him with disbelief, filled with joy. When a wide smile appeared on my face, Massimo grew cold, and his stare became impassive. He said, "Domenico will take you to the airport. The soonest flight leaves at eleven thirty."

I sat up, happy and afraid at the same time, looking out to the sea. I could go back! I heard the door to the apartment slam shut. Holding the duvet to my chest, I jumped to my feet and ran inside. Massimo was nowhere to be seen. I peeked outside to the corridor, but it was empty. I went back inside and dropped to the floor, my back sliding down the wall. All the events of last night flashed before my eyes like a frantic movie—the love we made to each other, the fooling around, the talking until the crack of dawn. My eyes watered—I felt like I'd lost something.

My heart ached. I could feel its beat. Was it possible I had fallen in love with Massimo?

I headed back to the terrace and picked up my dress. It was so crumpled I couldn't possibly wear it. I ran to the bedroom and quickly called reception and asked to be connected with Domenico's room. Amazingly, the receptionist knew who he was. My hands were shaking. I couldn't catch my breath. When the young Italian picked up, I was already crying. I said, "Please, come to me." Then I fell to the bed.

———

"Laura, can you hear me?"

I opened my eyes groggily and saw Domenico sitting next to me. There were some vials with medicine on the table, and an elderly man standing next to the bed, talking over the phone.

"What happened? Where's Massimo?" I asked, terrified, trying to get up.

Domenico stopped me and explained, "This is a doctor. He took care of you when I couldn't find your pills."

The older man said something in Italian, smiled, and left us.

"Where's Massimo? What's the time?"

"It's nearly noon. Massimo left," Domenico replied.

My head was spinning, and I felt nauseous. Everything hurt.

"Take me to him right now! I need some clothes!" I cried, wrapping myself in the sheets.

Domenico sent me a curious look, got up, and went to the closet.

"I ordered some of your things sent here before we arrived. The boat is waiting downstairs. We can go as soon as you're ready."

I jumped up and sprinted toward the closet. I didn't care what I wore. I grabbed a white Victoria's Secret tracksuit Domenico was holding, and a while later I was in the bathroom, frantically trying to put it on. I glanced at the mirror and yesterday's makeup on my face. I said I didn't care how I looked, but that would be too much. I wiped the makeup off and went back to the bedroom, where Domenico was still waiting.

The motorboat was too slow, despite ripping through the waves at maximum speed.

Nearly an hour later, I saw the hull of the *Titan* in the distance.

"Finally," I breathed, jumping to my feet.

I didn't wait until we were moored—I skipped to the deck of the yacht immediately. I ran, looking everywhere, opening all doors, but Massimo was nowhere to be seen.

Resigned and crying, I collapsed onto the sofa in the lounge. I was drowning in tears, and my throat felt so tight I couldn't breathe.

"An hour ago the helicopter took him to the airport," Domenico said, sitting next to me. "He's got a lot of work now."

"Does he know I'm here?" I asked.

"I don't think so. He left his cell phone in the room. I couldn't call him. Besides, there are some places where he can't take his phone."

Crying, I threw myself into Domenico's arms.

"What am I to do now, Domenico?"

The young Italian hugged me and stroked my hair.

"I don't know, Laura. I have never been in such a situation. We just have to wait for him to call."

"I need to go back," I said, getting up.

"To Poland?"

"No. Sicily. I'll wait for him to return. May I?"

I sent Domenico a wide-eyed stare, waiting for his permission.

"Of course. As far as I know, nothing has changed."

"So let's pack our things and go to the island."

I slept through most of the journey, with the help of sedatives. When finally I stepped into the SUV at the airport in Catania, it felt like I was returning home. The highway led along the slopes of Mount Etna, and the only thing I could think of was Massimo, smiling and telling me stories from his childhood.

When we entered the driveway, I noticed it didn't look like last time. The maroon stones had been replaced with dark gray ones and the drive was lined with new bushes and flowers. I barely recognized the place. Confused, I looked twice, making sure we were in the right spot.

"Don Massimo ordered it all to be replaced during our trip," Domenico said, stepping out of the car.

I entered the house and reached my bedroom, slipping into my bed and quickly falling asleep.

The subsequent days were identical. Some days I spent in bed. Others, I went to the beach. Domenico tried making me eat, but it was no use. I just wouldn't have anything. I wandered around the house, looking for something—anything—that would prove Massimo was there. I exchanged emails with Mom, but I couldn't talk to her—I knew I wouldn't be able to fool her, and that she'd immediately know that something was amiss. I watched Polish TV, which Massimo had ordered to be installed in my bedroom. At times I tried watching the Italian channels, but I still understood next to nothing.

And if that wasn't enough, all local tabloids and websites published the photo from the banquet—the one in which the Man in Black kissed me on the seafront. They were all captioned: "Who Is the Sicilian Potentate's Mysterious New Companion?" Most articles also mentioned my dance skills.

Days passed, and I felt it was about time to go back to Poland. I called Domenico, asking him to pack only those things I had brought with me from Warsaw. I wouldn't take anything that would remind me of the Man in Black.

Online, I found a cozy studio on the outskirts of Warsaw and rented it. What would come next? I had no idea, but I didn't care, as long as I stopped hurting so much.

The next morning, I was woken by the sound of the alarm clock. I drank a cup of cocoa, which I found on the night table, and turned on the TV. *Today's the day*, I thought. A while later, Domenico opened the door and sent me a sad smile.

"Your plane leaves in four hours." He sat down on the edge of the bed. "I'll miss you," he said, taking my hand. I squeezed it, feeling my eyes welling with tears.

"I know. Me too."

"I'll go check if everything's ready," Domenico said, getting up.

I stayed in bed, staring dumbly at the TV, skipping channels. I settled on some news before going to the bathroom.

"*The head of the Sicilian Mafia was shot in Naples. The young Italian was widely considered one of the most dangerous . . .*" I stormed out of the bathroom, back to the TV. The screen was showing a montage of scenes from the place of the incident—including two body bags and a black SUV. A hot, scalding feeling behind my sternum came next. I couldn't breathe. Then, a sharp pain, like someone stabbing my heart with a knife. I tried screaming but didn't manage even a croak. I fell to the floor, unconscious.

CHAPTER 11

I opened my eyes. The sun illuminated so brightly that I could barely see. I raised my hand to cover my eyes and inadvertently jerked on the IV tube. What the hell? As soon as my eyes became accustomed to the light, I took a careful look around. All the equipment around me suggested I was in a hospital.

What had happened? Then it struck me—Massimo was . . . My heart started racing, and all the devices surrounding me began whining. A doctor appeared in the room, followed by a nurse and Domenico.

I noticed my young assistant and started crying. Wracked by great sobs, I couldn't say a word. I coughed, sputtered, and choked, waving my arms in panic. The door opened and a figure appeared in the threshold: Massimo.

He passed everyone and fell to his knees next to me, taking my hand and snuggling his face against it, looking at me with eyes filled with fear and exhaustion.

"I'm sorry," he whispered. "Baby, I—"

I put my hand against his lips.

Not here. Not now. Tears rolled down my face, but they were tears of happiness.

"*Madam,*" the man in the white scrubs said, glancing at the medical report hanging from the bed frame. "*We've had to do a carotid revascularization. The state you were in was a threat to your life. We've had to insert a tube into your body. That's why you have a patch in your groin. Through the tube, we've inserted a guide wire into your carotid artery that allowed us to clear it. That's the short version, anyway. Despite your perfect knowledge of English, without walking you through all the specialist medical jargon, I wouldn't be able to explain the procedure in detail. But I don't think that is strictly necessary. What matters is that we've made it.*"

I could hear his words, but my eyes were fixed on Massimo. Nothing else mattered. He was here—alive and well!

———

"Can you hear me, Laura?" I felt someone raising my eyelids. "Don't do this to me or he'll kill me."

I opened my eyes slowly. I was lying on the rug, with Domenico nervously looking down at me.

"Thank God," he said as I started reacting.

"What happened?" I croaked, disoriented.

"You lost consciousness again. It's good I had the pills in the drawer. Are you feeling well?"

"Where's Massimo? I want to see him now!" I cried, trying to push myself up. "You said you'll take me to him anytime I want. Well, I want it right now."

Domenico studied me, as if searching for an answer to my question.

"I can't," he breathed. "I don't know what happened, but something went terribly wrong. Remember, Laura—the media doesn't tell the whole story. But you have to go back to Poland today. These are Massimo's orders. It's for your own safety. The car is already waiting. You have your apartment ready in Warsaw and an account in the Virgin Islands. Use the money however you want."

I stared at him, terrified, unable to believe him. He went on.

"All the documents, credit cards, and keys have been packed. A driver will pick you up and drive you to your new place. You have a car in the garage, and all your things will be sent from Sicily to Warsaw, according to your guidelines—"

"Is he alive?" I cut in. "Tell me, Domenico, or I'll lose it."

The young Italian went silent then, thinking.

"He's moving, that's for sure. Mario, his consigliere, is with him. So there's a chance he's alive."

"What do you mean moving?" I asked, frowning. "Can they both be . . ." I trailed off, afraid of voicing the word "dead."

"Don Massimo has a transmitter implanted into the inside of his left hand. A small chip, just like yours," he said, touching my left bicep. "We know where he is at all times."

For a moment I got lost in thought, absently fingering the little tube in my arm.

"So what is this, really?" I asked, feeling the anger rising in me again. "A contraceptive implant or a transmitter?"

Domenico didn't reply, as if he just realized I had no idea what I'd been implanted with. He only sighed heavily and pushed himself to his feet, pulling me with him.

"You'll take a public plane. It'll be safer this way. Now get moving. We have to go," he said, lugging my suitcases from the closet. "The less you know, the better, Laura."

Then he turned his back on me and disappeared behind the door.

For a long while I kept still, thinking about all the things I had heard. Despite the fury I was feeling, I was grateful to Massimo for taking care of everything. The thought that I might never see him again, that he might never touch me again, made my eyes tear up. The black thoughts soon lost the battle with hope, though, and I felt sure that he was alive. I knew I'd come back here one day. I packed my things, and an hour later, I was already on the plane. Domenico stayed in the mansion. He said he couldn't go with me. I was alone again.

The flight was short, even with the transfer in Milan. I don't know if it was the pills the young Italian had given me, or the apathy I descended into, but my fear of flying vanished. Leaving the terminal, I noticed a man holding a card with my name on it.

"I'm Laura Biel," I said in English. The power of habit.

"Good day. My name is Sebastian," the man said, and I grimaced, hearing Polish.

A couple of weeks ago I would have given everything to be able to talk in Polish with anyone, but now it only reminded me where I was and what had happened. My nightmare turned fairy tale had ended, and I was back at square one. There was a black Mercedes S-class parked by the entrance. Sebastian walked over to the car and opened the back door for me. We drove off.

It was September and the air was getting cold and smelled of the fall. I slid the window down and inhaled it. I don't think I had ever felt this bad in my entire life. The sadness and despair made even the hair on my head ache, and any reason was good to drown in tears anew. I didn't want to see anyone, talk to anyone, eat . . . or live.

We left the airport behind and the car headed toward the center of town. Oh God, not downtown . . . When we turned toward the district of Mokotów, I felt relieved. The car entered a closed-off residential estate and parked next to a low apartment building. The driver got out and opened the door for me, passing me my hand luggage. For a while I sat, rummaging through it, until I found an envelope labeled Home. There were keys there, as well as an address.

"I'll bring your bags upstairs and the car with the rest should be here anytime now," Sebastian said, offering me a hand.

I stepped out and headed to the door. When I reached it, another car stopped by the building. The driver exited and started to remove my things from the car.

I entered the hall and went to the reception, where a young man was waiting.

"Hello, I'm Laura Biel."

"Welcome. I'm glad you've arrived. Your apartment is ready. It's on the fourth floor, fifth door on the left. Would you like me to help you with the bags?"

"No, thanks. The driver will manage."

"See you, then!" the boy called out as I left, sending me a wide grin.

A moment later, I was in the elevator, going up to the top floor. I pushed the key into the lock with the number I had found in the envelope and entered the apartment. The first thing I noticed was a beautiful living room with windows spanning all the way up to the next floor. Everything was dark and modern—I could feel Massimo's hand in the decor.

The drivers brought me my things and disappeared, leaving me completely alone. The apartment was elegant and cozy. A large part of the living room was occupied by a black corner sofa made of soft Alcantara, with a white, fluffy rug laid out beneath it. There was a glass coffee table next to it, and the wall had a huge flat-screen TV on it. Next to that, there was the entrance to the bedroom, which housed a large fireplace surrounded with copper plates. As I entered deeper into the room, I saw a modern bed with LED lighting—it looked as if it was levitating. There was also a door to the closet and a bathroom with an enormous bathtub.

I went back to the living room and switched on the TV. The news channel. I opened my hand luggage and sat down on the rug, leafing through all the envelopes. Credit cards, documents, information. The last one contained a car key with three letters on it: BMW. To my surprise, I discovered that I was actually the owner of both the apartment and the car. After reading some more papers, I also found out that the seven-digit bank account was also mine. Why would I want all that if he wasn't with me, though? Was this his way of making those few weeks up to me? The way I felt now, I should have paid him for all the wonderful moments.

When I was finished with unpacking my bags, it was already evening. I was in no mood to stay here on my own. I took my phone, the car documents, and key, and took the elevator to the garage. I found the parking spot with the same number as my new apartment and discovered it was occupied by a large white SUV. I slid the key into its slot, and the headlights flared. *He couldn't find anything safer and more ostentatious*, I thought, clambering up to the bright leather interior. I pressed start and drove across the garage, looking for the exit.

I knew Warsaw pretty well, and I liked to drive around it at times, passing streets and avenues, mindlessly turning here and there. An hour later, I stopped by the house of my best friend, whom I hadn't talked to for weeks. I couldn't go anywhere else, so I just tapped in the entrance code, went upstairs, stopped at her door, and rang the doorbell.

We had been friends since we were five. She was like a sister to me. Sometimes younger, sometimes older, depending on the occasion. She was a hot brunette with an attractively curvy body. Men loved her. I don't know if it was because of her vulgarity, her promiscuity, or maybe her perfect face. Olga was definitely a beautiful woman with an exotic charm. She was half Armenian, and her Eastern genes gave her sharp facial features and—which I envied her the most—an olive hue to her skin.

Olga had never worked. She liked to make maximum use of the effect she had on men. Always a proponent of breaking stereotypes, especially those saying that a woman with many partners is a whore, she had a peculiar deal with men: she gave them what they wanted, and they gave her money in return. She was not a hooker—more like a mistress to men bored with ordinary, stupid girls. Most of her partners were deeply in love with her, but she didn't know what love was. She didn't want to change that, either. Olga was currently seeing an influential man, an owner of a big cosmetics company who didn't have the time or inclination to form any sort of serious relationship with anyone. So she accompanied him to official parties and dinners and massaged his head when he was tired. He, on the other hand, provided her with all the luxuries and comforts she could think of. From an outsider's perspective, it was a real relationship, but neither of them would ever admit that.

"Fuck me! Laura!" Olga exclaimed as she saw me in the doorway. "I'll kill you one of these days! I thought somebody kidnapped you. Come in, what are you waiting for?"

She grabbed me by the arm and pulled me inside.

"I'm sorry . . . I had to . . ." I stammered, and my eyes watered.

Olga froze, looking at me, terrified. She wrapped an arm around me and led me to the living room.

"Somehow I feel you could use a drink," she said, and a moment later we were sitting on her rug with a bottle of wine between us.

"Martin came to see me," she said, sending me a suspicious look. "He was asking for you. Told me what happened. That you disappeared, leaving him a letter. And then you came back before him and took all your stuff from his apartment. Jesus, Laura, what happened there? I wanted to call you, but I was sure you'd do it yourself as soon as you wanted to talk."

I watched her, sipping my wine and growing certain that I couldn't tell her the truth.

"I just had enough of all that ignorance. Besides, I fell in love." I raised my eyes and sent her a look. "I know how that sounds, so I don't want to talk about it. I need to get my shit together."

I knew she knew I wasn't telling her everything, but she was my friend and she always understood when I didn't want to spill everything.

"Okay," she snapped, flustered. "So, how was it? Everything in order? Do you have a place to live? Need anything?" She spewed questions one after the other.

"I'm renting a place from a guy I know. A large apartment. But he had to leave in a hurry and needed to leave it to someone he trusted."

"Cool, that's settled, then. How about work?"

She wouldn't back down that easily, it seemed.

"I have a few options, but I need to focus on myself for now," I muttered, playing with my glass. "I need to get some things in order first, but it's going to be all right. Can I stay the night? I don't want to drink and drive."

Olga burst out laughing and hugged me.

"Sure thing. When did you get a car?"

"I got it with the apartment," I replied, pouring us another glass. We sat and talked about the events of the last month late into the night. I told her about the charms of Sicily—the food, the alcohol, the shoes. After downing half of the second bottle, Olga asked, "All right, how about him? Tell me something about him. I'm going crazy here, pretending I'm not curious!"

Flashes of all the times I'd spent with Massimo whirled through my head. How I saw him naked for the first time, when he joined me in the shower. Our shopping spree and the moments on his yacht. Our dance at the banquet and that last night, after which he disappeared.

"He's," I began, putting my glass down, "special, commanding, haughty, tender, handsome, and very caring. Imagine your typical alpha male, who can't suffer any disobedience and always knows what he wants. Then add in a protector and guardian, with whom you always feel like a little girl. And finally mix in the fulfillment of all your sexual fantasies. And if that's not enough, he's six three, has not an ounce of fat on him, and looks like a sculpture made by God himself. Small ass, huge shoulders, wide chest . . . That's Massimo," I concluded, shrugging.

"Holy fuck," Olga said, "that sounds perfect. But, what about him?"

For a while I wondered what to tell her, but nothing smart came to my head.

"Well, we need time to think this through. Nothing's simple with him. He's from a wealthy Sicilian family. All traditional. And they don't normally approve of relationships with outsiders," I replied, grimacing.

"You're in over your head," Olga said, gulping her wine. "When you talk about him, you light up."

I didn't want to talk about the Man in Black anymore. Each memory hurt, because I knew we might not see each other again.

"Let's go to sleep. I need to go to my parents' tomorrow."

"All right, but promise you'll go somewhere with me on Saturday."

I frowned.

"Come on! It'll be fun. We'll spend a day at a spa and go to town in the evening. Party! Party!" she cried, jumping up and down.

Her glee and excitement only made me feel guilty about leaving her alone for so long in the first place.

"It's Monday today, you know, but okay. Let's have it your way. I'm reserving the weekend for you."

CHAPTER 12

The drive to my parents' took only a short time, despite the more than ninety miles that divided us. I didn't even have the time to think of what I'd say to them. I decided not to upset Mom anymore and just go with the lie Massimo had come up with.

I parked in the driveway and got out of the car.

"You vanish for a month and return in a car like that? How much do they pay you back there?" I heard my dad's amused voice. "Welcome home, honeybee," he said, hugging me tightly.

"Hi, Daddy. It's a company car," I explained, returning his embrace. "I've missed you."

Feeling his warmth and hearing his voice, so full of love, made my eyes water again. I felt like a little girl all of a sudden. I guess I still was one, deep down, and always ran to my parents with all my problems.

"I don't know what happened, but I'll listen if you'd like to tell me," he said, wiping away my tears.

Dad never pushed. He always waited patiently until I came to him and told him what bothered me.

"Jesus, you're so thin!"

We separated and I looked in the direction of the veranda, where my breathtaking mom appeared at the door. She was impeccably dressed and wore full makeup. Like always. I was nothing like her. She had long blond hair and grayish-blue eyes. Despite her age, she still looked no more than thirty, and I bet some twenty-year-olds would kill to have a body like hers.

"Mom!" I spun and ran into her arms, crying uncontrollably.

She was my fallout shelter. I knew she'd protect me from the world. Despite her overprotectiveness, she was my best friend. Nobody knew me like she did.

"See, I told you that trip wasn't a good idea," she said, stroking my hair. "You're crying again. Why are you crying?"

I couldn't tell her. I didn't really know.

"I just missed you two. I knew I'd be able to let go of all those emotions crowding in my head."

"You keep crying like that, your eyes will swell up and you'd have to cry all over again tomorrow when you see yourself in the mirror. Did you take your pills? We don't want any drama around here," she said, flicking the hair off my face.

"I did. They're in my bag," I replied, wiping my nose.

"Tom." She turned to my dad. "Grab us some tissues and make tea, would you?"

Dad smiled gently and went inside, while we sat down in soft recliners in the garden.

"So?" Mom asked, lighting a cigarette. "Will you tell me what this is about and why I had to wait so long for you to return?"

I sighed heavily, knowing this conversation wouldn't be easy. I knew I wouldn't be able to avoid it, though.

"Mom, I told you I had to fly a bit for my work in Sicily. I needed to get back to Italy for a while and it took longer than I expected. But for now, I'm staying in Poland. At least until the end of September. The company has branches here, too, so I can work in Poland. Besides, I have Italian lessons in Warsaw. So don't worry, I won't run off tomorrow. The company cares for me." I nodded at the BMW parked in the driveway. "They've also rented an apartment for me and given me a credit card."

Mother was looking at me suspiciously, but I didn't allow the lie to show, and she seemed to accept my story.

"All right, you've made me a bit calmer," she said, pressing the butt of the cigarette into the ashtray. "Now, tell me how it was."

Dad brought us tea, and I told my parents about Sicily, not skipping the geographical details. Some stories I took from guides I had read. The company I was supposedly working for owned hotels in Venice, too, so I could tell them about Lido and the festival. We sat together for hours and talked until I was too tired to continue.

When I was back in bed, Mom brought me a blanket and sat down on the edge of the bed.

"Remember: whatever happens, you've got us." She planted a kiss on my forehead and left, closing the door behind her.

The next few days, Mom took it as her ultimate goal to fatten me up a bit. She cooked and we drank gallons of wine. When Friday came, I thanked God I was going back to Warsaw. One more day and my stomach would have exploded. It's good that my parents lived by the forest. I could go jogging every day to burn off all the food that Mom had managed to stuff me with. I put on my headphones and sprinted ahead. Sometimes it took an hour, sometimes more. Throughout all this time, I had the feeling of being watched. I would stop and look around, but never saw anyone. I thought about Massimo—whether he was alive and if he was thinking about me, too.

On Friday afternoon, I got into my car and drove back to Warsaw. I called Olga, reporting in.

"Perfect timing! We're going shopping. I need a new pair of shoes," she said. "Give me the address and I'll pick you up in an hour."

"No, I'll come for you. I have something to do on the way."

When I arrived at Olga's, I saw her closing the entrance door and stopping, dumbstruck, in front of my car. She pointed a finger at it, circling the index finger of her other hand above her temple, wide-eyed. As soon as she got in, she cried, "Who gave you that ride?"

"I told you. Got it with the apartment," I replied, shrugging.

"Now I'm really curious how that apartment of yours looks."

"Oh, come the fuck on, it's a regular apartment. And the car's just a car." Her reaction got on my nerves, but what pissed me off even more was that I couldn't tell her the truth. She knew I was lying, and I knew I was making a fool of myself, ignoring the keenness of her intellect. "What's the difference?" Remember how we lived in that studio at Bródno?"

Olga burst out in laughter and fastened her seat belt.

"Yeah, with that crazy lady downstairs who always accused us of having orgies!"

"That wasn't entirely unfounded, you know." I sent her a meaningful look, reversing out of the parking lot.

"I might have moaned a bit loudly once or twice. Don't make it a big deal."

"Yeah, I remember getting back home earlier than I said once and thinking someone was torturing you."

"Oh, right, the little brat that fucked me back then was pretty rough, but his dad had a dentistry clinic."

"And he got you all the dental checkups for free."

"What he got me was a fuck so goddamn rough I scratched the plaster off the wall."

Thank God I managed to change the subject from my apartment and car. For the rest of the way our conversation focused entirely on Olga's rich sexual life.

Shopping never failed to improve my mood. We ran from boutique to boutique, buying shoes we didn't need. After a couple of hours of this crazy marathon, we were sated. Back in the multilevel parking lot, we had to find our car. It took a while, but finally we found it and started packing our stuff into the trunk.

"New ride?" I heard a familiar voice from behind.

I turned around and scowled, seeing Martin's best friend.

"Hi, Michał. What's up?" I said, giving him a kiss on the cheek.

"You tell me. Why did you leave us like that? Martin nearly dropped dead—he was so afraid for you."

"Yeah, believe me, I know all about just how afraid he was, fucking that Sicilian girl," I retorted, spinning back around and putting the last bag into the trunk. "He was so concerned that he simply had to blow off some steam, right?"

Michał froze, staring at me with his mouth agape. I closed the distance between us.

"What? You thought I didn't know? He fucked her on my birthday, the fuck!" I spat angrily and walked to the car door.

"He was drunk," Michał said, shrugging. I slammed the door in his face.

"Well, now he's going to know you're back," Olga said, fastening her seat belt. "Nice. Love that kind of drama."

"I don't. Especially when it concerns me. We'll go to my place, okay? You'll stay with me. I don't want to be alone today."

Olga nodded and we drove off.

"Fuck me," said my friend at the sight of the living room, not bothering to sound civil. "And that friend of yours rented it out to you just like that? And he threw in that car, too? Do I know him?"

"Oh, come on, it's more like a favor. And no, you don't know him.

It's someone I used to work with. The guest bedroom is upstairs, but I'd like you to sleep with me, okay?"

Olga wandered around the house, swearing once each couple of minutes, discovering new things. Amused, I watched her, thinking about what she'd say if she saw the *Titan* or the mansion on the slopes of Taormina. I took a bottle of Portuguese wine from the fridge, grabbed two glasses, and joined my friend upstairs.

"Come, I'll show you something," I said, climbing the stairs.

When I opened the door, she froze. We were on a beautiful, gigantic terrace taking up most of the roof. It had a table with six chairs, a barbecue, some chaises, and a four-seat Jacuzzi. I put the bottle on the table, pouring us the wine.

"Any questions?" I asked, raising my eyebrows and passing her one glass.

"What did you do for him to get that? Admit it. I know it's not your style, but somehow *I* never got a crib with a roof terrace for fucking anyone." She giggled, sitting in one of the comfy chairs. We covered ourselves with blankets and watched the flickering lights of downtown skyscrapers. Having people I loved around me did nothing to stop me from thinking about Massimo. Several times I even called Domenico, but he didn't answer any of my questions, instead asking his own, wanting to know if I was okay. I liked listening to his voice. It reminded me of the Man in Black.

CHAPTER 13

When we woke up the next morning and got ourselves more or less in order, I felt surprisingly good. Standing in front of the mirror, I tried telling myself that I simply had to live my life—get all my matters in order and start forgetting about the weeks I had spent in Italy. We had breakfast, rummaged through my closet and the stuff we had bought yesterday, looking for something to wear in the evening, and headed to the spa.

"You know what? I think I want to have some real fun today," I said as we left home. "Do we have a hairdresser set for today?"

Olga sent me a lordly look.

"Do you think I know how to do my hair on my own? Sure we have," she said with a laugh as I locked the door.

Our visit to the spa was something of a ritual we indulged in once every so often. Peels, massages, facials, nails, hairdresser, and finally makeup. When the time came for the penultimate point on our list, I sat down in the chair, and Magda, my stylist, rubbed a strand of my hair between her fingers.

"What do you want me to do, Laura?"

"Blond." I said simply. Olga jumped on her chair. "A bob with the back shorter and the front a bit longer."

"What?" Olga cried out so loud that all the other women turned their heads to look at us. "Are you out of your fucking mind? You've gone crazy!"

Magda laughed, running her hand through my hair. "It's not damaged, so the hair should be fine."

"You sure about that?"

I nodded and Olga collapsed back to the chair, shaking her head with disbelief.

Meanwhile, to make up for the delay caused by my whims, the makeup artists arrived and immediately went to work.

"Ready," Magda said after two hours, looking satisfied with her work.

The effect was breathtaking. The color of ripe wheat comple-mented my sun-kissed skin and black eyes simply perfectly. I looked young, fresh, and tasty. Olga stood behind me, ogling me with one brow raised.

"All right, I was wrong. You look fucking awesome. Now come on. We have a party to go to."

She grabbed me by the arm and pulled me to the car.

We parked in my apartment's underground garage and took the elevator upstairs. I pushed the key into the lock and turned it. I turned it twice, though I remembered locking it with only one rota-tion. After having a bottle of wine and changing into something less comfortable than our joggers, but at the same time infinitely better looking, we looked at ourselves in the mirror. We were ready.

For the night I picked a sexy black set: a high-waist pencil skirt and a tightly fitting long-sleeve short top. I left a two-inch gap be-tween the top and the skirt, subtly exhibiting my stomach muscles.

The outfit was topped off with black short-nosed stilettos and a studded clutch bag of the same color. Olga decided to emphasize her natural assets—large breasts and beautiful, full hips—by putting on a snug nude dress. She also wore high heels and grabbed a clutch bag, after throwing on some gold accessories.

"This night is ours," she said. "Just keep an eye on me. I'd like to return home with you."

I chuckled and pushed her outside, following in her wake. The biggest advantage of the life Olga was leading was that she knew most bouncers, managers, and owners of the local clubs.

We got into a taxi and drove to one of our favorite venues downtown. The Ritual, 12 Mazowiecka Street, where we used to eat and drink, and I'd like to say pick up guys, but I usually left that to my friend.

When we got out of the car, there were at least a hundred people queuing outside the club. Olga ostentatiously passed the whole crowd, making her way straight to the red line, and kissed the woman standing guard at the entrance.

She unpinned the rope blocking the passage inside, and later we were both in, greeted by the owner's wife, Monika. She fastened VIP armbands on our wrists.

"You look gorgeous," Olga said to the woman, who waved a hand dismissively, but smiled.

"You always say so." The cute brunette laughed and shook her head. "That's not going to stop me from buying you shots!" She winked at us and nodded for us to follow her.

We climbed the stairs and sat at a table. After instructing the waitress, Monika disappeared.

"Drinks are on me today!" I called, trying to outshout the music and pulling the credit card Domenico had given me from my handbag.

It was about time I used it. I only really needed one thing.

I waved at the waitress and ordered. A while later, she came back with an ice-filled bucket with a bottle of Moët Rosé. Seeing that, Olga jumped to her feet.

"Nice!" she cried, grabbing a glass. "What are we drinking to?"

I knew what I wanted to toast, and why I picked that specific champagne.

"Us," I said, sipping.

I wasn't drinking to me or to Olga. It was Massimo I was thinking about, and the 365 days that had never happened. I felt sad, but at the same time strangely calm—a part of me was accepting my new circumstances. After downing half the bottle, we went to the dance floor, moving to the rhythm, fooling around. My gorgeous shoes weren't exactly comfortable, so after three songs, I had to go back to the table. On my way there, I felt someone putting their hand on my shoulder.

"Hi!" I turned around and saw Martin.

I jerked away and stood rigid, glaring at him hatefully.

"Where were you all this time?" he asked. "Can we talk?"

I could see the photos Massimo had shown me. Back then, all I wanted to do was to rip Martin apart, but I stopped caring.

"I have nothing to say to you," I replied, and turned my back on him, heading toward my couch.

He wouldn't surrender that easily, though, and a second later he caught up with me.

"Please, Laura. Just give me a moment."

I sat down and glowered at him, sipping my champagne silently. That taste made me feel stronger.

"You can't tell me anything I don't already know."

"I talked to Michał. Please, let me explain. I'll leave you be after that."

Despite all the anger and revulsion I had felt after seeing those photos, I decided he deserved an opportunity to tell me his version of events.

"Okay, but not here. Wait a minute."

I went down to the dance floor and caught Olga, explaining the situation. She wasn't surprised or angry. She had already managed to find a replacement for me in the form of a charming blond-haired man.

"Go!" she called. "I don't think I'm coming back tonight, so don't wait up."

I went back to Martin and nodded at him, signaling that we could leave now.

When we were outside, he led me to the parking lot and let me in his car.

"You're not here to party, I assume," I said, stepping inside the white Jaguar XKR.

"I came here for you," he replied, and shut the door.

We drove across the city, and I knew where he was taking me.

"You look amazing with that haircut, Laura," he said quietly, looking at me.

I ignored him. His opinion was of no interest to me. I kept my eyes trained on the vista behind the window.

Martin pressed a button on his garage gate control, and we drove inside. He parked the car, and we took the stairs up. When I stopped by the door to his apartment, I nearly fainted. Even this place, not once seen by the Man in Black, reminded me of Massimo.

"Want something to drink?" Martin asked, going to the fridge.

I sat down on the sofa, feeling uncomfortable. I had a strange feeling that I was acting against the will of Massimo, breaking his ban by seeing Martin. If he saw us together now, he'd kill him.

"I think water will do best now," Martin decided, handing me a glass. "I'll tell you everything, and you'll do whatever you want."

I settled on the couch and gestured for him to start.

"When you ran away, I realized you were right. I went after you. One of the hotel staff stopped me at the reception, saying there was a serious malfunction of something in our room and that they needed my key to get inside. When we finished checking the alarm, it turned out it was only an error in the system and that everything was fine. I ran outside and looked for you until it got dark. I was sure I'd find you. I thought you hadn't gone far. That's why I didn't go back for my phone immediately. And when I finally got back to call you, there was that letter in my room. All the things you wrote . . . they were right. I fucked up." Martin dropped his head and started to play with his fingers. "I ordered drinks to the room and called Michał. I don't know if it was because of all the worrying, or the hangover from the day before, but I felt drunk after the first one."

He raised his eyes and looked into mine.

"Believe it or not, I don't remember anything else. When we got up the next day, Karolina told me what I did. I wanted to throw up." Martin took a deep breath and dropped his head again. "And when I thought it couldn't get any worse, reception told us we had to leave the hotel because our credit cards bounced. So we left the island. That whole vacation was cursed. Everything went wrong."

When he was finished, I hid my face in my hands and sighed. I knew everything he was saying sounded absurd, but with a little intervention on the part of Massimo, it could all have happened. All of a sudden, I wasn't sure who I was angrier with—the Man in Black for engineering this farce, or Martin for allowing himself to be mixed up in it.

"Does that change anything?" I asked after a while. "That you don't remember sleeping with that girl? Besides, the truth is that our expectations for our relationship were just too different. You wanted to have your cake and eat it, too, and I'll always need more attention than you're willing or able to give me."

Martin slid off the couch, kneeling in front of me.

"Laura," he said, taking my hands, "you're right. You're absolutely right. But during those weeks I realized how much I loved you. I don't want to lose you. I'll do anything to prove to you that I can change."

I stared at him, dumbfounded, feeling the champagne I had had rising in my throat.

"I don't feel too good," I muttered, getting up from the sofa and stumbling toward the bathroom.

I threw up long enough to completely empty my stomach. I was sick of that day and that conversation. I left the bathroom and tried putting on my shoes.

"I'm going home," I called, pushing my feet into the stilettos.

"Not going to happen. You can't go like that," he said, snatching my bag from my hands.

"Martin, please!" I was growing impatient. "I want to go home."

"All right, but allow me to drive you." He wouldn't accept my refusal.

We drove out of the garage and he turned his head to look at me, a silent question in his eyes. Right, he didn't know my new address.

"Turn left," I mumbled, waving a hand.

"Then go right and straight ahead."

Ten minutes later, we arrived.

"Thank you," I said, grabbing the handle, but the door didn't budge.

"I'll walk you to the door. I'd like to be sure you've arrived safely."

We took the elevator up. I really needed to be alone by now.

"It's here," I said, pushing the key into the lock. "Thank you for your help. I'll manage on my own now."

Martin didn't want to hear it. As soon as I opened the door, he tried slipping inside with me.

"What the fuck are you doing? Don't you get it? I don't want you around anymore!" I growled, stopping at the door. "You said what you wanted. Now leave me alone. Bye."

I tried closing the door, but Martin's strong hands stopped me.

"I missed you. Let me in," he said.

I let the door go, withdrew inside, and switched the light on.

"Martin, goddamn it, I'll call security!" I yelled.

My ex stood in the door, very still, staring angrily at something behind me. I turned around, and my heart nearly burst. Slowly, calmly, Massimo rose from the couch and started walking to the door.

"I can't understand a word of what you're saying, but Laura seems to want you out of here," he said, stopping a few inches from Martin. "Should I repeat it to you, so that you understand? Maybe you'll get it in English."

Martin tensed and, keeping his eyes pinned on the Man in Black, replied in a low growl, "See you around, Laura. Let's keep in touch." He turned away and went to the elevator.

As soon as he left, the Man in Black turned around and faced me. I wasn't sure if this was really happening. Fear and anger struggled for dominance with happiness and relief in my head. He was here, alive and well! For a long while, we stood like that, staring at each other. The tension between us was unbearable.

"Where the fuck have you been!?" I bellowed suddenly, slapping Massimo in the face, hard. "Do you have an idea, you goddamn egomaniac, what I've been through? You think I love fainting out of fear every fucking day? How could you leave me like that? Jesus!"

Resigned and exhausted, I collapsed to the floor, my back sliding down the wall.

"You look breathtaking, baby girl," he said, trying to lift me in his arms. "That hair . . ."

"Don't touch me! You won't touch me ever again if you don't explain yourself to me right now!"

My screaming made Massimo stand straighter. He loomed over me, looking more beautiful than I remembered. He was wearing dark pants and a dark long-sleeved shirt, emphasizing his perfectly toned body. Even now, furious at him, I couldn't not notice how extremely attractive he was. I knew he was a wild animal, ready to pounce, and that the attack would come anytime now.

I wasn't wrong. Massimo bent over and grabbed me by the arms, standing me up, and slipped his hand under my belly, throwing me over his shoulder, so I dangled head-down from his back.

My resistance and screaming wouldn't do me any good, so I just surrendered, waiting for his next move. He went through the door to the bedroom and threw me on the bed, quickly pressing his body to mine, blocking any movement I might have tried.

"You met with him even though I told you you weren't permitted. You know that I'll kill this man only to make him stop seeing you?"

I kept quiet. I didn't want to open my mouth, knowing that if I did, I would say more than I wanted. It was late. I was tired and hungry, and this whole situation was simply too much.

"I'm talking to you, Laura."

"I hear you, but I don't want to talk to you," I said quietly.

"That's even better. The last thing I'm in a mood for is difficult conversations," Massimo replied, and brutally pushed his tongue into my mouth.

I wanted to shove him away, but as soon as I felt his taste and his scent, all the days spent without him flashed before my eyes. What I could remember above all was the sadness and the pain.

"Sixteen," I whispered without breaking the kiss.

Massimo stopped and looked at me quizzically.

"Sixteen," I repeated. "That's how many days you owe me, don Massimo."

He smiled and ripped his shirt off with one fluid move. The dimmed light coming from the living room illuminated his naked chest, revealing fresh wounds, some still with bandages on them.

"Oh my God, Massimo," I breathed, squirming from under him. "What happened?"

I softly touched his body, as if trying to magically heal his injuries.

"I promise I'll tell you everything, but not today. Okay? I need you to be well rested, fed, and above all—sober. You're very thin, Laura," he said then, caressing my body, tightly wrapped in black fabric. "I'm getting the impression you're not feeling too comfortable in those clothes." He rolled me over to my belly.

Slowly, he unzipped the skirt and pulled it down my thighs, throwing it to the floor. He did the same with the top, and a moment later I was left only in my lace underwear.

Massimo watched me, unbuckling his belt. I studied him as he did it, recalling the drastic scene I had been part of in the airplane.

"This is a new set, isn't it?" he asked, pulling off his pants and boxers. "I don't like it. You should take it off."

I kept my eyes on him, taking off my bra. For the first time, I saw his manhood when it wasn't erect yet. His thick, heavy cock was slowly rising as I got rid of my underwear. Even in this form, it was wonderful—I couldn't stop thinking about how it would feel inside me.

Lying naked in bed, I lifted my arms above my head in a gesture of submission.

"Come to me," I said, spreading my legs.

Massimo snatched my foot out of the air and raised it to his lips, kissing my toes and slowly lowering himself to the mattress.

His tongue descended down my inner thigh, finally reaching the end. Massimo raised his eyes and shot me a glance, buzzing with desire. His stare told me this wasn't going to be one of those romantic nights.

"You're mine," he growled, sinking his tongue into me. He licked me greedily, reaching all the most sensitive spots. I writhed and squirmed, knowing that my orgasm would come very soon.

"No, stop," I said, putting my hands on his head. "Come here, come inside. I need to feel you."

Without hesitation, Massimo obeyed my order, sliding into me hard and fast, making both our bodies race together, like my heart was racing in my chest. He fucked me passionately, wrapping his arms around me tightly and kissing me deeply, taking my breath away. Suddenly, a wave of ecstasy spread through my body. I dug my nails into his back, moving them down, all the way to his buttocks, leaving trails of red. The pain I caused him was the final straw—his hot seed spilled inside me. We started and came almost simultaneously. Tears poured down my cheeks. I was so relieved. *This is really happening*, I thought, huddling against him.

"Hey, baby girl, what's going on?" Massimo asked, getting off me.

I didn't want to talk about it. Not now. I only rolled over, facing him, and hugged him tightly, hiding in his arms. He stroked my hair and kissed the tears away until I fell asleep.

I woke up as rays of the sun penetrated the drapes, illuminating the room. With my eyes half-closed, I reached to the other side of the bed. He was still there. I shot a glance at him and . . . jumped to my feet, screaming. The sheets were all blood-spattered, and Massimo was deathly still.

"Massimo!" I shook him, crying, and rolled him over. He opened his eyes, appearing disoriented. I collapsed back to the mattress, relieved. He took a drowsy look around and trailed a hand across his torso, wiping away the blood.

"It's nothing, darling. The stitches must have broken," he said, sitting up with a smile. "I didn't feel a thing. But we have to get cleaned up. We look like we've murdered someone," he added with amusement, running his clean hand through his hair.

"It's not funny," I snapped, and went to the bathroom.

I didn't need to wait long for him to join me. This time I was the one who washed him, gently stripping off the bloodied patches. When I was finished, I reached for a first-aid kit and applied new ones.

"You need to see a doctor," I said in a commanding voice.

Massimo shot me a warm, uncharacteristically submissive look.

"I'll do whatever you want, but first we need to have breakfast. Your fasting has come to an end," he said, stepping out of the bathtub and placing a kiss on my forehead.

I went to the fridge to look for something to eat, but the only things inside were wine, water, and some juices. The Man in Black went over, leaning his face over my shoulder, looking inside the empty fridge.

"Well, today's menu is rather limited," he said.

"I haven't been hungry lately. But there's a grocery store downstairs. I bet you'd like to feel like an ordinary human being for a change. Go get us something to eat. I'll make you a list and prepare breakfast," I said, shutting the fridge door.

Massimo took a step back and leaned over the kitchen table.

"As in: do grocery shopping?" he asked, frowning.

"Yes, don Massimo. Groceries. Butter, bread, bacon, and eggs. Breakfast."

With a chuckle, the Man in Black left the kitchen, calling out as he went, "Write me a list."

After telling him how to reach the store, which was located in the same building, about a dozen feet from the main entrance, I watched him get into the elevator.

I suspected it would take him more time than it should, but less than I needed to get myself made up. I rushed to the bathroom, combed my hair, applied some quick makeup—one of those "I have no makeup on, that's just how I look every morning" things—put on a tracksuit and sat on the couch.

Massimo returned faster than I thought, without using the intercom.

"When did you get to Poland?" I asked as soon as he came back.

He hesitated, glancing at me.

"Breakfast first, talk later, Laura. I'm not going anywhere. Not without you, anyway."

He put the groceries on the table and walked over to me.

"You make breakfast, baby girl, okay? I know next to nothing about cooking. Meanwhile, I'll need to use your laptop."

I pushed myself to my feet and headed to the kitchen.

"You're in luck. I love to cook and I'm pretty good at it," I said, and got to work.

In thirty minutes, we were sitting on the soft rug in the living room, having an all-American breakfast.

"Okay, Massimo. I've waited long enough. Talk!" I said, putting my fork down.

The Man in Black leaned against the couch and took a deep breath.

"Ask away," he said, pinning me with his icy stare.

"How long have you been in Poland?" I asked.

"Since yesterday morning."

"Have you been here while I was out?"

"Yes. When you left with Olga. Around three in the afternoon."

"How do you know the code and how many keys are there to this apartment?"

"I came up with it myself. It's my year of birth. Only the two of us have the keys."

Nineteen eighty-six. He was only thirty-two. I got back to my interrogation. It was more important than his age.

"Have your people been here since I got here?"

Massimo crossed his arms on his chest, smiling. "Of course. You didn't think I'd leave you alone, did you?"

I had known the answer to that question, even if only subconsciously. That feeling of being watched constantly—it hadn't come out of nowhere.

"How about yesterday? Did you send people to follow me?"

"No. I've followed you myself, Laura. I've been to all those places, including your ex-boyfriend's apartment. I can tell you this: when you got into his car at the club, I was this close to shooting the guy dead."

Massimo's gaze was cold and deathly serious. "Let's clear something up. Either you stop seeing him at all, or I get rid of him."

I knew negotiating wouldn't get me anywhere, but hundreds of hours of training on how to manipulate people didn't go to waste— I knew how to spin this.

"I'm just surprised you see him as a rival," I said impassively. "I didn't think you'd be afraid of any competition. Especially after I saw those photos, he's definitely not of any interest to me. Envy is weakness. You only feel it when you know your rival's worthy. So, at least as good as you, or even better." I faced him and kissed him softly. "I didn't think you had weaknesses."

The Man in Black sat still in silence, playing with his cup of tea.

"You know what, Laura? You're right. I can accept an argument if it's rational. What do you suggest?"

"What do I suggest?" I repeated his words. "Nothing. That part of my life is behind me. I don't care if Martin feels otherwise. He can keep pestering me. I don't care. Besides, just like you, I never forgive disloyalty. Oh, and while we're talking about him: What did you put into his drink on my birthday?"

Massimo set down his cup and sent me a discomfited look.

"What? You thought I wouldn't find out? That's why you forbade me to talk to him? So I wouldn't learn the truth?" I hissed, my teeth suddenly clenched.

"What counts is that he cheated on you. Not everyone feels the need to do that under the influence of what he got. It wasn't a roofie or MDMA. It was simply something that made the alcohol work faster. We only wanted him to get drunk quicker than normal. I won't lie to you. I had my hand in that. But he didn't go after you as soon as you ran away. I did slow him down, of course. But, just think—how much would that have changed? Would you really like the whole situation to have played out differently?"

He rose from the floor and took a seat on the sofa.

"Sometimes I get the impression you forget who I am. I can change for you, when I'm with you, but I won't change for everybody else. If I want something, I get it. I would have kidnapped you that day or some other one. It was just a matter of time and method."

His words made me angry. I knew he would have done what he wanted, but the knowledge that I had nothing to say about any of that was making me furious.

"You really want to dwell on the past? We can't change it now," he said, leaning toward me and squinting slightly.

"You're right," I conceded.

"What about Naples?" I asked, screwing my eyes shut at the thought of the words I had heard weeks ago. "The TV said you were dead."

Massimo stretched out on the sofa, leaning back. He studied me for a while, as if trying to gauge just how much of the truth I'd be able to bear. Finally, he started talking.

"When I left our hotel room, I went to reception. I wanted to give you some time to make your decision. Crossing the hall, I noticed Anna stepping into the car of her half brother. I knew that if don Emilio was here, something must have happened—"

I interrupted him. "What do you mean, don?"

"Emilio is the head of the family in Naples. Western Italy is their turf. After what she said when we met her, and knowing her character, I knew Anna was up to no good. I had to leave you. I knew she wasn't expecting that. And if she wanted to get you by going after me, I needed to mess up her plan. So I got back to the yacht and went to Sicily from there. In order to keep appearances up, I ordered one of the women from the staff at the *Titan* to join me. She put on your clothes and went home with me. Then we went to Naples. I've been planning to meet Emilio for weeks. We run some businesses together—"

"Wait," I cut in. "You dated another capo's sister? You can do that?"

Massimo laughed and took a sip of tea.

"Why not? Besides, I thought it a great idea at the time. The potential merger of two major families guaranteed peace for a long time, not to mention total dominance in most of Italy. You see, Laura, you have it all wrong. The Mafia is a company. A corporation. Like every business, mergers and acquisitions play a big part of our activity. The difference is that they're a bit more brutal than in normal companies. I've had a good education. I'm well prepared to run our business. I was taught diplomacy, and I resort to violence only when I have no other choice. That's why my family is one of the most powerful and wealthiest Italian mobs in the entire world."

"The world?" I asked, puzzled.

"Yes. We run our business in Russia, Great Britain, the US . . . well, to be honest, it would be easier to say where we *don't* run any business." The pride he took in his work was evident from the way he spoke.

"All right, but going back to what happened in Naples . . ." I said.

"Anna knew about my meeting with her brother. She was the one who suggested it in the first place back in the spring. I couldn't refuse only because we weren't together anymore. Emilio would feel disrespected, and I couldn't have that. So I went to the meeting spot, accompanied by Mario and several people who I ordered to stay in the cars. The negotiations didn't turn out to be as easy as I would have liked. Besides, I knew Emilio wasn't telling me everything. When we decided we wouldn't be able to reach an agreement, I left the building. Emilio followed me, spewing threats and calling me names. Saying that I've treated his sister badly and disrespected her, making her abort her unborn child. And then he said the most hated word. The one word in our business that always leads to something bad. *Vendetta*, or bloody vengeance."

"What?" I exclaimed, shocked. "Isn't that a thing only in movies?"

"Unfortunately not. The Cosa Nostra works like that. If you kill a member of a family or betray them, the entire organization is entitled to hunt you down. I knew I wouldn't be able to get it across to him that it was a lie. Talking any further would take us nowhere. If not for the place and time of our meeting, it would have played out then and there. But Emilio is not stupid. He needed it done as soon as possible. When we drove to the airport, two Range Rovers blocked our way. Emilio's people stepped out. He was there, too.

There was a shootout and he died. I think I got him. Then the Carabinieri arrived and Mario and I had to hunker down for a while. Wait until it all blew over. The cars we left were registered to one of my companies. The police only spilled the bare minimum of information, but the damned hacks wrote about the incident anyway, killing me instead of Emilio."

I was breathing loudly, staring at Massimo. Listening to him felt like watching a gangster movie. I didn't know if with my weak heart I'd have made a good mobster's wife, but one thing was certain—I was madly in love with the man facing me.

"Just so you know, Laura—there was no pregnancy and no unborn babies. I'm very cautious with those things."

I froze, hearing him say that. I'd completely forgotten about what Domenico had said to me before I left Sicily.

"Do you have a transmitter implanted under your skin?" I asked as calmly as I was able to be, under the circumstances.

Massimo made himself more comfortable in his seat, playing for time. His expression told me he knew what I was getting at.

"I do," he said simply, biting on his lip.

"Can you show it to me?"

Massimo took off his shirt and drew nearer. He stuck out his left hand, grabbed my fingers and placed them on the correct spot on his skin. I jerked away, as if it burned, before touching my left bicep.

"You're getting hysterical, Laura," Massimo said, putting the shirt back on. "That night I—"

I didn't let him finish.

"I'll kill you, Massimo. I'm serious," I growled. "How could you lie to me about something like that?" I glared at him, waiting for him to say something smart in response, while my head was spinning with thoughts. What if . . .

"I'm sorry. I just thought that the easiest way to keep you with me would be if I got you pregnant."

I knew he was being sincere, but normally it was women who played that trick on rich men, not the other way around.

I got up, grabbed my bag, and went to the door. The Man in Black jumped to his feet and followed me, but I waved him away and left. I took the elevator down to the garage, trying to calm my nerves, and drove to the mall not far from my new apartment. Having found a pharmacy, I bought a test and drove back home. When I got back, Massimo was sitting in the same spot. I dropped my things to the coffee table and said resolutely, "You've barged into my life, kidnapped me, stolen a year of my life, threatening to kill my loved ones, but it wasn't enough for you. You just had to try and fuck things up even worse by singlehandedly deciding to get me pregnant. Now, don Massimo, I'll tell you how it's going to be." My voice was loud and confident. "If it turns out I'm pregnant, you will leave this place, and I'll never be yours."

The Man in Black rose, inhaling loudly.

"I'm not finished," I said quickly, turning my back on him and walking to the window. "You'll see your child, but you'll never see me. The kid will never take over after you and live in Sicily. Is that clear? I'll have it and raise it, even though I don't want to. I always say that a family should be at least three people—two parents and a child. But I won't allow your behavior to destroy the life of a human being that is not even born yet. Do you understand?"

"What if you're not pregnant?" Massimo asked, taking a step toward me, stopping just a few inches away.

"Then you'll have some atoning to do," I said, turning away.

On my way to the bathroom, I took the test from the glass tabletop and shut the door behind me. I did what was necessary and placed the plastic test on the rim of the sink, crouching with my back to the wall and waiting for the result to show. I stayed there for much longer than necessary. My heart was pounding so hard I could see the blood pulsating in my veins through my skin. I was afraid I was going to throw up.

"Laura." Massimo knocked on the door. "Is everything all right?"

"Give me a moment!" I called out, standing and glancing at the sink. "Jesus Christ . . ." I whispered.

CHAPTER 14

When I left the bathroom, the Man in Black was waiting for me on the bed, his face contorted in an expression I had never seen before. It was fear, worry, anxiousness, and most of all unease. Seeing me, he jumped to his feet. I stopped him, reaching out with a hand clutching the test. It was negative. I let it go, and it cluttered to the floor. I went to the kitchen, took a bottle of wine from the fridge, poured myself a glass, and downed it, wincing. Turning my head, I shot a glance at Massimo, standing with his shoulder to the wall.

"Don't do this ever again. If we decide to become parents, it has to be either our mutual decision or an accident. Do you understand?"

Massimo closed the distance between us and hid his face in my hair.

"I'm sorry, baby," he whispered. "I'm sorry about that kid. It would have been a beautiful child."

He stepped away, laughing, as if knowing I'd hit him anytime. He snatched my arms as I swung at him, teasing me.

"If it were a boy but inherited your character, he'd be *capo di tutti capi* before he was thirty. Even I didn't manage that!"

I stopped fighting. "You're bleeding again," I said, unbuttoning his shirt. "We're going to a doctor right now. And that stupid conversation is finished. My son will never be part of the mob."

Massimo pressed himself against me, heedless of the red stains he was leaving on my clothes. With a wide smile, he looked me in the eyes and kissed me.

"So," he said, breaking off the kiss, "we're going to have a son?"

"Stop it, you! That was purely theoretical. Get changed. We're going to the clinic."

I dressed his wounds again and went to the closet, stepping out of the dirty clothes and putting on blue jeans, a white shirt, and my favorite Isabel Marant sneakers. When I was finished, Massimo appeared in the doorway and opened one of the four huge closets. It was filled with his things.

"When did you manage to unpack?"

"Yesterday. I had some time to do it. Besides, I had some help."

He put on worn dark blue jeans and a black sweater, finishing his look with a pair of casual loafers. I had never seen him wear clothes like that. He looked like an ordinary, young, well-dressed man now. He looked mind-blowing. He reached for a suitcase inside the closet and took out a small box.

"You forgot something," he said, clasping the watch over my wrist. It was the same one he had given me when we were driving to the airport on Sicily.

"Is this a transmitter, too?" I asked with a chuckle.

"No. That's just a watch, Laura. One transmitter is enough. Let's not get back to that subject again." He sent me a warning look.

"Let's go before your stigmata opens up again," I ordered, grabbing the keys to the BMW.

"You drank. You shouldn't drive," he said, putting them back on the table.

"Well, okay, but you can. Unless you can't. Drive, I mean."

Massimo stopped, sporting a sly smirk and raising an eyebrow.

"I've raced a bit in my time. I know my way around a transmission. But we aren't taking your car. Too big for my liking."

"I'll call us a cab, then."

I pulled out my phone, dialing a number, but the Man in Black plucked it out of my hand, pressing the speaker button. He approached the cupboard next to the door and opened the lowest drawer, pulling out two envelopes.

"You haven't looked in here, have you?" he asked ironically, opening the first one. "We have other means of transport in the garage. I like those others better. Come on."

We went down underground, and Massimo pressed a button on the remote he was holding. Car lights blinked in one of the parking spaces. We walked that way and stopped by a black Ferrari Italia. I froze, ogling the low, sporty, incredible supercar.

"Are any more of those cars yours"? I asked, watching as he got in.

"Whichever you want, baby girl. Hop in." Inside, the car looked like some kind of spaceship: multicolored buttons and knobs, and a steering wheel flattened on the bottom. To me it didn't make any sense. "How do you drive this thing without reading a manual? Could you get anything showier than this?"

The Man in Black pressed the ignition button and the car roared.

"There were some other options, but a Pagani Zonda was too ostentatious. Besides, Polish roads aren't flat enough for its suspension." He raised his eyebrows in amusement and stepped on the accelerator.

We drove out of the underground garage, and after the first couple of hundred feet I was sure he knew what he was doing. We passed intersection after intersection and I navigated, showing him the way to a private hospital in the wealthy Wilanów district. I had picked that specific place, as I knew a few doctors there. I had met them on one of the medical conferences I had organized. We clicked. They were party people, liked to eat and drink expensive cocktails, but most of all, they appreciated my discretion. I called one of them, a surgeon, telling him I needed a favor. Two young women sat behind the reception desk. I walked over to one of them, introduced myself, and asked her to point us to Dr. Ome's office. She practically ignored me, her eyes shooting glances at the handsome Italian accompanying me. I hadn't seen women reacting to Massimo like that before. In Italy, a darker complexion and black eyes were nothing special, but here it was something rare—exotic and novel. I repeated my request, and the receptionist gave us directions, blushing.

"The doctor is waiting for you," she muttered, trying to focus.

In the elevator, Massimo brushed my ear with his lips.

"I like it when you speak Polish," he whispered. "I'm just pissed that I don't understand a word. But that's okay. Our son will speak three languages."

I didn't even manage a riposte, as the elevator doors opened and we got out.

Dr. Ome was a rather plain-looking middle-aged man. This seemed to make Massimo happy.

"Welcome, Laura." The surgeon shook my hand. "How are you?"

I greeted him and introduced Massimo, telling the doctor we would be talking in English.

"This is my—"

"Fiancé," the Man in Black finished for me. "Massimo Torricelli. Thank you for having us."

"Paweł Ome. Call me Paweł. It's a pleasure to meet you. What brings you to me?"

Torricelli, I repeated silently. During those long weeks I hadn't learned Massimo's last name.

The Man in Black took off his sweater, and the doctor grew completely quiet.

"A hunting accident," Massimo said, seeing the reaction. "A bit too much Chianti," he added, feigning amusement.

"Believe me, I get it. Once, after a party, we decided to catch a train. Literally."

Recounting the story, Dr. Ome applied an anesthetic and stitched the wounds back up, writing a prescription for some ointment and an antibiotic, warning Massimo not to stress them too much.

We left the hospital and got into the car.

"Lunch?" Massimo asked, brushing a strand of hair from my forehead. "I can't get used to that color. I love it and it suits you well, but you're just so . . ." He thought for a while. "Different."

"I like it for now. Besides, it's only colored. I'll change it when I get bored with it. Let's go. I know a great Italian place."

Massimo smiled and tapped an address in the GPS.

"I have Italian food in Italy. Here, I'd like to try something Polish. Buckle up."

We drove across the city, passing narrow streets, and I was glad the Ferrari's windows were tinted—seeing the car, people turned their heads, trying to peer inside.

The supercar was a great match for Massimo: complicated, dangerous, hard to control, and very sexy.

We stopped downtown at one of the best restaurants in town.

We went inside and were greeted by the manager. Massimo told him something discreetly, and the man disappeared before directing us to a table. A while later, an older man with a clean-shaven head appeared. He wore a dark gray suit with crimson lining—clearly hand tailored—and a dark shirt with the top button undone. On his feet was a pair of breathtakingly beautiful shoes.

"Massimo, my friend!" he called out, giving the Man in Black, who barely managed to get up, a great hug.

No stress on the wounds! I scolded the Italian in my head.

"It's good to finally see you in my country."

The men exchanged pleasantries, only recalling that I was there, too, after a while.

"Carlo, please meet my fiancée, Laura."

The man kissed my hand and said, "Karol. It's a pleasure to meet you. You can call me Carlo, like he does."

I was a bit surprised that Massimo was friends with a restaurant owner in Warsaw, despite not having been here before.

"You probably won't find my question too unexpected, but how did you guys meet?" I asked.

Karol shot Massimo a quick glance, and the Italian replied, his eyes growing familiarly cold all of a sudden.

"Work. We do business together. Carlo's people drove you from the airport and protected you while I was gone."

"Have you ordered anything yet? If not, please, allow me to pick something for you," the host said, sitting at our table.

After several dishes and a couple of bottles of wine, I felt full and completely out of place—the two men started talking business. From what they said, I deduced that Carlo was half Polish and half Russian. He invested in restaurants and owned a big logistics company dealing with international shipping.

The sound of Carlo's phone interrupted their extremely boring conversation. The host excused himself and left. Massimo focused his eyes on me and reached out, taking my hand.

"I know you're bored, but this will become a part of your life. You will have to participate in some meetings. You'll be excluded from others. I need to discuss some things with Carlo." He lowered his voice, inclining his head my way. "But then we'll return home, and I will fuck you on each floor of the apartment," he said seriously, narrowing his eyes.

I felt hot suddenly. I loved rough sex, and the threat of it was something I treated more like a promise worth waiting for.

I pulled my hand out of his grip and took a sip from the glass, leaning back in my chair. "I'll consider it."

"I wasn't asking for your permission, Laura. I was informing you of what I'll do."

His expression told me he wasn't joking, but that was just one of the things I loved so much about him. He sat back, calm and composed, but inside he was burning. I knew that the more agitated he grew, the better the sex would be.

"I don't think I'm in the mood today," I said nonchalantly, shrugging slightly.

His eyes drilled holes in me with such intensity I could feel his gaze on me. He didn't speak, but smirked with self-assurance, as if he was asking if I was sure of what I had said.

Carlo's voice broke the silence.

"Do you remember Monika, Massimo?"

"Of course. How could I forget your lovely wife?"

The Man in Black stood up to kiss the woman on both cheeks, gesturing toward me.

"Monika, please meet my fiancée, Laura." The woman shook my hand vigorously.

"Hey, nice to see Massimo in the company of a woman for a change, instead of Mario. I know he's his main man, or consigliere, or whatever they call themselves, but I can't exactly tell Mario I love his shoes, can I?"

Despite the difference in age, I knew Monika and I would get along. She was a tall brunette with a delicate face. It was hard to tell how old she was—she had either alien DNA in her or a really good plastic surgeon.

"Nice to meet you. I'm Laura. And I was just about to say the same thing about your shoes. Aren't those the latest Givenchy boots?" I asked, pointing to her shoes.

Monika looked at me with a knowing grin.

"Ah, I can see we already have something in common. I don't know how interested you are in their conversation, but I'd suggest a trip to the bar with me. It's going to be fun, I promise."

She laughed, revealing a set of snow-white teeth, and pointed to a spot on the other side of the room.

"I've been waiting for someone to save me for an hour now," I replied, getting up.

Massimo didn't get a word of what we were saying. He shot me a look, seeing me stand.

"Going somewhere?"

"Yes. Monika and I are going to talk about something a lot more important than making money. Shoes, namely," I said, sticking out my tongue.

"Well, have fun. We don't have much time. As you recall, we have some things to take care of later."

I stood rooted to the spot, staring at Massimo with puzzlement. Things? His eyes grew darker, his pupils dilating. Oh, those things.

"As I said, don Massimo, I'll think about it."

When I started to leave the table, he gripped my wrist and shot up to his feet, pulling me toward him and pushing me against the wall. He kissed me passionately, behaving like there was no one else in the room, or at least as if he didn't care.

"Think quick, baby girl," he breathed, tearing himself away from me.

I stood for a short while, studying him. He was someone else when there were people around—he wore a mask that he took off only when we were alone.

Massimo sat back at the table and returned to his conversation with Carlo, while I headed to the bar to talk to Monika. The restaurant, despite serving Polish cuisine only, was not one of those rustic wooden shacks with folk decor. It took up the entire first floor of an old tenement building. High ceilings and wide columns holding up the roof gave the room an unmistakably prewar feel. There was a black grand piano in the middle of the room, played by an old, elegant man. Everything aside from the instrument itself was white: the tablecloths, the walls, and the bar. It all created a cohesive whole.

"Long Island," Monika ordered, perched on a bar stool. "Want the same?"

"Oh no. Long Island would be a bit too much. I had a rough night. A glass of Prosecco for me."

For a long while our main topic of conversation was her awesome boots and my sneakers. She spoke of this year's fashion week in New York, the support she offered to young Polish designers, and how hard it is to find good clothes in this country. But it clearly wasn't her reason for pulling me aside.

"So you do exist," she said at one point, changing the subject and looking at me with disbelief.

For a while I wondered what she was talking about, but finally I recalled the portraits in Massimo's mansion.

"I know, it's hard to believe, but it seems so. The only difference is I have blond hair now."

"When did he find you? And where? Tell me something. We're dying of curiosity here. Well, Karol not so much, but I'm positively bursting with it."

Some time passed before I told her our story, omitting some details. I didn't know how much I could tell a woman I had only just met. Even feeling like I had known her for years didn't change my approach.

"You have a difficult task ahead of you, Laura. To be such a man's woman is a great challenge," Monika warned me, glancing at her glass. "I know what our men do for a living, so remember—the less you know, the better you sleep."

"I noticed that questions aren't exactly welcome," I whispered, grimacing.

"Don't ask about anything. If he wants to tell you, he will. And if he doesn't, it means it shouldn't concern you. And another very important thing: never question his decisions when it comes to security." She turned to face me and pinned me with her eyes. "Remember—everything he does, he does to protect you. Once, I didn't obey," she said, rolling up her sleeves. "And I was kidnapped."

I glanced at her wrists, which had old, barely visible scars around them.

"They tied me with a wire. Karol found me a day later. I've never again second-guessed him when it comes to security or overprotectiveness. Massimo will be even worse—believe me. He has been looking for you for years, and he believes those visions of his. He'll treat you as his most precious possession, certain that everyone else is trying to take you away from him. So be patient. I think he deserves it."

I sat still, mulling over her words. Outside the bubble that being with Massimo had been, I was learning that I wasn't actually living a dream or a fairy tale. Massimo's voice woke me from my pensiveness.

"Dear ladies, it is time for us to go. We have some important business to attend to. Monika, it was wonderful to see you again. I hope you'll visit us in Sicily soon."

We said our goodbyes and headed to the exit. Before we left, Monika grabbed me by the arm and whispered, "Remember what I told you."

Her deathly serious tone terrified me. Would someone really want to kidnap me? Why? But someone had kidnapped her. It could happen to me too.

"Get in, baby doll," Massimo said, opening the car door for me.

I shook my head, chasing away the worrying thoughts, and did as I was asked.

"You'll drive? You drank!"

Massimo turned in his seat and stroked my cheek. "You drank. I had one glass of wine. Now, buckle up. I'm in a bit of a hurry to get home," he said, fastening his seat belt.

The black Ferrari zoomed through Warsaw, and I couldn't stop thinking about his plans. Various scenarios flashed through my head, only strengthening my curiosity and arousal. We drove into the garage without exchanging a single word on the way. It felt just like that time when we had been shopping together in Taormina. The difference was that now I knew he wasn't ignoring me. He was just thoughtful. As we left the car, a security guard approached us.

"Miss, there are packages for you in the reception on the ground floor."

Confused, I sent Massimo a look. He only watched me, narrowing his eyes.

"Not from me," he said, raising his arms defensively. "All your things from Sicily came here with you."

We took the elevator to the main hall. The entire space was filled with a sea of white tulips.

"Laura Biel," I said, approaching the receptionist. "There's supposed to be a package for me here."

"Yes. All these flowers are for you. Would you like me to help you carry them upstairs?"

My mouth agape, I looked around. There were hundreds of tulips. I drew near one of the bouquets and snatched the little card attached to it.

Does He Know What Your Favorite Flowers Are? it read. I went to another, reading another card. Does He Know How You Like Your Tea? I grabbed yet another. Does He Know Your Passions? Terrified, I read card after card, crumpling them all into little balls and stuffing them into my pockets.

The Man in Black stood behind me with his hands crossed on his chest, watching me until I read all the messages.

"You know what?" I said to the receptionist. "Send these back or throw them away. Unless you have a girlfriend. She would be happy if you give them to her." I pressed the elevator button. Massimo positioned himself next to me and went inside without a word. Upstairs, I went to the door and took the envelope that was taped to it. I went inside and sat on the couch, turning the white envelope in my fingers, finally raising my eyes and looking at Massimo. His eyes flared with hate and his jaw was working rhythmically. Terrified, I stood and drew nearer to him.

"He's disrespecting me," Massimo said through clenched teeth as I faced him.

"Come on, they're only flowers."

"Only flowers? What's in the envelope?"

"I don't know, and I don't care!" I cried, frustrated, flinging the envelope into the fireplace. I grabbed the remote and switched the flames on, incinerating the paper instantly.

"Better?" I gazed at the Man in Black, but he didn't react. "Shit, Massimo, haven't you ever fought for a woman? He has a right to try if he feels like it. And I have a right to make a decision." I lowered my voice a bit, holding his face between my hands. "And I've already made it. I'm staying with you. Even if a whole orchestra is going to play me a serenade and he's going to sing, I won't change my mind. He's dead to me, just like that man you shot in the driveway."

Massimo pinned me with his ice-cold stare. I knew he wasn't listening. He jerked his head away and pulled a step back, storming off to the bedroom. I heard him getting something from the closet and stomping back. He passed me on the way, loading his gun.

"I'll kill him," he hissed, pulling his phone from his pocket.

Terrified by the intensity of his actions, I just stood in place, gaping. I had no idea what to do to stop him.

CHAPTER 15

As calmly as I was able, I picked the phone from his hand and put it down on a cabinet next to the door. I took the key from the lock and put it down my panties, keeping my eyes on Massimo. With a burst of rage, he grabbed me by the throat and slammed me into the wall. His eyes were ablaze with desire and hate in equal measure. Despite all his strength, I wasn't afraid. I knew he wasn't going to hurt me. Or, at least, I hoped so. My hands hanging limply, I stood still, biting my lip and staring him defiantly in the eyes.

"Give me the key, Laura."

"Take it if you want it," I replied, unfastening the top button of my pants.

Massimo slid his hand into my underwear with too much force, his other hand still gripping my neck. As I moaned, feeling his fingers on my skin, I could see the hatred giving way to desire in his eyes.

"I think it might be deeper," I said, closing my eyes.

He wouldn't be able to ignore that.

"If you want to play it that way, baby girl, I have to tell you, I'm not going to be gentle," he warned me, rubbing his finger against my clitoris. "All my anger will focus on you, and I'm afraid you might not like the way I'll treat you. So just let me out of here."

I opened my eyes and looked at him.

"Fuck me, don Massimo . . . please."

Massimo tightened his grip on my throat and pressed himself against me, drilling me with his ice-cold eyes.

"I'll treat you like a whore. Do you understand me, Laura? And even if you change your mind, I won't stop."

It turned me on. His words, the fear, and the knowledge that a man's life depended on my behavior now. An internal compulsion I felt only stoked my passion, making me want it even more. And the thought of how brutal and ruthless the Man in Black could be took my breath away.

"So do it," I whispered, pressing my lips to his.

Massimo pushed away, dragged me across the living room, and threw me to the couch. He did it with so much ease—as if I were a rag doll. He pressed a button on a remote, and heavy blinds slid down all windows. Then he went to the wall to switch the lights off. Despite the early hour, the apartment was drowned in darkness. I didn't know where he was now. My eyes hadn't adapted to the gloom yet. All of a sudden, I felt his viselike grip on my throat again, and his thumb pressing into my mouth.

"Suck it," he said, pulling the thumb out and replacing it with his throbbing cock. "You'd like to be punished instead of your lover boy? All right."

He grabbed me by the hair and pushed himself into my mouth. I wasn't able to take a breath. He was moving faster and harder, choking me. Then his cock retreated, though only slowly, before sliding back in—slower this time, but also deeper.

"Open your mouth wider. I want to push my prick inside your

throat," he said, leaning my head over the headrest of the sofa and kneeling on the sofa.

I clutched at his naked buttocks and pulled him toward me. I felt the tip of his penis touch the skin of my neck, brushing against it and finally sliding inside my mouth. I moaned, delighted, tasting him, unable to resist touching him. I pushed at him gently, moving him away just a few inches, and grabbed his heavy testicles, fondling them and shoving his cock deep in my throat. Massimo propped both hands over the headrest behind me, panting loudly. I knew I hadn't sated him last night. If I tried, making him come wouldn't take me more than a couple of minutes. I sucked his cock fast and hard until he grabbed me by the hair and pulled my head away, pressing it into the pillow.

"You didn't think I'd let you finish that easily, did you? Lie down and don't move."

I didn't obey him, lifting my head from the pillow, trying to catch his prick with my mouth again. With a growl, Massimo seized my throat and pushed me painfully into the corner of the sofa, rolling me over to my belly and moving his grip to the back of my neck. He ripped my pants and thong off.

"Want to check how long you last, Laura? We'll see just how much you like pain."

This was beginning to sound scary. I jerked, trying to get free, but he was so much stronger that me. The Man in Black wrapped his arms around my waist and lifted me up, so I was on my knees, my butt sticking up, and my torso still on the pillows. His hand whooshed through the air, slapping my ass. I let out a yelp, but he didn't stop. Holding me by the hair and pressing my face to the pillow, stifling my screams, he hit me again and again. Then, gently and slowly, he slid his middle finger in my pussy, purring with satisfaction.

"I can see you like what I'm doing," he said, licking his finger. "I adore your scent, Laura. I'm happy you didn't take a shower," he added, his finger finding its way back inside me.

I pushed myself up, trying to stand, suddenly ashamed hearing those words, but the Man in Black's elbow landed on my back, pushing down. I was embarrassed, cringing. I wanted this to stop.

"Massimo, let me go right now! You hear me?"

He didn't react and I screamed on the top of my lungs. "Don Massimo, for fuck's sake!"

It only made things worse. His rhythmically stroking finger was joined by his thumb, which pushed into my anus.

"Your ass is so tight! I can't wait to feel it," he breathed, turning my head to the side.

His fingers rushed, picking up the pace, and I found myself in heaven. I didn't resist anymore, didn't want to pull away—it felt too good. The Man in Black felt my resistance dissolve and released my hair. He moved the pillow I had been lying on so that he was directly above me now. His chest leaned over my back, skin on skin, and his erect cock brushed against my thighs. He kissed the back of my neck and then bit it, his hand still moving inside me.

"I'll push myself inside you now, Laura. Relax."

I couldn't wait. My legs spread obediently. I was so turned on that if he wouldn't do it himself, I'd have impaled myself on his prick myself.

Massimo grabbed my hair again, as if thinking I'd try escaping.

"You misunderstood me, baby girl," he breathed into my ear and slowly pushed himself into my ass.

I tensed and stopped breathing, and he pushed harder.

"Relax, honey. I don't want to hurt you."

Despite all the violence of what he had done, his voice was tender, and he tried being as gentle as he could. I trusted him, knowing he wanted to please me and not hurt me. My lungs started working again, and Massimo's fingers traced back to my clit, massaging it softly.

"Good, baby girl, very good. Now, push that ass higher for me," he whispered, and I felt he was already all inside me.

Slowly he pulled out and pushed in again, never stopping the motion of his fingers, pressing and rubbing, driving me crazy. After a while he stepped up the pace, sliding his free fingers into my pussy. Now he was everywhere at once. I writhed beneath him, screaming with pleasure, and a moment later I felt myself being close. I moaned, "Harder!"

The Man in Black happily obliged, fucking me so hard that a whole series of orgasms flooded over me. I gnashed my teeth, unable to control myself under the avalanche of ecstasy. The sound of his hips hitting my buttocks sounded like applause. I felt him exploding inside me, and his movements slowed down. Massimo's entire body shook, and he let out a mighty moan, reminding me of a roar of a great animal. He collapsed on my back and kept still for a while. I felt his heart pounding as he tried to calm down his breathing.

He slid out and fell to the floor, panting. My legs all shaky, I stumbled to the bathroom to take a shower.

When I came back, Massimo was nowhere to be seen. Terrified, I ran to the door and grabbed the handle—it was closed. I switched the light on and saw that the was key lying on the floor, next to my thong. Don Massimo, wrapped in a towel, was slowly descending the stairs.

"I didn't want to interrupt, so I used the bathroom upstairs," he said, throwing the towel off and letting it fall to the steps.

The view made my legs wobbly all over again. His slim legs ending in that beautiful, toned butt. He walked down slowly, keeping his eyes on me. The wounds on his chest did nothing to make him look any less attractive. If anything, they only made him look better. He was perfect and he knew it. Stopping right in front of me, he kissed me on the forehead.

"Everything all right, baby girl?"

I nodded and took his hand, leading him to the bedroom.

"I need more," I said, lying down on the bed.

Massimo laughed and covered me with the duvet.

"You're insatiable. I like it. To tell you the truth, we forgot to buy condoms, so no can do." He shrugged. "So, either I fuck you in that sweet ass of yours again, or forget it, because I never stop halfway, and you told me it's too early to have a kid."

I sent him an amused look, making myself more comfortable.

"So what are we going to do?" I asked.

"What do people in Poland do on Sunday evenings?"

"Sleep. They have to go to work on Monday mornings," I replied with a smile.

Massimo hugged me and reached for the TV remote.

"So we'll do just that and turn in early. We have quite a day ahead of us."

I lifted myself on my elbows and shot him a worried look.

"What do you mean?"

"I have some things to take care of with Carlo. I want you to accompany us. We need to go to Szczecin. We could fly, but I know how you hate that, so we'll meet him there. Unless you want to stay, but my guys would have to keep an eye on you, then."

That reminded me of what Monika had said.

"Karol's people would protect me?"

"No. Mine. I bought an apartment on the other side of the street, so they're as close as they can be without bothering you. Each room has cameras, too, so I know what's happening here while I'm out. And they can have an eye on you, too."

"Excuse me? Aren't you overdoing it, don Massimo?"

He only rolled over on the bed with a laugh, throwing his leg over me.

"Don Massimo? Why not don Torricelli, if you want to keep it official? How's your little hole feeling, by the way?" he asked, running his hand between my buttocks. "Just to be clear, Laura: I still want to kill him, and I'll do it if he disrespects me again."

I fell into thought, gazing at Massimo. "Is that so easy to you? To kill a man?"

"It's never easy, but if there's a reason, it becomes bearable."

"Let me talk to him."

Massimo took a deep breath and rolled onto his back.

"Massimo. I love you. Just—" I stopped abruptly, suddenly realizing what I said.

He sat up, his eyes studying me carefully. I faced him, closed my eyes, and dropped my head. I wasn't ready for that, but I said it and it was the truth.

With a finger, he raised my chin and said in a serious, controlled voice, "Say it again."

For a long while I tried to catch my breath, but the words stuck in my throat.

"I . . . I love you, Massimo," I managed finally. "I first felt it when you left me on Lido, and then I grew absolutely certain when I learned you'd been killed. I've been pushing it away, because you kidnapped me and kept me against my will, blackmailing me . . . But when you allowed me to go, the only thing I could think of was how to stay with you."

As soon as I finished talking, I felt my eyes well up with tears. It was such a relief, telling him that.

Massimo stood up without a word and left the room, vanishing in the closet. *Great,* I thought, *now he's going to pack his things and leave me.* I sat on the edge of the bed and covered myself with a towel I grabbed from the floor. When Massimo arrived again, he was wearing joggers and held something in his hand.

"It wasn't supposed to go like this," he said, kneeling in front of me. "Laura, I'd like you to marry me." His fist opened, revealing a little black box.

Inside was the largest diamond I've seen in my entire life. Shocked, I gaped at it, unable to utter a word. I felt my blood pressure rising and my heart thumping dangerously fast. A wave of nausea overcame me. Massimo quickly realized what was happening, reached to the end table, and stuck a pill under my tongue.

"I won't let you die before you accept," he said in a whisper, pushing the ring onto my finger.

I felt the tension leaving my body and I felt better by the minute. Massimo wouldn't back down, though. Still kneeling, he waited for my decision.

"But I'm . . ." I stammered, without a clue what to say next. "It's too soon. We don't know each other, and we've started out on the wrong . . ." I was babbling.

"I love you, baby girl. I'll always protect you and I'll never allow anyone to take you away from me. I'll do everything to make you happy and you won't ever have to worry about anything. If I'm not with you, Laura, I'll never be with anyone else."

I believed his every word. I knew it all to be true, and I knew how much all that romantic openness was costing him. Did I have anything to lose? For my whole life I had been doing what others expected of me, or what was the most appropriate. I never took risks, fearing changes and afraid of letting others down. Besides, it's a long way from a proposal to a wedding.

"Yes," I breathed, falling to my knees, too. "I'll marry you, Massimo."

The Man in Black dropped his head and exhaled.

"Jesus, what am I doing?" I asked myself, leaning my back against the bed. "We're complicating things a lot with this, you know?"

He didn't respond, and his head didn't even twitch.

"Listen to me now, Massimo. I need to finish saying what I started. Martin and his life mean nothing to me now, but I still don't want you to make unnecessary mistakes on my account. You have me, I'm yours and only yours, and only I can make him understand that. A relationship should be about trust and sincerity. So if you trust me, you'll allow me to talk to him."

Massimo lifted his head and sent me an impassive look. "Even now. Even at a time like this, this goddamned piece of shit is between us. I'll only allow you to see him to get rid of that maggot once and for all. If you fail, we'll do it my way."

I knew he was being serious. I had exactly one chance to save the life of my ex-boyfriend. Or Massimo would take it.

"Thank you, darling," I said, kissing him softly. "Now come. As my fiancé, you have a lot more duties."

We didn't make love that night, but it wasn't necessary. Closeness and love were all we needed.

CHAPTER 16

I didn't like getting up early, but I had to. The Man in Black wouldn't let me stay. I dragged myself out of bed, went to the bathroom, and made myself ready in about twenty minutes. Massimo sat on the sofa with a laptop on his knees and a cell phone in hand, focused and composed. He wore the clothes I had gotten used to—a black shirt and dark pants—looking really dapper. I watched him, peeking around the wall and playing with the ring on my finger. *This is going to be my husband*, I thought, *and I'll spend the rest of my life with him.* One thing was for sure: this wouldn't be an ordinary, boring life—more like a gangster movie sprinkled with some porn. After some time studying Massimo, I went to the closet and picked an outfit that would fit his attire, packing a small suitcase. As I took the stairs down to the living room, Massimo raised his head and sent me an appraising look. My dark gray high-hipped pants and the impossibly high stilettos hidden beneath the loose legs made me look taller and thinner. To top the outfit off, I'd picked a cashmere sweater in a brighter hue of gray. I looked elegant and matched my fiancé very well.

"You look very attractive, Mrs. Torricelli," Massimo said, putting down the computer and drawing near me. "I hope those pants aren't hard to take off and don't crumple easily. Otherwise you might end up looking a little less ritzy when we arrive."

I smiled and returned his look.

"First, don Massimo, your wonderful Ferrari isn't well suited for what you're suggesting. It's not too comfortable even when you're fully clothed. Second, I'd be a bit distracted by your bodyguards. So forget it."

"Who said we're taking the Ferrari?"

Massimo raised his brows and fished out another car key from the drawer.

"Please," he said, opening the door for me and pointing me toward it.

Four men accompanied us on our way to the garage, so the elevator got a bit cramped. We must have been quite a sight—five guys, most of them well over two hundred pounds, and one petite blonde. The Man in Black spoke to the men in Italian, instructing them.

When the door slid open on the lower level, the entire security team got into two BMWs parked by the gate, while we went deeper into the garage. Don Massimo pressed a button on the remote, while I was trying to guess which car blinked its headlights in response this time. It was a Porsche Panamera, its windows tinted. I breathed with relief—the prospect of having sex in the Ferrari was a bit too much, even for someone as flexible as me. Massimo headed to the passenger door and opened it for me. As I stepped inside, he leaned over, drawing his face right up to mine, and said, "Every couple dozen miles I'll fuck you on the back seat, so I hope you like the car."

He always turned me on when he was so commanding. I liked

it that he didn't ask my permission, instead just telling me what he'd do. Besides, I loved teasing him. I made myself comfortable in the seat, and said, "It's nearly four hundred miles. You think you'll manage that much fucking?"

He laughed out loud and retorted before he shut the door, "Don't you provoke me, or I'll fuck you twice as many times."

We spent the drive to Szczecin talking, fooling around, and having sex in parking lots in the forests alongside the road, acting like teenagers who borrowed a car from their parents, bought an extra-large pack of condoms, and set out on an adventure. Each time we pulled over to a lot, the security detail stopped at a distance, giving us some privacy and freedom.

We spent the next couple of days in Szczecin—I went to the spa, and Massimo worked. Despite the multitude of meetings, we ate together, slept together, and woke up together.

On Wednesday, as we were driving back to Warsaw, my mom called.

"Hello, darling, how are you feeling?"

"Oh, just perfect, Mom. I have a lot of work, but everything's fine."

"Great! I hope you remembered your cousin's wedding on Saturday."

"*Kurwa mać*," I blurted out.

"You watch your language, Laura Biel!" Mother snapped, raising her voice at the sound of the cuss.

The word "kurwa" was one of the few Polish words Massimo knew, so he instantly knew I wasn't too happy with whatever my mother said over the phone.

"Judging by that terse exclamation, dear, I gather you've forgotten. Well, let me remind you, then. The wedding is at four but try to arrive a bit earlier."

"That was an expression of delight, Mommy. Of course I remember. Count me in. I'm bringing someone, too."

Only silence answered me for a while. I had a pretty good idea what I was going to hear next.

"Who?"

Yup, just as I suspected.

"I met someone in Sicily. We work together. I'd like to bring him with me, as he's in Warsaw for training right now. Will that be enough data for you, or do you need me to send you a birth certificate, too?"

"All right, have it your way. See you on Saturday," she replied, apparently offended, and hung up.

My eyes tried to focus on the landscape behind the window. How was I to tell Massimo he was just about to meet my parents? I shot him a glance and wondered what his reaction would be. He felt my eyes on him and knew something was amiss, so he took the first ramp off the highway and parked the car, turning in his seat to face me.

"I'm listening," he said, frowning.

Two black BMWs stopped behind us. A man stepped out of the first one and approached our car. Massimo rolled the window down and waved the man away, saying something in Italian. The bodyguard turned back, stopped by his car, and took out a cigarette.

"We need to go to my parents' on Saturday. I completely forgot about it, but my it's my cousin's wedding," I explained, grimacing, and hiding my face in my hands.

The Man in Black didn't hide his amusement.

"So? That's it? I thought something had happened. I need to start learning Polish after all. I tend to misinterpret some situations if I only understand the swearing."

"This is going to be a catastrophe. You don't know my mom. She'll pelt you with questions. And I'll have to be there, translating, as the only foreign language she knows is Russian."

"Laura," Massimo said placatingly, pulling my hands away from my face. "I told you my parents had made sure that I got a good education. Aside from Italian and English, I also know Russian, German, and French. It's going to be okay."

I stared at him, wide-eyed, and felt incredibly stupid then, being able to communicate in only a single foreign language myself.

"That doesn't make it any better."

The Man in Black laughed out loud, turning to the steering wheel and accelerating.

It was dark when we arrived. Massimo parked the car and pulled my suitcase out of the trunk.

"Go upstairs. I need to talk to Paolo," he said, and headed toward the two black cars parked on the other side of the garage.

I took my bag and went to the elevator, only to discover it was out of order. I opened the door and took the stairs instead. Having reached the ground floor, I stopped. My jaw dropped. The lobby was once again filled with hundreds of flowers. White roses this time. *Oh God, no!*

"Miss," the receptionist called out, seeing me. "It's so good to see you. Those flowers are for you."

I took a panicked look around.

"The elevator's down. He'll have to go through here," I muttered.

"Excuse me, but I don't quite understand," the receptionist said.

There were too many flowers to hide them quickly, and too little time to try to carry them out of the building. I snatched the little card attached to one of the bouquets. I Won't Give Up, it said.

"Fucking shit!" I cried, crumpling it in my hand.

That's when the door opened, and Massimo strolled in. He took a quick glance at the roses, balling his fists. Before I managed to say anything, he spun on his heel and stormed out. I stood in place, dazed, leaning against the wall, thinking about what was surely going to happen now. The sound of the Porsche and its screeching tires shook me out of my reverie. I sprinted to the stairs and skipped three at a time, reaching the door of my apartment in a few seconds. My hands were shaking, and aiming the key at the lock proved to be more difficult than normal. When I finally opened the door, I grabbed the key to the BMW from the table and rushed back downstairs. Driving out of the garage, I dialed Martin, praying that he picked up.

"I see my present was more to your liking this time," he said.

"Where are you?" I shouted.

"Excuse me?"

"Where the fuck are you right now?!"

"Why are you yelling? I'm home. Want to drop by?"

God, no, I thought, and stepped on the accelerator.

"Get out of there! Right now, you understand? Let's meet at the McDonald's by your place. I'll be there in five."

"You must have really liked those flowers, eh? Why won't you come inside, though? We can order sushi."

Annoyed and terrified, I sped across the city, breaking every traffic regulation on the way.

"Martin, for fuck's sake, just get out and meet me where I told you!"

I heard the intercom in his apartment chiming.

"Someone's at the door. Probably the food delivery. I'll be there, though. See you."

I screamed at him, but he wasn't listening anymore. He hung up. I dialed his number again, but he didn't pick up. I tried again and again. I hadn't been this scared in my entire life. It was all my fault.

When I arrived, I left the car in the middle of the street and sprinted to Martin's apartment block.

I punched in the code and rushed upstairs, grabbed the handle, and swung the door open. Inside, I saw Massimo's men. I crossed the threshold, feeling my strength abandoning me, and slid to the floor with my back to the wall.

Massimo was there, too, sitting next to Martin on the sofa. Seeing me, he jumped to his feet, Martin hot on his heels. The bodyguard standing closest shoved him in the chest, pushing him back to the couch.

"Where are your pills?" I heard the Man in Black asking, but his voice was fading away. "Laura!"

"I have some," Martin said.

When I opened my eyes, I was lying on the mattress in the bedroom with Massimo next to me.

"You're giving me more reasons to kill that guy than he has himself," he hissed angrily. "If not for the fact that you left your medicine here . . ." He trailed off, clenching his teeth.

"Let me talk to him," I said, sitting up. "You promised me. I trusted you."

Massimo kept quiet for a while before calling out in Italian. His men walked out through the doorway.

"All right, but I'll be here. You will talk in Polish, so I won't understand anyway, but I'll be sure he doesn't touch you."

I pushed myself up and slowly, groggily went back to the living room, where Martin was waiting on the couch, fuming. After he saw me, his glare became less hostile. I sat down next to him, and Massimo took the chair by the aquarium.

"How are you feeling?" he asked, worried.

"Want to hear the truth? I'm furious with both of you. I want to kill you both," I retorted. "What were you thinking, Martin?"

"What do you think I was thinking? I'm fighting for you. Isn't that what you wanted? Didn't you want me to fight for you? Give you more attention?" he asked. "Besides, I think you owe me some explanations. For example, who are those armed men, and what is that Italian prick doing in my house?"

I dropped my head, resigned.

"I told you it was over between us. You cheated on me, and I can never forgive that. And the man sitting in the armchair there is my future husband."

I knew those words would hurt him, but it was the only way to get rid of him and ensure he lived. Martin pinned me with an angry stare, grimacing.

"So that's what it was all about? You wanted to get married? And I didn't propose, so you found yourself some Italian gangster and now you're going to be his wife? You took your man on vacation only to find yourself another one? That's fucking evil."

Martin's mocking, derisive tone rubbed Massimo the wrong way. The Italian pulled out his gun and placed it on his knees. My fury with the both of them boiled over then. I'd had enough of all this. It was too much.

Switching to English so they both understood, I screamed at Martin, "I'm in love, get it? I don't want to be with you anymore! You cheated on me and humiliated me. You acted like a bastard on my birthday. Nothing is going to change that anymore. I don't want to see you again. And I've had it with you both now, so you can kill each other if that's what you want!" I turned to Massimo. "But that isn't going to change a thing. I decide about my life. Not either one of you. So, fuck off! Both of you!" I screamed, and stormed out.

Massimo called something to the men in the corridor and they followed me. I was faster, though, and knew the neighborhood better. I reached my car and drove off, tires screeching, leaving them behind. I knew normally they'd start shooting, but they couldn't.

My phone kept buzzing, the screen displaying "unknown number." I knew it was Massimo, but talking to him was the last thing I wanted right now, so I switched the phone off. Praying she was home, I drove to Olga's. I rang the doorbell, and a minute later the door opened. Standing in the doorway, Olga looked like she had an epic hangover.

"You're alive," she said, plodding back into her apartment.

"Come on in. My head's going to explode. I got totally trashed last night."

I closed the door and followed her to the living room, where she fell to the couch and wrapped herself in a thick blanket.

"I've partied with that blond guy from the club since Saturday. I think the poor bastard fell in love or something. Can't seem to stop calling me."

I sat still, saying nothing. It was dawning on me that I had left the two men with a gun and told them to kill each other.

"You're pale like Dominika's calves. Remember? That girl we used to go to school with?" Olga said, but seeing my expression, she added, "What happened?"

I shook my head, shooting her a glance. If I didn't tell her the truth, all the secrecy might kill me.

"I've lied to you."

She faced me, grimacing.

"I don't live at a friend's apartment. And I didn't meet just anyone in Italy."

Telling her the whole story took me the better part of two hours, and when I was finished, I fished out my engagement ring from a pocket and put it on my finger.

"This is the proof," I sighed, leaning my head back. "Now you know everything."

Olga gaped at the piece of jewelry with shock on her face.

"Holy fuck. What you said was something straight out of a thriller. An erotic one, at that. What happened to Martin?" Her eyes flashed with excitement.

"Jesus, girl, I don't even want to think about it! Why are you asking me this?"

We both grew silent for a while, but after a moment's hesitation, Olga reached for her phone, dialed a number, and put the thing on speaker.

"We'll see."

The next few seconds seemed to take ages. I knew whom she was calling.

Martin picked up after five long rings.

"What do you want, you nymphomaniac?" he asked in a low voice.

"Nice to hear you, too, darling. I was looking for Laura. Do you know where she is?"

"You're not the only one looking for her. I don't know and I don't want to know. I don't want to have anything to do with her anymore. Bye." He hung up, and we both exploded with laughter.

"He's alive, at least," I said, trying to stop my nervous giggling. "Thank God."

"Even the Sicilian Cosa Nostra was no match for him," Olga added, pushing herself up from the floor. "Well, since everyone's alive and well, and I finally know what's happening, you can stay at my place for the night. Maybe it'll do your fiancé some good to worry a bit before you go back."

I sighed with relief and nodded, but was immediately on alert again as someone knocked on the door.

"At this hour?" Olga asked, puzzled, walking across the living room to open it. "That's probably just the blond guy. I'll get rid of him in no time."

She opened the door and fell silent, taking two steps back, followed by Massimo. He pinned me with an icy glare, stopping in the doorway, as if waiting for something.

"Well, well, this is beginning to look like a proper mess," Olga said in Polish. "Will you keep sitting there, making him wait? Or should I leave you two?"

"What are you doing here?" I asked. "And how did you find me?"

"The car has GPS tracking in case it gets stolen. Besides, I know where your best friend lives. I haven't introduced myself," he said, turning his head to look at Olga. "Massimo Torricelli."

"I know who you are," my friend replied, shaking his hand. "Laura told me, and the way she described you leaves no room for interpretation. So. Will you two just keep ogling each other, or do you want to talk?"

Massimo's expression grew softer, and I fought off the urge to laugh. This whole situation was so ridiculous . . . Just like everything else that had happened to me during the last few weeks. I got up from the couch and grabbed the keys to the car, walking up to my friend and kissing her on the forehead.

"I should go now. We'll meet tomorrow at lunch, okay?"

"Go and fuck his brains out for me. He's even hotter than you said," Olga replied, slapping me on the butt. "Ask him if he has a friend looking for some company," she added as I passed the doorway.

"Trust me. You don't want that." I waved at her and left.

We went out without speaking. I pressed the button on the remote and got into my car. Massimo sat in the passenger seat.

"Where's the Porsche?"

"Paolo took it home."

I pressed the ignition button and started driving. We didn't speak at all the whole way home, both waiting for the other to start.

Back in our apartment, Massimo took a seat on the sofa and nervously ran his hand through his hair.

"Does your friend know who I am? Did you tell her everything?"

"Yeah. I had enough of all those lies, Massimo. I can't live like that. Back in Italy it was easier. Everyone knows you there, but here it's different. The people are different. They're my people. And each time I'm supposed to lie to them, I feel like shit."

He sat still, keeping his emotionless eyes on me.

"We're going back to Sicily after the weekend," he announced, getting up.

"Maybe you're going back. I'm not going anywhere. Besides, you owe me an apology."

The Man in Black drew near me, suddenly shaking with fury, his eyes growing utterly black and his jaw clenching.

"I didn't kill him, so you can't blame me for anything. I went there to show him who he was dealing with. To set a boundary he won't be able to cross."

"I know he's alive. I also know he won't be bothering me again. He told Olga he doesn't want to have anything to do with me anymore."

Massimo couldn't hide his amusement at that. He stuck his hands into his pockets and rocked on his feet.

"It would be strange if he still hoped to get you back after what he heard from you and me."

I frowned and sent him a questioning look.

"I didn't kill him. You should be grateful," he said, planting a kiss on my forehead and disappearing into the bedroom.

For a moment more, I stood rooted to the spot, thinking about their conversation. Finally, I followed Massimo. He was in the closet.

I passed him on my way to the bathroom and took a shower, dreaming only of going to sleep. When I got back, he was lying in bed, wrapped in a towel, watching TV and looking absolutely comfortable—not at all like someone who had recently threatened to kill somebody. He was fascinating.

In my eyes, he was the perfect man—an alpha male, a guardian and defender. For the rest of the world, he was an unpredictable and dangerous mobster. It was strange and exciting, but would I be able to cope with that in the long run? Since last evening, when he had knelt before me, I was wondering if spending the rest of my life with this man was a good idea.

"We need to talk, Laura," Massimo said suddenly, keeping his eyes on the TV. "You rejected my call today and then turned your cell phone off. I'd like that to remain the first and last time. This is about your safety. If you're not in a mood to talk to me, pick up and tell me. Don't make me do things such as tracking you."

I stopped in the doorway, fully prepared for an argument, but Monika's words reverberated in my head. He was right. I walked over to the bed, allowing the towel I was wrapped in to fall to the floor, facing Massimo naked. He didn't even look at me. Fuming with anger, I threw myself onto the bed, turned my back on him, and fell asleep nearly instantaneously.

I was woken up by a gentle touch on my clitoris. I felt two fingers sliding inside me. Suspended between sleep and wakefulness, disoriented, not sure if this was really happening, I asked, "Massimo?"

"Yes?" I heard his sensual whisper right next to my ear.

"What are you doing?"

"I need to get inside you. I'll go crazy if I don't," he said, nearing his hips to mine, his hard cock resting on my buttocks.

"I don't want you to."

"I know," he said, and impaled me.

He shoved his penis into my hole, wet with his spit. I moaned, my head snapping back, leaning against his shoulder. We were lying on the side, and his powerful arms snaked around me, tightening. His hips were still, and his hands slowly traced lines across my breasts. With a reverence approaching worship, he touched my body, pinching my nipples once in a while. His touch woke me up, stoking the passion inside me.

"I need to feel you, Laura," he said as my hips started to sway gently. "Don't move." I was pissed—he woke me up, made me horny, and now was ordering me to lie still like a piece of driftwood.

I slid him out, turning myself over and sitting astride him.

"You'll feel me now. Deeper and faster," I said, clasping my hand over his throat.

Massimo didn't resist. He gripped my hips with both hands, moving them gently. Even lying beneath me, he had to at least pretend to be in control. I tightened my grip and leaned in toward him.

"I am going to fuck *you* this time," I said, starting to rock my ass.

As my clitoris rubbed against his belly, I felt the need to feel more. My movements sped up, getting more ruthless and insistent. The Man in Black dug his fingers into my buttocks, painfully, and moaned loudly. I couldn't help myself and slapped him on the cheek with my free hand, immediately orgasming with incredible intensity. Wracked by spasms of ecstasy, all my muscles tightened, and I froze. Massimo clutched at me harder, starting to move my hips steadily. A moment later, I felt his finger slipping into my ass and I came again with a loud cry as he pushed himself inside me faster and harder.

"One more time, baby girl," he whispered.

I lifted the hand that was resting on his torso and slapped his cheek again. I have never orgasmed for so long and so intensely. Massimo rolled over, throwing me to my back—his dick never slipping out of me—and knelt. I was exhausted, but I wanted more.

"I'm not going to come," he said, stopping and lying down. "Besides, we left the condoms back in the car, and I never stop halfway."

Puzzled, I sent him a look, but I couldn't see his face in the darkness. I had always treated making him come as a personal challenge, more satisfying than my own orgasms.

"If you don't want to come, I'll do it for you," I decided, shoving his cock down my throat, keeping my hand wrapped around its base. His breathing grew heavy, and he writhed beneath me. His body told me he was nearly there.

I grabbed his hand and placed it on my head so he could control my pace. Massimo tightened his grip on my hair and pulled me closer to his hips, making me taste his entire manhood.

He started to come, and a wave of his seed flooded my throat. I couldn't swallow, and it spilled from my mouth. He didn't seem to care, lost in the ecstasy my lips were giving him. At one point, the grip on my head loosened. His hand slipped off, hitting the mattress. I raised my eyes and licked his belly clean.

"You're sweet," I said, lying next to him.

I pressed a button on the remote I found on the night table, making the LEDs under the bed light up, so I could see Massimo's face. He was perfectly still, drilling me with his eyes.

"You're a pervert, Laura," he breathed, unable to calm his breath.

"Didn't your visions have anything sexual about them?" I asked, provocatively licking the remains of his jizz from my lips.

"I often thought about what you were like in bed, but I always fucked you—not the other way around."

I moved closer to him and kissed his chin, gently stroking his balls.

"That's just me, you know. Sometimes I like to be in control. But don't worry. It doesn't come often. Usually I prefer to be the slave. And I'm not perverted. I'm kinky. There's a difference."

"Well, if it doesn't come too often, I think I'll allow it. And trust me, baby girl," he said, running his fingers through my hair. "You are perverted, promiscuous, absolutely debauched, and—thankfully—mine."

CHAPTER 17

The next two days were rather ordinary. I met with Olga, and Massimo met with Carlo. We ate breakfast together and watched TV before going to sleep.

On Saturday I woke up early and couldn't go back to sleep. I kept thinking about having to take the Man in Black to meet my parents. A few weeks back I had been afraid they'd die from his hand, and now he was about to meet them.

When he finally woke up, I could start preparing, pretending everything was fine. I went to the closet to rummage through my stuff in search of the perfect outfit, completely forgetting that all the best ones had been left on Sicily. Resigned, I collapsed to the soft rug, staring at the hangers, and hiding my face in my hands.

"Everything all right?" I heard Massimo ask as he leaned on the doorframe.

"Nothing but the standard dilemma of half the women in the world: I don't know what to wear," I replied, frowning.

Massimo took a sip of the coffee in his mug, keeping his eyes on me, as if subconsciously feeling that it wasn't the clothes that were the problem.

248

"I have something for you," he said finally, walking to his part of the closet. "It arrived on Friday. Domenico's pick, so I hope you'll like it."

He reached up and took out a hanger covered with fabric sporting a Chanel logo. Delighted, I jumped to my feet and immediately unzipped the cover. I gasped, seeing a short nude silk dress. It had short sleeves and a very deep, creased neckline. It was perfect—simple and modest, but at the same time extremely sexy.

"Thank you," I said, turning to Massimo and kissing him on the cheek. "How can I ever repay you?" I asked, slowly dropping to my knees and stopping with my face on the level of his crotch. "I'd love to show you how grateful I am."

Massimo leaned his back against the closet and grabbed me by the hair. I pulled his pants down and opened my mouth, allowing him to decide the course of action. The Man in Black watched me with eyes full of desire, but didn't move a muscle. Impatiently, I tried catching his cock with my mouth, but the hands in my hair tightened their grip, immobilizing me.

"Take off your top," he said, holding me in place. "Now open your mouth. Wide."

He slid into my throat slowly, so I could feel each inch of him on my tongue. I purred with delight and started sucking. Blowing him was something I loved to do—I adored his taste and the way his body responded to my touch.

"Enough," Massimo said after a dozen seconds or so, pushing away and pulling his pants up.

"You can't always get what you want. Also, you'll be late to the hairstylist."

Staying on my knees, frowning and horny, I watched him leave the closet. Why did he give up his pleasure? It was no accident—I was sure. I glanced at my watch and realized it really was getting late, so I rushed down to the kitchen, gulped some tea, and grabbed a sweet roll from the table. After the first bite, I felt nauseous. I sprinted to the bathroom, nearly toppling Massimo over on the way. A while later, I heard knocking on the door, rinsed my mouth, and left.

"Everything all right?" he asked, looking me up and down with a worried expression.

I dropped my head, resting my forehead on his torso.

"It's stress. The thought of you meeting my parents scares me. I don't know why I told them we'd come," I blurted out. "I'm nervous and tense, and I'd just like to stay home today."

Massimo smirked, seeing my resignation.

"Will you feel better if I fuck you so hard you won't be able to sit down?" he asked, his expression comically serious.

For a while I considered that. My nausea was quickly vanishing. I decided that sex might actually help me to release the tension and improve my mood. The thought itself was making me feel better.

Massimo glanced at his watch and took my hand, leading me to the living room, before pulling my pants down and stopping next to the glass table.

"Lean down," he said, pulling on a condom. "And now show me that sweet ass. I'll do it fast and hard."

He did as he promised, and a while later I was relaxed and decidedly calmer—ready to go to the hair salon.

An hour passed and I was back home, but Massimo was nowhere to be seen. I took out my phone and called him, but he didn't pick up. He hadn't said anything about any meeting, so I grew a bit worried, but he was a grown man—he knew what he was doing. After two more hours and about thirty more calls, I was really pissed, though. I went to the apartment on the other side of the street to learn something from Massimo's goons, but nobody opened the door. I shot a glance at my watch and cursed under my breath. We should have been on our way by now. All spruced up, in my tight-fitting dress and sky-high stilettos, I took a seat on the couch, wondering what to do now. I didn't want to go on my own, but Mom would kill me if I told her I would miss the party. I grabbed my bag and the keys to the BMW and took the elevator to the garage.

On the way, I thought how to explain the absence of my new partner, and settled on selling everyone some story about him catching a cold or some such. Around ten miles from my destination, I glanced in the rearview mirror, noticing a car quickly gaining on me. It overtook me and blocked my way. I stopped my BMW. It was the black Ferrari. Massimo stepped out gracefully and headed my way. He was wearing a smart gray suit that perfectly brought out his musculature. He opened the door and offered me a hand.

"Business," he said by way of explanation, shrugging.

"Come on."

I kept my hands on the steering wheel, staring ahead. I hated this feeling of helplessness I had to experience so regularly when Massimo's "business" interfered with our plans. I knew I wasn't allowed to ask, and even if I did, he wouldn't tell me, and that would only make me angrier.

A moment later, a black SUV stopped behind my car, and Massimo said, unable to hide his ire, "If you don't step out of that car right now, Laura, I'll have to pull you out by force and that might ruin your look."

Pouting, I gave him my hand and got into the black Ferrari. In an instant, Massimo stepped inside, taking a seat behind the steering wheel and placing a hand on my thigh. As if nothing had happened.

"You look gorgeous," he said, stroking my leg softly. "But I feel like something's missing."

He reached to the glove compartment and took out a small box that read Tiffany & Co. My eyes widened, but I was doing my best to hide my glee, faking impassivity.

"You can't buy me with bling you know," I said as he opened the box, revealing a necklace glittering with dozens of small diamonds.

He lifted it out and fastened it on my neck, kissing me gently on the cheek.

"Now it's perfect," he said, turning his attention to driving the car. "But that 'bling,' as you called it, is platinum and diamonds. I'm sorry if it doesn't meet your expectations."

I liked that sly smirk of his when he thought he was proving his superiority. It turned me on. Also, it made me see red.

"Where's your ring, Laura?" he asked, overtaking another car on the road. "You know you'll have to tell them sooner or later."

"But it's not going to be today!" I cried out, exasperated. "Besides, what am I going to tell them, huh? Oh, I know! 'Mom and Dad, I've met a guy who kidnapped me and told me he saw me in a vision. Then he kept me locked up threatening to kill you both until I fell in love with him, and now we're going to get married.' Is that what they want to hear? What do you think?"

Massimo looked ahead, keeping his eyes on the road, clenching his jaw. He said nothing.

"Maybe this time I come up with a plan? I'll tell you how it's going to be. In a few weeks I'll tell Mom I fell in love. Later, in a few months, I'll tell my parents we're engaged. It'll be more natural that way. Less suspicious."

Massimo didn't look at me. His anger was palpable.

"You'll marry me next weekend, Laura. Not in a few months or years. In seven days."

My jaw dropped. I stared at him with eyes wide and heart pounding so hard I could hear it. I hadn't expected him to be in such a hurry. I had assumed we'd get married at the beginning of summer. Not in a *week*!

My head whirled with thoughts, with one question especially nagging: what have I gotten myself into?

Massimo stopped the car by the gate to my parents' house.

"Listen up, baby girl. I'll tell you how it's going to work," he said, turning to look at me. "Next Saturday you'll become my wife, in secret, and in a few months, we'll marry again, so your parents are happy. Okay?"

He leaned over and placed a gentle kiss on my forehead. "I love you, and marrying you is the penultimate thing I want to do in my life."

He parked the Ferrari in the driveway.

"What's the last one then?" I asked.

"A son, of course," he replied, opening the door.

I sat in place, trying to catch my breath, still not able to believe what was going on—how my life had changed during the last two months. *Get your shit together, Laura*, I told myself, stepping out. I smoothed down my dress and took a deep breath. "All right. Let's get this over with," I said, my legs slightly wobbly. "I hope you remember our official version."

The front door opened, and Dad greeted us from the threshold.

Massimo chuckled and offered a hand to my dad.

They exchanged a few sentences in German—nothing important, I presume—and Dad turned to address me,

"Darling, you look beautiful. That blond hair suits you. I don't know whether its because of that man or that haircut, but you look positively aglow."

"I guess it's both of those things," I replied, kissing him on the cheek and allowing him to embrace me.

We went to the terrace and took seats on soft lounge chairs surrounding a large table. Massimo did as I had asked him, keeping at a slight distance. At some point his expression changed. He fixed his eyes on something behind me. I cast a curious glance behind me. There she was—my mother, wearing an amazing off-white long evening dress, was heading our way, gracing Massimo with a charming smile. I got up and kissed her on the cheeks.

"Massimo, please meet my mother—Klara Biel." The Man in Black stood up, dumbfounded, but he quickly gathered his wits, switched to Russian, and greeted my mom, planting a kiss on her outstretched hand. She put on her charm, sending him one of her more breathtaking looks, before turning her attention to me.

"Would you come with me to the kitchen, darling? I need a hand there," she said, still smiling. That smile was nothing but trouble.

She turned and retreated inside the house, leaving the men deep in conversation. I followed her.

As soon as I went inside, I saw her again. She was standing with her arms crossed, right next to the table.

"What's happening, Laura?" she asked. "You change jobs, apartments, how you look, and now you bring an Italian to my house. Tell me everything immediately. You haven't been entirely honest with me."

Her natural lie detector was working without pause, it seemed, and it was never wrong. I had known it wouldn't be easy to fool my mother, but I was still astonished she had figured it out as soon as this.

"Mom, it's only a new haircut. I needed a change. We've already talked about my trip. And Massimo is a work colleague. I like him and he teaches me a lot. I don't know what to tell you . . . I've only known him for a few weeks."

The less I told her, the better. I wouldn't be able to remember all those lies.

My mother stood straighter, her gaze focused on me and her eyes narrowing.

"I don't know why you lie to me, child, but have it your way. Remember, though, that I see a lot, and I know my way around people. I also know how expensive that car you arrived in is. And I don't think that a hotel employee would be able to afford one."

In my mind I was screaming and cursing at Massimo for making me leave my BMW for his Ferrari.

"Besides, I know what diamonds look like," she continued, trailing a finger along my necklace. "*And* I've seen Chanel's newest catalog. Remember, dear, that I was the one who showed you what fashion is all about."

She finished and sat down, waiting for an explanation. I didn't move and wasn't able to come up with anything smart. Resigned, I lowered myself to the seat next to hers.

"What was I supposed to tell you? That he's a filthy rich *owner* of the hotel I told you about? He's from a wealthy family and invests a lot. We're seeing each other and I'd like it to be serious. And I can't exactly dictate the prices of the gifts he gets me."

Mother kept her eyes on me, studying my face. With each second, her expression was growing less hostile.

"He can speak Russian, that's for sure. He's a very polite young man. Well educated. And he has good taste in women and jewelry," she said, getting up. "All right. Let's get back to them before Tom bores him to death."

My eyes bulged. I couldn't believe the sudden change of attitude. I knew my parents had always wanted me to marry someone rich, but her reaction still completely surprised me. After a long while, I managed to get myself in order and followed in my mom's steps, still a bit dazed.

Outside, the men were engrossed in an agitated discussion. I had no idea what they were talking about.

I didn't know a word of German, but I knew I had to come to Massimo's rescue and present him with the new version of our story. Unfortunately, though my dad didn't speak English, he understood a lot of it.

"Come on, Massimo, I'll show you to your room," I said, patting him on the back. "Besides, Dad, we need to be going in a while," I added, turning to my father.

"It is getting kind of late," Dad agreed, pushing himself to his feet.

Massimo and I went upstairs and halted at my brother's old room.

"This is where you'll sleep, but it's not what I wanted to talk about," I said in a conspiratorial whisper before bringing him up to date on our lies.

When I finished, Massimo grinned, sticking his hands into his pockets, looking around the room.

"I feel like a teenager again," he said with a laugh.

"Where's your room, baby girl? You don't expect me to really sleep here, do you?"

"I do, and you will. My room is on the other end of the hallway. My parents still think our relationship is strictly platonic, so let's keep them in the dark for a while yet."

"Yeah, just show me your room, Laura," he said, trying to remain serious.

I took his hand and led him down the corridor to my old room. It was smaller than what I had in Sicily, but I had lots of good memories here and didn't need much to keep me happy. A bed, a TV, a little dressing table, and hundreds of photos hanging on the walls reminded me of my school years.

"Did you have a boyfriend when you used to liv[e]" simo asked, studying the photos with a smile.

"Sure. Why do you ask?"

"Did you give him blow jobs in this room?"

Unsure of what to say, I widened my eyes and frowned at the same time.

"Excuse me?"

"There's no lock on the door, so I'm wondering where you did it. And how. Knowing that your parents could come in at any time, I mean."

"I leaned him against the door and knelt in front of him," I said, placing a hand on Massimo's torso and pushing him toward the door.

He now stood exactly where my erstwhile boyfriend had stood, slowly unzipping his pants. I dropped to my knees and pressed his butt to the door.

"Don't move, Massimo, and stay quiet. This house has thin walls," I ordered, putting his penis in my mouth.

I blew him quickly and violently, wanting him to come fast. After a few minutes I felt his seed spilling into my throat. I swallowed it all like a good girl and got up, wiping my mouth with a hand. Massimo could barely stand. He screwed his eyes shut and leaned limply against the door.

"I like it when you act like a whore," he breathed, zipping his pants up.

"Oh really?" I asked with an ironic smile.

We got ourselves in order and returned downstairs, heading out to church for the ceremony. Lublin was a lot smaller than Warsaw. There weren't a lot of cars as expensive as ours. As we drove by the church, all eyes drifted our way, taking in the sight of the black Ferrari.

"Cool," I muttered, happy with the reaction we got.

Massimo gracefully stepped out of the car, smoothed down his jacket, and went to my door, opening it for me. Leaning on his arm, I got out of the car and put on my sunglasses. The crowd grew quiet as Massimo and I walked hand in hand toward the church. *It's only your family*, I told myself repeatedly, like a mantra, grinning at everyone we passed.

My brother's voice got me out of that daze.

"Hey, sis, I see your fancy stories had something to do with the truth after all," he said, walking over to me and giving me a quick hug. "You look awesome. I like your style."

I embraced him tightly. We only saw each other rarely, living so far away from one another. He was my friend, my beloved brother, and an unparalleled ideal. He was also the smartest guy I knew—a true mathematical prodigy—and a real stud. When we still used to live at our parents' house, he scored with all my friends. He was the complete man—smart, handsome, stylish, and ruthless. We were polar opposites when it came to character and appearance. I was a petite brunette with nearly black eyes, and he was a tall blond guy with emerald eyes. When he was little, he had looked like a little angel, with those platinum blond curls.

"Kuba, my beautiful brother, how good to see you. I completely forgot you'd be here. Let me introduce you to"—I switched to English—"my . . . Massimo Torricelli. We work together."

The men exchanged looks, shaking hands, but it looked more like sizing each other up before a fight than an ordinary greeting.

"Ferrari Italia, four point five liter engine, five hundred seventy-eight horsepower. A true beast," Kuba said, nodding his head in approval.

"Oh, you know, the keys were on top of the pile," Massimo said nonchalantly, putting on his sunglasses.

He was disarming, but my brother didn't seem to think so. He watched the Italian carefully, trying to look right through him, it seemed.

The service was boring as hell and too long. The whole time my entire family was focused on the handsome Italian at my side. The only thing I prayed for during the ceremony was for it to end. When the party started, the guests would stop ogling my man.

As the couple recited their vows, I recalled what Massimo had told me during our trip here: we were going to be in the same situation as the young couple in another week. It's just . . . was I really ready for this? Would I want to marry a man I barely knew? Who terrified me and made me angry on a daily basis? And besides, would I want to be with someone who wouldn't let me have my own opinions? Someone so controlling? Someone who always had to be right, who always had to have his way, and who didn't allow me to do most of the things I loved, thinking that he was protecting me? The sad truth was that I was so in love with him that rational thinking stopped being something I was capable of. I couldn't imagine losing Massimo again. I would not leave him.

"Are you feeling well?" he asked in a whisper as the ceremony finally ended. "You're very pale."

That was true. I hadn't felt too well for the last couple of days. I was tired and had no appetite, but that was to be expected—with all that stress, I should be thanking God I was still alive.

"I'm a bit faint, but it has to be the nerves. It'll be over soon."

We left the church, and it was supposed to be downhill from there. Everyone went to congratulate the young couple and celebrate my cousin Maria's big day.

The party was to be held in a picturesque rustic manor about fifteen miles outside the city. It consisted of several buildings, a hotel, stables, and a great hall where the party proper would take place. We were the last to arrive, as I had asked Massimo not to draw too much attention. Surprisingly, he listened. Practically unseen, we flitted through the huge room and reached our table. I sighed with relief, seeing Kuba was to sit with us. My brother would usually come to parties alone, trying to pick someone up. He loved it when women gave him their undivided attention, allowed him to woo them, and finally landed in his bed. He was a collector. In my case, the subject of sex had always been a bit more complicated, and sometimes men hurt me. My brother didn't have that problem—the only way women hurt him was when one in a hundred rejected him, ruining his score.

When we sat at the table, it turned out one place was free. I scanned the familiar faces of people around us, trying to guess who was missing. I couldn't. The appetizers arrived a moment later, and I devoured mine—I hadn't been able to eat since yesterday, so when I finally felt the hunger, my appetite swiftly overpowered any good sense I might have had.

"*Bon appétit,*" I heard someone saying, and raised my eyes.

It was a miracle I didn't spit out the food I was chewing. The last seat at the table was now occupied. By my ex, whom I used to practice dancing with. *Fuck me*, I thought, *can it get any worse than this?*

My brother watched me from over his plate, smirking ironically, unable to hide his amusement. Fortunately, Massimo didn't notice, or at least I thought so. Lucky he couldn't understand a word.

Piotr took his seat and started nibbling at his food, keeping his eyes on me. And my appetite was gone, just like that. Disgusted, I pushed away the half-eaten pumpkin soup, grabbing Massimo's thigh under the table. He softly caressed my hand, shooting a glance my way, reading me like an open book. I knew there would come a time when I would have to introduce him to my ex. Sooner rather than later.

Piotr had been a part of my life that I really wanted to forget.

We had met when I was sixteen. It all started with the dancing, and ended up as a relationship, as it often does. At first, he was my instructor, then my partner, and in the end—my tormentor. He had been twenty-five, and all the girls loved him—charming, handsome, fit, confident, and a dancer to boot. Regretfully, he also had his demons, and the greatest of those was cocaine. At first, I hadn't seen it as harmful, at least until his addiction started to take its toll on me too. When he was doped, he never thought about me. The only thing that counted was himself. At the time, I was seventeen and I worshipped him with all my heart. I had no idea what a real relationship should look like, of how a woman should be treated. Of course, I wouldn't have lasted five full years in a totally pathological relationship—when Piotr was sober, he would do anything for me, and always apologized profusely for acting like he had when under the influence of the drug. He was the reason I had escaped, moving to Warsaw. I knew I wouldn't have been able to free myself from him otherwise. His voice shook me out of my reverie.

"Red, if I remember correctly?" asked Piotr, leaning over the table with a bottle of wine.

His green eyes stared at me hypnotically, his full lips stretching into a subtle smile. He hadn't lost his magnetism, that was certain. A prominent jaw and a clean-shaven head didn't really match with the image of a typical dancer, but they made him all the more intriguing. He had grown more muscular, heavier, through the years.

I sipped from my glass and narrowed my eyes.

"What the hell are you doing here?" I hissed through clenched teeth, sporting a fake smile so the other guests, especially that one I cared for the most, didn't notice anything suspicious.

"Maria invited me. Well, her husband did, to be precise. I've been helping them with their first dance, and we grew to be pals.

Besides, I met them before, at your parents' anniversary party, years ago. Remember?"

I was fuming, wondering how my cousin could do that to me, when Massimo's hand slid up my back.

"Can you speak in English?" he asked, and I saw he was growing agitated. "I can't stand not understanding anything."

I grimaced slightly and closed my eyes, wanting to die.

"I'm not feeling too good," I said instead, pushing myself to my feet and walking away, Massimo hot on my heels.

We crossed the hall and went out to the garden, heading toward the stables.

"Do you ride?" I asked, trying to take his mind off me.

"Who was that man, Laura? You grew tense as soon as he showed up."

Massimo stopped and fixed me with his stare, keeping his hands in his pockets.

"My former dance partner. You didn't answer me. Do you ride?" I repeated, not slowing down.

"Only a dance partner?"

"Jesus, Massimo, why do you care? He wasn't *just* my dance partner, but I don't want to talk about it. I don't ask you about all your exes."

"So you were together? How long?"

I took a deep breath, trying to overcome my irritation.

"Several years. I would like to remind you, I wasn't exactly a virgin when you met me. No matter how much you try to change that, those are the facts. You don't have a time machine to change it, so just stop thinking about it and don't make me think about it, either."

Furious, I returned to the building. The first dance was over, and the guests were crowding the dance floor. As I passed the door, my cousin grabbed the microphone.

"Our first dance wouldn't be possible without our amazing instructor, who is with us today. Piotr, please, come here. Show yourself," she said. "It's also a happy coincidence that his dance partner of many years and my own cousin, Laura, is here with us, too."

I swear I was going to faint hearing that. What was she thinking?

"It would be our pleasure to watch you two dance."

The room exploded with cheers, and Piotr grabbed me by the hand, pulling me to the dance floor. *I'm going to throw up*, I thought, plodding behind him.

"Enrique Iglesias, 'Bailamos,' please," Piotr called out to the DJ. "Salsa, honeybuns . . ." he whispered into my ear, and lifted his brows, tossing his jacket to a random chair with a satisfied smirk.

I took my position by his side, thanking God he hadn't chosen tango. When we used to be together, our tangos always ended up in bed.

The first sounds of the guitar flew from the speakers, and I turned my head to the entrance, noticing Massimo, standing with his back to the door, eyes blazing with fury. I also saw my brother leaning to his ear, saying something. I had no idea if he was trying to explain why Piotr and I were now occupying the center of the dance floor, or whether they were just talking. It didn't change a thing—Massimo's glare was wild with rage. I pulled away from Piotr and ran to the Man in Black, kissing him passionately, wanting him to know that I was only his. Then, with a wide smile on my face, spurred on by applause, I went back to my dance partner. The DJ started over and I assumed my position again. Those were the longest three minutes in my life, and the most exhausting dance I had ever experienced. When we finally bowed, the cheers and applause were deafening. Maria ran up to me, hugging both Piotr and me, while my mother graciously accepted congratulations from dozens of guests. I slowly withdrew toward Massimo.

His expression was impassive, utterly emotionless.

"I couldn't say no, honey. It's my family," I stammered, trying to placate him. "And it was only a dance."

Massimo stood immobile, saying nothing, before turning around and leaving. I wanted to go after him, but heard my mother's voice behind me.

"Laura, dear, I see your training hasn't been in vain. You were absolutely brilliant back there."

I spun on my heel and Mom fell into my arms, kissing me and stroking my hair. "I'm so proud of you," she said, close to tears.

"Oh, Mommy, it's all thanks to you."

We stood in each other's arms until I remembered Massimo's reaction.

"Has something happened, darling?" Mom asked, seeing the change of my expression.

"Massimo is a bit jealous," I whispered. "He wasn't too happy seeing me dance with my ex."

"Remember, Laura, you can't allow him to act like he owns you. He has to understand you're not his property."

Oh, how wrong she was. I *was* his property. I was his and only his. It wasn't about his permission, though, but the fact that I cared so much about what he felt and thought. I knew his authoritarian behavior was as much a result of his upbringing as the appearances he had to keep up throughout his entire life. It had nothing to do with wanting to make me his property.

I went outside and searched the entire estate, but Massimo was nowhere to be found. His Ferrari was still parked in the same place we had left it. Through an open window in one of the buildings I heard a conversation in English. I recognized my brother's voice and went that way.

"Good evening," I said to the receptionist. "I'm looking for my fiancé. A tall, handsome Italian."

The girl smiled and glanced at her monitor.

"Apartment eleven, third floor," she said, pointing me to the stairs.

I reached the right door and knocked, and my brother opened it a while later, sporting a wily grin.

"Hey, sis, what are you doing here? Petey's bored with the dancing already?" he asked sardonically.

I ignored him and entered the apartment, crossing a short corridor to the living room. There was Massimo, sitting on a leather sofa, turning a credit card in his fingers.

"Having fun, baby girl?" he asked, leaning over the coffee table.

There was a little pile of white powder in the middle of the glass counter, and Massimo was arranging it into short lines. I froze, staring at the scene, when my brother appeared, holding a bottle of Chivas in his hand.

"I like your man," he said, nudging me on the arm and sitting next to Massimo. "Knows how to party." Don Massimo put a finger to one of his nostrils, bent over the table, and snorted one of the lines of coke.

"Can we talk, Massimo?" I asked.

"If you want to ask me whether you can join us, the answer is no."

My brother burst out in laughter.

"My sister and cocaine? That would have been a deadly combination."

I had never tried any drugs. Not by choice, but rather out of fear. I knew what they did to people and how unpredictable they made them. The view of those two doing lines brought back the worst memories and a feeling of fear that I never wanted to experience again.

"Kuba, would you leave us for a while?" I asked.

Seeing my expression, he got to his feet and put on his jacket.

"I was about to leave anyway. That blonde at table three has the hots for me."

Before he left, he called out to Massimo, "I'll be back."

I stood and watched the Man in Black snort another line, washing it down with a sip of the amber liquor. I walked over.

"Is that how you're planning to spend the evening?" I asked, reclining in an armchair.

"Your brother is a great guy," he replied, ignoring the question. "Very smart. Knows his way around finance. I could use a creative accountant in the family."

The thought of Kuba joining the Mafia made me feel nauseous.

"What are you babbling about, Massimo? He'll never join the mob."

The Man in Black barked out a laugh and took another sip.

"That's not your decision to make. If he'd wanted, I could make him a very rich and very happy man."

My brother's main flaw, besides his love of women, was his love of money.

"Will I ever be able to have a say in anything? Will you ever take my opinion into consideration before making a decision? Because if not, I don't want that life!" I yelled, jumping to my feet. "I have enough of that! Of not having any influence over what's happening. Of not being able to decide about my own life!"

Fuming, I left the room, slamming the door behind me. I took the stairs down and sat in a gazebo in the garden.

"Fuck this," I hissed to myself.

"Trouble in paradise?" Piotr asked, sitting next to me with a bottle of wine. "Has your friend gotten under your skin?" He took a swig straight from the bottle.

I stared at him for a second and was just about to get up when I decided I didn't really want to run from him. I reached out, took the wine from him, and poured a generous portion down my throat.

"Chill out, Laura! You don't want to get wasted this early."

"I don't know what I want anymore. And seeing you here . . . Why did you come?"

"I knew you'd be here. How long has it been? Six years?"

"Eight."

"You haven't called me or responded to my emails. You never pick up your phone. You didn't even allow me to explain. Or apologize."

I turned, facing him, angry again, and snatched the bottle from his hand.

"What's there to explain? You tried to kill yourself in front of me!"

He dropped his head.

"Yeah. I was an idiot. But then I went to therapy and I've been clean ever since. I tried getting my life together, but after a while I realized you were the only woman I wanted to be with. So I stopped myself. I don't know what I was thinking. Maybe I wanted you to be alone, and maybe . . ."

I raised a hand to shut him up.

"Piotr, you're the past. The city is my future. I'm living a different life now and I don't want you in it."

He leaned back, flopping over the backrest.

"I know, but that doesn't change the fact that it's really nice to see you. You're even more beautiful now."

We sat there, talking about everything that had happened during all those years, about my life in Warsaw and his dance studio. One bottle of wine, then another, and a third.

CHAPTER 18

I was woken up by sunlight shining over my face and a grotesquely strong headache.

"Oh, God," I moaned, crawling out of bed. I took a look around and realized I wasn't in my parents' house. I walked across the apartment and found myself in the living room, suddenly remembering the events of last night. Massimo leaning over the white powder and talking to Piotr, and . . . nothing after that. I grabbed my phone and dialed Massimo. He didn't pick up. *At least he's consistent*, I thought, though deep down I really didn't want to talk to him hungover.

I went to the bathroom and took a long shower before walking to the window. There was a black SUV parked downstairs, and Paolo was standing next to it, smoking a cigarette. I glanced at the spot where the Ferrari had been parked last night—it was gone. I put on some clothes and went down.

"Where is don Massimo?" I asked Paolo.

He didn't reply, only gestured to the back seat of the car. I stepped in, and he closed the door. We drove to my parents' house, stopping at the gate leading up to the driveway. Paolo got out and opened the door for me.

"I'll wait here," he said, getting back in.

With my shoes in my hand, I crossed the driveway and rang the doorbell. My mother opened the door.

"Nothing like a French leave," she said with a grimace. "Come. Breakfast is ready."

"I'll be there in a minute," I replied, walking to my room to change.

As I sat at the table, Mom passed me a plate with eggs and bacon. *"Bon appétit."*

The smell of food made me retch. I sprinted to the bathroom and threw up.

"Are you all right, Laura?" Mom asked, knocking on the door.

I left, wiping my mouth.

"I had a little too much wine. Do you know where Massimo is?"

Mom sent me a quizzical look.

"I thought he was with you. How did you get here?"

There was no sense in lying, so I told the truth.

"A driver brought me. I told you Massimo had some business around here, too. One of his employees waited for me. Jesus, my head is killing me," I mumbled, collapsing onto a chair by the table.

"Well, then I gather the party moved outside after your dance."

I didn't move, trying to remember what had happened. Nothing came to my mind. I gathered my things and prepared to leave after breakfast.

"When will you visit us again?" Mom asked.

"Next week we're going to Sicily, so it won't be anytime soon, but I'll call you."

"Take care of yourself, darling," she replied, hugging me.

I slept through the whole drive to Warsaw, waking up only twice, trying to call Massimo.

"We're here, ma'am." Paolo's voice woke me up.

I opened my eyes and discovered we were at the VIP terminal at the Okęcie airport.

"Where's Massimo?" I asked.

"In Sicily. Your plane is waiting," he said, offering me a hand.

The sound of the word "plane" made me rummage through my handbag on instinct, searching for my pills. I popped two and went to the check-in counter. Thirty minutes later, I was sitting in the private jet, dazed, waiting for it to take off. Flying with a hangover wasn't too pleasant, but the pills at least made me sleepy.

After another four hours we arrived in Sicily, where a car was already waiting for me. Domenico greeted me at the driveway of the mansion.

"Hi, Laura! Good to see you," he said, embracing me in a bear hug.

"Domenico! I've missed you so much! Where's don Massimo?"

"He's in the library, having a meeting. He asks that you freshen up first. You'll meet at dinner."

"I didn't think we'd leave so fast. Are my things here?"

"They'll be brought in tomorrow, but I've made sure to resupply your wardrobe. You should have everything you need."

Walking down the corridor, I briefly stopped at the door of the library. I could hear voices from within, but I didn't go in, despite really wanting to.

I took a shower and got ready for dinner. Not really sure what had happened last night, I decided to dress up, just in case. I chose my favorite set of red lace underwear, then reached into the closet and picked a flowy black ankle-length dress. I slid my feet into a pair of wedge platform sandals and headed toward the terrace. Massimo was sitting at the table laden with food and illuminated with candles. He was talking on the phone.

I walked over to him, planted a kiss on his neck, and sat in the lounge chair next to him. Without interrupting his conversation, he turned to look at me with that dark, icy stare. It couldn't mean anything good.

Finally putting down the phone, Massimo took a sip of wine and asked, "How much do you remember from last night, Laura?"

"I think I remember the highlights. Such as you snorting tons of coke," I replied sarcastically.

"What about later?"

I thought about that, feeling the fear kick in again. I had no idea what had happened after the second bottle of wine with Piotr.

"I went out to have a chat and some wine," I replied, shrugging.

"So you don't remember anything?" he asked, narrowing his eyes.

"I remember having too much to drink. Shit, Massimo, what's this all about? Are you going to tell me what happened or no? So I blacked out—is that so bad? I was angry at you and what you did. I went to the garden and met Piotr there. He wanted to talk, and we had some wine. That's all. Besides, of course, you leaving me again without a word. To be honest, I'm fed up with your constant disappearances."

The Man in Black pushed deeper into his chair. His chest was heaving faster.

"That's not all, baby girl. When your brother returned sometime later, he told me why you reacted like that, seeing the cocaine. I wanted to find you then. And that's when I saw you."

His jaw clenched. "In the beginning you talked, but then your friend overdid it a bit with the openness and tried forcing himself on you, taking advantage of the state you were in." Massimo trailed off, and his eyes grew completely black.

He lifted himself from the chair and smashed his glass on the stone floor. It broke into hundreds of shards.

"That fucking little shit wanted to rape you then and there!" he roared, his hands balling into fists. "You were so out of it you thought he was me. So you let him do what he wanted. I had to stop him."

I huddled in my chair, terrified, trying to recall what had happened, but my mind was blank.

"Mom didn't tell me anything. What happened? Did you beat him up?"

Massimo laughed ironically, walked over to me, turning me and the chair his way, and propping his arms on the armrests.

"I killed him, Laura," he hissed. "But not before he confessed to what he did to you years ago, when he was drugged. If I knew that before, I wouldn't have allowed him to join us at the table. He'd never set foot in the same room as you." I could see the emotions threatening to rip out of him. "How could you not tell me about all that? How could you allow me to eat at the same table as that fucking monster?"

Shocked and terrified, I gasped for air, praying that he was lying.

"I think he must have been planning to fuck you the whole evening. My presence made it harder. So he waited for the right moment. He had drugs on him, and I think he spiked your wine. To prove that I'm not lying, we'll do a blood test."

Massimo took a step back, putting his hands on the table.

"When I think about what that motherfucker did to you, all I want to do is kill him all over again."

What was I feeling right now? Fear, fury, and helplessness in equal measure. A man had died because of me. Or maybe the Man in Black was only bluffing, trying to punish me again. Slowly I rose from my seat. Massimo drew near me, but I raised an arm to fend him off and careened back toward the house. Bumping from wall to wall, I reached my room and locked the door. I didn't want him here. I didn't want to see him. I popped a pill to calm my racing heart, took off my clothes, and cowered in bed. I couldn't believe what he had done. When the pills started to work, I fell asleep.

The next morning, I was woken up by knocking on the door.

"Laura," I heard Domenico calling from the other side. "Can you open the door for me?"

I walked over and turned the key in the lock, letting the young Italian in. He shot me a sympathetic look.

"I'd like you to do something for me, Domenico, but I don't want don Massimo to know about it."

My assistant turned to stare at me, disconcerted, deciding on how to respond.

"Depends what you're asking."

"I'd like to see a doctor. I'm not feeling well, and I wouldn't want to worry Massimo."

"But you have your own physician who can come here at any time."

"I'd like to go to another one. Could you arrange that for me?" I wasn't going to back down.

Domenico took a moment to study me. "Of course. When do you want to go?"

"Give me an hour," I replied, going into the bathroom.

I knew the Man in Black would learn about all this, but I needed to know if he had been telling the truth. If I had been drugged at the wedding party.

Before 1 p.m. we took a car and drove to a private clinic in Catania. Doctor Di Vaio didn't keep me waiting. He wasn't the cardiologist I had seen before, but a general practitioner—just as I had asked. I explained what I wanted to check and asked him to take the blood samples at once. Waiting for the results, Domenico took me to a late breakfast before driving me back to the clinic around three.

The doctor invited me into his office in English, sitting me down in a chair and turning his attention to a stack of papers in his hands.

"There are intoxicants in your bloodstream, miss. Ketamine, to be precise. It is a psychoactive substance that can cause amnesia. This is very worrying. We need to order more tests and consult with a gynecologist."

"A gynecologist? Why?"

"Why, you're pregnant and we need to make sure the baby's okay."

I clamped my eyes shut and opened them again, trying to come to terms with what he said. "Excuse me?"

The physician gave me a surprised look. "You didn't know? Your blood tests leave no doubt. You're with child."

"But . . . I took a test two weeks ago and had my period before that. How is that possible?"

The doctor smiled good-naturedly, propping his elbows on the table.

"You see, a period can still come even three months into a pregnancy. A pregnancy test's result is dependent on many factors, including the time of insemination. We'll order some more tests and a sonogram. The gynecologist will tell you more. We just need to take another blood sample first."

I sat still, squeezing my eyes tightly shut again, feeling I was going to faint.

"Are you one hundred percent certain?" I asked.

"That you're pregnant? Yes. Absolutely."

I tried swallowing, but my mouth was suddenly parched.

"Are you bound by doctor-patient confidentiality?"

He nodded.

"Then I'd like you to tell this to no one."

"Of course. The receptionist will point you to the lab and schedule a visit with the gynecologist."

I shook the doctor's hand and left his office, my legs shaky. At first I went to the nurse to have that blood sample taken before going back to the waiting room, where I met Domenico. I didn't even acknowledge his presence, instead passing him on my way to the car. Joining me, Domenico sent me a quizzical look. The events of the last couple of days, my anger, and all that suddenly became unimportant. I was pregnant.

"And? Tell me, Laura. Everything all right?"

I gathered all my strength and plastered a fake smile on my face, replying, "Yeah. I'm anemic. That's why I'm so tired all the time. I need to take some iron supplements and it'll all work out."

Everything was clear, but at the same time I couldn't comprehend it—it was like some kind of trance. I could hear pounding in my head, and my skin beaded with sweat, only to cover with goose bumps a moment later. I tried breathing quietly, but I gasped for air instead.

The car headed back toward the mansion and I fished out my phone, dialing Olga.

"Hiya, bitch," I heard her happy voice in the receiver.

"Are you free next week?"

"I don't know . . . Not counting the blond guy with his rocket dick, my schedule's clear. My main guy left to conquer new markets, so it seems I won't be doing much. What's up? Got a suggestion?"

Domenico watched me, understanding nothing, while I tried acting naturally.

"Want to come to Sicily?"

She didn't reply, staying silent for a long while.

"What's happening? Why are you already there? Everything okay?"

"Just tell me if you'll come," I hissed, irritated. "I'll set everything up, just come here, please."

"Sure thing, darling, I'll be there. Just let me know when. Did that godly Italian of yours do something stupid? If he did, I'll kill the motherfucker. I ain't afraid of no mob!"

I chuckled, leaning back in my seat.

"No, it's all right. I just need you here. I'll let you know when I've taken care of everything."

I threw the cell phone into my bag and looked at Domenico. "I'd like my friend to come over tomorrow. Can you arrange the flight from Poland?"

"Will she stay for the wedding?"

Fuck! The wedding. All this shit happening made me completely forget about it. "Was everybody aware of it? Was I the only one kept in the dark?"

Domenico shrugged apologetically and dialed a number on his phone. "I'll arrange everything," he said, putting the phone to his ear.

When the car stopped in the driveway, I stepped out without waiting for anyone to open the door for me and went inside the house. Traversing the labyrinth of corridors, I barged into the library. Massimo was sitting at a large table with several other men. They all fell silent as I entered. The Man in Black told them something and got up.

"We need to talk," I said, clenching my jaw.

"Not now, baby girl. I'm having a meeting. Can it wait until the evening?"

I stood motionless, glaring at him and trying to calm my nerves. I knew too much stress would do me no good, especially in my state.

"I need a car, but without a driver. I need to go for a drive and think things through."

Massimo studied me for a while, narrowing his eyes. "Domenico will get you a car, but you can't go anywhere without security," he whispered. "Is everything all right, Laura?"

"Yes. I just need a while away from this place."

I turned my back on him and left, closing the door behind me and heading directly to Domenico, who was standing in the corner.

"I need a car. Massimo said you'll get me one. Keys, please."

He turned without a word and headed toward the stairs leading to the driveway. He stopped in the doorway and said, "Wait here a minute. I'll bring your car."

A cherry Porsche Macan pulled up in front of me shortly. Domenico got out and handed me the key, saying, "It's a turbo version with a very powerful engine. It can go over 170 miles per hour, but please don't try that," he warned me with a laugh. "Why do you want to go all alone? Maybe you'd prefer to stay and talk to me? Don Massimo will work late today. We can have some wine together."

"I can't," I replied, taking the keys.

I got inside the car, finding myself in a luxurious interior padded with cream-colored leather, and froze: there were knobs, buttons, lights, switches everywhere—as if a car needed all that stuff. The young Italian knocked on the window.

"There's a manual in the glove compartment, but I can give you a rundown. This controls the AC, the transmission is automatic . . ." He started listing all the different functions, and I felt my eyes watering.

"All right, I know everything now, bye," I cut him off, stomping on the accelerator and driving off, tires screeching.

As soon as I left the estate, a black SUV started following me. I was in no mood for company, especially the controlling kind. As soon as I reached the highway, I stepped on the accelerator, feeling the enormous power Domenico had told me about. I was speeding like crazy, overtaking other cars until the black SUV disappeared from the rearview mirror. Then I took the first exit and drove toward Giardini Naxos. They wouldn't count on me returning to town.

I stopped the car at a parking lot next to the highway and got out, putting my sunglasses on and walking to the beach. I sat in the sand and allowed myself to cry. What have I done? I had come here two months ago, and now I was the woman of the head of the mob, about to have his baby! I wailed. Not cried, but wailed. Howled in anguish. Hours passed like minutes and still I sat there. Hundreds of thoughts sped through my mind. Even those that suggested getting rid of the problem inside me. What would I tell my mother? What would I tell Massimo? What was going to happen to me now? How could I be so stupid? Why did I go to bed with that man? Why had I trusted him?

"*Kurwa mać,*" I groaned in Polish, hiding my head between my knees.

"I know that word."

I lifted my head and saw the Man in Black sitting next to me in the sand.

"You can't run away from the security guys, baby girl. They aren't there to annoy you, but to protect you." His eyes were full of worry, probing me searchingly.

"I'm sorry. I needed to be alone. I didn't think this car would also have a tracker. Because it has one, right?"

Massimo nodded.

"They'll be in real trouble for letting you go. If a woman eluded them, how are they supposed to protect me?"

"Will you kill them?" I asked, terrified. The Man in Black laughed out loud and ran his hand through his hair.

"No, Laura. That's no reason to kill a man."

"I'm an adult. I can take care of myself."

Massimo wrapped his arm around me, pulling me toward him. "I don't doubt it. Now, tell me, what was that about? Why did you go to that doctor?"

Thanks a lot, Domenico, I thought, disgusted by his lack of discretion.

I stayed in Massimo's embrace, pushing my face into his torso. Should I tell him the truth? Or should I keep lying for a bit longer?

"I've had too much of everything. The stress. I went to the clinic to check if you've told me the truth. You were right. There was ketamine in my bloodstream. That's why I can't remember anything. Did you really kill him, Massimo?" I asked, pulling off my sunglasses.

The Man in Black turned to look at me and took my face in his hands.

"I hit him and then took him to the pond by the stables. I wanted to scare him a bit, but when I started, I couldn't stop. Especially when he confessed to everything. So, yes, Laura. I killed him, and Carlo's man took care of everything else."

"Jesus," I breathed, feeling my eyes tear up again. "How could you? Why'd you do it?"

Massimo got up and lifted me, holding me by the shoulders. His eyes were black and cold as ice.

"Because I wanted to. Now don't think about it anymore. As you said: you don't have a time machine, so you can't do anything about that now."

"Leave me. I need to stay here alone a bit longer," I breathed, collapsing to the sand again.

I knew he wouldn't give up, and I needed to tell him something that would break through his walls. Paradoxically, I wasn't as worried by Piotr's death as I was about having to give birth to a child of the man now looming above me.

"You've killed a man and it's my fault. Now I have a guilty conscience and I can't live like that! The only thing I want now is to get on a plane and never see you again. So either you do as I ask, or this'll be the last time you see me."

He paused for a moment, but then headed toward the promenade.

"Olga will be here tomorrow at noon," he said, leaving, and disappeared into the SUV. The sun was about to set, which made me realize I hadn't eaten anything today. I couldn't allow myself to stay hungry for long now. Not anymore. I got up and crossed the beach, wandering from one colorful restaurant to another, finally stopping by the one where I had met Massimo for the first time. A shiver went down my spine, but at the same time my skin beaded with sweat. It hadn't been that long ago, but so many things had changed since then—nearly everything.

I went inside and sat at a table overlooking the sea. A waiter appeared immediately, greeting me in fluent English, and vanished equally as fast, leaving the menu. Leafing through it, thinking of what to have, wondering if there were some foods I shouldn't have in my state, I finally settled on what seemed the safest pick—a pizza.

I pulled my legs to my chest, wrapping my arms around them, my phone in my hands. I needed to talk to Mom. In any other circumstances, she would have been the first person I would have called with the happy news. Not this time, though. The news was anything but happy, and I would need to own up to all the lies I had told her, probably breaking her heart in the process.

When I was finished with the pizza and a glass of juice, I passed the waiter my credit card, not even bothering to look at him. My eyes were focused on the sea, nearly black by now.

"I'm so sorry, Miss Biel," he said. "I didn't recognize you with that hair." I turned my head, shooting the man a glance, a silent question in my eyes.

The young waiter was standing at attention by my table, the credit card lying in his outstretched, shaky hands.

"Wait a minute. What do you mean?"

"We have your photograph. Don Massimo's men sent it to us. You're supposed to be a VIP guest. Please accept my apologies. You don't have to pay for anything."

"Okay. One more tomato juice, then," I said, turning back toward the dark sea.

The thought of returning to the mansion and seeing the Man in Black made my stomach cramp.

The next hour passed quickly. It was time to go back home and get some sleep. Olga would be here tomorrow, and everything would be better. I would be able to cry as much as I'd like.

"I can see you're bored. Allow me to keep you company." A young, dark-haired man took the seat next to mine. "I heard you talking to the waiter. Where are you from?"

I sent the man an angry, frustrated look. "I'm not in the mood for company."

"Nobody is when they want to be alone. Sometimes, though, it's better to spill your problems on someone you don't know. That way, you don't have to be afraid of being judged. Plus, it'll be a relief. Trust me."

That won him a small smile, but also did nothing to dispel my anger. "I get it. Trying to hit on me, playing the easygoing friendly guy. Well, first of all, I really want to be alone right now. And second—you can get in trouble just by sitting next to me, so *you* trust *me*: go pester someone else."

The man wouldn't back down, instead sliding his chair closer to mine.

"You know what I think?"

I didn't give a shit, to be honest, but I knew he wouldn't shut up anyway.

"I think the guy you're thinking about doesn't deserve you."

I cut in, not allowing him to continue. "I'm thinking about the fact that I'm pregnant and about to get married on Saturday, so get your ass up and check if you're not needed at the bar."

"Pregnant?" I heard a voice from behind.

The dark-haired guy jumped to his feet as if his ass were on fire. Don Massimo took his place.

My heart was racing as he drilled me with those big black eyes of his. I caught my breath and spun around, looking over the sea, just to avoid eye contact. "What was I supposed to tell him? That you'll kill him? It's easier to lie. And safer. What are you doing here, by the way?"

"I came to have dinner."

"No food left in the fridge at home?"

"You weren't there, and I was missing you. Besides, I'm leaving tomorrow. I wanted to say goodbye."

I turned back to him, frowning. "Leaving?"

"I need to work, baby girl. But don't worry—I'll be back in time for our wedding," he said, winking. "I wanted to take you with me, but since your friend is coming over, why don't you go out somewhere? You deserve a bachelorette party. The credit card I left you with the keys to the apartment is yours. You might as well start using it. And you still haven't got a wedding dress."

His warm and tender voice calmed me down, assuring me that it wasn't time to tell him yet. I was lost—who was he? I mean, for real. At the same time, that unpredictability was one of the things I loved about him.

"When will you be back?" My voice told him I was mollified for now.

"As soon as I get to some kind of arrangement with the family overseeing Palermo. Emilio's death caused me some trouble, but you don't need to concern yourself with that," he replied, getting up and planting a kiss on my forehead. "If you've eaten and you're ready, let's go. I'd like to say my goodbyes back home."

We got to the Porsche and I passed him the keys.

"You don't like it?" he asked, opening the door for me.

I got in and waited for him. "It's not that. The car's beautiful, but it's too complicated. Besides, I like it when you drive."

For a while I hesitated, thinking if I should fasten my seat belt— I'd read somewhere that pregnant women shouldn't do that.

"How did you know where I was?"

Massimo laughed and stepped on the accelerator, making the wheels spin, tires screeching.

"Remember, baby girl, I always know what you're doing."

A few minutes later he parked the car in the driveway, stepped out, and opened the door for me.

"I'll go to my room," I muttered, gently stroking my belly.

"Okay, but I've relocated you. Let me show you to your new place," Massimo said, taking my hand.

"I liked the old one," I groaned as he led me down the corridor.

CHAPTER 19

We stopped by a door on the top floor. Massimo grabbed the handle and opened it. Behind it was a room that took up the entire floor.

The walls were lined with dark wood from floor to ceiling, and there was a gigantic C-shaped sofa in the middle, facing a large fireplace and an equally sizable flat-screen TV on the wall. Deeper into the room there was a series of tall windows and a flight of stairs leading to a mezzanine that housed a spacious bedroom with an enormous black bed supported on four columns—it made me think of a bedroom of some great monarch. The bedroom led to a closet and a bathroom, and finally to a terrace with a view of the sea.

"This is your new room, Laura. You're staying with me from now on," Massimo said, pinning me to the terrace railing as I paused to enjoy the breathtaking view. "I ordered your things brought in, but you won't need them tonight."

I felt his lips wandering down my neck and his hips pressing against mine, pushing gently. I turned to him and inhaled. "Not today, Massimo."

The Man in Black propped his hands on the railing, enclosing me between his arms. His gaze was penetrating. "What's happening, baby girl?"

"I'm not feeling too good. I think it's still from what I had at the party on Saturday."

I knew my argument wasn't a strong one, so I changed my strategy.

"I'd rather just snuggle up against you, watch some TV, and go to sleep. Besides, we're going to get married in a couple of days. Let's at least keep the pretense of propriety and hold back until then."

Massimo was clearly amused by that. He stared at me, unable to believe what he was hearing.

"Propriety? I come from a Mafia family, remember? But okay, honey, we'll do it your way. I can see something's wrong, so I'll just wash your back and that'll be enough for me tonight."

He led me through the apartment.

"Oh no you won't. We both know how taking a shower together would end."

An hour later we were lying in bed watching TV.

"You'll have to learn Italian at some point, you know that. If you're about to live here, you should know the language. We'll start on Monday," Massimo said, switching the channel to local news.

"Will you learn Polish, too? Or will I have to talk in English even when we visit Poland?"

"How do you know I'm not already learning it?" he asked, hugging me and running fingers through my hair. "I'm glad Olga will keep you company for the next few days. I think some freedom will do you a world of good. But don't even think you'll lose the bodyguards again. I don't want to have to worry about you." He took my hand with a tight grip.

"If you'd like to go diving or go to a party, tell Domenico. He'll have everything prepared," Massimo said seriously. "Remember that a lot of people already know who you are. I'm very concerned with your safety. You'll have to cooperate with my men if we want this to work."

The sense of those words got me thinking. So did Massimo's worried expression.

"Am I in danger?"

"Baby girl, your life was in danger from the very first moment you arrived. So just let me take care of things so you stay safe."

On instinct, I put my hand on my belly, under the sheets. I knew I wasn't responsible only for myself anymore, but for the little human growing inside me. "I'll do whatever you ask."

Massimo lifted himself on his arm, sending me a puzzled look and frowning. "What's with the sudden obedience, Laura?"

I knew he had the right to know about our baby. I also knew that conversation wasn't something I could run away from, but I didn't want to talk about it just before he had to leave. This wasn't the proper moment. "You're just right. I get it now. I'm a clever girl."

I kissed him and slid right back under his arm.

Around seven in the morning I was woken up by gentle prodding. Massimo's erect phallus was pressing itself against my buttocks. I turned my head his way, discovering with some amusement that he was still asleep. Slowly I slid my hand between us and grabbed his penis, starting to stroke it. Massimo moaned softly and turned onto his back. I propped myself on my elbow and watched his reaction. My grip tightened and my movements grew faster. Suddenly his eyes snapped open, but when he saw me, he closed them again. His hand slid under the sheets and started to softly rub my lace panties.

"Harder," he whispered.

I did as he asked and felt his hand venture deeper, reaching my wet snatch. Massimo inhaled sharply and started to play with me, writhing in ecstasy. His phallus grew longer and harder.

"Get on top of me," he said, licking his lips and throwing the duvet off the bed.

The motion revealed his astounding erection, and I suddenly felt hot.

"Not going to happen, love," I replied, kissing his chin. "I want to pleasure you this way."

"But I want to be inside you."

He turned to the side and pressed himself to me, hooking his finger under the fabric of my panties and drawing it away before roughly shoving his cock inside me. I cried out, my fingers digging into the skin of his back. He fucked me hard and violent, until he remembered that he couldn't finish inside me—we had no condoms. So he pulled out, panting heavily, and moved up over my head, placing his hands on the wall behind the bed.

"Finish me off," he whispered, sliding his cock into my mouth.

I sucked him passionately, my fingers delicately stroking his balls.

A moment later I felt his body growing tense, and a wave of sticky semen flooded my throat. He bellowed loudly, his hands clutching the headboard. When he was finished, Massimo collapsed onto the mattress next to me, trying to catch his breath.

"You can wake me up like that every morning," he breathed, smiling.

I tried swallowing his load but felt myself gagging.

I jumped out of the bed and sprinted to the bathroom, slamming the door shut behind me. I leaned over the toilet and threw up. When I was finished, I sat down with my back to the wall, suddenly becoming acutely aware that I was pregnant. *Jesus, this is bad*, I thought. If each blow job was going to end in throwing up, I wouldn't be able to do it at all!

Massimo stepped into the doorway, crossing his arms.

"That pizza last evening must have been bad. I knew something was wrong with it."

"The pizza, huh?"

"Yeah. Plus, drugs can change the taste and smell of semen, so think of that next time you're in a mood to snort some coke," I said, getting up and grabbing a toothbrush.

The Man in Black leaned against the doorframe, taking a moment to study me.

I finished brushing my teeth and kissed him on the cheek on my way to the bedroom.

"It's early. I think I'll lie down for a while more."

I slid into bed and switched the TV on. Massimo was still in the doorway but turned and was now facing me. I was switching channels mindlessly, feeling his eyes on me.

"I want a physician to take a look at you before I leave," he said, walking across the room to the closet.

My heart skipped a beat. I didn't know which doctor he would call, but even a witch doctor wouldn't be able to discover I was pregnant only from taking my pulse. Or so I hoped.

Twenty minutes later, Massimo stopped by the bed. He looked exactly the same as when I had first seen him back at the airport. Black suit and black shirt, bringing out the color of his skin and his eyes. He was authoritative, unyielding, and looked like a real gangster. Keeping the last vestige of calmness, I turned to the TV and said, "I don't think a bit of indigestion is enough of a reason to have me checked out by a physician, but whatever. I can diagnose myself and even come up with a treatment. Some stomach bitters, black tea, and stale bread. Want me to prescribe you something for that anxiety, too?"

Massimo took a step closer, smiling gently.

"Better safe than sorry, right?" I grabbed him by the belt. "Wasn't that morning blow job enough of a treatment, Mr. Torricelli? Maybe you're not satisfied with the service?"

The Man in Black laughed, stroking my face.

"I always want more, but we don't have time to sate me for now. Get ready for our wedding night. We'll have a lot to make up for, baby girl."

He leaned over me and kissed me on the lips passionately before going down the stairs.

"Remember. You promised you won't run away anymore. I have an app on my phone that allows me to see where you are. I installed the same app on your phone. Domenico will show you everything. If you don't like the Porsche, the drivers will take you everywhere, but please don't take any of the sports cars. I'm afraid you won't be able to handle them. I've got some surprises planned for you so you don't grow bored. You might want to have a look around. I hid them in the spots where we had our first times together. See you Saturday."

When he left, I felt my eyes watering. I rushed out of bed and chased after him, jumping into his arms, wrapping my legs around his hips, clinging to him like a koala bear on a tree branch.

"I love you, Massimo."

He purred with delight, holding me against the wall and sticking his tongue into my mouth in a luscious kiss. "I like that you love me. Now get back to bed."

He put me down and walked away, and I stood there, tears threatening to spill down my cheeks, watching as he opened the door. "I'll be back," he whispered, closing it behind him.

For a long while I kept still, wondering if this would be how I felt every time he left—praying that he returned safely. I forced the thought from my head and went to the terrace. Another beautiful day was beginning in Sicily—the clouds were slowly retreating, making way for the sun to warm the island. I took a seat in a lounge chair and stared out to the calm sea. A while later I felt a soft blanket sliding down around my shoulders.

"I brought you tea with milk," said Domenico, sitting next to me. "And a few pills for your anemia."

He placed vials with medicine on the table between us and started listing them: "Folic acid, zinc, iron, and all the rest you need in the first trimester."

I froze, gaping at him. "You know I'm pregnant?"

The young man smiled and nodded, making himself comfortable in his seat. "Don't worry. I'm the only one who knows. I won't tell anyone. This is between you and Massimo."

"But you didn't tell Massimo?" I asked, unable to contain my fear.

"Of course not. There are things even family has no right to meddle in. You have to tell him yourself. Nobody can take that away from you."

I sighed with relief and took a sip of the tea. "I'm praying it's a girl," I said with a melancholy smile.

Domenico turned his head to look at me and chuckled good-naturedly. "A girl can become the head of the family, too, you know," he replied with a half smile, raising his brows.

I punched him on the shoulder. "Don't even say that. It isn't funny."

"Have you thought about a name yet?"

I hesitated, watching him. I'd known about the pregnancy for only a day. Thinking about a name hadn't really crossed my mind yet. "First, I have to go see a doctor to help me understand the process. I'll think of the details later."

"I booked you a spot for tomorrow, three in the afternoon. Same clinic as yesterday. Now, come put some clothes on and let's go have breakfast. Me knowing your little secret means I've got to take a bit more interest in your diet."

As we crossed the bedroom, I noticed a large box occupying the center of the bed.

"What's that?" I asked, turning to Domenico.

"A gift from don Massimo," he explained, giving me a big smile and heading toward the staircase. "I'll be waiting in the garden."

I opened the box, revealing two smaller packages with the Givenchy logo on them. I took them out and opened them, too. Both held the beautiful boots that Carlo's wife had had on when we met in the restaurant in Warsaw. I was in love with those shoes, but nobody in their right mind would have paid what they cost. I jumped up and down, squealing with joy. Both pairs were the same, only differing in color. I grabbed the boots, hugged them to my chest, and went to the closet, scanning all the gorgeous things on the hangers. I wouldn't be able to fit into any of those things in a few months. I'd miss the New Year's Eve binge and all the parties with Olga . . . How the hell would I explain all that to my parents? Resigned, I plopped down in an armchair, still clutching the boots, thinking about all that frantically.

Then it dawned on me: I needed to go see my mom before my pregnancy showed. Then I'd be able to get away with not visiting if I sold her some story about work taking up too much of my time. My master plan had only one fault—the child would be born sooner or later, and that wouldn't be so easy to explain to my parents.

"Goddamn it, what a shitshow," I groaned, getting up. As long as my figure was still perfect, I decided to take as much advantage as possible of the contents of my closet. For my first day with Olga, I picked the boots I had gotten from Massimo. They'd go great with white shorts and a flowy gray shirt with long, rolled-up sleeves. I applied some delicate makeup and brushed my hair, putting my perfect bob in order. It was past ten when I was finished. I moved my things to an off-white Prada handbag and put on gold aviators. Before leaving the apartment, I stopped to look at myself in the mirror, unable to keep myself from letting out a gasp. My outfit had cost as much as my first car! Not counting the ridiculously expensive watch. Including that, the total price would probably reach that of a whole apartment. I felt attractive and very, very chic. But was this still me?

I hadn't thought Domenico would be so concerned with my condition. When I joined him for breakfast, he fed me, practically against my will, just like my mom used to do.

"Domenico, for fuck's sake, I'm not starving, you know," I groaned, irritated when he put another portion of eggs on my plate. "I don't want to eat any more. I'll only get nauseous again. Let's go already. I don't want to be late."

The young Italian gave me a disappointed look. "Maybe at least take an apple for the road?"

"Jesus! Take it yourself! And quit overfeeding me, you psycho!"

The road to Catania passed weirdly quickly. Or maybe it just felt like it. I had a lot to think about. I picked a car with a driver this time so Massimo wouldn't have to worry.

We parked by the airport terminal. I was glad I could spend some time with Olga alone—Domenico had sensed I needed it and stayed at the mansion. When I saw my friend emerge from the building, I didn't wait for the driver to open the door for me, instead running straight at her.

"Are those the Givenchy boots I can't afford?" Olga asked as soon as I fell into her arms, hugging her tightly. "Holding me like that won't get you anywhere. I'll still steal them!"

"Hi! It's so good to see you," I said.

"Well, your voice when you called me was so terrible, I knew I had no other option."

The driver took her bags and opened the door for us.

"Oooh, this is serious," Olga said, getting inside. "We get a private driver? I'm curious about the rest."

"Bodyguards, servants, and constant surveillance," I replied, shrugging. "Transmitters, wiretaps, and gangsters wherever you look. Welcome to Sicily." I spread my arms wide, smiling sardonically.

Olga frowned, giving me a quizzical look. "What's happening? I haven't heard you like that in a while."

"I wanted to sell you some lie, but that wouldn't work. Not with you. I'm getting married on Saturday and I want you to be my maid of honor."

Olga froze, staring at me in shock, her mouth agape.

"Are you out of your fucking mind?" she screamed. "I can understand falling for that gangster guy and wanting to take a shot at being with him, especially since he's offering you a life straight out of a fairy tale, has a knee-length dick, and looks like a god . . . But marrying him? After, like, two months? I am supposed to be the one who believes in divorce, not you! You always wanted it to be romantic, till death do us part, house, kids, and all that stuff. What's happening to you? He made you do it, right? I'll fucking rip him apart! He can't keep making you do things. You left the country, he turned you into some kind of doll straight out of *Vogue*, and now this!" she yelled, barely breathing at all.

I turned my head away from her, unable to listen to her anymore.

"I'm pregnant," I said.

Olga fell silent. Her eyes bulged, and I was sure they'd pop out and roll down to the floor.

"You're what?"

"I learned yesterday. That's why I wanted you to come here. Massimo doesn't know about it yet."

"Can we stop? I need to have a smoke."

I asked the driver to stop at the first place he deemed suitable. Olga jumped out of the car and lit a cigarette with shaking hands. After having one, she immediately lit another. She took a drag and said, "You're living in a gilded cage, but it's still a cage. And now this. Are you aware of what you're getting yourself into?"

"What am I to do, huh? Tell me. It's already happened. I can't get rid of the baby." I remained in my seat, glaring at her, raising my voice as I continued. "You yell at me as if I'm some kind of idiot, clueless as to what I have done. Yeah, I was stupid. Yeah, I wasn't careful, and I fucked up, but I don't exactly have a fucking time machine. So unless you have one, shut the fuck up and start being supportive! Fuck!"

Olga stood there, perfectly still, watching me as tears streaked down my face. "Come here," she said, flicking the cigarette away and getting back into the car to hug me. "I love you. And the kid . . ." She hesitated for a moment. "At least it's going to be good-looking. With parents like you, it has no other option."

We spent the rest of the way in silence, each one of us trying to get our thoughts into some semblance of order. I knew she was right. Her words were what I had thought, only feared to say aloud. That didn't change the fact that my life had really slipped out of my hands. I had no control.

When we were nearing the mansion, I turned to look at Olga. "Let's try and have some fun at least. I don't want to think about all that."

"I'm sorry," she replied, her eyes hidden behind sunglasses. "But you didn't exactly prepare me for the news." The car pulled up to the house, and Domenico was already waiting for us. Olga scanned her surroundings, shocked at what she was seeing.

"Holy mother of fuck! This is like *Dynasty*! You live here on your own or do you run a hotel?"

That made me laugh. I was glad Olga's good humor was back.

"Yeah, I know, it's a bit too much, but you'll like it. Come with me," I said as the young Italian opened the door on my side of the car.

I introduced the two and saw they immediately liked each other. That had been pretty likely—Olga loved fashion and charming, handsome men.

"He's gay, I think," she whispered to me as we walked down the corridor. "Good thing he can't understand us."

"I'm going to disappoint you right there—the word 'gay' is the same in many languages, so I think he might just have gotten a hint there," I whispered back.

Passing my former room, I recalled Massimo's words as he spoke to me about our first times together and the surprises he had left for me. "Wait a second," I said, grabbing the handle.

I went inside, feeling strangely anxious. Everything was . . . mine. So familiar. Untouched. Only the sheets had been changed, and the closet emptied of my things. There was a black envelope lying on the bed. I sat down on the edge of the bed and opened it. Inside there was a voucher for a luxury spa and a short note: *Whatever you like.* I hugged the note to my chest, already missing my Man in Black.

He could surprise me even when he wasn't around. I took out my phone and called him.

"We'll be at the end of the corridor," Domenico said, pulling Olga along. Three rings later, I heard the familiar voice.

"I can't stop thinking about you," I breathed to the receiver.

"Me too, baby girl. Something happened?"

"No. I just found the envelope and wanted to thank you."

"Only one?" he asked, surprised.

"There's more?"

"You have to do better, Laura. There was more than one first time for us. Has Olga joined you already?"

"Yes, thank you, we're already home."

"Have fun. And don't worry—everything is going great."

I hung up and went to search for the other surprises.

I could think of at least a few options, but I didn't know where to begin. It would be logical to retrace the steps of our recent past.

"The library," I whispered, and headed that way. There was another black envelope on the seat of the armchair where I had sat that first night. I opened it and found a credit card with another note: *Spend it all.* Oh, God, I didn't even want to think how much money was on that thing.

Then I went to the garden, where I first kissed Massimo. I found another black envelope on the canopied beach sofa. Inside, an invitation to our wedding and the few words I wanted to hear: *I love you.* I pressed the envelope to my chest and went back to the house in search of my friend and Domenico. I found them standing on the terrace of the bedroom located at the end of the corridor, not far away from my old room. It appeared that they both liked each other.

"Champagne for late breakfast," Olga said, rising a glass of Moët Rosé. "Your mafioso did his homework."

She pointed to a huge vase filled with ice, with several bottles of my favorite drink sticking out. Domenico shrugged apologetically, passing me a glass of tomato juice.

"I ordered two nonalcoholic sparkling wines from France, but they won't arrive until tomorrow."

"That's okay," I said, sitting in a large white armchair. "I can do without alcohol for a few months."

Olga pushed herself into the seat, pressing me into the armrest.

"Why, though? If you're about to get married and Massimo knows nothing about the child, you should pretend everything's normal. A bit of champagne-flavored sparkling water won't kill you."

I was afraid of the thought of having to rearrange my whole

life, fully submitting to the needs of someone who hasn't been born yet. And that was just the beginning. I knew the most difficult part would come in a few months.

"Domenico, I'd like to have lunch in town. Would you book us something?"

He poured another glass for my friend and left.

"Why didn't you tell Massimo about the kid?"

"As long as he doesn't know, I have a choice. I didn't want this child, Olga. But I also know I won't be able to get rid of it. Besides, Massimo was just about to leave, and I didn't want him to change his plans because of me. I'll tell him after the wedding."

"You think he'll be happy?"

For a moment I stayed quiet, looking out to the sea. "I know he'll be. You could say that this unplanned pregnancy was his plan."

I grimaced, shrugging, while Olga kept staring at me. "The fuck does that mean?"

I told her how I got the "implant" and about our first night on the yacht, explaining why he had lied to me. I also told her that this had all happened during my fertile days, and about the test that had shown nothing.

"So I think, however stupid this sounds, that I got pregnant when we made love for the first time."

Olga sat in silence for a couple of seconds, mulling over the story, before taking a sip from her glass and saying, "I don't want to sound like some crazy fortune-teller, but you know these things don't happen very often. So maybe it's fate? Maybe it just had to happen? You used to tell me everything in life happens for a reason. Have you thought about a name yet?"

"It all happened so fast, I haven't had the chance yet."

"Polish or Italian?"

I looked at her, trying to come up with an answer. "I don't know yet. I'd probably like both at the same time, but I'll wait for Massimo. Let's not talk about this anymore. Come on, let's grab something to eat."

We spent the afternoon talking and reminiscing about our childhood. We had always known that we'd become mothers someday, but the plan was to . . . well, plan it, instead of counting on a happy accident. It was late when we returned home, and Olga was clearly tired.

"Come sleep with me tonight," I said, making begging-puppy eyes.

"Sure thing, darling."

I grabbed her by the hand and pulled her with me upstairs. She stopped, dumbfounded, as soon as we entered my apartment.

"Ho-ly shit," she said with that natural charm of hers. "How much money does he have, Laura?"

I shrugged and took the stairs to the mezzanine.

"I don't have any idea, but probably a fuckload. It's really a bit overwhelming, but I got to tell you one thing—you get used to all the luxury real fast. I've never asked him for anything, though. I didn't have to—he gets me everything I need."

We sat on the bed, and I pointed to the opened door leading to the closet. "Want to see something really excessive? Go in there. You could buy a couple of apartments in Warsaw if you sold those clothes."

I followed Olga through the door. The light flashed on, revealing the enormous space in all its glory. The wall opposite the door was lined with shelves filled with expensive shoes—Louboutin through Prada. There was a rolling ladder affixed to the shelves, allowing me to pick even those pairs that were on the very top. In the middle of the room there was an illuminated cabinet with watches, sunglasses, and jewelry, and above it hung a gigantic crystal chandelier. The interior of the room was black, the individual sections divided by tall mirrors. My things took up the right side, and Massimo's the left. There was a comfy padded leather armchair by the door to the bathroom. Olga collapsed on it, shocked.

"Fuck me. I don't know what to say, but I can't say I feel sorry for you."

"Me neither, but sometimes I just think I don't deserve all this."

Olga got up from her seat, walked over to me, and placed her hands on my shoulders. What are you talking about?" she exclaimed, shaking me. "Laura, you're with a millionaire, you love him, and he loves you! You give him all that he wants, and now you're going to have his child. You don't need to be as rich as he is to give him what he wants and needs. And if he wants to buy you all that stuff, where's the problem? You've got to change your attitude!" She wagged a finger at me. "For him, spending ten grand is like buying bubble gum. Don't try to compare your finances to his. It's a whole different world."

That actually sounded pretty logical.

"If you had as much cash as he has, wouldn't you want to buy him everything?" she asked.

I nodded.

"So you see? Just be grateful for what you get and stop overthinking it. Now let's get to sleep, Mommy. I'm exhausted."

CHAPTER 20

The next day we had breakfast too late to even call it that. We spent the morning in bed, doing nothing until noon.

"You need to do me a favor," I said, rolling to the side to look at Olga. "I'm going to see a gynecologist today, but the visit has been booked in your name, so you're the patient. At least officially."

Olga sent me a skeptical look, raising one eyebrow.

"I don't know how deep Massimo's control reaches. The plan is to tell him that you forgot your birth control pills and we had to go to the clinic. That way he won't be suspicious of our visit to the clinic, if he checks where I am."

Chewing a sweet roll and washing it down with coffee, Olga said, "You're out of your fucking mind, you know that? He'll learn about everything, but we can do it your way. Whatever."

"Thanks. We'll go to Taormina after my checkup. I want to buy my maid of honor some clothes. Besides, I need a wedding dress myself," I said with a smile. "You know what that means?"

"Shopping!" Olga exclaimed, kicking her feet in the air, the sweet roll sticking out from her mouth.

"Massimo gave us a credit card, and we're supposed to wipe the account clean. I'm a bit afraid of how much we'll find there. Anyway, I'm going to call him now. I need to get this done." I headed toward my favorite divan.

The Man in Black bought the story about Olga's pills, only making sure it wasn't anything serious aside from the birth control. He swiftly switched subjects, starting to talk about our wedding. He said we wouldn't have a wedding party and that it would be a very private ceremony. At the end, he fell silent. Completely unlike him.

"Everything all right, Massimo?" I asked, suddenly anxious.

"Yeah. I just wish I were home already."

"Only three more days and you'll be back in Taormina."

Silence was my answer. Finally, he sighed and whispered, "It's not about the place, but the fact that you're not with me. Home is where you are. I don't care about the building, Laura. Especially since we also have an apartment in Palermo."

We—it felt so good when he said it like that. I'd really started missing him, but only realized that when I'd dialed his number.

"I need to go, Laura. I might be off the grid until Friday, but don't worry. Use the app in your phone if you feel the need."

I returned to the table, hugging the phone.

"You really love him, don't you? That's a new one," Olga said, rocking on her chair. "You hear his voice over the phone and you suddenly look like you'd give him a blow job through the receiver if only that was an option."

"Oh shut up and come on. Let's find something pretty in my closet. After we're done with the gynecologist, we're going to spend some cash, so let's look like *Vogue* babes."

Rummaging through my things took us too much time. If not for Domenico, I would have been late to my appointment.

We stopped in the doorway, ready to go out. I put on the same boots as before, the black ones, with a black bandeau dress. Olga chose the "rich hooker" style, putting on the shortest possible high-hipped white Chanel shorts that barely covered her butt and a top of the same color. To finish it off, she selected a pair of enormously tall Giuseppe Zanotti stilettos with golden insets, plus a pair of white-rimmed sunglasses. We didn't look like a pregnant girl and her broke friend, that's for sure.

Dr. Ventura was surprised when two women entered his office. I explained quickly that I needed my friend's support, as my fiancé had left. The gynecologist accepted her presence during the examination, which took place behind a privacy curtain anyway. When we were finished, I put my clothes back on and sat down next to Olga. The doctor scanned through some papers after putting on his glasses.

"You are definitely pregnant. Six weeks, it seems, considering the sonogram and the tests. The fetus is developing correctly, your results are acceptable, but I'm a bit worried about your heart disease. There may be some issues during the birth. We need to consult a cardiologist and change your medication. Also, no stress for you, young lady. No strong emotions and anxiety," the doctor said sternly, and turned his attention to Olga. "You have to take good care of your friend now. The coming weeks will be the most crucial for the child's growth. I'll prescribe some supplements, and if there are no more questions, we'll see each other in two weeks."

"I have just one question: Why am I losing weight?"

Dr. Ventura reclined in his seat and took his glasses off. "This happens sometimes. Women may gain or lose weight in the beginning of pregnancy. You need a balanced diet and to refrain from overeating, even if you're hungry. When you don't have any appetite throughout the whole day, make yourself eat something anyway. The child needs food to grow."

"How about sex?" Olga asked.

The doctor cleared his throat, shooting me a puzzled look.

"With my fiancé, of course. Are there any contraindications?"

The man flashed a friendly smile and replied, "None whatsoever. You can have as much sex as you want."

"Thank you very much," I said. I shook his hand and we left.

"High five! We're pregnant," Olga said with a grin as we drove to Taormina.

"We need to drink to that! I mean, I need to drink. You'll just watch me."

"You're a dumbass." I trailed off, thinking. "Jesus, it's good everything's fine with the baby. I drank so much during those last weeks. And those drugs . . ."

Olga frowned, turning toward me. "Drugs? You never did any drugs."

I told her the story of the wedding party, omitting the detail of Piotr's death.

"What a prick," she spat. "I've always told you he was an asshole. I wish he died, the fuck."

Well, actually he did, I replied in my mind, shaking my head to get rid of the uncomfortable memory.

On our way shopping, we picked up Domenico from the mansion. Nobody knew the most expensive and best boutiques in town like he did. Taormina was a beautiful, gorgeous place, but there was nowhere to park.

"All right, we'll just hop off here and take a walk," Domenico suggested, and opened the door.

Two security guards got out of the car following us. They stayed at a distance, but didn't stop trailing us.

"Will they always have to follow me, Domenico?" I asked, grimacing.

"Unfortunately, yes. You'll get used to it. Where do we start? The maid of honor or the bride?"

I knew it wouldn't be easy to find me a dress, so we started with me. I didn't really care, as nobody was going to see me anyway, but at the same time I wanted to look beautiful for Massimo. We hopped from designer store to designer store but didn't find even one thing that I could use. If not for the fact that Olga was lugging close to a dozen bags like some kind of fashion-frenzied vagabond, I would have been fuming by this time, but her joy made up for everything.

"All right, we're not going to find anything here," said Domenico. "I'll take you to my friend's atelier. She's a great designer. We'll have lunch there first, and then find you something. I'm sure she'll have what you want."

We walked down a narrow street, passing niches with stairs leading up and down and little cul-de-sacs, finally stopping in front of a small, dark purple door. Domenico punched in the code and we entered, taking the stairs up.

He must know the owner well, if she lets him pop by her workshop like that, I thought.

It turned out to be one of the most magical places I'd ever been to. The house was a large open space supported only on several pillars decorated with cotton ball lights in white and gray. All around the space, there were dozens of hangers exhibiting a wide array of evening, wedding, and cocktail dresses. A tall mirror hanging on the wall, flanked by windows overlooking the bay, reached the ceiling, at least thirteen feet high. The floor in front of it was covered with red carpet, which led to a huge white padded leather sofa. A door opened, and a woman appeared—tall, slim, and incredibly beautiful. Her long, straight, black hair fringed her thin face. She had unnaturally large lips and enormous eyes, like a Japanese manga doll. She was simply perfect. Dressed in a short skirt that brought out her impossibly long legs and very small breasts, she resembled me a bit. It was apparent that she worked out a lot, but her figure was very feminine and sexy.

Domenico walked over to the woman, allowing her to embrace him. For a few seconds, they stood in each other's arms, as if neither of them wanted to let go first.

Slowly, I approached them, reaching out with a hand. "Hi, I'm Laura."

The beautiful woman released Domenico and kissed me on both cheeks, her lips spreading in a wide smile.

"I know who you are. You look even better with blond hair," she said. "I'm Emi. I saw your face on dozens of paintings in Massimo's house."

Her words wiped the smile from my face: "Massimo's house." Why had she been there? Are they close? I recalled Anna, Massimo's gorgeous ex. Was Emi part of his collection, too? Domenico wouldn't have exposed me to something so stressful, would he? My head was aching with all these questions.

"Domenico." She turned her attention to the young Italian. "How is your brother? I haven't seen him in a while, and I'm sure he could use some new suits."

"Brother?" I repeated, frowning, sending Domenico a quick look.

He turned, his face impassive, and said, "Massimo and I had the same father. We're half brothers. I can tell you all about it if you'd like. Back home. For now, let's take care of your wedding dress."

I stared at the two of them dumbly while Olga ogled the clothes hanging all around us. Meanwhile, I was wondering what was more interesting: Emi's relation with Massimo or the fact that Domenico was my fiancé's brother.

"Laura." Emi turned to me. "Have you thought of anything specific? A shape? Material?"

I shrugged, making an uncertain face.

"Surprise us, my love," Domenico said, slapping Emi on the butt.

My jaw dropped. I had been sure he was gay until now. "Wait a minute," I said, raising my arms, while all three pairs of eyes turned to me. "Explain something to me. I'm lost. Who are you all to each other?"

Emi and Domenico burst out laughing, and the woman wrapped an arm around my young assistant.

"We're friends," she said, smiling. "Our families have known each other for years. Massimo and Domenico's father was best friends with my dad since primary school. I even had a crush on Massimo back in the day, but he wasn't interested. So I allowed the younger brother to take his place." She planted a kiss on Domenico's cheek. "If you need specifics: yes, we sleep together. A bit less often since you've arrived, but we manage," she said, winking at me. "Want to know anything more, or shall we pick you a dress? I don't fuck Massimo, if that was your next question. I prefer my men younger."

I was embarrassed, but at the same time a wave of relief washed over me. Emi's terse depiction of their relations brought back my good humor.

"I'd like it in lace. The more, the better. I want it Italian. Classic. Light and sensual."

"Very specific indeed. But as it happens, I've made one dress lately that might just be your style. Come." She took me by the hand and led me behind a heavy drape. "Domenico, order us some lunch and get some wine from the fridge, please. I always find it easier to think after a glass of white."

Ten minutes of struggling with the dress and having it pinned with what felt like a million sewing pins, I left the changing room and stepped on the dais between the white sofa and the mirror.

"Fuck me sideways," Olga grunted. "You look . . ." She trailed off, and tears streaked down her cheeks. "You're so beautiful, honey," she whispered, stopping behind me.

I raised my eyes and looked at my reflection. I was speechless. For the first time in my life, I had a wedding dress on. It was the most beautiful thing I'd seen.

It wasn't pure white, but slightly, delicately peach colored. The dress featured a bare back and was covered with thin lace. It was tight fitting from the waist up, while the lower part was flowy and loose, with a very long train—at least six feet long. The perfect V-shaped neckline went perfectly with my small breasts, allowing me to wear no bra. There was delicate crystal embroidery beneath the breasts, perfectly complementing the gown with its gentle glimmer. It was perfect. Ideal. I knew Massimo would love it.

"You need a veil," Emi said. "One that will cover your back. We're in Sicily, you know, and priests around these parts are crazy about those things." She drew a circle on her temple with her index finger. "But I have something that will work." The designer disappeared in the forest of hangers, only to return a moment later and cover me with thin, nearly translucent lace that shrouded me entirely like a cocoon. I was still visible beneath it, but at the same time it obscured my bare back enough for the priest to be happy.

"Now he won't bother you," Emi said, nodding with satisfaction.

Olga was sitting on the couch, drinking her third glass of wine. "I didn't think it'd work. That was too easy, but you look amazing."

That was a fact. I did look amazing, and I knew Massimo would think the same. The longer I kept looking at myself in the mirror, the clearer it became that I was really getting married. Slowly but surely, happiness came with that thought.

"All right, take it off me unless you want me to start crying," I said, stepping down from the dais and trailing the train and the veil behind me.

When we freed me from the dress and I returned to the main room, the table by the sofa was already laden with various seafood delicacies. We sat on white chairs and dug into our dinner.

"It'll be ready tomorrow," Emi said between bites. "Domenico will bring it to the mansion. I hope you'll lend him to me for this one night."

I laughed, hugging Olga, who was sitting next to me.

"I already have a companion for lonely nights, so you can have him." I turned to the young Italian. "Maybe it's even better that you stay and watch over her, so she finishes on time."

"I'm always watching someone. Either my brother's runaway girlfriend or my own, always sewing something new. That's my fate, it seems. One is a don, the other a seamstress."

Emi dug an elbow into his side, shooting him a provocative glare. "You don't have to watch over me if you don't like it."

Domenico leaned toward her and whispered something into her ear, making her lick her lips lusciously. I was jealous. Not of my assistant, or rather future brother-in-law, but of the fact that they had each other and could enjoy one another openly. Massimo and me? It was highly likely we wouldn't be able to behave like this with other people present.

"What about me?" Olga asked. "With all those things we bought me, there still isn't a single thing that would match your dress."

Emi put down her fork, chewing a piece of octopus, and went to one of the hangers. "I can see the hooker style is something you're familiar with," she said, returning with a dress. "But it won't do this time. Not in the church Massimo picked for you. Try this on."

Olga made a face, but took the dress. Before she vanished into the dressing room, she called out, "Look how I sacrifice my values for you, Laura." When she returned and stopped by the mirror, she had a change of heart. The dress she was wearing was the same color as mine, but had a different length and shape—it was a pencil dress with shoulder straps made of delicate matte silk. Very elegant. Perfect for Olga's shape—large, round backside, flat belly, and large breasts.

"I'm glad there won't be a party after the wedding. I can barely walk in this," she said. "Only good for slow dancing, but it sure looks awesome."

I sighed with relief, seeing my friend looking so good, knowing we were ready for my big day.

When we finished our food, it was getting late, and Taormina was already shrouded in darkness.

"Laura," Domenico said as I was saying goodbye to Emi. "If anything happens, call me."

"What is there to happen?" Olga asked, annoyed. "You're worse than her mother."

"I'll walk you to the car," he offered.

"You know what? I'm not that tired. I'd like to go for a walk. How about you, Olga?" I asked.

"Why not? It's warm outside, and I've been here for two days and haven't seen anything."

Domenico didn't look so happy with our idea, but couldn't exactly say no, especially since we had our security team. "Give me a moment. I'll call the guys. When you go downstairs, wait for them if they're not already there. Or . . . you know what? I'll walk you downstairs."

"You're impossible, Domenico," I cried, pushing him through the door. "I'm nearly thirty and I've always coped without a band of armed men. I'll be all right, so quit being so overprotective."

The Italian stood watching me, arms crossed on his chest. "Just wait for them, please," he hissed as I slammed the door shut.

"See you tomorrow. Bye!" Olga shouted, and we ran down the stairs.

We waited a moment for the stone-faced bodyguards and headed down a street chosen at random.

The evening was beautiful and warm, and the streets of the small town were filled with tourists and locals alike. Taormina buzzed with life, music, and the smells of Italian cuisine.

"Would you ever move here?" I asked Olga, walking arm in arm with her.

"Here?" she asked, surprised. "I don't know . . . nothing really keeps me in Poland, but there's nothing for me here aside from you."

"Is that too little?"

"I don't know, but remember how much time it took me to move to Warsaw? I don't like changes. And I'm afraid of drastic ones."

Right. It had taken me ages to talk her into moving with me.

I had been living in Warsaw for the past eight years, having moved there to escape Piotr's pathological love. When I finally relocated to the capital, I had nowhere to live, and the job I had been offered was right for me in every aspect aside from the financial. My mother still couldn't accept that I had chosen the option that I had, but I knew it had been the right thing to do. There had been two opportunities for me. The first one had been a job as a manager of a five-star hotel, but with the wages of a part-time worker. The pros had been that I would get my own business cards and a boost to my ego. On the other hand, there had been that exclusive beauty salon that had wanted me as a new stylist—that would mean I'd have to serve rich, haughty old crones. The paradox had been that as a manager I earned three times less than what they had offered me at the salon. In the end, the lure of a prospective career that would grow had won me over and I went with the hotel. After that there had been other hotels and other failed relationships—when you work in that industry, your job is your life. There's no time for anything else. It can be awesome if you're single, but when you're in a relationship, it just doesn't work. The choice between your job and the person you love is a constant struggle. It's exhausting. So you fuck up either your relationship or your job. In the end, I decided to be single and climb the steps of the corporate ladder, finally reaching the position of sales manager. That's when something broke inside me. I had saved a lot of money, so I could quit my job and look for something more satisfactory. Martin had supported me in that decision. He used to say they were using me at work. The truth is that he had simply needed a full-time cook and cleaning lady at home.

"You know, Laura." Olga's voice brought me back to reality. "I can come here once in a while when the child is born. I know next to nothing about kids, though. They scare me. They shit themselves all the time. But I'll manage somehow. For you."

"Better tell me how am I going to manage?" I snapped, shaking my head. "Normally I would call Mom to come to the rescue, but if she sees all this—the armed bodyguards, the house, the cars . . . she'll kill either me or herself. Or them."

"How about Massimo's mother? Won't she help you out?"

"His parents are dead. They died in a boat accident. It was probably an attack, but it was never proved that anyone else had something to do with the explosion. Massimo told me his mom was incredible. She loved him very much. He doesn't like to talk about his parents, but when he does, his eyes change. And his dad? Well, you know . . . head of the family. More of an authority figure than any kind of emotional support. The only member of his family I've met is Domenico."

"Why did they hide the fact that they're brothers?" Olga asked, leading me down another narrow alley.

"I don't think they've been hiding it. They just didn't tell me, and I didn't think to ask. I think Massimo picked him as my guardian because he trusts him the most."

"Remember Mariusz, the guy from real estate? He got you a guardian, too, no?" She laughed sharply. "That was a weird one, right? Total psycho."

I nodded, frowning at the memory. I used to go out with a guy who really liked to show off, trying to conquer my heart by playing someone he was not. He had lived above his means, as it turned out, but in the beginning there was this one situation when he told us that he couldn't go with us to a club, but he'd send "his man" with us instead. He gave the guy some cash to pay for our drinks and so on, and at first he really did his job, shooing away all my potential admirers. But at some point he had one too many and it turned out he was a psycho. He started hitting on Olga and me, making scenes, shouting and swearing, but—as my friend knew all the bouncers at all the clubs—our guardian ended up on his ass, outside the club, with a black eye and crying like a baby.

"Yeah, that was pretty intense. But I have a better one. Remember when we went to a club on our own, and everyone thought we were hookers?"

"Oh yeah!" she exclaimed. "We wore white and that guy had his birthday. What a party!"

I huddled against her arm.

"You know it's not going to be like that anymore," I said regretfully. "Everything is going to change now. I'll have a child, a husband, the whole package. All that in only two months!"

"You're overreacting," Olga replied. "You can hire a nanny. You'll have to, anyway, with all of Massimo's trips. You won't have to cope alone. Besides, who will you leave the kid with when you go to a ball or some formal dinner? You better start thinking about it already."

"Why would I?" I asked, shrugging. "I know he'll decide for me. I won't have a say in anything. It'll be about his child's safety." I shook my head, suddenly afraid. "Jesus, he'll lose it. He'll be too scared to leave us for even a minute."

Olga burst out in laughter, and a while later I joined her.

"Or he'll keep you in a cellar, just to be sure."

We walked for another hour, reminiscing the not-so-old times, until it got really late. Stopping for a while, we allowed our bodyguards to catch up with us and asked them to take us home.

CHAPTER 21

The next day I woke up alone. Olga was gone. *Why did she wake up this early?* I thought, looking for my phone on the nightstand.

"What the fuck?" I swore, seeing it was already 1 p.m.

I didn't know I could sleep this long, but the doctor had said something about sudden exhaustion. Apparently it was natural for someone in my current state.

Still dazed, I went to the bathroom to get myself ready to leave and headed out to look for my friend. I went to the garden first, where I found Domenico. He was sipping coffee.

"Good day. How are you feeling? I have some papers for you," he said, pushing a stack my way.

"I don't know how I'm feeling, really—I'm still super sleepy. Where's Olga?"

The young Italian took out his cell phone and dialed a number. A moment later a boy joined us, bringing me tea with milk.

"Olga is sunbathing on the beach. What would you like for breakfast?"

I covered my mouth with my hand. The thought of eating made me want to throw up. I waved away Domenico's question. "I'm nauseous. I don't want anything for now, thanks. I'll go to the beach." I grabbed a bottle of water and went to the wharf.

On the way I finally stopped feeling queasy. The motorboat berthed at the quay reminded me of my panicked flight from the shower, from the horny Massimo and his hard cock.

"Why are you ogling that poor boat as if you'd like to fuck it?" I heard a voice, and saw Olga, half-naked, emerge from the water.

"You two fucked on that boat, didn't you?" she asked.

With a mysterious smile, raising my brows, I turned to face her as she approached.

"I like your boobs," I said. "Now I know why Domenico was so awkward."

"Yeah, he came here and brought me a bottle of wine, doing his best to look me in the eyes. You should have seen it. Slept well?" she asked, lowering herself to a chaise.

I lay down next to her, closing my eyes and turning my face to-ward the sun. "I'm not sure. I think I could sleep through the day. Weird."

"You've nothing better to do anyway, so go get some sleep or grab a bathing suit and let's catch some sun before that wedding."

I didn't know if I even could sunbathe. I hadn't thought to ask the doctor. "Can I sunbathe pregnant?"

"I don't have an idea. I'm not much of a mother myself. Ask Uncle Google."

Right. That would be logical. I took out my phone and tapped in my question. A while later I rolled to the side, facing Olga.

"No sunbathing for me. Listen to this: 'The sun allows the skin to produce vitamin D, which is particularly important for the child. It is enough to take walks in the shade to reach the right level of the vitamin. Sunbathing isn't recommended, as one cannot fully pro-tect the skin against harmful UV rays. A pregnant woman's skin is overly sensitive, and the sun may irritate it, causing discoloration. Besides, the body quickly dehydrates in the sun, which is detrimental to the child.'"

Olga turned to me, sliding her sunglasses halfway down her nose, and said, "You've binged on wine like crazy and you were pregnant for a while now. How is a bit of sun going to top that? Bullshit."

"Well, now that I know I'm pregnant, I'm not going to risk getting an ugly hormonal splotch on my chin or something. Anyway, we have an invitation to a spa, so choose—either you stay here and grow old by the second with all that UV light, or we go have some fun."

I grew quiet, waiting for a response, as she stood by the chaise with her bag in her hand, putting on a beach wrap.

"So? Are we going or what?"

In another hour, we were ready to leave, and Domenico parked my cherry Porsche on the driveway. He left the car and frowned slightly. "Don't run away this time, okay?" He pointed to the black SUV, which stopped right behind my car. "Massimo gets furious when you do that, and the guys always suffer for it."

I patted his shoulder and opened the door. "We've discussed it with the boss already. You can stop worrying. Did you program the route to the spa in the GPS?"

Domenico nodded and raised a hand to wave goodbye.

"What a fucking spaceship," Olga groaned, looking around the interior of the car. "Who the fuck needs so many buttons? This is supposed to be a car! A steering wheel, three pedals, a gear stick, and four seats. What does this one do?"

"Jesus, don't push them! It'll catapult us through the roof or something."

I slapped her hand away as she tried touching some other unidentifiable button. "Don't touch it." I shook my head. "I said the same thing when I got it, but they tell me its safe," I added, shrugging with resignation.

When we drove out and reached the highway, I decided to show her what my Macan could do and stepped on the accelerator. The engine roared and the car shot forward, pressing us both into our seats.

"This thing is fucking *fast!*" Olga cried out in delight, turning the music up.

"You'll see how the security guys start panicking now. I've lost them once already."

I drove, weaving between other cars, overtaking them all. I was suddenly glad that I had learned how to drive from a man. My dad had always told me to drive safely and steadily, always in control, so both my brother and I had had to learn how to cope in the most dangerous and extreme situations on the road. Dad's lessons hadn't been meant to make us road hogs, but to prepare us for the various threats in traffic. Suddenly I heard the sound of a police siren. In the rearview mirror I glanced an unmarked Alfa Romeo with two men inside.

"Just fucking great," I muttered, stopping on the side of the road.

A uniformed man walked over and said something in Italian. I spread my arms and tried explaining in English that I couldn't understand him. Neither he nor his colleague knew the language, but from his gesticulation I deduced that I was supposed to show him my license and registration papers. I pulled the documents out and handed them to the policeman.

"Oh shit," I hissed, turning my head to look at Olga. "I forgot my license." She shot me a withering glare and stuck out her chest.

"Well then, I should probably go and give those two a blow job."

"This isn't funny! I'm being serious!"

The black SUV caught up with us then and stopped right behind us. Two of our bodyguards stepped out. Watching them, Olga said, "Now we're really screwed." The two groups approached each other and shook hands. It looked more like a meeting between colleagues than a police inspection. They talked for a moment, and then the officer walked back to me and handed me the papers.

"*Scusa*," he muttered, and saluted briefly.

Olga shot me a surprised glance.

"He even apologized . . . Weird."

The patrol car left, and one of the security guards walked over to me and leaned down, sticking his head through the window.

"If you'd like to test the car like that, we can go to the racing track. We're authorized by don Massimo to take it away from you when you try to lose us again. So. Either you drive slower, or you go with us," he said impassively.

I frowned but nodded. "I'm sorry."

The rest of the way passed without incident. We took our time. The spa was luxurious and opulent. It offered a wide range of treatments and rituals, including options for pregnant women, so I could partake without worrying about the fetus.

We spent almost five hours there. Hearing that, a man would have thought us crazy, but a woman knows how long it takes to really take care of herself. Scrubs, massages, facials, pedicures, manicures, and getting your hair done. Thinking about Saturday's ceremony, I picked colors similar to that of my wedding dress. I needed to be 100 percent ready for the occasion. I trusted the hairstylist and told him to touch up my roots only. The man's name was Marco, and he was as gay as it got. He dealt with the dye perfectly, so I decided to shorten my hair a bit, too. Smelling like heaven and totally relaxed, we took our seats on the terrace while a waiter served us dinner.

"You're not eating enough, Laura. This is your first meal today. You shouldn't do that."

"Oh, give me a break. I constantly want to throw up. I wonder if you'd have an appetite if you felt like that. Besides, I'm already nervous with the wedding in just a couple of days."

"Got doubts? Remember: you don't have to do this. A kid doesn't automatically mean you have to get married, you know? And a marriage doesn't have to be forever."

"I love Massimo and I want to marry him. And I want to tell him we're going to have a child. I'm tired of keeping this a secret," I said.

After an appetizer, soup, the main course, and the dessert, I could barely breathe. We waddled back to the car and managed to get inside.

"I'm nauseous again. This time from overeating," I said, turning the engine on.

I saw the lights of the black SUV in the rearview mirror and started driving, punching in the address Domenico had marked as Home in the GPS. The traffic was practically nonexistent by that time, and the highway was empty. I pressed the cruise control button and leaned my head on my arm, which was propped on the window. The automatic gearbox had this advantage (or disadvantage, depending on where you stand on such things) that you didn't know what do to with your hands while driving. Well, one of them, at least. Olga was scrolling through her phone, completely ignoring me, and I felt sleepy.

Driving along the slopes of Mount Etna, I watched the majestic mountain and the stream of lava running down its summit. The view was incredible and terrifying at the same time. My eyes on the spectacle, I didn't notice the black SUV gaining on us. I turned to glance in the mirror, but in this moment the car lurched, hitting us from behind.

"What the hell are they doing?" I screamed. The car bumped

into the Porsche again, trying to push us off the road. I stepped on
the accelerator in an effort to lose them, tossing my bag to Olga
and calling out, "Find my phone and call Domenico!" With shaking hands, panicked, Olga rummaged through my bag, finally fish-
ing out my cell phone. The dark SUV wasn't backing down. Thank
God the engine in the Porsche had more power. I had a chance to
lose them.

"Just dial the number! The phone is connected to the car speakers."

Olga did as she was told, and I listened to the ringing, praying
for Domenico to pick up.

"What are you doing there so late?" Finally my future brother-
in-law's voice reverberated through the car.

"Domenico! They're chasing us!" I cried.

"What's happening, Laura? Who's chasing you? Where are you?"

"Our bodyguards went crazy! They're trying to push us off the
road! What do I do?"

"It's not them. They called me five minutes ago, saying that
they're still waiting at the spa."

I felt a chilling wave of terror wash over me. I couldn't panic.
Not now. But I had no idea what to do.

"Don't hang up," Domenico said.

I heard him shouting something in Italian before getting back to
me. "The security team is on its way. I'll have your location in a moment. Don't be afraid. They'll catch up with you in a minute. How
fast are you going?"

Shaking with fear, I glanced at the speedometer.

"Nearly 130 miles per hour," I stammered, suddenly terrified
with how fast I was driving.

"Listen to me, I don't know what car is chasing you, but if you
thought it was one of ours, it's probably a Range Rover. It can't go as
fast as the Porsche, so if you're up to it, you can lose them."

I stepped on the accelerator and felt my car gaining speed, seeing the lights of the SUV shrinking in the rearview mirror.

"In about nine miles there's going to be an exit leading to Messina. Take it. My people are already on their way. The security team is around twenty miles behind you. After you take the ramp off, the road is going to be blocked by a tollbooth, so you have to slow down. But remember: if you can't lose them until then, do not roll down the windows or step out of the car. The car is bulletproof so you're safe as long as you're inside."

"What? They're going to shoot at me?"

"I don't know. All I'm saying is you stay inside. You're safe there."

I listened to Domenico, hearing a ringing in my ears. My heart was pounding. I was holding on by the barest thread. Shooting a glance at the mirror, I saw the lights of the car following us slowly disappear. I picked up speed. *Either I'm going to die in a car crash, or they'll shoot me dead*, I thought. Then a sign appeared on the road. The exit.

"I can see the exit, Domenico!"

I heard him saying something in Italian before speaking to me, switching back to English. "Good. My people are nearly at the tollbooth. A black BMW with four people inside. You already know Paolo. When you see him, stop as close to him as you can."

I started braking to take the exit from the highway, praying for Domenico's men to hurry. Passing the turn, I saw the black BMW stopping, and the four men jumping out. I stepped on the brake pedal and the car skidded to a halt, nearly hitting the security detail.

Paolo opened the door and pulled me out of the Porsche. I was shaking uncontrollably. He tossed me back inside, to the back seat, got behind the wheel, and drove through the tollbooth, tires screeching. I was doing my best to breathe steadily, to calm down my racing heart. I heard Domenico's voice calmly explaining something to the driver.

Where was Olga? I completely forgot about her. I looked up and saw her sitting in the front passenger seat, looking straight ahead. "You all right, Olga?" I asked, grabbing her by the arm.

She turned abruptly, and her eyes were full of tears. She unfastened her seat belt and scrambled to the back seat, pressing herself into my arms, crying. "What the fuck was that, Laura?"

We sat hugging each other, tears streaking down our cheeks, and shaking as if the interior of the car were minus twenty degrees. I felt how absolutely terrified she was. I had never seen her like that. Despite feeling like that myself just a moment ago, I knew I needed to support her now.

"It's okay. We're safe now. They only wanted to scare us."

I didn't really believe that, but I had to calm my friend down.

Domenico was already waiting for us when we got back to the mansion. As soon as the Porsche ground to a halt, he opened the door for me. I slid out, falling into his arms.

"Are you all right? How are you feeling? The doctor is on his way."

"I'm fine," I breathed, holding him tight.

Olga stepped out of the car and snuck into our embrace, joining us.

Domenico took us to the grand lounge on the ground floor. The doctor arrived twenty minutes later, checking my blood pressure and giving me some heart pills. I wasn't hurt. Then he turned his attention to Olga. She still couldn't cope with what had happened, so he gave her some tranquilizers and sleeping pills. Domenico took her to her bedroom. When they disappeared, the doctor told me to see a gynecologist right away, to check if the child was okay. I felt all right, as much as one can feel fine after experiencing something like that, and I was sure the baby was okay. The collision with our car wasn't that serious. The seat belt only grazed my collarbone, not

really tightening over my belly, but better to be safe. Domenico returned after a while, and the doctor said goodbye and left.

"Listen to me, Laura. You need to tell me what happened. All
of it."

"We left the spa, the valet passed me the keys to the car—"

"What did he look like?" he cut in.

"I don't know. Like an Italian. I didn't take a look. When we got
into the car, a dark SUV started following us. I thought it was the
security. Then we drove to the highway and it all started. You know
the rest. I talked to you the whole way."

Domenico's phone rang, and he left the room, fuming. Worried,
I followed him. Domenico nearly ran through the main entrance,
heading toward my bodyguards, who were just parking their car on
the driveway. When the men stepped out, he slammed his fist into
the first one's face, toppling him to the ground, and then did the
same to the second one, kicking him as the man went down. The
men from the BMW parked a couple of feet away stepped in and
held the driver to the ground, while Domenico pummeled him with
his fists, furious.

"Domenico!" I screamed, terrified at what I was seeing.

He slowly rose from the ground, leaving the poor man unconscious, and headed my way.

"My brother will kill them anyway," he said, wiping his hands
on his pants. "Come. I'll take you to your room."

I sat down on the bed while Domenico went to the bathroom to
wash his hands. I felt my medication starting to work, feeling dazed
and sleepy.

"Don't worry, Laura. This will not happen ever again. We'll find
whoever chased you."

"Please, promise me you won't kill them," I whispered, looking
Domenico in the eyes.

His face crumpled in an ugly grimace as he leaned against the doorframe.

"I can promise you that, but the decision is Massimo's. Don't worry about that now. The most important thing is that you're all right."

I heard knocking on the door. Domenico went to open it and returned with a mug of hot cocoa.

"Normally I'd have given you some alcohol," he said, putting the mug on the nightstand. "But the situation is what it is, so you're left with milk. I've got to go now, but I'll wait until you change and lie down in bed."

I went to the wardrobe and put on Massimo's T-shirt, went back to the bed, and slid under the duvet.

"Good night, Domenico. Thank you for everything."

"I'm sorry," he said quietly, going down the stairs. "Remember, there's a button by the bed. If you need anything, just press it."

I rolled over and turned the TV on, used the remote to switch off all the lights, and put my head on the pillow. I started to watch a news channel, but fell asleep quickly.

I woke up in the middle of the night. The TV was still on. I turned to grab the remote, which lay on the nightstand, and froze. The armchair next to the bed was occupied. It was Massimo, watching me closely. For a moment, I stayed still, unsure if I was still asleep or if this was really happening.

A few seconds passed before Massimo rose, only to fall to his knees by the bed, resting his head on my stomach.

"I'm so sorry, my love," he whispered, wrapping his arms around me.

I slipped from his embrace, got out of bed, and knelt on the floor by him, hugging him tightly. "You can't kill them, okay? I've never asked you for anything, but now I'm begging. I don't want anyone else to die because of me."

Massimo didn't speak, keeping perfectly still in my arms. We stayed like that for a very long time, with me listening to his calming breath.

"It's my fault," he said finally, pushing himself away and lifting me in his arms.

He lay me in bed, covering me and sitting down at my side. I shook off the remaining sleepiness, watching him. It was clear Massimo had come in a hurry. He hadn't even had the chance to change clothes and was still in his tuxedo. I caressed the lapel of his jacket.

"Was there a party?"

The Man in Black dropped his head, pulling at his bow tie.

"I've let you down. I promised I'd protect you and that nothing bad would ever happen to you. I went away and you've just barely avoided death. I don't know who sat behind the wheel of that car or how this all happened, but I swear I'll find the one responsible," he growled, and rose.

"I don't know if it is a good idea for you to say here, Laura," he said. "I love you more than anyone else in the world, but I can't bear the thought of you losing your life because of me. By bringing you here I acted like an absolute egoist. And now, with the situation so unstable, I can't be sure of anything."

I looked him in the eyes, terrified of what I was hearing.

"I think you need to leave for a while. There are going to be a lot of changes, and until they happen, you're not safe in Sicily."

"What are you saying, Massimo?" I cried, jumping to my feet. "Now you want to send me away? Two days before we're supposed to get married?"

He spun around, shooting out his arms and grabbing me tightly by the shoulders.

"Do you even want that? Maybe I really should be alone, Laura. I chose this life. I didn't give you a choice. I'm condemning you to be with me, to be in constant danger."

He let me go and started walking toward the stairs. "It was stupid of me to think it could end any other way. That we could be together." He paused and turned his head toward me. "You deserve someone better, baby girl."

"I can't believe it!" I cried out, running to catch up with him. "*Now* you start thinking about me? After two months? After proposing to me? When I'm about to have your child?"

ACKNOWLEDGMENTS

We all have someone in our lives who believes in us more than they probably should.

For me, such a person is my sister by choice—Anna Mackiewicz.

Thank you, darling, for effectively and regularly pushing me to publish this book.

Thank you for believing in me.

Mom, Dad—thank you for raising me to be who I am. A person who can talk about sex, love, and emotions.

I love you so much!

But I owe the biggest thanks to the man who left me, broke my heart, and inspired me to act, making it possible for you, dear reader, to hold this book now.

KM—thank you.